A PLACE CALLED SORRY

Caitlin Press Inc.
8100 Alderwood Road,
Halfmoon Bay, BC von 1y1
caitlin-press.com

Text design by Vici Johnstone and Kathleen Fraser.
Cover design by Vici Johnstone.
Cover photo courtesy of the Grant-Kohrs Ranch National Historic Site, National Park Service, image number GRKO 16234.1.
Edited by Jane Silcott, Rebecca Hendry and Kathleen Fraser.
Printed in Canada.

Caitlin Press Inc. acknowledges financial support from the Government of Canada through the Canada Book Fund and the Canada Council for the Arts, and from the Province of British Columbia through the British Columbia Arts Council and the Book Publisher's Tax Credit.

Library and Archives Canada Cataloguing in Publication

Milner, Donna, 1946-, author
    A place called Sorry / Donna Milner.

ISBN 978-1-927575-94-9 (paperback)

    I. Title.

PS8626.I457P53 2015   C813'.6   C2015-904039-6

A PLACE CALLED
SORRY

DONNA MILNER

CAITLIN PRESS

Dedicated to
Addie Hamm.

Thanks for listening, my friend.

History is the stories we tell—and the stories we don't tell.

1.

Calling Sorry a town, in my mother's oft-stated opinion, was an impertinent stretch of the facts. To her, the scanty little settlement located twelve hard bush miles from our ranch was simply the place where a number of side roads, not much more than widened paths, converged onto the trail that once led to the Cariboo goldfields.

Even Grandfather's fanciful stories of how Sorry came to be did nothing to alter her judgment. According to him, and he had good reason to know, at the start of the gold rush in the mid-1800s, someone had come up with the misguided notion to build a roadhouse on that exact spot to accommodate the steady flow of gold-fevered travellers in pursuit of the motherlode. In the beginning, the roadhouse was a roaring success, with the owner charging exorbitant prices for supplies, and the only civilized place to lay one's head on the last leg of the arduous journey. Over time, however, the fortune seekers found a shorter route, and the traffic along the wagon road dwindled down to a few hardy homesteaders and trappers who had little need of a place to lodge. By the turn of the century, all that remained of the failed enterprise, besides the weathered shiplap building, was an oversized sign high on a pole in front of the abandoned inn. The bold letters painted across it read "SORRY," and in much smaller print below, as if an afterthought, was the word "closed." The sign, which could be seen from some distance, became a landmark. Over the years, the "closed" faded, causing locals giving directions to say, "When you come to a place called Sorry, take this road—or that."

Long before I was born in 1925, an enterprising Dutchman who was visiting his sister in the area fell prey to the lure of the Cariboo and decided to make it his home. He purchased the abandoned roadhouse at the wilderness crossroads for next to nothing and immediately applied for a postal outlet in the grocery store he intended to open in the restored building.

Surprisingly, perhaps in an effort to please the area's widely scattered population of ranchers, miners and trappers, the government approved his application. More importantly, the new owner brought in a power line. Before long, a few houses, a one-room school and a small church sprang up like mushrooms on the crossroad corners.

The Dutch grocer, who had a sense of humour, repainted the sign in front of the building, inserting the words "THE" and "GROCERS" before and after the "SORRY." As the tiny community grew, so was it branded.

Eventually, my father, the area's only notary public, set up a desk in a corner of The Sorry Grocers, where, from nine to noon every Saturday, he would meet with locals in need of his services. While he waited for clients, he often amused himself by reading the notes and messages posted on the bulletin board near the front door. The corkboard, which the grocer, Mr. VanderMeer, had installed as a courtesy to his customers, quickly became an important message centre, overcrowded with various handwritten notes. Offerings of items for sale or trade, from livestock to machinery, second-hand scythes to free puppies, were scattered willy-nilly among help-wanted pleas for extra hands during branding, haying or ice-harvesting time. Personal messages of all kinds: announcements of who was pregnant, sick or in need of urgent information to be passed on to remote friends or relatives were scratched out on scraps of paper and tacked to the board.

The abundance of overlapping notes, along with the many rumours repeated to the shopkeeper by lingering customers, caused my father to say to him one day that he could publish a newspaper with all the information that was brought in to his store. Whether it was Father's remark, or the fact that Mr. VanderMeer prided himself as a bit of a writer, the grocer was eventually inspired to include his interpretation of local happenings in his printout of the store's weekly specials. He gave his publication the grandiose name of the *Sorry Times*. Every Saturday morning, the latest edition was stacked on the counter beside the cash register. Before long, Saturday became the store's best trading day, and if you waited until Monday morning to pick up a copy of the folded four-page circular along with your mail, you were likely to be disappointed.

No one enjoyed the *Sorry Times* more than my grandfather. Some of my earliest memories are of his Saturday after-dinner ritual when he would sit at the head of the kitchen table reading the messages and local stories aloud, never resisting the temptation to pass along comments laced with tongue-in-cheek judgment of the goings-on of our neighbours. I remember Father teasing him once, saying, "If I were you, I'd be a mite careful that I wasn't mistaken for an old gossipmonger."

Grandfather had removed the unlit pipe from his mouth—for Mother could not tolerate the smell of tobacco smoke in the house—and said with a shrug, "If that's the worst a body's ever mistaken for, well then I'd say he's led a pretty blessed life."

Years later, when he was in his eighties, my grandfather's eyesight would begin to fade. He fought the encroaching shadows with the same intensity with which he had beaten back the wilderness from the land he had ranched for over sixty-five years, as if sheer strength of will and a stubborn refusal to give in could stave off this new enemy. The darkness came anyway. As his vision slowly dimmed, his voice grew louder. Deep and gravelly with age and years of pipe smoking, his voice was often the voice of comfort during my childhood. But as the volume increased, so too did the harshness. Anyone within hearing distance would not have been blamed for attributing that brittle edge to a demanding, cranky old man. They would never have made this mistake if they knew him as I did.

Eventually, he would have to strain to make out the words on the page, and it would become my job to read the *Sorry Times* out loud. By the time I turned thirteen, every Saturday afternoon, the minute Father walked in the door after returning from town, Grandfather would demand the "newspaper."

"Come, boy," he would call out, as if I were a dog, but a favoured dog, for affection always softened his rough-edged summons. And I would be compelled to join him wherever he happened to be—at the kitchen table, in his overstuffed chair in the parlour, or in the rocking chair out on our front porch—waiting to hear the latest edition. I'm not certain if his insistence on hearing every single word, every story, announcement and advertisement, in that weekly paper was for his benefit or mine, but each and every time, after I read the final word on the back page, he would lean back and say, "Well done, boy."

If my father was in the room, his eyes would meet mine and an expression both sympathetic and apologetic would cross his face. He would shake his head but remain silent. I, too, had nothing to say. By then, I had stopped bothering to remind Grandfather that I was a girl.

2.

There were worse things going on in the world than my grandfather's diminishing eyesight and memory during those years history would brand the Dirty Thirties.

Throughout my teenage years, every evening, Father would fiddle with the huge wooden dials of the upright Victrola Radiola in our parlour until the radio announcer's sombre voice crackled into the room, too often bringing bleak reports of economic decline, falling commodity prices and Germany's march across Europe.

But when I was very young, long before I would take any notice of the woes of the outside world, my grandfather was the centre of mine.

He hadn't always been under the illusion that I was a boy. In those early years, before my brother Evan was born, I was proud to be called Grandfather's "cowgirl sidekick." According to family legend, he had taught me to sit a horse before I could walk, and from the moment I was a toddler, he allowed me to shadow his every step. Then one day, to Mother's horror, she discovered the two of us lying on the edge of the back field, me with a rifle in my five-year-old hands, and Grandfather instructing me how to sight down the long barrel.

That little incident caused quite a hullabaloo at our dinner table that evening.

Mother had slammed down platters and bowls, with little regard for spillage, while describing the scene she had witnessed to my father. Leaning back to avoid the hot stew splatters, Father, a man of few words, said, "I think I'll bow out of this one, Fern." He then uncharacteristically added that since he was raised on a ranch and knew the value of early learning, "I tend to sympathize with Dad's position."

"But a gun? My God! Addison."

"Ah, but the gal's got a good eye," Grandfather said, flashing me a conspirator's wink from the head of the table. "A regular Annie Oakley."

Mother spun around to glare at him. "Chauncey Beynon Beale, don't you start!" That's when everyone at the table knew how serious she was, and we all sat up a little straighter.

The admiration between my mother and her father-in-law was real, and everyone knew they held a genuine fondness for one another. She usually called him Dad, only using his proper names when she was exasperated with him. He lived to avoid that.

That evening, her anger at him dissipated just as quickly as it rose, and she dropped down into her chair and said with a sigh, "She's just a child."

Taking the serving ladle in hand, she pointed it at Grandfather, and like a teacher admonishing a student, she waved it under his nose, saying, "I don't want her playing with guns!" She reached for his dinner plate and filled it while he waited, appearing sheepishly contrite. With an exaggerated click of her tongue, she scolded, "And letting her lie in the dirt with her new frock on."

"I've been meaning to talk to you about that, Fern," Grandfather said, accepting the steaming plate of stew. "Don't you think it would be better if our Addie wore overalls?"

When the ladle clanged loudly against the crockery bowl, he quickly added, "I'm not saying all the time. Just when she's outside. Wouldn't you like that, Addie?"

Nodding fiercely, I glanced from his face to Mother's, surprised that he would test her this way, especially when she was in a mood. But she only shook her head with a furrowed expression. "Oh, please," she said. "I've asked you not to call her that. She's enough of a tomboy already."

I didn't mind one little bit when Grandfather called me Addie— Mother's pet name for Father—but she always took exception to it.

She resumed serving in silence, as if she was contemplating his words. Then, glancing at me and catching what I hoped was a pleading I'll-be-a-good-girl smile, she turned back to him and said, "All right, I'll sew some overalls for *Adeline*. But only for around the ranch. And I want you to promise that there will be no more playing with guns."

"Oh, I give you my word, Fern," Grandfather agreed, tucking into his stew. "It won't be play."

By the time I was six years old, with my new twenty-two rifle—a birthday gift from my grandfather—I could pick off a gopher's head as it popped up from its hidey-hole in the back pasture. And thanks to him, I was an accomplished rider. Whenever he went after cattle, I would follow behind his dappled mare on my Welsh pony, which he had bought from a neighbouring rancher whose children had outgrown it.

But when I was eight years old, my world was turned upside down. Mother was expecting, and everyone was hoping for a boy, when one day I overheard her telling a neighbour how obviously disappointed my grandfather had been when I was born a girl instead of the grandson he had anticipated.

If his disappointment was obvious to her, it hadn't been to me. And if what my mother said was true, and I had no reason to doubt her word, then Grandfather had kept his disenchantment with my gender well hidden. Up until then, I had never questioned his love. It was seldom spoken out loud or fussed about; taken for granted, it filled the ranch house like the wood stove's comforting warmth. Only after Mother unwittingly revealed the truth did I begin to study Grandfather's every act for signs that my failure to be born male had tarnished his affection for me.

Still, as my father was fond of saying, "If a child goes searching for reasons to feel sorry for herself, she's certain to find them." For a while, all of Grandfather's attentions held different meaning to me, and his previous generosities were lost to my suspicions that his actions were guided by only one reason—his wish that I was a boy.

When I was nine, my brother, Evan Harrison Beale, was born. On a rainy spring day, with the crocuses pushing up along the edges of our mud-bogged road, my father brought Mother home from the hospital in Quesnel. Grandfather had to hook up the team and pull our Ford pickup truck through the last half mile of thick gumbo. When they finally came up the porch steps and into the kitchen, I was sitting sulking in the parlour, pretending to be reading. The two men, both fussing over Mother and encouraging her to rest, escorted her and the mewing bundle through the ranch house and into the master bedroom. Before long, Grandfather came back out. I kept my nose in my book but watched from the corner of my eye as he crossed the room, looking strange and somehow even more gigantic cradling the tiny baby. He squatted down in front of me and without a word offered to place my new brother in my arms. Fully expecting my grandfather's affection to be transferred to his grandson, leaving none for my pitiful self, a mere girl, I instantly resented the intruder. Refusing the package, I jumped up and escaped to my room in the loft.

In the following weeks I remained sullen and rude with Grandfather. Yet even when I sassed him back for no good reason, his tolerance never wavered. Seeing no sign that he favoured the baby over me, I realized that our relationship was not going to change. Relieved of jealousy over my baby brother, I was free to adore him.

I believe little Evan was born with a smile on his face. He woke each morning in the crib at the foot of my parents' bed cooing and waiting to be picked up. There were no shortages of arms waiting to cuddle this "angel baby," as Mother called him. Cherubic and sweetly cute, with a shock of ginger hair—the same dark shade as hers—he soon became the centre of our lives, entertaining us all with his innocent blue-eyed antics.

Before the baby was a month old, Grandfather ordered a black metal pram with nickel trim and wheel covers. Although my father said he could not imagine what use a fancy baby buggy could possibly have out here in the wilds, my mother loved it. When Evan was tiny, it allowed her to bring the sleeping baby to whatever room she was in—the kitchen, the parlour or out on the screened-in front porch. After he learned to sit up, I would push him around the yard and down the dirt road as far as I was allowed to go. With the barking ranch dogs running alongside, the buggy's rubber wheels bumped and careened over the hardened ruts while Evan bounced and shrieked with delight. Until Mother, ever watchful, called a stop to the wild ride.

If my grandfather, and my father for that matter, showed no favouritism, Mother could not help herself. Evan was the apple of her eye. From the moment he was born, her life on the ranch seemed less of a burden.

It was no secret how much my mother missed the city. She and Father had met in Vancouver in 1920 while she was taking her nurse's training and he was studying law after returning from the Great War. More than once I heard her lamenting how, when they first started dating, she had assumed that when he became a lawyer he would set up a practice in Vancouver. Before he finished his degree, however, he fell victim to homesickness and returned to the ranch. Instead of becoming a solicitor, he settled for notary public, a profession he felt would serve him and his neighbours better at any rate. He and my mother kept up correspondence for a few years. Then one summer, after she completed her nurse's training, Father drove down to visit her in her childhood home in New Westminster and ended up proposing. Whenever she told the story, she always added that she still didn't understand how he had convinced her to leave the city, and her career, to marry him.

Their return to the ranch as husband and wife came as a welcome surprise to Grandfather. He insisted on giving up the master bedroom, the only bedroom on the main floor of the ranch house, allegedly saying he'd sleep out in the barn if it meant the possibility of grandsons. Not willing to climb up into the loft, which had been Father's room as a child,

Grandfather built a lean-to addition off the parlour. For the rest of his life, that room, with its own wood heater and a heavy wooden door to separate it from the main house, served as his bedroom.

According to Grandfather, Mother tried hard to become a rancher's wife. But after the first few long winters, she began to suffer bouts of sadness. Once I was born, her homesickness lessened, but it never fully left her. From the beginning, Grandfather did everything within his power to make the life of his son's wife easier. At no small expense, hydro lines were strung down the three-mile stretch from the main road, bringing electric power to the ranch house. Recognizing her love of music, and in hopes of staving off the despondency of long winter months, Grandfather purchased the RCA Victrola Radiola, a combination radio and gramophone, which still stands in the ranch house parlour these many years later.

When I was young, Mother measured the progress of my growth against the height of that polished mahogany centrepiece. By the time I was five, my head was even with the top; at six, I was tall enough to peer into the phonograph bed. The year Evan was born I towered over it.

I don't recall my mother smiling so easily and so often as she did in the months after his birth. Oddly enough, I felt no resentment of her fawning over my baby brother. It allowed me far more freedom. All her energy went into worrying about him instead of me. Despite her worry, he thrived, and we were all held captive to his precocious behaviour. Still her mindfulness was beyond obsession, as if he would be snatched away from her at any moment.

3.

In the evenings, Evan would fall asleep draped like a contented kitten on Mother's lap while she sang him lullabies. On Saturday nights, after he was tucked into his crib, if the mood struck her as it often did, my mother would lift the Victrola's hinged top and place one of her glossy black records on the turntable inside, and she and my father would dance to the music of Duke Ellington or Tommy Dorsey.

Grandfather enjoyed the music as much as anyone and sometimes let himself be coaxed into dancing. The only dance he ever admitted to knowing was a wild stomp he used to do with the Hurdy Gurdy Girls during his mining years in the boom town of Barkerville. His strong arms would swing my startled mother, and sometimes me, up into the air, showing us how the miners used to hoist the tavern girls. "Sometimes we lifted them so high," he boasted, "that their feet would touch the ceiling."

Mine never came close to our ceiling, but I liked to imagine my nightie billowing out like he said the girls' hoop skirts did as they came back down.

It's a wonder the baby slept at all on those evenings, but the blaring Victrola and our stomping feet never seemed to bother him. As much as I enjoyed the music and watching my parents dance, for me, the real thrill always came on the nights we lost our electric power. Whenever the warning flicker of light bulbs foretold the collapse of a snow-burdened tree somewhere along the miles of hydro lines, I would look forward to everyone gathering in the darkened parlour to listen as Grandfather, his face aglow in the orange light of the hurricane lamp, spun tales of the olden days.

After all these years, I am uncertain if my memories of those snowbound winter nights and the stories and conversations inhabiting them are exact. Or have I filled in the gaps with what I would learn much later about my grandfather's past?

I do recall, however, how he would finger the empty pipe in his hands as he kept us spellbound with colourful stories of his years in Barkerville during the gold rush.

Yet something was always missing from those tales. It was as if his life had begun the day he, in his own words, "hoofed it, alone in the world, into that wild town." Father, never one to pry into anyone's privacy, always refrained from asking about the years before his gold-mining days.

Mother had no such reservations. Her many prodding questions and Grandfather's masterful way of avoiding them were like a game of one-upmanship between them. The amused expression playing at the corners of my father's mouth during those good-natured volleys betrayed the fact that he took some secret joy in their verbal sparring. If Mother pushed too hard, Grandfather would act as if he hadn't heard her. Without missing a beat, he would launch into yet another long-winded description of the burgeoning town of Barkerville, at one time the largest western town north of San Francisco.

One evening he made the mistake of mentioning that after the Great Fire of 1868, which all but demolished the town, he had struck out on his own yet again to homestead this ranch.

Mother's eyebrows knit together as she did some mental arithmetic. "Gosh, Dad," she said, "that would make it 1864 when you first arrived in Barkerville. What in heaven's name was a fifteen-year-old boy doing walking through the wilderness alone? And where on earth were you walking *from*?"

"Oh, that's not a story for our young Addie's ears," he said.

"*Adeline*," Mother reminded him.

"Right," Grandfather relented. "But I'm sure she would be more interested in hearing about her namesake, her grandmother Adeline Beale."

And without waiting for anyone's agreement, he lit into the story about how he had found his future wife waiting tables in the rebuilt mining town's Wake-up-Jake café.

"I was thirty years old by then and pretty darned set in my ways," he said. "Every now and then, though, I would make a trip in for supplies and a bit of human company. Barkerville was never the same after the fire. The gold rush was petering out. The Hurdy Gurdy Girls had all left. With a real church and a schoolhouse, the place was all of a sudden more suited to families, so most of the women were married. Truth be told, I wasn't in the market for a wife. But the moment I laid eyes on my Adeline, that all changed. To begin with, she was the first female I'd met who was almost as tall as I was. Must have been close to six feet. Good, hardy stock. And it was clear from the start that she took no guff from anyone." He smiled at me. "She was like you, Addie," he said. "She had spunk."

I grinned with pride at the comparison to the grandmother I'd never known.

"It occurred to me right off," he continued, "that she would make the perfect ranching partner. She agreed. We didn't waste any time courting before she asked to see the ranch. Well, I'd been batching it for twelve years. All that time I lived in a windowless one-room cabin dug into in the hillside. I fully expected that the minute she spied my chimney pipe poking up out of the mound atop my underground dwelling, she would turn on her heels, climb onto the wagon and order me to take her back to town. But she did no such thing." He smiled with remembrance.

"She wasn't much impressed that we had to stoop to go in the door, but after a quick look around my subterranean home, all she said was, 'We'll need to find a way to knock out a window to get some light in here until we build ourselves a real house.' The very next morning, we started falling trees."

He glanced down at the pipe in his hands. "If I didn't exactly fall in love with that woman when we first met," he said, "I certainly did then."

On that snowbound winter night, I heard for the first time how my grandparents had built our hand-hewn log house, the only home I have ever known. When it was completed, Grandfather added on a wide front porch so his new bride could sit and watch the sunset, and he made plans for expansion, in anticipation of the large family he coveted. For years it appeared that his dream of sons, who would help work the ranch, was an illusion. Countless miscarriages later, after he had all but given up hope and believed his wife was too old to have children, she gave birth during another winter snowstorm in 1895. The eleven-pound baby boy, my father, was too much even for my hardy grandmother. She died, as Grandfather said, "before the midwife could tie off the umbilical cord."

When Grandfather stopped speaking, the room became so silent I thought I could hear the snow falling outside. And then in a low voice, he began to sing. "My Adeline, sweet Adeline, you're the flower of my heart, sweet Adeline."

Perhaps it was only the reflection of the flickering lamplight that made it appear my stoic grandfather grew misty-eyed as he sang the old song. When he was done, he said, as if to himself, "I still thank the good Lord every single night for that woman. For without her in this world there would be no Addison. No Evan. No Addie."

And for once my mother did not correct him.

4.

Evan took his first wobbling steps across the linoleum kitchen floor into my arms, much to Mother's chagrin. As if sensing her overprotectiveness, her unwillingness to let him try, it was me he reached for. After that he would toddle behind me, shadowing my every step, just as I had once shadowed Grandfather's.

By that time, my grandfather was eighty-three. His once tall and lean frame—like Father's, with taut muscles stretched over lanky bones—was beginning to stoop. His diminishing stature and advancing age caused Mother to monitor his every action with my brother. On the day he announced he believed it might be time to let the boy sit a horse for the first time, Mother reluctantly agreed. "But only long enough to snap a photograph," she said, handing me the Brownie box camera.

With one-year-old Evan on her hip, she followed us outside. My Welsh pony—which I believed I had outgrown, and I was vying for a full-sized mount of my own—stood tethered to the corral fence. As we approached, the pony shifted his weight onto his hind end. Mother gasped at the sudden movement and took a startled step back. For a moment I thought she was going to change her mind, but then my brother let out an excited squeal, his chubby legs and arms kicking with delight at the sight of the animal.

"It'll be all right, Fern," Grandfather said gently, reaching for the baby. "He's going to love this, aren't you, little fella?" Hesitantly, Mother surrendered Evan to him, but her fingers trailed after, refusing to lose touch of his little body even as he was placed on the pony's bare back.

She glanced over her shoulder at me, her eyes wide with unwarranted fear. "Take the picture, Adeline," she ordered. "Hurry!" I snapped the photograph, but all the blurred image would attest to in later years was Mother's hovering like a worried hen over her chick. Seconds later, refusing to let Grandfather lead the pony around the yard, she scooped Evan off its back and fled into the house.

Why mother was so much more fretful with my little brother than she ever was with me was always a mystery. Maybe it was because by then, having given in to my desire to always wear jeans or overalls around the ranch and to my opting for outside chores, she had come to accept her loss of control over me. Whatever caused her apprehension with Evan, she clung to that baby until we all feared he would become as housebound as she.

Mother was not an outdoors person. She kept herself busy in the house, cooking, baking, polishing and cleaning so much that the sight of a pine needle or speck of mud on her floor could throw her into a tizzy. The farthest she ventured outside was to the screened-in front porch, blaming her lack of adventure on the mosquitoes and blackflies that plagued any exposed skin during the spring and summer, and on the sharpened teeth of the wind during the fall and winter.

I never knew her to ride a horse. Unlike other ranchers' wives, no one expected her to help with haying, cattle roundup or branding. In the dead of winter when our two draft horses, King and Prince, were harnessed to the sleigh, she could never be convinced to join us on the ride out to Sucker Lake behind the back field where we would harvest blocks of ice for our icehouse.

On a brittle January morning in 1937, one month before I would turn twelve, and two months before Evan's third birthday, Father suggested that we bundle him up and take him along to the lake for our first load of ice that day. The idea threw Mother into a frenzy. Insisting he was far too young and that he would only be a baby for such a short while, she demanded to know why Father would "rush it." He tried to tease her out of it, suggesting that at this rate the boy would be going to school before she untied the apron strings.

With a bitterness that I would not have believed her capable of, Mother snapped back, "I have precious little else when I'm alone in this God-forsaken place, Addison. Don't take him away from me, too."

In the shocked silence that followed her words, Grandfather ushered me out to the porch. I don't know what was said between my parents, but through the kitchen window I saw Father gently wipe a tear from Mother's cheek. Then he folded her into his arms, where she stood unyielding as he murmured something into her ear. When she finally laid her head on his chest and returned his embrace, I breathed a sigh of relief. Moments later Father joined us outside. With Grandfather at the reins, we headed out in the sleigh, leaving Mother standing framed in the kitchen window, Evan held safely in her arms.

As much as my mother shunned outside chores, I begged for them. I preferred any outdoor job to the menial domestic ones that could keep a girl captive indoors. Those winter trips to Sucker Lake—simply another ranch chore if we wanted our food not to spoil in the summer—were like a holiday to me. I looked forward to riding on the flatbed sleigh as it glided behind the horses' rumps, its runners slicing through the deep snow, sending white waves in our wake. I loved the musky scent of hay and horse sweat, the sting of snowflakes landing on my cheeks and the anticipation of the warmth from the bonfires that would crackle beside the lake while the men cut and loaded the huge ice blocks and I gathered up the smaller chunks for Mother's icebox.

Late that afternoon, we returned home to find the kitchen table set with Mother's good china and best lace tablecloth. The air was filled with the aroma of roast beef and Yorkshire pudding. A fluffy Boston cream pie, Mother's specialty and Father's favourite, sat on the sideboard. After dinner, as if in apology for her outburst that morning, little Evan was permitted to stay up later than usual. The rug in the parlour was pushed back and mother brought out her record collection and a bottle of sherry.

All my life, my grandfather and father had always been teetotallers, but I never knew either of them to begrudge Mother having a glass of sherry as she sometimes did on special occasions and on those music-filled nights.

By then, Grandfather had taken to wearing wire-rimmed eyeglasses at home—although his vanity would not allow him to wear them to town, where he often mistook one person for another. In the dim evening light in the parlour, he often set his spectacles aside and was content to listen to the radio or Mother's music. That night, he sat on the sidelines, his empty pipe playing across his lips, his toes tapping in rhythm, while the rest of us took turns dancing with each other, often with Evan's feet planted on ours, his arms hugging our legs.

Why my father, who usually preferred a slow dance, decided to swing my mother into the air, I'll never know. But when Duke Ellington's "The Waltz You Saved for Me" was over, and the record exchanged for the rousing instrumental "It Don't Mean a Thing (If It Ain't Got That Swing)," Father surprised us all by continuing to dance. Imitating Grandfather's old miner's stomp, he took Mother around the waist and swung her up into the air, hoisting her higher and higher with each whooping lift. After the song ended, laughing and out of breath, she fell back into her chair. When Father changed the record on the phonograph, she begged off, encouraging me to take her place. As she sat back sipping her sherry, Father, to my delight, swung me in the same Hurdy Gurdy Girl fashion to Benny Goodman's "Sing, Sing, Sing." Evan, bouncing on Grandfather's knee, threw up his arms and cried out repeatedly, "Me, Dada, me." So when we were done,

Father replaced the Victrola's bulky needle arm on the spinning record and then swept my brother up into his arms. Mother, relaxed by her second glass of sherry, did not stop him.

"Up, up, Dada," Evan cried. And just as Grandfather had so often done with me when I was a toddler, Father threw my giggling little brother up in the air, letting him free-fall back into his waiting hands.

"Again, Dada," Evan begged, "again." And Father obliged, tossing him higher and higher. It all looked so innocent, so harmless, my father's huge hands catching him easily and launching him back up again, over and over.

In the shadows' glowing edges, I caught the flicker of alarm in my mother's eyes, her mouth opening in a silent O. She pushed herself up from her seat just before Evan landed awkwardly in my father's arms and whimpered, "Ow. Dada. Hurt."

Before Father could check him over, Mother snatched my little brother away and took him to her chair, laid him in her lap and examined every inch of his body. Finding no marks—for surely, as my bewildered father was saying, the child was nowhere near the ceiling—she nuzzled him in her arms crooning her "hush little baby" lullaby. Within moments he was sleeping, and our evening's dance party came to an end.

Later, in the eerie light of predawn, I was awakened by a caterwaul of hysterical screams and animal-like keening. I bolted from my bed and scurried down from the loft, my bare feet scarcely making contact with the ladder rungs. I raced through the kitchen toward the sliver of yellow light bleeding from my parents' bedroom, arriving at their doorway just behind my long-john-clad grandfather.

We stood there together, frozen in place by the scene before us. Next to the crib, at the foot of the bed, my father was doubled over, his shoulders heaving in silent agony. Beside him, slumped on the wooden plank floor, my sobbing mother rocked back and forth. It took a moment to register that the limp bundle clutched to her breast was Evan's pale and lifeless body.

5.

No one would ever know when, or why, Evan took his final breath. He was sleeping peacefully when mother laid him in his crib the evening before. In the early hours of morning, perhaps instinctively sensing the stillness in the room, she had woken from a fitful sleep. Rising to check on him, as she often did during the night, she found him gone from this world.

Growing up on a ranch it's impossible to be sheltered from the harsh realities of life. By the age of eleven I had witnessed the many forms of heartache that living off the land brings. I was well acquainted with the truth of birth, and the necessity of death. If we wanted to eat, to survive, animals had to breed, and animals had to die. I had witnessed the butchering of steers, cows, pigs and chickens. On many occasions I watched, even helped, gut and dress out their carcasses, until they became nothing more than meat to be stored in the icehouse.

I don't believe I was jaded, but I understood early that death was a part of life. Familiarity with death in animals, however, gives no immunity against the shock of seeing its brutal truth on the face of someone you love.

As I stood in my parents' bedroom doorway in the dark morning light, my mind struggled to take in the unimaginable. I wanted to run into the room and shake my brother out of his endless sleep. But my grandfather's firm hand restrained me, and all I could do was choke out a hoarse "Wake up, Evan. Wake up."

At the sound of my voice, Father's head lifted. When I saw the bewildered sorrow in his red swollen eyes, the full force of the truth hit me like a blow; my father, who I believed could fix anything, could never fix this.

He looked down at Mother and lightly placed his hand on her shoulder, perhaps in an effort to make her aware that I was there. She flinched at his touch and shrank away, hugging Evan tighter to her breast, as if shielding him from my father. At the sight of the renewed agony on Father's face, my grandfather soundlessly closed the bedroom door.

Taking my hand, he whispered, "Come, child. Your folks need us to be strong now."

I let him lead me through the darkness into the kitchen, where he pulled out a chair and sat down. With a strength that I thought he had lost, he lifted me, bewildered and trembling, onto his lap and held me close. Morning shadows crept across the room while I clung to him with my arms around his neck and sobbed into his shoulder.

When I was finally spent, I sat up and he gently ran his hand down my face and then his own, wiping away our mingled tears. Reaching beyond me he swept an arm over the table, his fingers searching for his eyeglasses. I stood up and retrieved them from the sideboard. He hooked the wire frames around his ears, cleared his throat and said, "Okay, Addie. There's things need doing."

There's something to be said for routine, and that morning he knew it was needed more than ever. He kept me busy fetching kindling to restart the smouldering fire in the cookstove, finding the matches and carrying in wood to keep it stoked. I helped him search the cupboards for the coffee canister and rolled oats. While we measured out the coffee grounds and the oatmeal into their pots, I listened for my parents, but the only sound in the house was the crackling of the fire and the mantel clock ticking away the minutes.

After the coffee finished perking and grew cold, after the porridge that no one would eat was cooked and then congealed, my parents' bedroom door was still closed. Grandfather placed everything in the warming oven above the stove and told me to go upstairs to get dressed.

Outside, the growing light of dawn cast long winter shadows across the hushed landscape. From somewhere in the purple haze beyond the meadow, a lone wolf suddenly howled and the ranch dogs took up an answering chorus. Their plaintive cries echoed through the morning, as if in sympathy with our sorrow.

With the weight of the grey sky pressing down on me, I shivered and hurried after Grandfather as he crossed the yard to his workshop. "Stay close to me, boy," he called back, then stopped short. He shook his head. "Sorry, Addie," he said, turning back to me. "I don't know where that came from."

That day was the first time he called me boy. He looked down at me and tried to smile. "Guess it's just that this morning you remind me so much of your pa," he said, touching my shoulder. "He was always a real trooper, too."

The inside of Grandfather's workshop smelled of sawdust and cold metal. When he slowly began searching through a stack of lumber, holding each board up to eye level to check the grain, I didn't need to be told what he intended to build. I made my way to the back corner of the shop where a pile of neatly cut lengths of cedar, sanded to a fine satin finish, were stored. Gathering up an armload of the cedar boards, meant for the hope chest Grandfather intended to build for me, I transferred them to his workbench. He squinted down at them and then back at me. I solemnly nodded my offer, and without a word passing between us, he nodded back acceptance. Grabbing a hammer and a can of nails, I waited for his instructions. But Grandfather shook his head slowly. "No," he said, taking the tools from my hands and setting them down next to the boards. "This can wait. Your ma doesn't need to hear any hammering on this day."

He went into the storage room, rummaging around until he found what he was looking for. Startled, I watched him wheel out the black metal buggy and push it across the workshop. He opened the door, picked up the pram in his arms, and went outside. I ran after him as he carried it across the yard, worried that he had somehow lost his mind with grief. But instead of heading back to the house, he ducked into the icehouse. I realized then that my grandfather was not crazy at all. And I knew that the pram, the baby buggy that Evan and I had had so many hours of fun with, would be where my brother would lie waiting until we could bury him.

Father was standing on the other side of the kitchen door staring numbly out its window as we crossed the yard. While we stamped our boots free of snow and hung our coats in the winter-enclosed porch, he watched as if he had not seen us do this countless times before. Once I was inside, without a word, he knelt down and folded me into his arms.

The rest of the morning passed in a blur. I remember Father checking on Mother in the bedroom every now and then, Grandfather dishing up bowls of porridge and urging us to eat. Wanting to please him I tried but couldn't choke back a single spoonful. Like Father, though, I accepted the warmed-over coffee. It was a first for me and something that, on a normal day, Mother would have heartily disapproved of. But this was not a normal day. I sipped the hot, creamy liquid, and then when tears blurred my vision again, I folded my arms on the table and buried my head in them. I dozed off, waking with a start some time later to hear Father's and Grandfather's hushed voices at the table. My mother still had not come out of the bedroom.

Seeing my head rise, Grandfather sent me up to the loft, insisting I would be more comfortable napping in my own bed. Then he and Father went in to Mother. I could hear them gently urging her to allow them to take Evan, her responses little more than animal whimpers.

"Let me take care of the boy, Fern," Grandfather said, as if talking to a frightened child. "See. I've got these nice warm blankets to wrap him in until Reverend Watts comes."

His patient and tender coaxing went on until Mother relented with a final wail, and moments later he carried my brother, swaddled in his old baby blankets, through the kitchen below and out to the icehouse.

In the silence that followed I heard Father murmuring something to Mother. Abruptly her weeping ceased and in a voice devoid of emotion, she said, "Leave me."

From conversations that drifted up to the loft that morning, I learned that Evan was to be buried beside my grandmother on the knoll overlooking the east meadows.

In the early afternoon, heavy snowflakes began to drift down. While Mother remained in her bed, Father drove into Sorry to fetch the church minister, Reverend Watts, and to use The Sorry Grocers' telephone to call the coroner in Quesnel. I stayed home, curled up on the divan in the parlour, while Grandfather went out to build a bonfire to thaw the frozen ground in the ranch's lonely little cemetery.

Not long after they were gone, I heard Mother stirring in her room, and then the door opened and she emerged. Wearing her flannel nightgown, her long curly hair loose and gone wild, she shuffled by without noticing me there. She made her way through the parlour and into the kitchen by holding onto the backs of furniture, the counters, the walls, like a doddering old woman. Hearing the door creak open, I jumped up and raced after her. By the time I reached the kitchen doorway, she was trudging through the snow in Grandfather's boots, heading toward the icehouse. Worried about how lightly dressed she was in the bitter cold, I tugged on my boots, grabbed my jacket and Father's mackinaw and hurried after her.

As long as I live I will never be able to erase the image that stopped me at the open icehouse door. Inside, illuminated by the shaft of grey afternoon light, Mother was sitting among the straw-covered ice blocks. Her breath escaping in tiny puffs of frozen vapour, she was gently rocking my brother's baby carriage and singing, "Hush little baby, don't say a word, Mommy's going to buy you a mockingbird."

I approached slowly and laid the mackinaw around her trembling shoulders. She lifted her head, and although for a moment she appeared to struggle for recognition, her blue lips attempted a smile and she uttered, "Thank you, dear." She allowed me to lead her back into the house, where I rubbed her feet and hands with Pond's cold cream while she disappeared inside herself.

I had known my mother to do this before. But she was always aware of it, and if I had to prod her sometimes when she stared vacantly while

I was speaking, she would say with a start, "Oh, silly me, there I go, wool-gathering again."

I learned early to recognize the first warning signs in her faraway look, and I knew how to draw her back by asking questions about her life in the city. Father, too, was not oblivious to her sinking into blue moods, and he often encouraged her to take the Greyhound bus down to New Westminster for a visit, but she would decline, saying she couldn't bear to go without him because she would miss him far more than she ever missed the city.

There was no question that she adored my father, but watching her shrink away from his every touch in those grief-filled days, I began to fear that her heart was locked against him forever. For although I never heard the words spoken out loud, then or ever, it was clear Mother blamed Father for Evan's death.

It was Grandfather who would finally convince her to take a mouthful of soup, a sip of tea. And after a sudden storm arrived, delaying the burial, it was only he, or I, who could lead her back to the house every time she drifted outside like a sleepwalker heading to the icehouse.

She barely uttered a word during that week, but the night after we finally laid Evan to rest, when the last mourner had left our house, she knelt down beside me in the kitchen. Her cheeks pale and her eyes empty of anything except sorrow, she gently took my face between her hands. For a brief moment I thought I saw a spark of her old self return to those tormented eyes. She reached up to brush a wisp of hair from my forehead, and then, her voice flat and lifeless, she said, "I'm sorry, Adeline. Please forgive me."

During the night a chinook swept over the countryside, the warm winds of a false spring taming the fury of winter's jaws for a while. I awoke long before daybreak to the sounds of Father and Grandfather getting ready to ride out in search of three pregnant heifers who, fooled by the mild temperature, had found their way through a section of broken fence and wandered away from the feeding pasture. I sleepily considered getting up and going with them but escaped back into slumber. I woke much later to discover sunlight streaming in through the small window above my bed and Jack Frost's handiwork melting down the glass.

Maybe it's only the passage of time that has led me to believe that, even before I hurried downstairs, I knew my mother was gone.

6.

Downstairs, the fires crackled in the kitchen and parlour stoves, but as I raced from room to room, nothing had ever felt as cold or empty as our ranch house did on that January morning. In my parents' bedroom, Mother's clothing spilled out of open dresser drawers and lay strewn around the floor. Her armoire doors stood wide open and inside, to my dismay, only her large green tapestry suitcase remained. The smaller matching travel bag, normally stored beside it, was missing. In the kitchen, the Magic Baking Powder tin where she kept the money she had inherited from her mother lay empty upon the counter, the tightly wrapped roll of bills nowhere in sight.

I yanked back the kitchen curtains and peered outside, thinking Father must have come back from the fields and driven off somewhere with her. But there was the tail end of our pickup truck parked in the machine shed. I threw on my coat and boots and ran out into the yard. I searched the empty icehouse, the outhouse, my voice becoming more and more frantic as I called out for my mother. Even in my growing panic, I knew enough not to stray far from the house to search for her. Grandfather had always been a stickler for plans, instilling in me that survival in the country hinged on being prepared. If any one of us was lost, my job was to stay at home while the adults searched. It was an emergency plan that had never been tested until then.

Her missing tapestry travel bag and the empty baking powder tin indicated that wherever Mother had gone, she had gone of her own accord. Yet I couldn't help but fear that she may have become disoriented and wandered astray in a landscape unfamiliar to her, except from the windows of our home or truck. For it was hard to imagine that my mother, who never ventured farther than the corral fences in the best of weather, would walk off in the middle of winter.

Driving the stray cows into the feeding pasture, Father and Grandfather heard my frantic cries echoing across the fields. Moments later my father raced into the yard. With the ranch dogs in hot pursuit, his horse's hooves kicking up clumps of snow, he pulled to a standstill a few feet from where I stood and leapt to the ground.

Leaving his horse in my care, he willed his cold truck to a cranky start and followed the trail of footprints I had spotted in the melting snow, which testified to the truth: my mother had indeed walked away.

Her tracks disappeared after the first bend in our road. Three miles later, in the churned-up snow on the main road, Father found some indentations that may or may not have been footprints. At The Sorry Grocers, a sympathetic Rose VanderMeer, the grocer's wife, had not seen Mother. Father came to the conclusion that one of our neighbours must have picked her up somewhere along the road and given her a ride into Wells or Quesnel. No one ever owned up to the deed.

There was no sign of her in Wells. In the Quesnel bus station, a pressured clerk reluctantly admitted that he might have sold a southbound ticket to a woman matching her description earlier that morning. He couldn't be certain, but the bus was long gone at any rate. In hindsight, Father would tell Grandfather much later, his harried appearance must have led the clerk to wonder if a woman might not have had good reason to leave him, and in some misguided way the clerk felt he was protecting a wife from an overbearing husband. Father drove back to the ranch, packed a bag and left for the coast.

In New Westminster, Mother's bachelor brother, Walter Wagner, her only living relative, denied any knowledge of her whereabouts. But he could not meet Father's eyes as they stood in the doorway. Describing the scene afterward, Father concluded that either Uncle Walter was feeling guilty for not showing up at Evan's funeral, or he knew more than he was saying. Still, neither Father's pleas nor his accusations changed his story. He offered to let Father search the house, which he did without hesitation, but there was no sign of a woman's presence. My father returned to the ranch, his hopes of finding Mother's trail ending on the doorstep of the New Westminster house where she grew up. For a long time he would drive into Sorry every weekday to check the mail, hoping she would send word. And once—sometimes twice—every month, he would head down to the coast, where he would sit outside her childhood home on the chance he might catch sight of her. He never did.

The fact that there was no trace of her beyond those few footprints in the melting snow weighed heavily on us all. While Father concentrated his search on the belief that she had made her way south, on that first day Grandfather and I had searched closer to home. We rode out on horseback, making wider and wider circles from where her footprints ended, looking for any clue that she had wandered off the road and into the bush. A fresh snowfall the next morning rendered the search impossible.

In the following days, I woke each morning listening for familiar sounds coming from the kitchen below that meant Mother was up and busy mixing pancake batter or kneading bread dough. The smell of brewing coffee wafting up to the loft, the crackle of wood burning in the cookstove, would lull me into a sense of well-being in those first few waking moments, and I would imagine her with her hands and apron dusted in flour from some delicacy that would be ready by the time I got up for school. When I was fully awake, the reality of her absence would harden me for the day. After a while, I stopped hoping each waking moment for her return. I refused to give in to the urge to run to the window to peer hopefully down the road every time the dogs started barking outside. By spring I had steeled myself to her absence.

7.

The women of a community hold it together. It is the women who look out for and care for one of their own when they are down. And so it was with the women of Sorry and the ranches surrounding it. If the little place called Sorry was the hub of our community, the back roads spreading out from that tiny hub were like spokes on a wheel. It was down those dirt roads that the ranchers' wives travelled to deliver their children to the one-room schoolhouse, to worship at the Protestant church, to visit Reverend Watts—or more often, his wife—in times of need, to shop in The Sorry Grocers and to see my father at his makeshift office in the corner.

There are no secrets in a small community. Even in one as spread out as ours. Fern Beale's disappearance was common knowledge within days of her leaving. The women passed it on in hushed tones upon meeting, tut-tutting their tongues and shaking their heads sadly at our family's misfortune of having one tragedy following directly on the heels of another. When their husbands encountered my father or grandfather, it was with little more than oblique glances, brief nods or grunted greetings. Not so their wives. Father said that he barely had a free moment at his desk on Saturday mornings anymore for all the ladies who stopped by to utter words of sympathy, to offer advice and, in not so subtle ways, to inquire if there was any news of Mother. Some took it upon themselves to visit the ranch house that spring—something they had seldom done when my mother was with us.

By her own admission, Mother had never fit in with the ranchers' wives, who she always maintained were standoffish because they considered her too "citified." But one would have thought she had a passel of best friends, the way they lamented her absence.

Father and Grandfather tolerated the women with good grace whenever they showed up with baked offerings or jars of preserves in hand. I would scurry up to the loft to wait hidden from view while they sat at our table below and inquired in hushed voices about how I was faring with all of this. Many offered to take me in until my mother's return. I imagined them looking around at the state of the ranch house, taking note of the dirt and dust-covered floors, the cluttered counters and the dish-filled sink.

Neither Father nor I was much for housekeeping, and Grandfather's poor eyesight forgave the muck and pine needles we tracked in and ignored. I knew my mother would be horrified if she could see how quickly her spotless home had turned to such rack and ruin. My refusal to keep a tidy house, my newfound slovenliness, was my only way of punishing her, and I did it with relish, allowing the mess underfoot to grow deeper and deeper until my father would take a broom to it himself. His only admonishment regarding my lack of interest in housekeeping was to say, "Well, Addie, like a true rancher, it appears that the land is more important to you than the house."

I made a half-hearted attempt at cooking, but my grandfather rescued me from that fate after he tasted a few of my concoctions. He took over the kitchen, surprising me but apparently not my father, with loaves of sourdough bread and pots of bubbling stew.

The first time I dug into one of his meals and marvelled that he could cook at all, he laughed out loud. "How do you think your father and I survived alone all those years?" he asked.

Until then I hadn't given much thought to how he had raised my father by himself. Before I could respond, though, Grandfather continued, "When you're left with a child on your own, you learn a lot more than you bargained for. Oh, the local gals wanted to help back then too," he said picking up his fork. "Someone was always showing up on the doorstep ... to make sure I was keeping the baby alive, I suppose. Mostly they wanted to take him home with them. But I figured, if they can learn all this stuff, so could I. I figure I did all right. Your dad didn't turn out too bad, eh, boy?"

Father glanced up from his meal, surprise arching his eyebrows. "Boy? Don't you mean Addie, Dad?"

"Yeah, of course. Guess I just got stuck in the past there for a moment."

From that night on, Grandfather did most of the cooking. It would eventually come to a point where he needed my eyes to help gather the ingredients, but once they were in his hands he threw meals together fearlessly. If they sometimes turned out a tad too salty, or perhaps slightly burnt, neither Father nor I complained.

In appreciation of his proficiency in the kitchen, I eventually relented and took over the dishwashing, although I have to admit not well and not consistently. That and my spit-and-a-promise efforts at cleaning were my concessions to doing my share in the house. But Father was right. I would far rather tackle any outside chore.

Life after Mother was different, and not necessarily always worse. Although we no longer played records on the phonograph or spent evenings dancing in the parlour, no one enforced my bedtimes or corrected my language. And out of the blue every once in a while when I was helping Grandfather in the kitchen, he would break into a version of "Sweet Adeline." I loved hearing him sing the song that connected me to the grandmother I was named after.

"My Adeline, sweet Adeline, you're the flower of my heart, sweet Adeline," his deep baritone voice would croon as his hand deftly reached out like a surgeon's, waiting for me to pass the next ingredient for whatever creation he was cooking up. Sometimes, if my father was in the room, he would join in, their voices harmonizing, and for those moments, my anger at my mother was forgotten.

There were other freedoms that came with being a motherless twelve-year-old. No one objected to the fact that I had taken to drinking coffee, and no one climbed up to the loft to check the tidiness of my room, as she had done once a week. Most of all, no one told me what clothes to wear. I shunned the dresses, the skirts and the blouses with their scratchy collars and now lived in overalls or dungarees and Father's cast-off shirts. I tossed out the collection of ribbons and either pulled back my long blonde hair into an elastic band or let it hang loose. When winter melted into spring, and spring gumbo slowly hardened into dirt roads, my only acquiescence to the change of seasons was to trade out my heavy snow boots for rubber waders or cowboy boots.

The change in my attire, more than anything, drew the attention of the women in our community. I could feel their eyes on me whenever I accompanied my father to his grocery store office on Saturdays. The one person in town whom I could count on not to raise her eyebrows at the state of my clothing was the grocer's wife, Rose VanderMeer. The only indication that she noticed at all was when Father found a smaller version of his flannel work shirts laid out on his desk at the store one Saturday morning. When I unwrapped his purchases at home that afternoon, along with the two new shirts, I found she had slipped in a handful of leather ties, the same as the ones she used to fasten her own hair.

I liked Mrs. VanderMeer. And it was obvious to me that both Father and Grandfather favoured her as well. Perhaps it was because she was a quiet woman who minded her own business yet, like Mother, had been the subject of much whispered tittle-tattle herself. Or perhaps it was because, although both were politely tolerated by the other women, they were clearly considered outsiders.

Most of the ranchers' wives were born to the life, daughters and granddaughters of pioneers and homesteaders. Rough-hewn and sharp-edged, they worked the land alongside their husbands, producing offspring like livestock and comparing the numbers of their brood like badges of honour. And so for years, whenever Mother showed up in Sorry wearing her best city dress with only one child in tow, they couldn't help but search for flaws. They held up their competency and plainness against her beauty and fine ways, and they found themselves wanting.

With Mrs. VanderMeer, I came to suspect that some of their stand-offishness was because she was the only Native woman in the community. And, as Father noted, it didn't help that she was the one whom those proud women often had to ask for an extension of credit at The Sorry Grocers during hard times.

She always had a ready smile whenever Mother and I walked into the store, though. The two women couldn't have been more different. Rose VanderMeer's glistening ebony hair, worn in a thick braid down her back, was in stark contrast to my mother's unruly red mop, which she always wore tucked tidily into a crocheted snood. And Mother's freckled alabaster skin appeared wintery pale next to Rose VanderMeer's smooth, coppery complexion. Yet to me they were the two most beautiful women in our community.

If they were never exactly close friends, they at least had an unspoken respect for each other. Like Mother, the grocer's wife was not one to join in the ladies' huddled conversations at church or in the store. But whenever she and Mother met, her strange midnight-blue eyes—irises so dark they appeared almost black—sparkled with warmth.

From the beginning there was much hushed speculation about those eyes.

Little was known about her past. Her reserved ways kept everyone guessing when years ago the Dutch grocer brought her home to Sorry after a trip to Williams Lake. He offered little by way of explanation to his curious customers other than to introduce her as his wife and her seven-year-old boy as his stepson.

It was when she registered the boy for school, giving his birth name as Alan Baptiste, that the chin-wagging started in earnest. It was rumoured that she was the daughter of a Chilcotin chief. When I wondered out loud if that made her a real Indian princess, or if I mentioned her odd blue eyes, it was one of the few times Grandfather refused to comment on local gossip.

All I knew was that she was the mother of my best friend—in truth, my only friend—Alan Baptiste.

It hadn't always been so. Not long after they came to live in Sorry, when I was six and Alan was seven, for some reason my father had the notion that we would make great playmates. Maybe it was because all the other kids in the area had brothers and sisters to spare. And at the time, I, like Alan, was an only child, with neither of us having a single sibling, cousin or otherwise to call our own. Whatever Father's reasoning, on Saturday mornings, he started taking me with him when he went into his office at The Sorry Grocers.

I don't know what made him think the solemn boy would be interested in playing with me on Saturdays when he clearly wasn't during the week. At school he sat slumped in his desk, treating me with the same disdain he seemed to hold for the other kids in the class. Although he had good reason to dislike them, I resented him lumping me in with those bullies who taunted him so mercilessly or ignored him completely.

Our teacher, Mrs. Parsons, was no better. From the start she begrudged his presence, disregarding him for the most part, except for those times when he would disappear in the middle of a school day. The sight of his empty desk after lunch would cause her to purse her thin lips and mutter some disparaging remark about Indians not belonging in her classroom. As she scribbled his name on the blackboard for punishment the next day, the rest of the class, her daughter Enid in particular, would giggle while I glared at her back and wished that I too could escape to the hillsides above our school like Alan Baptiste.

Still, no matter how hard I tried to get his attention, he treated me as nothing more than an annoying girl. One morning during recess, in an overture of friendship, I offered to share my peashooter with him. He looked down at it, then at the dried peas in my other hand, kicked at the dirt, then strode away muttering, "Stupid girl."

As much as the rejection stung, it was somewhat understandable. At that time, my mother was still insisting I wear a dress whenever I left the ranch. Worse yet, as curly as her hair was, mine was poker straight, so every school morning she heated up the curling iron on the kitchen stove and rolled my hair into huge sausage ringlets. Hard as I tried to rake them out with my hands on the way to town, I am certain that in Alan Baptiste's eyes I looked just like a Pollyanna.

The first Saturday we were thrown together at the store, it appeared that his mother was just as hopeful as my father was for our friendship. Alan was polite enough—until we were out of her sight. The moment the door closed behind us after we went outside, to "go play," as she suggested, he hurried down the porch steps and headed across the road. Behind the school he glanced back over his shoulder. At the sight of me still following, his dark eyes—the same midnight blue as his mother's— narrowed, and he said, "Get lost."

Sitting on a swing in the schoolyard watching him climb up the hillside, I decided that I didn't like him much. Yet there was something about the boy that drew me to him. Besides, there really was no one else near my age in Sorry. Except for Enid Parsons, and I would rather have eaten glass than claim our teacher's prissy daughter for a friend.

So I continued to go into town on Saturday mornings in hopes that, like Father said, Alan would eventually come around.

Then one morning during the summer after Evan was born, I discovered Alan out in the back lot behind the store with a slingshot in his hands. He didn't notice me standing at the side of the building as, with one eye closed, he took aim at the pop bottles lined up on the stumps in the distance. He took his shot, and the stone fell miserably short of any target. When a second and third shot failed to shatter any glass, I couldn't help myself. The laugh barked out of my mouth before my hand could cover it.

Alan swirled around. "Buzz off," he muttered when he saw me standing by the corner of the building.

"Great shooting," I said

"Yeah? And I suppose you can do better?"

"Bet I can."

"Okay, Miss Smarty-pants," he said, offering the homemade weapon. "Let's see."

"Swell." Before he could change his mind, I strode over and grabbed the slingshot. I tested the wooden handle in my grip, then bent over and retrieved a stone from the neat pile at Alan's feet. Loading it in the leather pad, I stretched back the rubber as far as it would go and let it fly. A split second later a puff of dust rose from the ground in front of a distant stump.

"Yeah, great eye," he scoffed.

"Just testing the sight," I said, picking up another pebble. I quickly loaded and without hesitation pulled off a shot that ended with the satisfying explosion of glass. And then, to prove it wasn't a fluke, I took shot after shot until every bottle was in shards on the ground. Years of Grandfather's marksmanship lessons were not for nothing.

Alan grabbed the metal bucket at his feet and headed over to clean up the mess. "Pretty good for a girl," he grudgingly conceded.

I followed behind and helped pick up the glass shards. "Oh yeah?" I said, dropping chunks into his bucket. "Well, if I had my rifle here I could show you some real shooting."

"Yeah, sure. As if you have your own gun."

"Do too. Go on in and ask my dad if you don't believe me."

A strange expression flickered across his face. It struck me then that living in a store, having a stepfather who never hunted, Alan was not likely to have access to a rifle. His struggle to hide his envy made me ashamed of my boasting.

Too carelessly, I reached for another piece of glass and felt the sharp edge slice my finger. I glanced down at the crimson blood dripping onto my palm. Smiling sheepishly at Alan, I held up my hand, playfully offering, "Blood brothers?"

He shook his head in disgust. But I was pretty certain he fought a grin before he turned away muttering, "Stupid girl."

Our reluctant friendship slowly grew from there. It was sealed forever after my brother Evan's death. When I finally returned to school, while all the other students were nervous around me or avoided me altogether, it was Alan who came and sat down beside me on the school steps and said quietly, "I'm sorry about your brother."

At lunch hour he invited me over to the store. After that we fell into the habit of escaping from the school grounds at noon break and heading over to The Sorry Grocers to eat our lunch on the porch, or inside at the counter during poor weather. And sometimes, just as she had on that very first day, his mother would fetch us a bottle of Pepsi-Cola from the cooler, and we would pass the dripping bottle back and forth as we ate our sandwiches.

By the time we entered grade six, Alan was the eldest of the twenty-one students in Sorry's little one-room school. Although he was a year older than me, he was in the same grade. Not, I believed, because he was any less intelligent, but because there was nothing in that classroom to hold his attention.

He confided in me once how much he envied the ranchers' sons, who were allowed to quit school to work alongside their fathers the moment they turned thirteen. But unlike all the other boys in Sorry, Alan, at his mother's insistence, was obliged to remain in school until he graduated, regardless of how long that took.

Mrs. Parsons was just plain mean-spirited about Alan's continued presence in her classroom. Even the length of his hair was a cause for complaint. His mother began tying back his shoulder-length hair and tucking the ponytail under his shirt collar—her only concession to the teacher's constant notes home. It made no difference.

At the supper table I would often bemoan Mrs. Parsons' treatment of Alan. Father and Grandfather would neither agree nor disagree but let me rant on about the unfairness of her punishments for the simplest of things. Of course, playing hooky was not considered a minor thing, but surely staring out the classroom window, or not responding to some question, did not warrant Alan sitting on a stool facing the corner all afternoon, or receiving a razor-strap lashing on the palms of his hands.

Every time Alan was singled out in this way or had his intellect berated, I wanted to ask our teacher exactly how many languages she could speak. For I knew first-hand that Alan and his mother spoke two fluently. But something warned me that this knowledge was their private business. It was not for me to betray something I had learned by accident one day when I walked into the store's backroom and overheard them speaking in a strange and unfamiliar dialect. Mrs. VanderMeer noticed me there in the doorway and stopped talking. While Alan went back to stocking shelves, she explained that whenever they were alone they always spoke the language Alan had grown up with on the reserve because she was afraid that over time he might forget their people's native tongue.

The childish schoolyard taunts aimed at him lessened as time went on and the older boys left school, but Mrs. Parsons' castigations only got worse. He suffered her with a smouldering glare and a hardening of his jaw. Still, as he grew older, I could see it took everything he had to hold his temper, to honour his promise to his mother and remain in that schoolroom.

I was not so restrained and often found it difficult to keep my mouth shut when I believed our teacher was being unfair. My questioning her authority did little to improve her temper and would only make it harder on Alan, so I soon learned to hold my tongue. But it came a little too late, and although my punishments were never as harsh as Alan's, it seemed that Mrs. Parsons looked for any excuse to reprimand me. Until Mother left.

8.

In the months after my mother's departure, Mrs. Parsons took a renewed interest in my well-being. Then, one Sunday afternoon in late spring, she drove out to our ranch in the school's Willys sedan. When she and Enid climbed out of the mud-splattered car, Grandfather beat a hasty retreat to the parlour.

"Don't you dare leave me down here alone," Father said when I headed for the loft.

Reluctantly I joined him on the porch to greet them. Watching my teacher and her daughter gingerly making their way along the plank boards laid across the muddy yard, I ungenerously imagined them losing their footing and toppling into the soupy muck.

"Good afternoon, Mr. Beale. Adeline," Mrs. Parsons called out when they safely reached the porch steps. "It's such a beautiful spring day for a drive, isn't it?" Without waiting for an answer she climbed the stairs, wiped her feet on the mat and handed Father a pastry box. "Hope we didn't come at an inconvenient time," she said, peering past him at the kitchen table still cluttered with lunch dishes.

"No, of course not," Father said, holding the door open and ushering them inside.

I busied myself filling the teakettle, leaving him to help with their coats and hats. After everyone was settled awkwardly around the table and had exchanged pleasantries about the weather, Father cleared his throat and asked, "Is everything all right with Addie's schooling, then? I know I have been a bit neglectful..."

"No, no, Adeline is doing fine," Mrs. Parsons said, smiling sweetly at me, then added, "Well, perhaps falling a little behind in lessons, but that's to be expected, given the circumstances. And I am certain she will get back on track soon, won't you, dear?"

Oh, if sugar had a sound it would be the honey silkiness of her voice as she looked from me to Father. The whistling of the kettle on the wood stove saved me from responding. I jumped up to pour the boiling water into the teapot.

"Since you mention it," Mrs. Parsons continued, "I know this has been a difficult time for your family, and it's completely understandable, but I can't help noticing that Adeline must have outgrown her spring clothes. One of the reasons I came out here today was to offer my services. A woman's touch, if you will, to help her shop for some appropriate school outfits."

The teapot almost slipped from my hands as I returned to the table.

Father spoke before I could let loose the curt reply forming on my tongue. "Thank you, Mrs. Parsons," he said, "but I believe Addie is fine in the wardrobe department."

Looking pointedly at my mud-stained overalls, Mrs. Parson said, "For the ranch, perhaps." She pushed her cup and saucer forward for me to pour. "But the fact is that we do have a dress code, and wearing trousers or overalls to school doesn't set a very good example for the younger girls, does it?"

"I don't know about that," Father said. "But my guess is that, as you say, 'given our circumstances,' the girls, and the school, might have some tolerance for Addie's choice of clothing for the time being."

I gloated inwardly at the sight of Mrs. Parsons' lips growing thinner as she tried to maintain her smile. Beside her, Enid remained silent, studying her hands. I felt sympathy for her, just as I sometimes did at school. Imagine your mother being the teacher and daily pointing out your work and your manners as an example to the rest of the class. But my sympathy didn't extend to friendship with a girl whose idea of excitement was to let someone push her on the schoolyard swing, and whom I found, to use Grandfather's expression, "as dull as dishwater."

Regaining her composure, Mrs. Parsons picked up her teacup. She took a sip, then set it back in her saucer and conceded, "Perhaps you're right, Mr. Beale, and for now we'll let it go." With a renewed smile at Father, she reached over and patted her daughter's hand. "As a widow, I know what it's like to raise a child alone. And so I would like—well, Enid and I thought it would be nice—to invite Adeline to spend some time with us in our home, to spend the night every now and then, if you will."

Her sudden shift in the conversation was as startling to me as her suggestion. "No!" I blurted. Then, when even Father appeared taken aback by my outburst, I mumbled, "Thank you, but I have my chores."

"Well, it's an open invitation," Mrs. Parsons said, "We'll leave you to consider it."

After they were gone, Father said, "Perhaps spending time with Enid's not such a bad idea, Addie." It was more a question than a statement.

"That'll be the day," I snorted. "She's thirteen years old and still talks about her dolls, for crikey's sake!"

From the parlour behind me came Grandfather's barked laughter. He had remained hidden while our company was there; his admitted distaste for my teacher stemmed, I suspected, from my complaints about her treatment of Rose VanderMeer's son.

9.

By the beginning of the new school year, it was clear to me that Mrs. Parsons' interest in my father was much more than a teacher's concern for a student. Her newly developed habit of popping into The Sorry Grocers on Saturday mornings, the rouge and lipstick she took to wearing—which only served to make her narrow face appear sharper—and the change in her hairstyle, from a tightly knotted bun to falling loose whenever she was around him, gave her away. Worst of all, the way she looked at him was downright goo-goo-eyed.

During the summer she showed up at our ranch a number of times, always with some flimsy excuse of delivering books she thought I might be interested in, or outfits that Enid had outgrown, which would be "perfect for me in the new school year." It never occurred to her—or she chose to ignore—that, although Enid was a year older, she was barely an inch taller than I was. I did search through the books she brought and had to grudgingly admit, if only to myself, that many of them were interesting. But without even looking through the bundles of clothing, I took them out to the storage shed where, for all I know, they are still being used by mice for nesting.

Other than being his usual polite self, my father showed no interest in or encouragement toward Mrs. Parsons, so I held no fears that he would in any way succumb to her not-so-veiled flirtations. Still, when I returned to school in the fall, she started her campaign in earnest: asking after my father's well-being at every opportunity, singling me out for special favours in class and extending the constant invitations for which I was fast running out of excuses to decline. And then, one Friday afternoon in the middle of September, she handed me a note to deliver to my father requesting that he stop by the school for a parent-teacher meeting after his office hours the following day.

Father read the note at the dinner table. When he was finished, he carefully refolded the paper, looked over the top of his reading glasses and asked, "Is there something I should know, Addie?"

"Yeah," I said, swallowing the last of my gravy-sopped biscuit. "My teacher's got a crush on you."

At the head of the table Grandfather chuckled under his breath.

Father turned to him. "Well then, maybe I should send you in to meet with her instead, Dad."

"Nope. It's not me that woman has her sights set on," Grandfather replied, his bushy Beale eyebrows arching mischievously.

Sometimes on Saturday mornings, if all my work was done, I would go into Sorry and hang out with Alan while my father kept his business hours. The next day, wild horses couldn't have held me back from racing through my chores so I could be ready when he climbed into the pickup truck to drive to town.

At noon, after Father had stamped his last document and bid good day to his final client, he grabbed his jacket and pushed on his wide-brimmed cowboy hat. As Alan and I dumped buckets of ice chips into the pop cooler at the front of the store, I watched my father stroll across the road as if in no great hurry to reach his destination. When I was certain he was inside the schoolhouse, I followed. Alan declined to come with me, even when I tried to persuade him that we could pretend we were real Indian scouts on a spying mission.

"I *am* a real Indian, pale face," he said with a teasing grin, but he still wasn't tempted to join my eavesdropping plan.

Behind the school, I crouched below an open window. Above the drone of autumn-lazy insects I heard Mrs. Parsons say, "I am greatly concerned about Adeline's complete lack of interest in making friends with any of the other girls in class."

There was nothing surprising in her words. I had received her opinion on the subject many times, and by "other girls" I knew she meant Enid. The rest of the females in our class were all so much younger that no one could expect us to have anything in common.

"To be perfectly honest with you," she went on, "I worry that she spends her recess and lunch times either alone, with her nose in a book— not that there is anything wrong with reading, mind you—or running off to God-knows-where with that Indian boy."

She knew perfectly well that God-knows-where was usually across the street at the grocery store.

"Alan's a good lad," my father said. "And I'm grateful that he and my daughter are friends. He's been a great comfort to her in this last while."

"We have all tried to be of comfort, Mr. Beale."

When there was no response from my father, she continued. "Be that as it may, I don't feel that it is proper for a girl of her age to be running around with an …" She hesitated for a moment. "The truth is that I can't help but see that Adeline is growing wilder and wilder with the passing months."

My father's continued silence must have encouraged her because she suddenly asked, "May I be perfectly frank with you, Mr. Beale?" Without waiting for a reply, her voice sugar-coated once again, she continued, "Adeline is twelve years old, almost thirteen, a very vulnerable age for a young lady, and I believe she is suffering from the lack of a woman's influence. And, well, dare I point out that you and I are in a similar position, aren't we? I am a widow with a daughter who has never known her father—God rest his soul—and she could certainly benefit from having a man around. It has occurred to me that you and I could be of some … well, of some advantage to each other. And, if I could be so bold, I would like to suggest that we could start keeping each other company, seeing each other, as it were. So," she drew an audible breath, "on that note, I would like to invite you over to dine with us one evening, Addison. Or, if you prefer, we could drive into Wells and have a quiet dinner first, just the two of us, to get to know one another."

Her sudden change in the conversation startled me as much as the use of my father's given name. I sat up quickly, my back scraping against the rough wood siding.

Inside, the silence was so complete that I could hear the school clock ticking off the seconds before Father said, "I'm a married man, Mrs. Parsons."

"It's been nine months, Addison. Do you really believe she's coming back?"

"I hold out hope."

His quiet response touched something in my heart, and I felt tears that I had held in check for months threaten. His next words stopped them.

"And let me be perfectly clear, Mrs. Parsons," he said, his chair scraping across the floor, "if anything were to happen to change my marital status, I would not want to give you false hope that I would be interested in pursuing a relationship with you. Now or ever."

How I wished I could have seen her face then, but hearing his retreating footsteps, I jumped up and rushed off before my father came out of the schoolhouse.

At home, the interview with my teacher was never mentioned. At school the following Monday, it was clear that my father's rejection had bittered Mrs. Parsons' tongue toward me. All week long the secret knowledge of Father's rejection empowered me, and her harsh barbs failed to find their mark. And then, at lunch on Thursday, the sunshine on the hills and the warm September wind were too tempting for Alan. For the first time he invited me to go with him, saying, "There's something I want to show you." I didn't hesitate.

I followed him along the narrow animal paths winding up the grass-covered slopes. The children playing their games in the schoolyard below grew smaller, their voices fading in the distance as bunchgrass gave way to dirt and gravel, brush turned into forest. The grade grew steeper and I had to scramble to keep up with Alan, who was familiar with the difficult terrain. After a while, I broke out into a clearing where he waited. He pointed to the darkened ridge rising above us. "Up there," he said. I nodded and hurried across the clearing. By the time I reached him, he was yanking the leather tie from the ponytail at the back of his neck. "Real Indians," he said shaking his hair loose, "wear their hair long."

I pulled the tie from my own ponytail and stuffed it in my pocket, letting my hair fly about in the breeze. Slipping on loose stones and grabbing at roots and branches to steady myself, I tackled the steep hill, refusing to give in to the need to rest in fear of losing sight of my friend. Sometime later, I pulled myself up onto the ridge to find him sitting beneath a sway-back pine tree.

Sucking wind and dripping with sweat, I leaned over to catch my breath. When I straightened up, I turned about in a slow circle, taking in the view that stretched forever and forever in every direction. It felt as if I were standing on the top of the world beneath a dome of blue sky.

"Wow, this is swell!" I said collapsing down beside Alan.

"Yeah," he said. "Too bad they aren't there today."

"Who?"

"The wild horses," he said, scanning the valley floor. "Sometimes a herd shows up in the meadows down there. Out on the reserve we called them slicks."

From somewhere above came the screech of a hawk in flight. Alan glanced up and searched the sky until he found the bird gliding on the wind. As he watched it soar in the afternoon sun, I noticed for the first time the tiny flecks of brown in his midnight-blue eyes. At the same time, I saw something else I'd seldom seen in those eyes—a peaceful look of contentment.

"Do you miss it?" I asked. "The reserve?"

The change in his expression made me instantly regret my question.

"No. Not really," he replied after a moment. "I don't remember a whole lot about it. I was five when my mother moved us into town—before the government men could come and take me away to residential school." His gaze returned to the rolling hills and meadows below.

"They took her there when she was a girl," he continued. "She hated that school. The first day they chopped off the girls' braids. Shaved the boys' heads. They threw away their clothes and made them wear uniforms. Told them they couldn't speak their own language anymore and beat them when they did. She ran away after a few years ... Found her way back to the reserve. She hid in her grandmother's house there until she was too old for school."

"Golly!"

"That's why she wants so bad for me to finish school in Sorry. Why she wants me to keep our people's language," he said, still staring down into the valley. "But my mother, she doesn't see that I don't fit in either world. Out on the reserve the other kids teased me about my blue eyes, called me 'not Indian.' In Sorry, I'm teased because I am."

I hugged my knees to my chest and set my head on them.

We were silent for a long while. Then he said quietly, "I remember out there they had a saying: 'The land is forever. Everything starts and ends with the land.'" He shrugged. "Maybe that's why I like it up here so much. Because it's like I can see forever."

"Yeah, me too," I agreed, glad of his shift in mood.

"I guess so," he laughed. "Since most of that land's part of your grandfather's ranch."

"Grandfather's?"

He nodded and swept his arm to indicate the entire valley below us.

"My grandfather owns all that land?"

"Yeah, I guess," he conceded. "As much as any man can own something that's forever."

Disoriented, I studied the valley floor, not recognizing any of the landmarks. And then, on the far side of the valley, I spotted a familiar clump of autumn-yellowed trees. It took a few moments before I realized that the little knoll beside the poplar grove was the spot where my brother Evan was buried. At the sight of the tiny fenced graveyard in the distance, I swallowed back a lump in my throat and felt a warmth in my chest that had nothing to do with the afternoon heat.

Beside me, Alan lifted his face to the sun's rays and closed his eyes "Maybe the horses will still come today," he said. "Maybe not."

I lay back in the grass, my head resting in my hands. Before long the silence gave way to the hum of insects and the rustle of wind in the branches above us. My eyelids became heavy and for a time I dozed off, waking only when clouds scudded across the sun, chilling the air. Lazily, I turned toward Alan, sensing rather than seeing a movement beyond him. I had to stop myself from gasping at the sight of the animal standing not ten feet away. Unaware of or unconcerned by our presence, an enormous buck with its heavily antlered head lowered to the ground ripped out the soft green grass, roots and all. The grinding of his teeth and the air snorting from his black nostrils as he chewed sounded loud above the wind. Finally the stag slowly raised his head and swung around toward us. For what seemed like forever, the animal's dark eyes remained locked on us while we both held our breath. Finally he took one more mouthful of grass, turned and slowly walked away. At the edge of the ridge, the buck stopped and stood motionless, his head held high, his antlers reaching to the sky. I had seen many male deer in my life, but never one so huge. I hadn't finished counting the many points on his antlers to tell my father and grandfather about later before the animal stepped down onto some unseen path and disappeared from view.

"Golly," I whispered, "have you ever?"

"Yeah," Alan replied, rising to his feet. "But never this close."

Later, making our way down from the ridge, even though his wild horses hadn't shown up that day, I felt privileged that my friend had chosen to share this special place with me.

The afternoon sun was sinking in the sky as we descended, and I began to worry that I had missed the school bus. But as we broke out of the forest, I saw that some of our classmates were still playing in the schoolyard below.

And standing in the schoolhouse doorway, watching us descend, was Mrs. Parsons.

10.

I could feel our teacher's cold gaze as we came out of the shadows and started down the grassy slopes. When we arrived at the bottom, she strode across the schoolyard toward us. She reached Alan first. Seizing him by the ear, she pulled him along, snarling, "Inside with you!" Glancing back at me she hollered, "You, too! Inside. Now!"

I had no choice but to follow behind them. For a brief moment it occurred to me that they looked comical. Alan, almost the same height as Mrs. Parsons, could easily have pulled himself away and just walked off, but he offered no resistance. He even had to trot to keep pace as, still tugging on his ear, she yanked him forward up the stairs and into the schoolhouse. She didn't let go until she had hauled him to the front of the classroom. As she withdrew her hand, she shook something unseen off her fingers. Her eyes narrowed as she looked closely at Alan's head.

"Lice!" she hissed, wiping her hand on her sleeve.

My heart leapt into my throat as she leaned over to study the top of my head. When she stepped back, her lips stretched into a thin line, I knew that what was about to happen was far from comical.

"You both have lice," she said, sounding satisfied with this discovery. Sliding two wooden stools against the wall, she unceremoniously shoved us onto them.

Confused, I glanced at Alan and saw anger darken his face. But he remained on the stool, watching her stride over to her desk. When she opened the bottom drawer, reached inside and brought out the scissors and hair clippers, his eyes narrowed and his hands tightened into fists.

As she came at him with the scissors, I fully expected him to knock them from her hands and shove her away. I'll never know if it was his respect for his mother or respect for authority that kept him silent and un-flinching while she hacked away at his beautiful long hair. Without mercy, she ran the clippers over what was left on his tufted scalp, and I could tell that it took everything he had to remain still.

Then she turned to me. I cringed and shrank back. I knew this was wrong. Knew that if I stood up and ran from the room there was little she could do to stop me. I glanced over at Alan. And it struck me that the strange expression on his face seemed almost triumphant. In that moment I decided that whatever the reasons he had allowed this, I could do no less. As the cold scissors snipped away, I kept my head lowered and my eyes squeezed shut, not wanting to see the handfuls of blonde hair fall to the floor.

"This is what you get, young lady." *Snip. Snip. Snip.* "For playing with savages." *Snip. Snip. Snip.* "I warned you." *Snip. Snip. Snip.* "Warned your father!" *Snip. Snip. Snip.* "But would he listen to me?"

I tried to drown out her ranting by concentrating on listening to our classmates playing stickball outside in the schoolyard. Playing, I had no doubt, with one ear open for the sounds of the punishment going on inside the classroom. Determined to give neither them nor Mrs. Parsons the satisfaction, I refused to allow the threatening whimpers to escape from my lips as the clippers worked away, cutting and digging into my scalp.

When she was done and had turned away, her shoulders heaving with spent energy, I reached up and touched my head. My fingers came away red. Beside me, Alan glanced down at my hand, slowly ran his over his own scalp, then smeared his bloodstained palm on mine. In a hardened voice he said, "Blood brothers."

Feeling the sticky warmth pressed between our hands, I glared at our teacher's back. "Yeah," I said, my own voice shaking in defiance. "Real Indian blood brothers."

Without turning around, Mrs. Parson hissed, "Heathens! Both of you! Get out!"

11.

When Alan and I showed up in the grocery store that afternoon, Mrs. VanderMeer took one look at us and her hand flew to her mouth. She came out from behind the counter. Holding back tears, she gently touched each of our heads and then, without asking who was responsible, said, "This is sinful."

Flipping over the sign in the window—the first time ever I'd seen the "closed" side displayed on a weekday—she locked the door and went into the backroom to fetch her husband.

Mr. VanderMeer was not so calm. Catching sight of us, he stopped short in the storage-room doorway. "Vut der hell!" he cried, rushing to his stepson. "Who in Gott's name did this?"

Fearing I might break into girlish tears, I remained silent as Alan explained what had happened. When he was done, to my surprise, he looked at his mother and said with what sounded suspiciously like satisfaction, "I told you it's no different here."

His stepfather ripped off his apron. Tossing it aside, he spat, "Well, she won't get away with this, by Gott."

"Wait, Dirk." His wife's words stopped him before he reached the door.

Stepping between Alan and me, Rose VanderMeer placed a hand on each of our shoulders and said quietly, "Let's speak with Addison Beale first."

The four of us sat squeezed together on the bench seat of the store's delivery van as it bumped and careened over the dirt roads on the way to the ranch. Mrs. VanderMeer sat as mute as Alan and I, while at the wheel her husband cussed out Mrs. Parsons every few minutes, his Dutch accent growing heavier and heavier until I had trouble understanding anything he said—which was probably just as well.

Father was latching the corral gate when we pulled into the ranch yard. Although his eyes betrayed his dismay at the sight of Alan and me climbing out of the van, he listened without comment to the grocer's sputtered indignation and then quietly ushered everyone into the house. Inside, Grandfather was in his room having his afternoon nap, and I was relieved by that. Lately he had taken to calling me boy more often. Certain that my shorn head would only serve to reinforce his mistaken notion, in that moment I wished to neither add to nor explain his growing confusion.

At our kitchen table, in response to Father's patient questions, Mr. VanderMeer vented his ire. He firmly stated that in his opinion, the teacher should be confronted, reported and fired. His anger was punctuated by fits of deep-throated coughs. After a particularly long bout of hacking, he took out his handkerchief, wiped his mouth and muttered, "If you ask me, the voman shut be horsewhipped."

When he was certain Mr. VanderMeer was finished, my father turned to us, carefully searching our faces. "And what do you two believe should be done?" he asked.

"Nothing," Alan answered before I could open my mouth.

"Nothing?" Dirk VanderMeer straightened up in his seat. "We can't let her get away with—"

His wife put her hand on his, stopping his words with the simple gesture. She turned to Alan and said, "I'll speak with her."

Slumped in his chair, Alan shook his head. "Won't make any difference."

Father turned to me. "And what about you, Addie? What would you like us to do?"

"Nothing," I said, agreeing with Alan. "It will just make it worse."

"All right," Father sighed. "If you're certain that's what you both want." Alan nodded.

"It's only hair," I said. "It'll grow back."

"Yeah, that's the thing about hair, isn't it?" Father smiled wanly. He reached out to gently touch the side of my shorn head. "It's not what I would choose to do. But it's your decision. Either way, as you say, your hair will grow back, as lovely as before, whereas I suspect that you're both right—if confronted, Mrs. Parsons' disposition will only grow nastier."

During this exchange, a ruddy-faced Mr. VanderMeer sat with his arms crossed, his jaw set. Both Alan's mother and my father promised not to confront Mrs. Parsons. The storekeeper gave no such assurance.

The next morning, Alan and I ignored our classmates' sideways glances and made our way to our desks amid the din of muffled giggles and whispers. Rose VanderMeer had done her best to tidy up what was left of our hair, gently smoothing out the choppy clumps, cleaning and disinfecting the nicks and cuts and then oiling our scalps. Still, the mirror told me that my tufted head appeared somewhat like that of a newly hatched chick.

As we took our seats, Mrs. Parsons stood ramrod straight at the front of the room, her hands raised in a command of silence. As the buzz died down, her gaze skimmed over the class, searching for any place to rest that didn't include Alan or me. Did I detect a hint of remorse in her thin-lipped expression?

I will never know, for at that moment the back door flew open and Dirk VanderMeer came storming in. Striding between the rows of desks, his eyes fixed on the teacher, he ordered, "Outside, kiddies, you have an early recess."

A few feet shuffled, but everyone remained seated, staring at the gape-mouthed Mrs. Parsons.

"Sir!" she finally sputtered. "School is in session!"

"Not until I speak with you it's not." The storekeeper gestured toward the bewildered class, demanding, "Go on now! Outside. All of you."

As the students jumped up from their desks to stampede from the room, Alan and I remained seated.

Mr. VanderMeer made his way to Alan's desk and in a softened voice said, "Son, please wait outside."

I expected my friend to argue, but, resigned, he pushed himself up and headed toward the back door. I stood and followed, glancing back over my shoulder on the way out.

At the front of the class, Mr. VanderMeer dragged a stool across the floor. Placing it beside Mrs. Parsons' desk, he sat down, saying, "Now you and I shall sit and talk about this in a civilized manner."

Outside, curious students crowded around the porch. Instead of joining them, Alan and I ducked into the cloakroom. Standing amid the coats and jackets with their scent of dirt, cow dung and grass filling our nostrils, we pressed against the dividing wall to peer between the cubbyholes. Through the cracks I could see little more than blurred forms at the front of the room, but I could hear Mr. VanderMeer's heavy breathing.

Finally, Mrs. Parsons broke the silence. "I am authorized to cut students' hair in the event of lice," she said.

"Madam, we live right across the road. If there vas a problem, you could have brought the youngsters over."

"I am under no such obligation. And it was my duty to get rid of the lice before the other students could be infested."

"My wife checks the boy nightly for head lice. I vould doubt that they breed so quickly as a single day."

"Well, those two hooligans were playing hooky, gallivanting in the bush all afternoon. Ticks. It must have been wood ticks, then."

"Ticks? Lice? Vitch?"

"I am no expert on bugs, Mr. Van—"

"This is not the season for wood ticks, Mrs. Parsons. The truth is you had no reason for such harsh action."

"I did what I thought was right—"

"I am a director on the school board," he said, cutting her off. "Dit you know that? And I am of a mind to report you, to see you lose your job." He took a deep breath. "But my son has asked that we not interfere, and—"

"He's hardly your son, now, is he, Mr. VanderMeer," she snapped. "The truth is he shouldn't even be in this school. He's Indian. He belongs with his own people in the residential school at—"

The sharp report of a hand slamming down on the wooden desk echoed like the crack of a shotgun in the room. "Madame, stifle it, by Gott!" Mr. VanderMeer ordered. And then, his voice dangerously low, he said, "Now, I intend to honour my *son's* request, but I warn you, if you ever so much as attempt to repeat any shenanigans like this again—if I ever hear a single complaint from *any* student—I won't be responsible for whatever consequences either I or the school board deem fit."

"Are you threatening me, Mr. VanderMeer?"

"You bet your sweet britches I am!"

By the time he stormed out the back door, the students had scattered, and Alan and I stood waiting at the bottom of the steps.

"I'm sorry, son, but that had to be done."

Alan touched his arm and said, "It's all right, Father." It was the first time I had ever heard him call his stepfather anything other than sir.

The storekeeper's threat to Mrs. Parsons' career evidently carried some weight. After that meeting she left Alan and me alone. Completely alone. She ignored our presence as if we didn't exist. All the lessons and instructions were directed at the other students. Any schoolwork we chose to complete was not checked. If we failed to return to our desks after recess or lunch, nothing was said. Her punishment played out like reward.

We neither minded nor, I believed, took too much advantage of the circumstances. In our isolation in the classroom, Alan and I turned to books. That fall and winter, I was surprised by his complete engrossment in the stories once we started choosing our own reading material instead of what the school dictated. Outside of class we would spend hours discussing the unfolding plots of favourites like *The Call of the Wild*, *The Red Badge of Courage* and *All Quiet on the Western Front*, or scoffing over the unlikeliness of the Native characters and their dialect in *The Last of the Mohicans*.

Being deprived of our teacher's direction was not a hardship, and neither of us felt any compulsion to inform our families of the situation.

12.

In the ten months since Evan's death and Mother's disappearance, Grandfather's eyesight had worsened. He claimed he could still see well enough outdoors in the daylight to work around the ranch, but inside, in the artificial light of electric or coal-oil lamps, even with the help of his eyeglasses, reading and writing had become strenuous. He had always been a voracious reader, and when he lamented the loss of this ability, in addition to the *Sorry Times*, I began reading to him from the same novels Alan and I were enjoying. I didn't mind; after all, it was Grandfather himself who had instilled the love of reading in me. Still, there were moments I had to fight impatience when he forgot that I had already read a certain passage in a book, or the latest edition of the *Sorry Times*, and ask me to do so again and again.

More and more lately he was confused by the simplest of things in daily living, sometimes tripping over his tongue trying to come up with the name of some common item. Yet his mind seemed as sharp as ever when it came to the business of the ranch.

On any given day, he could give a precise mental count of the cows, bulls and steers, the location of the range where they were grazing and the current price per head they would fetch at the auction ring in Williams Lake. As recently as the previous month, after the United States had imposed a tariff on Canadian beef causing the price to plummet, he told Father, "I'll be damned if we'll give our cows away."

Complaining that American buyers counted for less than 10 percent of the sale of Canadian beef, yet they controlled the price, he said, "We don't have to be held captive to these rock-bottom prices. We've had a bumper crop of hay this year, so we can just hang onto the entire herd, feed 'em over the winter and hope for better prices come spring. Maybe by then this whole cockamamie idea of tariffs will go away. If not, we've got a good cushion."

I had a pretty fair idea of what that cushion was. Over the years, Grandfather, who held little faith in paper money or stocks and bonds, had always bought gold with any ranch profits. After the stock market crashed in '29, according to him, his stockpile of gold was suddenly "shinier than its colour, leaving us sitting pretty." That, along with his stubborn refusal to do more business with banks than he was forced to, kept the ranch solvent during the lean years. Unfortunately, our neighbours had not fared so well. Grandfather and Father refrained from discussing finances anywhere other than behind the closed doors of the ranch house, and usually when they thought I was not around. Lately though, Grandfather would often forget himself and include me in the conversation.

Early one Saturday morning in the late fall, I came in from the barn while he and Father were once again discussing the plans for wintering the herd this year. Heading up to the loft to change into my go-to-town denims, Grandfather's voice stopped me. "You don't mind doing a little extra work feeding cattle over winter, do you, boy?"

By that time he was calling me boy more often than not, and I was resigned to it, perhaps even enjoying it at times. And certainly my new haircut, courtesy of Mrs. Parsons, didn't help matters. Before Father could correct him, I answered quickly, "Yeah, as long as my monthly allowance is raised from two dollars to four."

Grandfather chuckled. "Right. We can do that."

My raise in wages came with conditions.

For as long as I could recall, every Sunday evening, Grandfather would sit at the kitchen table and record the ranch's weekly numbers and business in black notebooks. Lately, though, he had stopped keeping track of the details in writing. That Saturday morning I watched with envy as my father headed into Sorry. Left behind, I was not only to be Grandfather's reading eyes but was destined to become his writing hand as well.

I reluctantly followed him into his bedroom to retrieve the record books he intended to update. When he began unbuckling the leather straps on the trunk at the end of his bed, my regret over being deprived of spending time with Alan that day lessened somewhat. Curious to see the inside of the mysterious chest—which up until then had remained, if not exactly forbidden to me, Grandfather's private territory—I helped him unfasten the straps. As we lifted the heavy lid, the musky scent of aged paper and mothballs wafted into the room.

Inside the trunk there appeared to be nothing more than old clothes, newspapers and stacks of the familiar black record books. More than somewhat disappointed by the contents, at Grandfather's bidding, I gathered up a pile of the ranch books. As I did so, I noticed a battered old leather volume at the very bottom of the pile. Because it seemed so out of place among the others, I scooped it up along with them and headed back to the kitchen.

At the table, Grandfather sat across from me while I picked up each book and fanned through pages looking for his latest entry. The years fluttered by in his declining handwriting, from fancy script to hastily scrawled notes. Most were nothing more interesting than the recording of livestock births, facts and figures regarding hay production, weather and cattle prices.

March 15, 1930: Six new calves dropped during the night. 5 below and windy ...

April 2, 1932: Two-week-old calf lost to wolves in the south meadow. 33°F and raining ...

April 22, 1934: White-stocking filly born to bay mare, Nellie.

June 5, 1935: Joined branding crew at the Millers' ranch. 68°F and sunny.

I leafed through the pages quickly, flipping from front to back, going forward in time until I came to what appeared to be his latest entry. The date and the lone sentence at the beginning of an otherwise empty book stopped me.

January 8, 1937. Evan Harrison Beale. Passed away peacefully. Aged 2 years, 10 mos.

My breath caught at the sight of my brother's name, and my mind went right back to that day, remembering how Grandfather had taken care of us all in our sorrow. Swallowing back the lump in my throat, I turned the page.

"Okay, Granddad," I said, uncapping my fountain pen. "I'm ready."

For the rest of the morning he dictated while I wrote down tedious details about recent ranch activity: the bringing in of the cattle from the summer range, the amount of feed stored for the winter, the beaver dams blown to drain our meadows, the current weather and cattle prices and the reasons for the decision to winterize the herd this year.

Finally he said, "That should do it. From now on it will be your job to record updates every Sunday night."

Relieved, I restacked the books to return to the trunk in his bedroom. Before I did, though, I picked up the stained leather volume. Carefully opening the book to reveal its brown-edged pages, I immediately recognized the handwriting. Although his penmanship had grown shaky over the years, the fancy script was unmistakably Grandfather's.

"What's that you got there?" he asked rising from his chair, his empty coffee mug in hand.

"Looks like an old journal of yours," I said, watching him walk over to the stove.

As he reached for the coffee pot, I read the first entry. "We arrived in the Queen's colonies on this the eleventh day of February, 1864, after sailing from San Francisco to Fort Victoria on the paddle steamer SS *Brother Jonathan*."

He hesitated for a moment, then finished pouring his coffee. Seemingly in no great hurry, he slid the pot to the back of the stove and returned to the table. "Yep, that's mine, all right," he said. He set his mug down and I placed the leather-bound book into his outstretched hand. Stroking the cover, he smiled with remembrance. "This was my first journal," he said. "Started on that very day. I'd just turned fifteen."

He sat down and opened the brittle-with-age book. Squinting, he slowly turned the first few pages. "The SS *Brother Jonathan*," he muttered, shaking his head. "As long as I live I'll never forget the putrid stench, the vomit and filth of all those men, miners and fortune seekers, crowded together with no room for a decent breath during that voyage north. Pa called it a ship, but it was nothing more than a decrepit, vermin-infested tub."

He closed the book carefully. "Worse yet, what we didn't know, wouldn't find out until much later, was that two years previously, that same ship had carried an ailing San Francisco miner to Fort Victoria. By the time we arrived in '64, tens of thousands had perished in the new colonies. Mostly Indians, whole villages, tribes wiped out by the smallpox within months of that ship's docking.

"Had Pa known, had he any inkling of how that bloody epidemic would be tied to our fate, perhaps he wouldn't have booked passage on that boat. But then, no one could have foreseen the horrors that awaited us." He pushed himself up from the table and, without another word, headed to his bedroom.

Later when I looked in on him, he was napping peacefully. On the night table beside his bed—with its secrets from a past my grandfather had always held close—lay the old journal.

13.

Later that evening, I went to Grandfather's room. As usual I found him sitting propped up against his pillows, his hands folded on his lap just like an expectant child waiting for the latest instalment of a bedtime story. All his life it had been his habit to read in bed before he went to sleep each night. Now that he could no longer see well enough to do it himself, he liked me to "read him to dreamland," as he put it.

That night, instead of picking up *White Fang*, which I had frankly grown tired of after the third go-round, I reached for the journal on his night table.

"Granddad," I asked. "Would you like me to read from your journal?"

He shifted a little against the headboard. "Ha. Curiosity got to you, did it?"

Before I could respond, he added, "And why not? I guess you have every right to hear your family history—while I still have a mind to explain it."

I opened the old book.

"Now hold onto your horses," he said. He held out his hand and I reluctantly handed over the journal.

Hugging it to his chest, he said, "If you're to know the whole story, I should start at the beginning, the real beginning, with my pa. Your great grandpa, Edwin Vincent Beale."

He smiled with some private recollection. "He was more than a bit of a dandy, that man. Never too proud to admit—maybe boast is a better word—that he had left behind more than a few broken hearts when he sailed from England to seek his fortune in America. He was an explosives man, a trade in great demand in a growing nation."

He cleared his throat. "Now where was I?" he asked himself. "Ah, yes. Pa. When I was a boy, the dispute over slavery in the American States was intensifying. Talk of secession from the Union was the main topic of conversation among visitors to our home. But it was clear that all of that was of little interest to my pa. The only things that held his attention were his work, his whiskey and the 'turn of an ankle' ... *any* ankle, according to my mother. On more than one occasion I overheard her accusing him of spreading his seed all across the South, not caring if the recipient was white, brown or black. I was the seed that sprouted, I gathered—or at least the only one that he was ever called to answer for—although truth be known, it is more than probable that I have half-brothers, or sisters, of all ilks, down south."

He gave the notion some eyebrow-knitting thought and then resumed his story as if he were speaking to some stranger instead of a young girl, or more aptly to him—in that moment, perhaps—a young boy.

"It was no secret that it was my birth that trapped Pa in Alabama, and in a marriage he never wanted. I was eleven years old when the State of Alabama seceded from the Union, but I can still remember how the formation of the Confederate States caused even greater friction between my parents. 'You're nothing but a yellow-bellied coward,' Mother often accused him, agreeing with the Confederate officers every time they came calling for Pa, with his expert knowledge of explosives, to join them. 'It's not my cause, Margaret,' he would insist if he was sober. If he was drinking, which often was the case, he answered in much harsher terms, accusing her of being a slavemonger. Their battles escalated right along with the war."

From out in the parlour came the muffled sound of the radio, and I wondered if Father was aware of any of this family history, and how he would feel about me hearing all this at my age.

"Late one night in the summer of '63," Grandfather went on, "not long after the Union victory at Gettysburg, Pa shook me awake in the darkness, asking if I wanted to go on a little Wild West adventure. His nocturnal adventures when he was in his cups were nothing new; I had often tagged along sleepy-eyed while he stumbled through the night to end up in some plantation cabin or around a campfire, singing and drinking. But that night I knew something was different. He handed me a battered valise and told me to pack whatever I could fit inside, saying if I wanted to see some real cowboys and Indians, I was going to have to take a little holiday from school. Well, by golly, he didn't have to ask me twice. I was fourteen years old and figured I had already learned more reading and arithmetic than I would ever need in a lifetime.

"It took us many long hard months riding trains, stagecoaches, buckboards and shank's pony before we reached California. The only cowboys I saw along the way were those I spied from the train, riding horseback behind longhorn cattle in Texas. The only Indians were those Pa pointed out in the distance as our stagecoach passed through the Arizona Territories. By that time, I had begun to fret over my mother being left all alone.

"It was on the back of a buckboard bumping our way out of Yuma that he told me the truth. Or his version of it. Ma was gone. Run off with the same Confederate officer who had accused Pa of being a traitor. 'Do you know what conscription is, Son?' he asked me. I was still wrestling with the idea that my mother had run off with another man when he informed me that conscription was a law that would force all able-bodied men to enlist in the army. It was coming as certain as sunrise, according to him, and he wasn't going to wait around and be forced into going to a war that wasn't his. He was still a British citizen, not American, not Yank nor Confederate, he insisted. But worse than the risk of his conscription was mine. 'I have seen lads younger-looking than you marching off to fight,' he told me. 'And it's just a matter of time before they come for you. So, I'm sorry,' he said with no regret at all, insisting that he had no other recourse. 'Your ma is hell and gone, and there's no going back.' That was the last he ever spoke of it.

"We spent most of that winter in California. Enough time for Pa to reach the conclusion that the gold rush was dwindling down, and work was becoming scarce for a blasting man. Even that far west he was considered at best a turncoat. And at worst, a deserter. By December he decided that we would head to the new goldfields in the Queen's colonies to the north.

"From then on, it's all in here," he said, stroking the leather journal as if it were a small animal. "Well, most of it, anyways. So." He offered up the book. "Still want to read it?"

"Yeah," I replied, eagerly accepting the journal. Who wouldn't after his ominous comment this afternoon about the horrible fate that awaited him and his Pa on their journey north?

"Okay, then. Have at it," he said, settling back in his pillows.

Excited, I turned to the first page and began to read.

14.

We arrived in the Queen's Colonies on this, the eleventh day of February, 1864, sailing from San Francisco to Fort Victoria on the paddle steamer SS *Brother Jonathan.*

The final hours of the voyage had me forget for a while the vile state of the overcrowded tub of a boat they call a ship. Over the last four days we have endured the torture of high seas—frightful winds—and the constant pounding of the rain. This morning I woke to sunny skies. I hurried to the rails to find we were steaming through a peaceful inside water passage. To our east, beyond the dark outline of the mainland's craggy shoreline, forested hills and mountains stretched north and south with snow-capped peaks visible in the distance. To our west, rocky outcroppings and islets jutted from the depths all along the rugged coast that is the Colony of Vancouver Island. On either side of our bow, huge barnacle-covered beasts humped through the water like giant sea monsters—my first sighting of the whales of which the seafaring men have spoken. Above us flocks of squawking and screeching seabirds swirled around our masts, dissipating as we neared our port.

When we finally crept into the sheltered harbour at Fort Victoria, there were so many ships at anchor and docked along the wharfs that I could hear their rigging creaking and chattering in the wind. At the sight of the Union Jack fluttering from a flagpole in the distance, Pa removed his hat and lowered his head. From the deck of the SS *Brother Jonathan*—with the reek of human misery still heavy in my nostrils—the hodgepodge of buildings crowding the sloping hillsides on shore looked to me like salvation.

Unlike Pa, who was one of the few passengers not suffering from seasickness during the voyage, I have neither the stomach nor sea legs for that method of travel. Each day at sea I swore that once I set foot on dry land, never again would I leave it. Pa maintained that his lack of seasickness was due to his daily dose of whiskey. I have no reason to doubt him and so when he offered to share it with me I took my first swallow. The scorching mouthful burned all the way down my throat and then all the way back up again—just as had everything else I tried to hold down while I was on board. Liquor is another thing I swore off during the wretched journey. Pa laughed out loud at that oath. He barked with the same laughter this afternoon after we disembarked and I once again vowed that this would be my last day aboard any ship.

—Look around you, son, he said. Unless you plan to live in Fort Victoria for the rest of your life, then you're bound to break that oath.

He swept his arms around in a dramatic gesture.

—The Colony of Vancouver Island, he said with another laugh. Island!

Pa's teasing wasn't meant to be cruel, but his words found their mark. Dumfounded, I stood on the bustling dock while the miners and prospectors with whom I had shared such close quarters jostled against us in their haste to leave the ship, every one of them anxious to get a head start seeking passage to New Westminster and the fortunes being made in the goldfields of the Colony of British Columbia on the mainland. Pa's destination.

It wasn't that I was unaware of his plans. He had shared them on our departure from San Francisco. According to him, as an expert powder man, he is guaranteed a sure fortune blasting out a wagon road through the Fraser Canyon to the goldfields. Fort Victoria is a free port. New Westminster is not. And so all cargo—human and otherwise—must first enter the Colony by way of Vancouver Island. Pa's laughter served to remind me that as soon as he procures a position with the road crew we will once again set sail for the mainland.

In that moment, with my legs still feeling the motion of the ship even though I was standing on solid ground, the thought of another boat trip was more than I could bear and I felt my shoulders sag under the weight of it. Pa put his arm around me.

—Don't despair, my boy, he said. Crossing the strait will take mere hours. At any rate, we have days before that to enjoy this fine town.

The first thing he did after finding us lodging—in what I can only describe as a flophouse—was to order a hot bath for each of us. The proprietress's face was so heavily made up that her skin creased as she grinned and named her price. Five dollars seems like a great deal of money to me but Pa pulled out a silver coin and told her to include a shave and haircut. Since I have turned fifteen this last week I ordered a shave as well, which brought a chuckle from Pa. He told the woman to go ahead but not to charge any more as shaving my jowls would do no more damage to her straight razor than scraping it over a baby's bottom.

He took his bath first, leaving me with his scummy water and suds. After his words I abandoned the idea of a shave and soaked myself in the metal tub until the tepid water turned cold. A few hours later Pa returned from his exploring of the town, bringing me fully awake from my slumber by tossing a brown paper package onto our shared bed. I sat up and untied the string and pulled away the paper to discover late birthday presents of a bone-handled nib pen, a bottle of India ink, two well-used books and this journal. The gifts came with the pronouncement that now that our Wild West adventure is over, we need to think about getting back to work—he to his profession and me to my education. Pa is so proud of his purchases that I don't have the heart to tell him that I've already read *The Last of the Mohicans*. But it's a welcome diversion and I shall read it again just as I will make use of the other book, *The Imperial Dictionary of the English Language*, because I have always enjoyed the learning of new words. I also declined to inform him that for me, our journey ceased to be an adventure some time ago. Somewhere along the trail crossing through the Indian Territories, the excitement and fear of the unknown became nothing more than the drudgery of travel and the boredom of lonely hours spent cooling my heels while he satisfied his needs in ways he believes I am too young to understand.

15.

Feeling a blush rise to my cheeks as the meaning of the last sentence sunk in, I glanced up quickly, but Grandfather had dozed off.

I studied the map of wrinkles that crisscrossed his weathered cheeks and high forehead, trying to picture him as a boy of fourteen—little more than two years older than I was—leaving his childhood home, travelling across an entire continent and then sailing off to unknown territories. As hard as I searched, I could not imagine that teenage boy.

I pulled up the patchwork quilt and tucked it around him. Taking the journal with me, I tiptoed from his room.

Out in the parlour, Father glanced up from his book.

Ever since Mother's disappearance in January—for that is what we had come to call her leaving whenever we spoke of it, which was seldom—Father had become a night owl. He would sit alone in the parlour reading, sometimes falling asleep in his chair, often not taking to his bed until dawn threatened.

That evening he smiled and wished me a good night, giving no indication that he had heard anything from behind Grandfather's closed door.

Long after I retreated to the loft, long after the parlour light had finally gone out and my father's weary footsteps took him to his room, I lay awake thinking about everything Grandfather had told me. I couldn't help wondering how a man who—too often, these days—had difficulty remembering exactly what it was he had been doing or saying five minutes before could recall with such vivid detail the events of so long ago.

But he was right. Curiosity had gotten to me. How had it been for him being motherless, just as I was, at such a young age? Exactly what had he meant when he referred to the horrors that awaited him and his pa on their journey north? Unable to sleep, I switched on the lamp and picked up the journal.

Normally I am a fast and fluent reader, but Grandfather's youthful penmanship, with its flourishes and curls, the ink blots and smudges, made it slow going. The words did not seem those of a fifteen-year-old boy, and I had to constantly remind myself that they were written over seventy years ago, that times were very different then, and that the boy was my grandfather.

16.

Pa is in no hurry to leave this place. He seems intent on visiting every saloon and dance hall this bustling and overcrowded fort town has to offer. Walking through the downtown area in the light of day, I marvel at the number of these nighttime establishments. Small wonder that I have heard this place called the Sodom of the Pacific. I'm grateful for my books and this journal to help pass the evening hours. Pa has added his discarded copies of the Colony's daily newspaper to my reading supply and I'm glad of it. The *British Colonist* is packed with local stories and announcements as well as shipping news and court reports. In the last week I have learned more about the nature of this place and its citizens from these newspaper pages than I have from exploring the maze of crowded streets. According to the number of advertisements for pills and excelsior and the lists of ailments they cure, one could conclude that most of the females in Fort Victoria must suffer from dropsy, melancholy and headaches and the men from liver and bowel disorders. Pa chuckles at the ads for these snake-oil remedies, as he calls them. But he despairs at the many advertisements offering second-hand prospecting supplies and staked claims for sale. He suspects that if miners are already abandoning claims all the way from the Fraser Canyon to Williams Creek and Richfield, then perhaps things are not as rosy as he has been led to believe. I clipped this notice from today's newspaper to press here between these pages.

> *To Intending Speculators in Cariboo*
> *Mining Claims and Property*
>
> *A GENTLEMAN JUST ARRIVED FROM the Cariboo*
> *who will probably remain in Victoria about 14 days before*
> *returning to the gold region will be glad to extend his as-*
> *sistance and advice to persons about to invest as above.*

> *He has resided in various parts of the Cariboo for over 4*
> *years and is intimately acquainted with the goldfields and*
> *everything regarding the present positions and has ex-*
> *pert knowledge of that richly endowed country, part of*
> *which is not developed yet. Any person wishing to consult*
> *the aforementioned may hear of him by applying at this*
> *newspaper office or by letter addressed to the same place.*

Pa says this advertisement only proves that speculators are already out to milk the dreams of pie-in-the-sky fools.

The other bit of gossip that is concerning him is that many of the labourers carving out the Yale to Cariboo wagon road are Chinese. This information is concerning because he has heard that the Chinamen receive next to nothing for their work. And worse yet, Pa says there are many explosives experts among these immigrants from across the sea. Experts who are unafraid to risk their lives in the rush to complete the Royal Engineers' wagon road before a private company carves out a competing route farther north.

The alternate route would cut weeks off the journey to the goldfields. But Pa has heard that it is a route so treacherous that even the Chinamen will not work on it. None of this must concern him too greatly, as he has made no effort that I know of to search out either the government or the private company said to be hiring workers. I fear our money will run out before he does. I have gone so far as to suggest that I find work while we are here but Pa simply flipped his lucky twenty-dollar gold piece in the air as he often does. He winked and told me that there is plenty more where this one comes from. He insists that I leave the worry to him—that my only job is to continue to study and educate myself.

February 25, 1864

While Pa sleeps during the daylight hours I am left with a lot of time to explore the fort. I have wandered to the edges in all directions until the ground becomes too soggy or the forest too dense. Much of the town is a hodgepodge of hastily thrown-together clapboard houses and whipsawed lumber shacks. They crowd in among the sturdier square-hewn whitewashed log homes and the fancier two-storey brick ones with their white-picket-fenced yards. The smell of freshly cut lumber is everywhere. The government buildings above the harbour hold no interest for me but the main street is a hubbub of clamour and excitement. Women in full-skirted dresses sweep over the plank-board sidewalks hurrying from merchant to merchant. Men wearing anything from suits with starched, white-collared shirts to mud-crusted woollen pants and ragged overcoats stride with determination between the banks and false-fronted stores. Cobblestone streets in the finer areas of town give way to hardpack dirt roads where embedded boulders cause sparks to rise under horses' hooves and make for rough rides for the occupants of wagons and carriages.

Down in the harbour, ships come and go daily. From a safe distance on shore I find it interesting to watch them unload their cargo and, according to the *British Colonist*, reload with fortunes in gold headed south.

Today the sun was shining and it was a fine a day, as if spring had already arrived. Down on the Hudson's Bay Company wharf I ran into four boys who all appeared to be around sixteen or seventeen years old. Given my height I had no trouble pretending to be the same age and fell in with these cocky fellows. After we got past establishing who I was and why I wasn't in school—a question I might have asked them as well because if I am not mistaken today, being Thursday, was a school day—they shared their plans to "borrow" a skiff and row across the harbour to Dead Man's Island. When they invited me to join them in their mischief I couldn't see any way to get out of it without being taken for a sissy. Lucky for me, the day was calm and the small rowboat rode much smoother across the gentle waves than I expected. Still, I was relieved when our hull scraped bottom on the small island and we hauled the boat ashore. Beyond the sandy beach, young trees grew among a tangle of charred and burned tree trunks. As we gathered driftwood for a campfire, the boy who called himself James hinted responsibility for a wildfire that had caused the destruction on the island. Later, while we sat around in the firelight, the story came out that one summer day a few years ago they had rowed over to the island for a swim and had built a bonfire on the beach. Later they had to beat a hasty retreat across the water while at their backs a growing inferno overtook the island. There was some good-natured ribbing between these school chums as they recalled that day. And there was more than a hint of boasting in their words that the fire had gotten away accidentally-on-purpose. It seems that the island is a kind of cemetery for the local Songhee Indian tribe. The boys gave a morbid description of corpses packed into old trunks or wooden cracker boxes that littered the island. Suspended high up in the trees and stacked on the ground, the tinder-dry makeshift coffins had burst into flames as easily as matchboxes. I am still taken aback that there seemed to be little remorse among the boys for their mischief. I kept my counsel, though, as I needed a ride back over the waters.

Earlier this evening, over our dinner of salmon chowder and baking powder biscuits at our lodging, I repeated the story about their fire destroying an ancient burial place to Pa. He shook his head, saying he was not surprised by the unfortunate lack of sympathy my comrades displayed for the Natives' culture—blaming only the ignorance passed down by their parents.

He went on to tell me that when the smallpox epidemic came to the colony two years ago, most of the whites had already been inoculated. According to Pa, as the sickness spread through the Indian settlement outside the walls of Fort Victoria, the governor of these colonies, James Douglas, sanctioned the Hudson's Bay Company to inoculate the Indians as well. But by the time his pleas were heard it was too late.

I recalled the fuss I made over getting inoculated against the smallpox in San Francisco and was suddenly glad for Pa's steadfast insistence.

—Poor buggers, he said, pushing his soup bowl aside and wiping his mouth with his napkin. No immunity and no sympathy either. In order to stem the epidemic the Natives were banned from the island. They were forced to load their sick and dying into canoes and paddle north escorted by a gunboat. Of course their sickness spread with them all the way up the coast.

Pa shook his head at the pity of it all and threw back the last of his dinner drink.

He is a kind man, my pa, and cares to see no man suffer. When he is sober.

When he is drinking he is quick to temper and it is best to stay out of his way. It is of the time in between sober and drunk that I have learned to be leery. I watch for the shift from his being his jolly self with only a drink or two under his belt to the time when the smallest gesture—the most innocent word or simple look—can push him over the edge into the beast who lashes out without warning. In my early childhood I have been on the receiving end of those lashes—cuffs to the head and whippings whenever he forgets who he is. And always— if he remembers the next day—his remorse is almost as unbearable.

I have learned to steer clear of him when he gets near to that dividing edge. During this past week, though, after sharing dinner with me he goes out on the town and then stumbles home in the early morning hours to fall into bed, snoring almost before he hits the pillow beside me. Tonight he concluded our dinner conversation by speculating that perhaps the good governor's sympathy for the Natives stems from the fact that his wife is a half-breed—her father a Hudson's Bay chief factor and her mother the daughter of a Cree Indian chief.

—I saw her today, Pa said. She was riding by in her carriage this afternoon wearing as fancy a dress and as fine a bonnet as the ladies of San Francisco, and even though she must be over fifty years of age she is still a handsome woman—one that I would not kick out of bed for farting.

It was then that I knew Pa had had more to drink than his after-dinner brandy, and I decided to beat a hasty retreat to our room and leave him to his night's gallivanting.

17.

During those fall months, every now and then, Grandfather allowed me to read a few pages of his journal to him instead of the latest novel at hand. Each time I did, I enjoyed a shamefully smug pleasure in remembering all those years Mother had tried every trick to pry his past from him, while he had chosen to share it with me.

For the most part, though, the entries were disappointing. Little more than wordy observations about his surroundings, and about as exciting as the ranch records. Before long my interest waned, and so too, it seemed, did Grandfather's.

In the meantime my hair was slowly growing out. As the soft blonde down covered my scalp, I was surprised to discover that I didn't miss having long hair. I enjoyed the new-found freedom of not needing to brush it out every night, and not having to braid or tie it back to keep it from tangling during the day. I decided that I would keep it short. I had Mrs. Parsons to thank for that—but little else.

At school, Alan and I continued to be invisible to her. So we came and went from class as we pleased. Fall edged toward winter. The anticipation of the coming cold months of isolation drew Alan to the forests and hillsides more and more. I gladly followed along. Hiking through the countryside, we fell into a friendly competition over who could be the first to identify animal tracks and droppings, sometime coming close to fisticuffs over who was right. But I have to admit that he often spotted the live animals long before I was aware of their presence: rabbits and weasels, their coats changing colour with the season; deer grazing between the trees; a black bear hightailing it into the bush as we passed nearby. And more than once, in the distance, he pointed out the regal buck we had encountered up on the ridge on the afternoon we came down from the hillside to have the hair shaved from our heads.

We often returned to that lofty spot on the ridge. We would sit beneath Alan's watching tree, as I had come to call the lone pine on the summit, and pass my grandfather's field glasses back and forth. It was from this vantage point one day that I first spotted my father, riding his strawberry roan across the meadow below. Squinting through the field glasses, I followed horse and rider's unhurried progress until they came to a standstill beside the poplar grove. Father dismounted, and leaving the reins loose so his horse could graze, he entered the little graveyard on the knoll. Feeling like an intruder, I watched for only a few moments before I set down the binoculars. An hour later, when Alan and I left the ridge, the roan was still waiting patiently by the graveyard fence. I never mentioned anything about it at home, but after that, whenever Father saddled up to go riding alone, I followed him in my imagination and pictured him as I saw him through the field glasses that day—kneeling at my brother's grave.

One late afternoon, Alan pointed out a movement near the poplar grove. Thinking it might be my father again, I took up the field glasses. At first I could make out nothing more than the distant flicker of dappled light among the trees and their autumn-stripped branches. And then the movement took form, and one by one the wild horses that Alan had talked about emerged like phantoms from the shadows to graze in the meadow grass. I counted over a dozen ponies of various sizes and colours.

Beside me Alan shifted. "The stallion," he said. I lowered my glasses and followed his gaze to the slope on the far side of the meadow, where a solitary buckskin horse stood, his black mane lifting in the rising breeze. "He's a loner," Alan said in a hushed voice.

Twice more during the waning months of autumn, we spotted the stallion overlooking his herd. In the meadows below, the wild ponies would graze peacefully among the deer until the sharp crack of a rifle would scatter them all to the trees. I began to worry, reasoning that if we had spotted the deer so easily then surely the hunters could too. I feared that they might find and bring down the buck. Alan shrugged off my worries, saying, "That stag didn't grow so big being stupid."

But I wasn't so confident. There were a few "No Hunting" signs posted on the rail fences along our road and nearby fields. Up until then I had given little thought to the signs; they had done their job, and there had never been a problem with hunters near the ranch house. But after seeing how far our ranchlands stretched beyond those fields and fences, and the wild animals that inhabited them, I began to worry that there were not enough signs posted. So one night at dinner I brought up the subject of hunters trespassing on our land.

Father put down his fork and thought for a moment. "Those hunters need to eat too, Addie," he said. "And as long as they leave our cattle alone and steer clear of where we live, then we can't deny them the chance to get their winter's meat." ·

I worried out loud about the stag from the ridge. Grandfather and Father had also spotted the heavily antlered buck over the years, and they knew which one I was speaking of. But they agreed with Alan. Like him, they believed the old buck was probably wise enough to make it through another hunting season without our help. "If not," Grandfather said, "he's a wild animal, and you can't herd or protect a wild animal."

"I just don't want the hunters to shoot them on our land," I insisted. "Couldn't we put up more 'no hunting' signs?"

"Not *we*," he said. "But if you have a notion to, go ahead. Although I have no idea where you would start."

But I did. The following Saturday morning, with black snow clouds rolling up on the northern horizon, I, and a reluctant Alan Baptiste, headed out with my newly made signs.

The crisp autumn air smelled of rotting leaves, smudge fires and chimney smoke as we hiked the ranch's eastern meadows and fields, posting signs on fence posts and trees. Our final stop was up on the ridge. By then the sky was turning dark, and we headed down the mountainside the moment we nailed the last sign to the lone pine tree.

With daylight fading quickly, I hurried to keep up with Alan. Skidding and sliding on the steep path behind him, I realized that we had stayed too long and our folks were bound to start worrying. Perhaps it was the fading light, or our haste to get home before darkness set in, that made Alan careless. Hurrying around a corner, he neither saw nor sensed the shadowy form on the narrow animal path before the horse reared up before him. I slid to a stop close behind and watched in horror as the buckskin stallion's forelegs pawed at the air just inches away from my friend. And then to my amazement, Alan lowered his head. With his gaze fixed on the ground, he waited, as if in submission, as if waiting for those hooves to strike. I held my breath as the horse took one last paw at the air, and then his heavy front end dropped back down onto the path. The animal was so close that its black mane brushed against Alan's shoulder when it swung its massive head to the side to study him with its huge dark eye. I could smell the stallion's breath, hear the air rushing out of his flaring nostrils and see it turn to vapour in the late-afternoon air. Alan remained unmoving as the horse inspected him. Finally, the stallion snorted and took a step backward. As if in imitation, Alan too stepped back. They each took cautious steps backward, and the sudden meeting became a respectful retreat. Only after the horse had made a full about-turn and stepped off the path did I let the breath escape from my lungs. After the buckskin's powerful hind end disappeared into the darkening woods, I saw that as calm as Alan had appeared during the brief encounter, his body was now shaking so fiercely I feared he might crumble to the ground. He turned to me, his eyes wide with delayed fear.

"Golly," I whispered.

"Yeah, golly," he said to himself. Then, as if afraid to break the spell of what had just happened, we continued downhill in silence.

By the time we reached the grassy hillside above Sorry, the sky was dark. Yellow light glowed from the town's windows. Fat snowflakes drifted down, whitening the ground and causing our feet to slip and slide as we quickened our pace. Certain that my father, and Alan's parents, would be worried, perhaps even angry at our late return, we hurried across the road and up the store's porch steps. But when we pushed open the door, we found their concern was not for us. Beside the counter, with undisguised fear upon his face, my father stood hovering over Mr. VanderMeer, who was slumped in a chair, a bloodstained handkerchief pressed to his face.

A wild-eyed Rose VanderMeer spun toward us. "Stay back," she said, motioning us away. "That teacher woman, she's put the pox on him."

18.

"It's not smallpox," Father said on the heels of Mrs. VanderMeer's startling words. "But you're right, Rose. They should stay back."

Mr. VanderMeer was seized by a fit of coughing. Ignoring the warning, Alan rushed forward. Father raised his arm, halting him before he reached his stepfather.

"Best to keep your distance right now, son," he said. "I suspect your father has consumption, and he may be contagious." He motioned toward the storefront. "Turn the sign over and lock the door, please," he said.

Alan obeyed, but I could feel him strain to keep himself in place while his mother went behind the counter and came back with a hand towel to replace the blood-soaked cloth her husband was coughing into.

Father knelt down before Mr. VanderMeer. "Dirk, I'm going to drive you into the hospital in Quesnel," he said. "We need to find out from the doctor if it's tuberculosis, for your sake and your family's."

Breathless, Mr. VanderMeer nodded, and while Alan's mother fetched clothes and extra towels for the journey, my father took him aside. "Your mom and I will take him to town in the grocery van," he told him. "He'll be more comfortable if he can lie down in the back for the trip." Pulling the pickup keys from his pocket, to my surprise, he handed them over to Alan. "I don't know how long we will be. Until then I think it's best if you and Addie head on out to the ranch."

How my father knew that Alan could drive was a mystery to me, but after a few jerky false starts, we made the twelve-mile trip to the ranch without incident. We arrived to find Grandfather snoozing in the parlour, his eyeglasses still perched on his nose. When I gently shook him awake, he startled, grabbed the arms of his chair and squinted up at me as if trying to place me.

"Hello, Mr. Chance," Alan said behind me, addressing my grandfather by a name which up until then I had only known his mother to use. At the sound of Alan's voice, Grandfather's gaze flickered past me and his face ashened.

"Willum?" he croaked, his voice barely audible.

"No. Granddad," I rushed to explain. "This is Alan. Alan Baptiste. Remember? Rose VanderMeer's son?"

Staring hard, he adjusted his glasses. The panic slowly drained from his face with recognition. "Alan. Of course," he said, pushing himself up from his chair. "You've grown some, boy."

I realized then that of course, since Grandfather rarely went to town anymore, and certainly not on weekends, it must have been years since he had seen Alan at the store.

We followed him into the kitchen, where I explained about Mr. VanderMeer. "Sorry to hear that, Alan," he said, the misunderstanding forgotten. "Dirk's a good man. Let's hope for good news."

After dinner, Alan and I scraped our barely touched bowls of stew into the slop bucket to feed to the dogs. Grandfather retired to the parlour and played with the Radiola knobs until he picked up the Canadian Broadcasting Corporation.

The previous year, the new radio station had started to broadcast hockey games every Saturday night, games which had fast become the highlight of our weekends. On this night, though, I sat listening to but hardly hearing Foster Hewitt's scratchy voice call the play-by-play action between the Montreal Maroons and the Toronto Maple Leafs. Only after Grandfather lifted his dozing head and yawned did I realize the game had come to an end. He switched off the Radiola and announced that he was going to bed. "You two head on up to the loft, now," he said. "It could be morning before they're back. Best to get some sleep now."

I saw no sense in arguing. Grabbing some extra blankets from the linen closet in the kitchen, I said to Alan, "He gets confused sometimes. Thinks I'm a boy." I laughed half-heartedly, then added, "And who for crikey's sake is Willum?"

A strange expression flickered across Alan's eyes before he turned away, announcing that he was going to the outhouse.

"We have an inside toilet now," I told him.

"That's okay."

Watching him leave, I knew his need was more about being alone than preferring to use the outside privy. While he was gone I climbed up to the loft and pulled out the mattress pad we kept stored under my bed for company, unrolled it onto the floor and made it up with the extra blankets. It was only much later, after he had returned and settled down on the makeshift bed next to mine without a word, that I felt the awkwardness of the situation. He was so close to me I could smell the fresh snow melting in his hair. And for the first time, I felt the unsettling stirrings of something other than friendship for Alan Baptiste.

19.

Sometime during the early hours of morning, I woke from a fitful sleep in the grey light of dawn. Glancing over the side of my bed I discovered that Alan had already risen.

I sat up as Father's voice drifted up from the kitchen

"They'll be taking him to the TB sanatorium outside of Kamloops this afternoon," he said quietly. "Your mother is staying with him until the sanatorium ambulance arrives."

"How long will he be gone?" Alan asked.

Father took his time in replying. As if carefully measuring his words, he finally said, "I wish I could give you an answer, but even the doctor won't predict it with any certainty. It could be some time. More than a few months in all probability."

"I'd like to see him before he goes."

"Yes, I can understand that. All right, then. I promised to draw up some papers for him. When I'm done you can come with me when I head back to the hospital. I don't know if they'll allow you into his room, son, but we can try."

I stayed home to help Grandfather with the chores. We had started feeding the cattle in the holding fields the weeek before and it was a two-man job.

In the light of day, Grandfather stubbornly insisted his vision was still fine, but as he sat behind the wheel of the tractor, squinting and zigzagging precariously through the fields while I yelled directions from the hay wagon, I decided it was time I learned to drive. Surely if Alan could do it, so could I.

It was past dinner hour before my father, Mrs. VanderMeer and Alan returned. I learned later that at the hospital, when Father tied a sterile white mask over his nose and mouth, he handed one to Alan and without asking permission took him into Dirk VanderMeer's quarantined room. Before a nurse came in to shoo him out, Alan had the opportunity to say goodbye to his stepfather, promising to take care of his mother while the grocer was away.

Sitting over his untouched mug of coffee at our kitchen table that evening, Alan announced that he intended to quit school to help in the store. It was during Rose VanderMeer's strong protests that he let it spill that he was learning nothing at school anyway, because our teacher no longer spoke to us or gave us any new lessons.

Startled at this revelation, Father glanced from Alan to me and then said that Mrs. Parsons would certainly have to speak to him. He would see to it that we each got the required lessons for our grade from her. I could see in his expression that he would also be talking to me about keeping this bit of information from him.

"Thank you, sir," Alan said, "but I need to learn the business of the store now."

"This situation is temporary," Father said gently. "Quitting school is permanent."

"Still." Alan shrugged.

Father held his gaze. "Let me ask you something," he said. "Is that what you want to do with your life? Do you plan to become a storekeeper?"

Alan looked down at the table. "No, sir."

"Have you given any thought to what it is that you would like to do?"

Without raising his head, Alan hitched his shoulders again, as if it were irrelevant, then thought better of it and mumbled, "Ranching."

Father let the reply settle for a moment. Then he glanced over at Mrs. VanderMeer. "Rose, you know that I help Dirk with the year-end accounting. According to the books, your business is doing well enough that you can afford to hire someone for the busy hours during the week. You're closed Sundays, and I'll be around on Saturday mornings, as always. So how does this idea sound to you? And to you?" he asked, turning to Alan. "We could use some help around the ranch this winter. If you stay in school, as your mother wishes, then I'll pay you to work out here on the weekends and holidays, and your mom can hire someone for the store if she needs to."

Before Alan and his mother drove away that evening a deal was struck. Every Friday, after school, Alan would come home with me and stay until we went back on Monday morning. It made everyone happy in a moment when happiness seemed beyond us: Father and Grandfather would have the extra help for those days; Mrs. VanderMeer was relieved that Alan would stay in school and he was more than glad to be a ranch hand for at least two days each week. The only one who had mixed feelings about all this, it appeared, was me.

I don't know what Father said to Mrs. Parsons on Monday morning, but from that day onward, although she still continued to ignore us, a lesson plan was written out on the blackboard each morning. And on the weekends, when all our chores were done, Father insisted that Alan and I sit at the table and do homework to catch up with the missed schoolwork and to prepare to write our year-end exams in the spring.

The first weekend Alan came to work at the ranch, Father solved my initial apprehension. Unlike Grandfather, who'd seen no reason the two of us shouldn't share my room in the loft, Father was less liberal. Without my having said a word, he'd set up a cot in the corner of his own room for Alan, relieving my worry over the sleeping arrangements.

On Friday, when we all walked into the kitchen after school, Grandfather looked up from the sink where he was scrubbing potatoes. Startled by the sight of Alan with us, he once again called him Willum.

"It's Alan Baptiste, Granddad," I said quickly. "Remember? Rose VanderMeer's son?"

"Ah yes, Rose's boy," he replied, and went back to concentrating on the potatoes.

I glanced at Father and mouthed, "Who's Willum?"

He shook his head, the expression on his face saying, *I have no idea.*

On more than one occasion during the next two days, I noticed Grandfather studying Alan with a perplexed expression on his face. Over the weekend, he seemed to grow more and more agitated by his presence. And then, after dinner on Sunday night, when I sat down at the kitchen table to work on the ranch books as usual, he waved me away, saying, "Not now."

Glad to be relieved of the weekly recording, I gathered up the books and my fountain pen and ink bottle. But he instructed me to bring them to his room later, explaining that he needed me to put pen to paper on his behalf before his memories were "all dried up and blown away."

That evening, leaving Father and Alan in the parlour listening to the Radiola, I found Grandfather in his bedroom, pacing the floor in his long johns.

"Close the door behind you," he ordered.

I did so, then stood waiting while he continued pacing. "Just gathering my thoughts," he mumbled. After a moment he seemed to come to some conclusion, settled himself in his bed and gestured to the chair beside it.

I sat down and opened the latest record book I had brought with me.

"No, not in that one," he said with a note of impatience. Searching his night table, he came up with a fresh notebook, which was set beside his old journal. He passed it to me and settled back once again.

"Okay. Let's start." He took a deep breath. "I need to set the record straight about something that's missing in that journal."

Before I could uncap my fountain pen, he began dictating. "This is the statement of Chauncey Beynon Beale, as to the events occurring on the Homathko River above the Bute Inlet, in the Province of British Columbia, during the …" His words, which up until then had been rushing out, came to a grinding halt. His eyebrows knit together. "During the … during the …"

"How do you spell the name of that river, Granddad? I've never heard …"

"Don't interrupt me, boy," he barked, then apologized, explaining that he was anxious to get it all down before he lost his train of thought. "Darn," he said, "I may already have. Read back what you've got so far."

As I did he nodded along. "Right," he said. "During the last day of April in the year of our Lord … eighteen sixty-four?" He appeared to give that some thought, then, as if satisfied it was correct, said quietly, "The telling comes over seventy years late, but it is no less the truth as I recall it."

I wasn't certain if he meant this to be recorded, but unwilling to interrupt again, I kept my pen nib scratching across the page. When I was done I blew lightly on the wet ink, then glanced up, waiting for him to continue.

Staring intently beyond the iron rails at the foot of his bed as if he could see into the corner shadows, Grandfather remained silent for some time. The minutes ticked by on his night table clock until he finally held up a shaking hand and motioned toward his journal.

"Jog my memory," he said. "Read to me from where we left off last time."

And so I traded my pen and notebook for the old journal. Finding the page marked by the attached ribbon, I began reading.

20.

March 6, 1864

Our plans have changed! It appears that Pa is not as reluctant about finding employment as I have credited him with. After word got around that he turned down work with the Royal Engineers on the Yale-to-Cariboo wagon road, he was sought out by the foreman of the Bute Inlet Road Company. Pa refuses to negotiate wages with the foreman and so tonight the parliamentarian and founder of the private road company Alfred Waddington himself came to our boarding house.

Our proprietress placed a lace cloth on the table and banned the other tenants from the room while the meeting took place. A portly man, but not overly tall, Mr. Waddington commanded respect without uttering a word. Like Pa he is a clean-shaven man except for the neatly trimmed lamb-chop sideburns, which run down his jowls to meet under his double chin. He wore a formal black waistcoat suit with a stiff, high white collar and bow tie. A gold pocket-watch fob and chain hung from his vest. Pa—not having bothered to change from the trail clothes he wears daily—was not intimidated. After shaking the gentleman's offered hand he waved away our hostess, instructing me to close the door behind her. I was allowed to stay and will attempt to report the conversation that took place between them as I recall it. Mr. Waddington spoke first.

—I hear you are an expert blaster, he said.

—That I am, Pa replied.

—By your word. And how do I know it is not the boast of a man looking to find a paid passage to the goldfields?

—It's no boast. I know powder and I know her moods, which just like a woman's change with the season, the weather and the time of day. I know how to set my charge to take out a mountain of rock with half the powder and half the risk.

Pa removed a cigarette from his case and bent over the table candle to light it. Leaning back in his chair, he blew out a cloud of smoke.

—But I will not work for the wages your foreman, Mr. Brewster, is offering, he said.

Mr. Waddington waved away the cigarette case my father offered.

—If what you say is true, Mr. Beale, I can offer you compensation that would make it worth your while to join our expedition.

—I'm listening, said Pa.

Mr. Waddington stood and pulled out the long parchment roll that he had carried in under his arm. I helped Pa move the steaming teapot, the candles and the china cups over to the sideboard. After the table was cleared, the paper was unfurled and laid out flat, revealing an intricate hand-drawn map of the island and mainland coastline. Mr. Waddington placed a fat sausage finger on the spot marked Fort Victoria and then ran it north up the waterway between Vancouver Island and the mainland's coastline to the mouth of a narrow inlet. He followed it inland until his finger came to rest at the head of the channel.

—Bute Inlet, he said. This is where my road begins.

—I have heard say that this road is nothing more than a fool's folly, Pa said.

—We completed forty miles of this folly and thirty-six bridges before last winter set in. With the right men, we will blast our way to the top of the plateau and complete the entire route by fall.

Mr. Waddington swept his hand across the map and slapped his palm down on the eastern side of the wandering line that marked the Fraser River.

—The Cariboo goldfields, he proclaimed, sitting back in his chair. This route will be weeks and miles shorter than the so-called Great Yale Wagon Road. And we will finish ours long before the Royal Engineers and their crew finish theirs.

—Tell me the truth, Pa said. From the number of burnt-out prospectors I see returning with nothing to show for all this glitter that is supposed to be there for the taking, I am wondering if this Cariboo gold rush is also folly.

—Oh, the gold is there, all right. But the trek to the goldfields is a long and difficult journey. Most of the fortune seekers arrive expecting to find nuggets strewn about on the creek beds waiting to be picked up by hand, only to find that it is backbreaking work extracting it from the ground. More don't succeed than do. That's true. But there are many who are taking out fortunes each and every day. This discovery makes the California gold rush look like child's play. And the thousands of anxious prospectors and miners will be more than willing to pay a hefty road toll to shorten their journey.

—And the Indians? asked Pa. What do they think about your road passing through their territory?

—We already have some in our employment, packing and guiding. The people of the Chilcootan area up on the plateau, as I am sure you have heard, are in great decline from the smallpox epidemic, and those left are glad to have work to feed their families. No, there will be no trouble with them.

Mr. Waddington paused.

—I too have a concern, Mr. Beale, he said, his gaze hard on Pa. I have heard that you like your liquor.

—That I do, said Pa. But it has never interfered with my work.

He held up his hand.

—A man cannot have the tremors if he is to set charge. You can see for yourself that my hand is as steady as the rock I blast. I expect to continue to have my whiskey at night when my day's labour is done.

—Many of our men do, Mr. Waddington told him. The company supplies a nightly rum ration for those who imbibe. You are welcome to bring your own as well. But I must caution you that it must be for your personal use only. As an elected Member of the House of Assembly, I was responsible for the bill outlawing the selling of intoxicants to the Natives and I mean for my road crew to keep that law.

—I am not in the habit of selling liquor.

—Then we are agreed.

The rest of their conversation involved the negotiations of Pa's wages, which I will not recount here, as it is his private business. But I will say that he was satisfied with the cash advance offered and the generous bonus promised if the road reached the plateau before the first week of August.

Before they concluded, Pa added one more condition. In order for him to agree to take the job, he said, the company must also hire me.

—I do not employ children, Mr. Waddington said.

—My son is a young man of seventeen years.

One of the gentleman's thick eyebrows lifted. He turned to study my face. I held his gaze, knowing that my height gave credence to Pa's lie. And just like the boys I had accompanied to Dead Man's Island, Mr.

Waddington did not question my being seventeen years of age instead of the true fifteen I have just turned. He offered to take me on as cook's helper, saying he would not have one so young working with powder.

—Nor would I, said Pa.

Mr. Waddington offered me a dollar a day. Before I could answer, Pa said to make it two and we would have a deal. I would have been happy with the dollar but was glad of Pa's tenacity when Mr. Waddington readily agreed to double that.

So it's done. We sail north with the road crew within the next two weeks. My excitement over becoming a wage-earning man is overshadowed by the thought that I must endure another paddle steamer journey up the coast to Bute Inlet.

21.

I finished reading the final line of that day's journal entry and glanced up. Seeing the even rise and fall of Grandfather's chest, I realized he had dozed off. A sudden snore gurgled from his throat and it was clear he was asleep for the night.

The very next evening he had forgotten about the writing he'd asked me to do for him.

In the following months, for the most part, the journal remained on my night table. Eventually, the times when I took it to Grandfather's room to try to jog his memory grew fewer and farther between, so caught up was I in my own world with Alan Baptiste.

Alan took to ranching as if he had been doing it all his life. No chore was too tedious. From chopping wood to mending fences, mucking corrals to scrubbing pots and pans, nothing was beneath him. Rising early—which for us was habit born of necessity—he would embrace each new job without complaint, as if it were amusement rather than toil. The first time we went searching for strays, he surprised me in the way he sat our bay gelding, with his shoulders rising and falling, moving in complete harmony with the animal. He claimed to have learned to ride when he was a young child on the reserve in the Chilcotin but said he had not been on a horse since. Whether he had or hadn't, Dad said he was simply a natural. I scoffed that it was just like riding a bicycle—something you never forget.

I had always harboured a secret pride in the way I handled a horse, yet even I knew that there was a great sight more air between the saddle and my bouncing rear end than Alan ever allowed whenever he cantered by me to rein a stray calf back into the fold. Still I had to admit I felt a sting of jealousy at my father's open admiration for his ability. My consolation came that summer after I talked Father into teaching me to drive the tractor. When he saw how quickly I learned to handle the machine, it took little to convince him to allow me to transfer my new-found skill to our pickup truck. Although my driving was far less jerky than Alan's clumsy double clutching, Father never did call *me* a natural—perhaps because he was aware of all the extra hours I had put in practising in the yard whenever he was off riding range. But he would allow me to take the wheel every now and then when we headed into town, which I did with a not-so-hidden smugness if Alan was with us.

The last months of '37 were harsh. The ushering in of the new year brought even lower temperatures, which plummeted to forty below by February. For days the ranch was in a deep freeze and we ventured outside only when necessary. Still, the livestock needed to be fed. Fingers grew numb inside double-layered mittens, and frost grew heavy on woollen scarves tied over faces while we struggled to toss clumps of frozen hay from the wagon. The cattle bunched together in the fields nearest the house, their hides dusted with frost, their breath thick vapour clouds rising from nostrils heavy with icy snot. For an entire week, there was no school, so Alan stayed out at the ranch and worked alongside the rest of us.

When thin-ribbed deer showed up on the edges of the herd, grazing on whatever loose hay they could steal, I worried out loud about them and the wild horses, in particular the buck from the ridge and the stallion, whom I had come to think of as ours. Afraid they would not find enough to eat in this harsh weather, I suggested that we take feed to some of the pastures where they grazed in the fall, and where they would not have to compete with the cows for it. Alan disagreed with me. Father did as well, saying he didn't mind putting out extra hay during the cold spell, but he would not consider delivering it to them.

"They're not pets, Addie," he admonished. "You don't want to make them dependent on our feed. With dependency comes a loss of freedom, the birthright of a wild animal."

Grandfather agreed, and I was outnumbered. Yet I noticed that everyone was more generous when spreading hay in the fields during those sub-zero days.

That February, Alan and I turned fourteen and thirteen within days of each other and Father promised that we would celebrate by going to a movie at the new Sunset Theatre in Wells as soon as the cold snap broke. The following Saturday, three days after Alan's birthday and the exact day of my mine, we stoked the home fires and bundled ourselves up to drive into Sorry, where Alan's mom had the grocery van warmed up and ready to go. We switched vehicles, and with Rose VanderMeer sitting between the men on the front seat, and Alan and me perched on wooden boxes in the back of the van, we drove to Wells. Grandfather had tried begging off, saying he couldn't see much of anything nowadays and the price of a ticket would be wasted on him, but Dad refused to accept his protests. "The screen's pretty big," he told him. "And you can still hear, can't you?"

It was only by chance that the film playing at the Sunset Theatre that night was *Monkey Business*. I was astonished when the four Marx Brothers popped out of biscuit barrels singing "Sweet Adeline," thinking that Father had planned it, but he was as surprised as I was. Beside me, Grandfather jerked up in his seat and then whispered, "Why, Addie, they're singing your song." Startled, I watched his profile silhouetted in the screen's flickering light as he sang along with the rest of the song. It's possible that he was thinking of my grandmother. Still, listening to his deep baritone voice singing my name in perfect harmony with the comedians went a long way to easing the sting from the fact that this was my second birthday without my mother.

I don't know if it was the song or something else that triggered his memory, but after we arrived home and had stoked up the dying fires, Grandfather touched my cheek and said, "Goodnight, sweet Adeline." I stood open-mouthed and watched him retreat into his bedroom humming the tune under his breath.

The next day I was back to "boy" again. Late in the afternoon, while Alan and Father were unloading ice blocks from Sucker Lake, Grandfather and I prepared Sunday dinner. More and more lately I was doing the work while he directed, and I was learning to cook in spite of myself. All of a sudden, without turning from the sink where he was scrubbing carrots, he asked, "So, how are you making out reading my old journal?"

Reaching down to open the oven door, my hand stopped in mid-air. Taken aback that he was aware I had his journal in my possession, I was suddenly flooded with guilt. In the past months he seemed to have forgotten that night in his room, when he'd asked me to record some personal memory for him. Since then I'd read very little of his journal, to him or to myself.

I stalled for an answer while I peeked at the sizzling roast. After I closed the oven door, I joined him at the sink, picking up the bowl of soaking potatoes. Draining them, I said with all the nonchalance I could muster, "Okay, I guess. It's, umm, well, your handwriting's kinda hard to figure out sometimes."

He chuckled. "Yeah, I imagine so. When I was a lad, our schoolmarm was a stickler for that fancy script. Had my knuckles rapped with the ruler a good number of times until I got it right."

He was silent for a while and just when I thought he was done with the subject, he asked, "How far have you read? To what date?"

"Uh, I don't remember the exact date. It's mostly about Victoria—"

"Haven't got much further then, have you?"

I blushed at this truth. Grandfather, of course, took no notice. "Fort Victoria," he said with a note of wonder in his voice. "Not quite the little wilderness outpost we had expected. In all our travels across the States I had never seen so many different folks all in one place." He finished scrubbing the last carrot, turned from the counter and wiped his hands on a dish towel. "Rich men, poor men, beggar men, thieves, doctors, lawyers and Indian chiefs." He repeated the nursery rhyme in an off-key, singsong voice and then added, "Pa and I were just two more faces in that crowded little port town."

Slicing up the vegetables, I peered out the window above the sink for any sign of Dad and Alan. When I was certain they were still in the icehouse, I asked, "Didn't you miss your mother?"

When he didn't respond right away, I began to regret voicing the question that had been bothering me. There had been no mention of his mother in his boyhood journal and I wondered why. I would never have asked if Dad had been around, because I didn't want him to think my question had anything to do with me missing my own mother. And I didn't want to cause him any more hurt by bringing her to mind.

I busied myself placing the vegetables around the roast, taking Grandfather's silence to mean he had taken abrupt leave of the conversation, as he often did these days. He stoked the fire and took a seat at the table. And then, as if there had been no lull between question and reply, he said, "Not at first. It was too much of an adventure. Course, when my pa fessed up the situation with Ma, I fretted for a while. She was my mother, after all. But the truth was that she was never exactly motherly. Even as a wee lad I felt her lack of affection, her indifference to me. You have to remember that she was a Southern belle, and the life she had with my pa was not exactly what she'd bargained for."

"Did you ever see her again?"

"No, never did. After I settled in Barkerville, I sent some letters to our old address in Mobile, Alabama. My inquiries eventually found their way to an old friend of Ma's. She answered, saying my ma had followed her beau to Georgia, where she had perished in the siege of Savannah. A civilian casualty in Sherman's march to the sea." He heaved a sigh at the memory. "For a long time I blamed myself. Thought if I hadn't run off with Pa so easily, maybe, well, maybe things would have been different."

"But you were just a kid. What about your father?"

"Pa? Well, you'll have to read the rest of my journal to understand. But the truth is, he was never meant to settle with any woman. Maybe that's why I, same as your dad, have always been a true dyed-in-the-wool one-woman man."

I didn't question how he could say that about Father with such certainty, because I too believed it to be true. It was unthinkable that anyone else would ever take my mother's place. Even in my own mind I imagined a distant future when it would be just him and me running the ranch.

I pulled out a chair at the table. "So, in your whole life," I asked sitting down across from him, "there was no one else except Grandmother Beale?"

"Hummff," he grunted at the question. Worrying the frayed edge of his shirt sleeve, he stared straight ahead as if in his dim vision he could see something that I could not. "Yeah," he said after a moment. "I guess you could say there was someone, once upon a long, long time ago. But she was a woman, and I was but a boy."

Just then footsteps pounded up the porch steps. Grandfather pushed himself up from the table. "Best we finish getting this supper ready," he said. Walking over to the counter, he reached up and felt around for the stack of plates. Out on the porch, Dad and Alan removed their coats, scarves and gloves. By the time they exchanged their work boots for house slippers and came into the kitchen, my conversation with Grandfather, like the cloud of frigid air that had rolled in with them, was already dissipating into a memory.

Later that evening, feeling the guilt of my recent neglect, I went to his room. Closing the door behind me, I held up his journal and offered to read to him.

He hesitated briefly, then waved me to the chair at his bedside.

22.

We're almost there! Yesterday Pa and I boarded the schooner HP *Green* along with sixteen other road crew men and steamed out into the strait in the early-morning fog. I have found that staying on deck and keeping my eyes on the not-so-distant shores helps keep my stomach level. Still I will be glad once we reach our final destination. Tonight we are anchored in a small bay awaiting daylight before entering the narrow channel at the mouth of Bute Inlet. I will be glad to set foot on solid ground once again.

March 22, 1864

Words fail me. I am afraid that no matter how I try I will be unable to pen the sights and experiences I have had this day. But I shan't soon forget them. There is nothing that will ever erase the memory of lashing myself to the rails while our ship entered the heaving waters rushing into the channel. Roiling currents and whirlpools tossed and turned our hull until at last we shot out on the other side of the rapids and into Bute Inlet. After she came about, our ship steamed slowly forward on the calm waters that stretched for miles before us. Pa called the waterway a firth. He spelled it out so I could look it up in my dictionary and record a new word in my journal. But the definition I have found—a long, narrow arm of the sea—seems inadequate. It does nothing to describe the emerald waters or the heavily forested mountains and sheer rock cliffs rising on either side of our ship and keeping us in the morning shadows. Waterfalls, rivers and creeks spilled spring runoff into the inlet. Sleek-coated otters slipped in and out of the water to feed on mussels along the rocky shores while hundreds of bald-head eagles competed for fish at the mouths of creeks and rivers.

As we steamed along, most of the road crew stood crowded on the starboard side of the ship to gape in mute awe. It was as if we had entered another world—a hushed, mist-shrouded sanctuary. Not far from where Pa and I leaned at the rail, Mr. Brewster—the foreman of the road crew—pointed out the sights to the red-headed fellow beside him. I have watched this man sketching in a large notepad on deck during our voyage. I hear that he is a famous artist by the name of Frederick Whymper who has been commissioned by Alfred Waddington to paint images of the scenic route that his road will follow. If the mainland is as impressive from shore as it is from the decks of our boat, the artist will have plenty to inspire him.

When we sailed around the final bend I had my first view of the foreboding mountains through which Waddington's road will cut. Soaring thousands of feet above the timberline, their jagged snow-capped peaks cut into the eastern sky. In the shadows below lay the mouth of the Homathko River and the small settlement known as Waddington Town. Our ship's destination.

Beside me, Pa whistled under his breath, his gaze on the towering blue-black mountains in the distance.

—I hope Waddington knows what he's doing, he said to no one in particular.

Along the shore, signs of human life began to appear. Wisps of smoke rose above the treetops. Dugout canoes rested on the shore. One of our shipmates pointed out signs of a Native encampment where a moment before I had detected nothing but forest. On closer inspection I spied primitive dwellings constructed of branches and bark. In front of one stood two men watching our progress. Slowly, others began to appear among the trees. They headed out to the beach until it seemed an entire village was making its way to greet us. Several half-naked children ran alongside, oblivious to both the spring-chilled air and the barnacle-crusted rocks beneath their bare feet.

As we drew nearer to the head of the inlet a number of log buildings and canvas tents took shape on the shore. Suddenly it seemed the little settlement was alive with inhabitants. And it appeared that all of them were Indians. As we drifted closer I strained to hear the foreman's explanation of the various dress, adornments, tattoos and piercings that distinguish the different clans gathering on the long wooden wharf. I am uncertain how to spell the strange names he gave them. Euclutat and Homalco. But I was struck by the robust appearance of these Indians compared to the sickly few I had encountered on the outskirts of Fort Victoria. Most surprising to me was that they seemed to welcome our arrival as they competed to catch the bowlines being tossed from our ship.

Mr. Brewster's words confirmed my observations as he explained the abundance of seafood that keeps these coastal tribes supplied with food year round.

—The buggers are glad enough to see us coming, though, he said. But their joy isn't at the sight of us—it's for the goods we bring to trade for their salmon.

Suddenly he swore in a voice loud enough for all to hear.

—Jesus H. Christ! What the hell are they doing here?

I followed his gaze to where it rested on a small group of Natives who were watching our arrival from the shore at the end of the wharf.

—Klatsassin! Mr. Brewster told his companion with contempt. He's a Chilcootan war chief and has no bloody business being here.

The foreman swore again using a word I don't care to write down here.

A war chief! Well, my heart jumped into my throat at the thought of seeing a real chief, and I scanned the half dozen or so men and women until I located the one I was certain Mr. Brewster had called Klatsassin. Tall and imposing, the man stood out in his leather breeches and heavy fur robe. A thick animal pelt sat upon his head making him appear much taller than the rest. Regardless of his height, and even from a distance, he appeared to be as menacing a figure as I could ever imagine. With wide-set eyes and a strong square jaw, his handsome face betrayed no emotion as he scanned the crowd at the ship's rail. His gaze paused only briefly as it moved from one face to another. When it passed over me I felt a shiver and a sense that I would not want this man for an enemy. None of the others standing with him appeared quite as regal or robust as he did with their hide clothing hanging loose over lean frames. My first thought was that they all could use a good feed of potatoes.

One of the road crew explained that this group did not belong to any of the coastal tribes but were Chilcootans from the plateaus beyond the mountains.

—We already have a Chilcootan chief working for us as a guide, he said. A hereditary chief by the name of Talhoot who's proven to be trustworthy—as far as Brewster believes savages can be trusted, that is. But you won't see our foreman dealing with a war chief.

Something's not right for them to come down to the coastal territory so blatantly. There's no love lost between the Chilcootans and the coastal tribes, that's for sure.

Our cargo was unloaded with Pa overseeing the handling of his trunk like a worried mother hen. Not trusting anyone else with it, he insisted that I lift one end and we carried the heavy trunk from the wharf ourselves.

At the end of the pier the war chief was watching the passengers come ashore. Ahead of us, Mr. Brewster strode off the wharf and headed deliberately toward him. As we drew nearer I was startled to discover that the chief's piercing glare was even more disarming because his eyes were dark blue in colour!

When all of a sudden a young fellow and girl appeared at his side, I slowed my pace, forcing Pa, at the other end of the trunk, to do the same.

The young man stepped forward to address the foreman.

—My uncle asks where is the old Tyee from Victoria?

Mr. Brewster stopped short. Keeping his gaze fixed on the chief, he gave his answer.

—Tell your uncle that Mr. Waddington did not come across the big drink with us. Tell him that if you people want work, you will have to deal with me. But not in this place. You must come to our camp upriver. Tomorrow.

Even as Mr. Brewster spoke, the young man addressed the chief in their own language. His words caused disappointment to flash across the chief's face.

Intrigued, I dropped my end of Pa's trunk in pretense of needing a rest. But the chief was finished with the conversation. He turned and strode up the beach, his people following on his heels.

During the hike to our base camp, we learned the reason for his distress. The word is that one of the war chief's daughters has been kidnapped and is being held for ransom by a coastal tribe—a common occurrence among these people, according to the gossip among the road crew. Klatsassin has come here with his family to ask for Mr. Waddington's help in negotiating her return.

—Old Waddy's got no business getting in the middle of these people's disputes, Mr. Brewster complained. It does no good to be a bleeding heart. He's intervened in tribal quarrels before and should know by now that it never does any good. Theft and kidnapping is a way of life between these savages and I say let 'em argue and murder each other and then they'll leave us alone.

Perhaps his bitter words were sparked by the disturbing news he'd received when we reached the ferry landing at the Homathko River this afternoon. The ferryman—who had stayed the winter to guard the road company's cache of supplies—reported with some agitation that he had woken one morning a few weeks ago to discover that twenty sacks of flour had gone missing from the storehouse during the night. He has no proof, but he told the foreman he believes the Chilcootans are the culprits.

—The smallpox and hunger have made them desperate, the ferryman said. I ain't saying that excuses them, but it sure looks to me to be reason to suspect them.

Mr. Brewster cursed in words that once again I cannot record. He swore that he would get to the bottom of this. He vowed that when he did rout out the thieves, he would see to it that they would never be hired to work with his road crew.

Once we were safely on the other side of the river I breathed a sigh of relief and hurried off the precarious wooden ferry. Before Pa and I started lugging his heavy trunk up the last leg of the trail to our camp, I glanced back over my shoulder at the treacherous river we had just crossed. At that moment a group of Natives arrived on the far bank to await the ferry's return. Among them I spotted the young fellow who had spoken to Mr. Brewster on behalf of the war chief Klatsassin. The chief was not with the group, but the girl I saw at the wharf when we disembarked earlier today was.

Tonight Pa and I are settled in our tent. As I sit on my bedroll writing by the light of our paraffin lamp, I cannot explain why I can still picture the girl's face so clearly. Or why I find myself hoping she is with the group of Chilcootans who are camped nearby.

23.

"Is that true, Granddad? Did the war chief really have blue eyes?"

"Yeah. Odd, but it happens sometimes," he said, then added in a tired voice, "That's enough for tonight."

He tugged the covers up and turned on his side, his back to me. But from the way his jaw muscles worked as he tried to settle, I doubted that he would find sleep any time soon.

I rose to leave, wondering what memory had triggered such agitation. Before I reached the door, he surprised me by saying, "Leave my journal." He held up a trembling hand and gestured toward his chest of drawers.

I set the journal on the dresser top next to the photograph of my grandmother and left the room.

The only trace left of the grandmother I was named after was that old sepia photograph on Grandfather's bureau. I remembered being told when I was very young that I had inherited her blonde hair and her green eyes, and it was clear that I would also have her height. But looking at that photograph, I always imagined more similarities than physical appearance. I recognized myself in the unflinching stare that seemed to follow me whenever I was in the room. I saw myself in the set of her jaw, in the unyielding, unforgiving expression. Without being told, I knew this woman had been no quitter. Like my mother was.

Growing up, I had often bemoaned the fact that I did not look like Mother but took after my father's side of the family. I was now glad of that fact. Sometimes I would pick up Grandmother Beale's photograph to study her serious face and something deep inside me would whisper, *Am I like you?* I wanted to believe I was, but I knew little about her beyond this faded image and Grandfather's sparse stories about how they met. He and Father rarely spoke of her, just as they rarely mentioned Mother now. It was as if once their women left, there was no point in discussing them. I sometimes wondered, if I were suddenly gone, would they cease to speak of me?

Even the house had given up any trace of my mother's scent. In no small part thanks to me. One weekend when Father was away at the coast,

I gathered up all the clothes she'd left behind, stuffed them into her re-maining green tapestry travel bag and dragged it out to the storage shed. I took her perfume bottles, her fancy powder boxes, her jars of Pond's cold cream—with their perilous memories of her slathering the excess cream from her hands onto mine—and out of Father's sight, I lined them up on the fence and used them for target practice. Before long, a pungent male odour took over every corner of every room in the ranch house. Where once the air was heavy with her soft fragrances, it now reeked of hard sweat and wood smoke, old leather and unwashed woollen socks, making it a sadder but safer place.

As another winter crawled into another spring without my mother, my anger at her festered. In all that time, Father never uttered one harsh word against her. In my heart, I believed he blamed himself for her leaving, just as I knew without it ever being said that he, like Mother, held himself responsible for Evan's death.

He asked me once to forgive her, saying quietly that sorrow can cause people to think and behave in strange ways. A part of me understood her crazed grief. But what I couldn't come to terms with—the resentment that I would carry around like a sack of rocks for far too long—was that there had been no note, no letter, not one word from her to ease our fears that something horrific had befallen her.

A deeper part of me was frightened that everyone was wrong. What if Mother had not simply run off to the city, but had lost her way that day, wandered into the frozen woods never to be found? Whenever those thoughts threatened to rise to the surface, I pushed them back. It was far easier to be angry at her than to believe her to be dead.

By that second spring, if Father had not exactly accepted her leav-ing, he had come to some kind of peace with it. The winter had been hard and perhaps the extra work with the cattle and his concern for the Van-derMeers kept him busy, but I was glad he had stopped driving down to the coast only to return empty-handed and empty-hearted. Now, once a month, he drove Alan and his mother down to Kamloops to visit Mr. Van-derMeer in the TB sanatorium.

To say Alan visited is not quite correct. He told me he could only wait outside while they went in, but it brought him some kind of comfort to see his stepfather wave down from his window.

I think something about Alan's presence comforted my father as well. Perhaps having a boy around filled a small part of the empty space left by Evan's death. I don't know. But as the months passed by, I could see them growing closer. I didn't mind. Alan spending so much time at the ranch made it feel as if he truly was my brother in more ways than our crude blood-brother oath. And like Father, I suppose, I too found that Alan filled an empty space inside me, an empty space I was trying hard to pretend wasn't there.

In May, Alan and I wrote the grade seven exams. Given the hours of study that Father had insisted we do, and the confidence we both felt after writing the tests, I wasn't worried. On the final day of school in the middle of June, Mrs. Parsons walked around the class handing out report cards. She dropped the brown paper envelopes on each of our desks without a word, but something in her expression as she delivered Alan's made my stomach sink.

Dismissed from school for the summer a few minutes later, we left the classroom among the chatter and excitement of the other students who were jostling to get outdoors, all glad to see the last of our teacher's face for a few months. Alan and I walked across the road together, our unopened report cards in our hands.

"My mother'll be disappointed," he said as we approached the store's porch.

I stopped in my tracks. "Why?"

"I failed."

"How can you know that? Didn't you say you thought you had done okay on the tests?"

"Yeah. But I failed."

"Let's look," I said, plunking myself down on the steps.

He sat down beside me. Over in the schoolyard, our classmates were celebrating their freedom. We were not supposed to open our envelopes before delivering them to our parents, but as usual everyone was ignoring the rule. From the sounds of joy coming from those waiting for Reverend Watts and the school bus, and the other students whooping and running to their nearby homes waving their report cards in the air like prizes, all were excited with their results.

I nudged Alan to open his. While he did, I ran my finger along the sealed flap of mine and removed the yellow report card. Before I could glance at it, Alan passed his to me.

I took it from his hands. "This can't be," I blurted, looking down at the columns of Ds and Es in every subject. There was not a single teacher remark, only a hastily scrawled FAILED on the bottom.

Returning it to him, I opened my own with trepidation. I had passed to grade eight, but barely. All my marks were Cs and Ds.

Behind us, the store's screen door screeched open and Mrs. Vander-Meer came out onto the veranda, a dripping bottle of Pepsi-Cola in each hand. When neither of us made a move to accept the offered soda pop, she set the bottles on the railing and reached down to take the report card from Alan's hand.

She studied the paper. With her eyebrows furrowed, her teeth pressing on her bottom lip, she silently formed the letter F. As realization hit her, a woman who rarely displayed her emotions, confusion flickered across her face. But she quickly gathered herself together and handed the report card back to him. She retrieved the Pepsi-Colas from the railing and passed one to each of us, saying, "Next year, you'll do better."

"That teacher's going to keep me in grade seven forever. It's a waste of time to go back," Alan said.

"Going to school is never a waste of time," Mrs. VanderMeer replied before going back inside.

Later at the ranch, Alan and I sat at the kitchen table while Father studied our report cards. Finally, shaking his head, he laid them aside, saying, "This doesn't make sense. I know you are both capable of better grades."

Alan took the failure as just another reason he should quit school. While he bemoaned the waste of sitting in a classroom for another year, Dad nodded with understanding. Encouraged by my father's silence, Alan added hopefully, "Then I could work out here full-time."

Father's nod turned to a slow shaking of his head. "Sorry, son, but that wasn't the deal. If you quit school, you quit the ranch."

Beside me, Alan's shoulders slumped. Even I was surprised at Father's harsh response, and I blurted out, "He's right, Dad. Mrs. Parsons isn't teaching us anything new. The daily lessons she scribbles on the board we could do just as well at home."

"Mrs. Parsons isn't the point," Father interrupted. "Receiving a diploma is." He pushed his hand through his hair as if gathering his thoughts, then said, "Your mother doesn't need any more worry right now, Alan, so I'm asking you to wait awhile and continue working here for the summer before making a decision. Can you do that?"

Alan reluctantly agreed, and so it was settled for the moment.

A month later I learned that my father was far more conniving than

I ever gave him credit for. After dinner on a hot evening at the end of July, he told Alan he had something to show him. I followed them outside and across the yard. The still evening air was heavy with the aroma of summer dust and freshly cut hay. When we reached the corral, Father unlatched the gate and held it open for Alan. As he followed Dad inside, I climbed up and sat on the top rung. On the side of the corral, our sorrel mare lifted her head from the manger. Her tail swishing away lazy summer flies, she watched them approach. Following Father's lead, Alan slowly circled the mare, his eyes inspecting, his hands running across her flanks, down her belly and over her teats. Finally he lifted her tail, stepped back and said, "She's with foal."

"That's right," Father said, stroking the mare's withers. "But it wasn't our stud that caught her. She got out of the field in April. I found her a week later in the east meadow with the herd of wild horses." He stopped for a moment to let the information sink in. And then, glancing over his shoulder at Alan's reaction, he said, "Yeah. The buckskin stallion. I've been keeping an eye on her to see if she took before saying anything. So now here's a new proposition for you to consider."

I couldn't read anything in Alan's expression as Dad strolled to the mare's front end.

"The foal should be born sometime next March," he said, his hand caressing her velvety nose. "If you're still working for us then, it's yours." He gave the mare's neck a final pat and then sauntered away without looking back.

After that day, whenever my imagination ran to a distant future of ranching with my father, the visions included Alan.

Looking back with the understanding time brings, I would see that neither my father's bribery nor my dreams were enough to save Alan from his eventual destiny. But unlike Father, I would find myself hard pressed to forgive when just like Mother, Alan quit on us too.

24.

That summer of 1938 forgave and erased any reminder of the harshness of the past winter. Perhaps only in reminiscence was it so perfect, for surely there must have been the usual swarms of blackflies and mosquitoes, and a relentless sun to plague us during the long hot days spent branding, haying or harvesting winter firewood. Still, my memories of that time are all good, filled with sunshine and Alan, who lived and worked with us every day for the entire two months.

Our chores left us precious little free time, but if we were not too tired at the end of the day, after dinner we would grab our fishing poles and hike down to the creek at the bottom of the south field. Other times we would saddle up our horses and ride until twilight descended. We would often leave our mounts grazing in the east meadows and climb the ridge to sit beneath Alan's watching tree in hopes of catching sight of the wild horses.

Inevitably an unspoken rivalry emerged between us. Whether we were riding range, roping strays or catching rainbow trout in the creek, we were always trying to outdo each other, particularly if Father was within sight. The only time it was no contest was whenever—in a futile attempt to control their population in our fields—we went out shooting gophers.

I clearly had the advantage, since my grandfather had me using the pests for target practice at an early age. According to him and Father, killing the rodents was a necessary evil in order to keep them from overrunning us, from ransacking our grain and root cellar.

Still, I was taught early to never kill for the sake of killing. The lesson was brought home to me a few years before, when I was lying spread-eagle on the edge of the back field one day "keeping the gophers' numbers down." Just as my father came up behind me, a sparrow lifted from the fence and took to the sky. In a moment of vanity, wanting to show off my marksmanship, I swung my rifle to sight the bird in flight. Even as my finger squeezed the trigger I knew my mistake. Seeing the bird flutter broken-winged into the autumn stubble, I felt shame flush my cheeks. With the gunshot still echoing in my ears, Father bent down and folded his lanky frame through the fence rungs. Straightening up on the other side, in his unhurried way, he bid me to put aside my rifle and come with him. Out in the field, I stood with my head hung while he knelt beside the wounded bird and gently took it in his hands. With blood, slime and tiny down feathers streaking his palms, he offered up the struggling bird, telling me quietly to "put the poor creature out of its misery."

Although I wanted to shrink away, I knew better than to refuse. I knew full well, without his saying it, that I had to take responsibility for the bird's suffering: that in wanting to cause death I was about to feel it.

The lesson I learned in the field that day would stay with me. By the time Alan started hunting gophers with me, I never celebrated my kills. It was tempting, though, because even using my grandfather's high-powered scope, Alan was such a darned lousy shot.

His lame marksmanship was still a sore point, so even when we were target practising using tin cans, I refrained from gloating too much about my superior shooting.

Yet I noticed nothing stopped him from teasing me when it came to physical activities. In brute strength he now had me hands down. Even though I was tall for my age, all of a sudden Alan towered over me. There seemed to be no bottom to his appetite, and putting away a meal became yet another activity where he outshone me. Over summer, his lean body filled out and he seemed to grow taller by the day, causing even his mother to comment whenever she saw him.

Rose VanderMeer came out to the ranch every Sunday afternoon that summer. After dinner, she and Father would work on the store's books. It was during those evenings, while they sorted through the weekly receipts, that I began to realize the limited extent of Rose VanderMeer's education and understand her passionate desire for Alan to complete his. Her child-like scrawl on the receipts, sometimes with backward-facing letters—using B to indicate bread, C for canned goods and so on—was how she kept track of customers' purchases. Oddly enough, she had no problem with numbers and could add and subtract quicker than I.

Watching her and Father huddled at the table while Alan and I did the dinner dishes, there were moments when it felt as if we were a family. A strange one, to say the least: a father who was married but had no wife; a daughter whose grandfather, more often than not, mistook her for a boy; a husbandless wife whom no one really knew anything about before she showed up in our little community with her six-year-old son; and a son who would surely be too big to fit in his wooden desk when we returned to our classroom in the fall.

On the first day of school in September, the startled expression that crossed Mrs. Parsons' face when Alan walked in and folded himself into his old desk at the back of the room was almost comical. Still, every morning our separate lessons would be chalked out on the blackboard once again.

But Father had other plans. "Never mind the lessons she puts up for you," he told Alan. "Just do the same ones as Addie. When it's time for the provincial exams next spring, I'll arrange for you both to write the grade eight finals in Quesnel."

All summer, Grandfather's journal remained set aside. I was too preoccupied with my own adventures and he never mentioned it, so it lay untouched on the top of his dresser. Grandfather's memory, like his eyesight, was declining, and I wondered now and then if he even remembered the journal, or the unfinished statement he had asked me to write for him. Recalling his agitation the last time I read the journal to him, I was reluctant to bring it up.

In Mr. VanderMeer's absence, there were no editions of the *Sorry Times,* so on Saturday evenings, Grandfather no longer insisted on my reading to him and was content to sit in the parlour listening to the news on the Radiola before retiring early. Even the Sunday night ranch records seemed forgotten. Selfishly, I was secretly relieved to be released from the task and glad to be free to spend more time with Alan.

Yet every now and then, I would guiltily promise myself that I would take the very next opportunity to gently remind Grandfather about the journal, and the part he said was missing from it. The time never seemed quite right, though—until the last weekend of September.

That morning, Father took Alan and his mother to visit Mr. VanderMeer at the TB sanatorium. The trip to Kamloops was over five hours each way and so, in order not to have to stay overnight, they set out in the darkness before dawn and would be gone until late that night.

After breakfast, when the rising sun was nothing more than a sliver of yellow light beneath a heavy grey sky, I headed outside. In the barn, with no one to impress, I took my time cleaning out the stalls. I filled the water troughs and stoked fresh hay into the mangers, giving extra to the pregnant mare, whom Alan had been blatantly pampering all summer. Her ears twitching, she nickered with entitlement as I stroked her neck.

By the time I was finished in the barn, any pretense of sunlight was gone from the sky. A cold drizzling rain found its way under my collar and trickled down the back of my neck as I went about my outside chores.

Back at the house a few hours later, I found Grandfather, who had taken it in his head to bake bread, stoking the fire in the cookstove to get the kitchen warm enough for rising dough.

"Dad brought bread from the store yesterday, you know," I reminded him, shaking the rain from my hat and hanging it by the door.

"Yeah, well, I got a hankering for something more substantial," he said, sliding back the stove's cast iron lid with a loud scrape. "Not that fluff they try to pass off as bread." He shuffled over to rummage around in the cooling cupboard.

I came up behind him, reached for the mason jar of sourdough starter on the shelf right in front of him, pulled it out and placed it in his hands. As he turned away I realized with a start how much taller I had grown in comparison to him. Or, more correctly, how much he had shrunk. When did this all happen, this loss of height? And weight? He had never had any extra fat on his tall, lanky frame, but suddenly he appeared downright skeletal. I stepped back and watched him take the jar over to the counter. Halfway there, a phlegm-filled cough rattled up from his lungs, causing him to stop to catch his breath before continuing with his shoulders stooped, his legs wobbling with each measured step. When had he become so feeble?

I had never given much consideration to Grandfather's age—had never thought of him as *old*. Watching him in that moment, I did a quick calculation and was startled by the conclusion that he must be close to eighty-nine now. A deep sadness overcame me with the realization that for him, time, like his body, was winding down. It was impossible to imagine life without him.

We worked side by side at the counter in silence, me passing him ingredients and he turning them into a huge, sticky lump of dough. As he dumped the dough out onto the floured counter, a sudden sense of urgency prompted me to speak.

"Do you still want me to do some writing for you, Granddad?"

"Writing?"

"Remember? The night you asked me to write down something you said was missing from your journal?"

"Ah," he said, deftly kneading the dough. "Where is that old journal?"

"It's on your bureau," I reminded him, then added quickly, "And, you know, well, uh … I was thinking maybe I could read some more of it to you."

"Why, that sounds like a great idea. Once we set this dough to rising and make ourselves a bit of lunch, why don't you just go fetch it?" And in a moment of surprising clarity, he added, "After all, we've got the whole day to ourselves, haven't we?"

After the sourdough was patted down in a basin, covered with a damp tea towel and set on the sideboard, after our lunch was eaten and our dishes stacked in the sink, I went to Grandfather's room to retrieve the journal. When I returned, he was sitting at the table chewing on the end of his unlit pipe.

Since Mother had gone—in defiance of her leaving, I admit—I had often encouraged him to smoke in the house. I didn't mind the sweet smell of his pipe tobacco. But he never took me up on the offer. Perhaps out of respect for her, or for my father's hopes of her return, the only place he ever lit the pipe was outside or on the screened-in front porch.

As I slid into a chair across from him, he leaned forward, folded his hands on the table and said, "Okay. Have at it."

I put aside the notebook and pen, which I'd brought along just in case, and carefully opened the journal.

"Start right from the beginning, now," he ordered.

So with rain pounding on our roof and streaming from the eaves outside the kitchen window, I began to read from the very first page of his boyhood journal. After the first few lines, I glanced up every now and then to check his reaction. He remained relaxed back into his chair, listening with a faraway look on his face. Sometimes he nodded as if in agreement, and sometimes a smile, wistful and sad, would flicker across his lips at some memory that was not recorded on those pages. "Ah, yes," he would interject, "I remember that."

If one of the passages went on too long about the weather, or with some wordy description of the countryside, he would wave it off, indicating I should skip that part and move on to the next date.

"My, wasn't I the flowery writer?" he declared at one point. Chuckling, he added, "I always did find putting my thoughts on paper far easier than saying them out loud. Could be sometimes I went a tad too far."

We interrupted the reading only to form the dough into loaves and set them on the sideboard for one final rise. By the time the loaves were ready to go into the oven, I'd finally reached the date where I had last left off. I peeked up as I began reading his description of sailing into Bute Inlet, but Grandfather appeared unperturbed by the entry, which had seemed to upset him so much last time. So I chanced it and continued on.

"… As I sit on my bedroll writing by the light of our paraffin lamp, I cannot explain why I can still picture the girl's face so clearly. Or why I find myself hoping she is with the group of Chilcootans who are camped nearby."

I read the final words of the day's entry and looked up again. Across the table, Grandfather had set aside his pipe and sat staring down at his hands folded in his lap. Either he was in deep thought, or he had gone to some far-off place in his mind that he seemed to retreat to more and more lately.

Suspecting that the girl might be the older woman he had mentioned during our interrupted conversation of months ago, as I rose to put the bread into the oven, I asked, "Was she very beautiful?"

"Who?" Grandfather raised his head, his bushy eyebrows furrowing in confusion or annoyance, I couldn't read which.

"You know who," I teased. "The Native girl in your journal." Wiping my hands on the tea towel, I sat back down.

Grandfather remained silent for a long time, the muscles of his face twitching, as if with conflicting emotions. Then he smiled and said quietly, "Yeah. She was a real beauty, was Rose."

"Rose?"

Thinking I had pushed too far, that he had grown tired and was confusing the girl from his past with Alan's mother, I corrected him. "No. Not Mrs. VanderMeer. I mean the girl at Bute Inlet. The one with the Chilcotin war chief."

While the rain drummed on the roof and the faint aroma of baking bread seeped from the oven, Grandfather's face worried with some private notion of his own. After a few moments of silent consideration, he said, "Yep. Coincidence, eh? But sure enough, that was her name. Rose."

He nodded toward the journal lying before me on the table. I picked it up and continued reading.

25.

March 28, 1864

Rain! Will it never stop? The downpour started two days after we arrived. The ground is sodden and water lies in great puddles everywhere. It seeps from moss-covered deadfall and drips relentlessly from overhead branches. The last thing I hear at night and the first thing I hear in the morning is the rain's constant drumming on our tent.

Pa is vexed, for his powder can quickly turn useless in such weather, and he works hard to protect it from becoming damp. The roadwork has slowed. The men return wet to the bone for meals. They sit in the openings of their tents hunched over tin plates and stare out through the grey curtain of rain with frowning faces.

I spend most of my day in the cook's tent learning my duties from a reluctant Mr. Laitmere and his helper—his klootchman, as the rest of the crew call the gap-toothed Indian woman who not only does the cook's bidding all day but lives with him as his wife at night, sharing his tent and his meals. She speaks no English but shows her displeasure at me by slapping my hands whenever I touch anything she deems to be her territory. I have finally been delegated to fetching water and firewood and cleaning up after meals. Still she watches my every move with hard eyes, and I have come to the conclusion that she is afraid of being replaced.

I can hardly blame her. Food appears to be in short supply at the Chilcootan camp. Women and children often appear in the shadows beyond the circle of our campfire, their gaunt faces silently begging for our after-dinner scraps. But Mr. Brewster has forbidden us from sharing any food with them. Besides still being angry about the stolen flour, he believes that feeding the Natives only encourages them to be lazy. Even those Chilcootans who work for the road company are only paid in trade—muskets and blankets and pots and pans—but no food. And so our scraps go to the dogs and not to the pot-bellied children whose wide eyes watch us from the edge of the trees. Every now and then, one will dart over if someone tosses a crust aside, but if our Mr. Brewster is around, he will snatch the bread away, insisting these people hunted and fished for centuries before we came and if they need food that is what they should bloody well do now.

It's not easy to watch. Pa and I have taken to putting aside a portion of food each meal and he doles it out as he can. This has caused some disagreement between him and the foreman because Pa makes no attempt to hide his actions. I wish I had his confidence to place chunks of bread or pieces of bacon in those reaching hands. In particular I would like to share something as an offer of friendship with the young man and the girl whom I saw with the war chief on the shores of Bute Inlet. The pair never come to beg for food. I sometimes catch glimpses of them foraging in the underbrush or along the banks of the river. They seem to communicate with bird-like whistles when they are at a distance from each other. A sucking in of air through unmoving lips rather than Pa's pursed, blowing-out whistle that I have never mastered. Each time I hear the repetitive call of a chickadee, I assume that the couple are close by. I stop whatever chore I'm doing to scan my surroundings and am often rewarded with a sighting. If they are aware that I'm there they give no sign, and I feel like a voyeur ducking out of sight and watching them in silence.

I have come to the conclusion that they are brother and sister, so alike are their coppery faces with high cheekbones and strong noses. He is almost feminine in his handsomeness, and her beauty is so fierce that I am startled that no one else has mentioned it.

Only Pa seems as fascinated by them as I. In one day he has learned more about the elusive pair than I have in five days of spying.

This morning, to get a feel for the lay of the land, he engaged an English-speaking Chilcootan by the name of Crooked-Eye to guide him on a trek through the canyon trails leading up to the plateau. Pa returned this evening drenched to the skin and a little down in the mouth over the terrain ahead but full of information he has gleaned from the guide. After dinner and his nightly helping of whiskey, Pa shared what he's learned. I was correct in my guess that the couple are brother and sister. Twins. The son and daughter of a Chilcootan chief, they are the only survivors of the smallpox that wiped out their entire village. Saved—according to Pa's guide—by a white man.

The story is that when they were small children, a trapper had built his cabin near their winter camp. In exchange for the chief's permission to remain in their territory, the trapper had taught the twins to speak English. During the twins' fifteenth year, the white man's sickness came. Within days it swept through their village, sparing none. Except the twins. The guide told Pa that it was believed that the lives of the chief's son and daughter had been saved by the small boxes of magic sniffing tobacco that the trapper shared with them.

Snuff, Pa explained to me.

He had heard of this dubious remedy in the old country, he said. A mixture of European and Chinese medicine. Snuff—laced with finely ground scabs from smallpox victims. Immunization by exposure. Not unlike the inoculations we had in San Francisco, Pa claims.

Now under the protection of Klatsassin, the orphaned twins are camped somewhere nearby hoping that the brother will gain work with the road company.

I asked Pa if his guide told him their names, and he said yes, but he couldn't understand or pronounce their Chilcootan ones.

Neither could the old trapper, apparently. He gave them both Christian names. Rose and Willum.

March 29, 1864

The rain has stopped! This afternoon the sun beats down so hard that steam rises from the saturated forest floor. The air is so clean and fresh it is easy to forget the misery of the constant damp. As I was fetching buckets of water from the river early this morning, a fleeting movement in the undergrowth caused me to pause. I spun around to catch a quick glimpse through the glistening cedar branches of the girl Pa says is called Rose. All morning while I worked I felt her furtive eyes watching me just as though the tables have turned and she is now the one spying on me. But the moment I sensed her presence and glanced up, she disappeared in the mist as if by the trick of magician's smoke. Then, after lunch today, I had a strange encounter with her. After our cook and his woman had retired to his tent, leaving me alone to clean up and tend the campfire, I pushed aside my unfinished meal and took the opportunity to fetch my journal and write by the light of day. As I stepped out of our tent I stopped short at the sight of the girl standing in the trees not ten feet away. Believing she had been tempted by my unfinished lunch, I nodded toward the table, silently inviting her to take whatever she wished. But she remained motionless. Her un-flinching eyes held mine until I was the one to look away. Not wanting to frighten her off, I walked slowly over to the camp table, all the while keeping her in my peripheral vision. Certain she was still watching me, I busied myself settling down to write. I filled my fountain pen and opened the journal. Jotting down today's date, I glanced up quickly and caught the stricken look that flashed across her face at the sight of my pen moving across the page. She shrank back and then, just as if it had been a loaded weapon I held in my hands, she turned and fled.

I have since learned the cause of the girl's horror.

Earlier this evening a group of men from the neighbouring camp—led by the man Crooked-Eye—showed up asking for the boss man. Among them was the twin brother. He stood off to the side scowling as our cook informed the group that Mr. Brewster was at the forward camp and wouldn't be back until tomorrow night.

—But even if he was here he ain't about to hire any of you until he has the names of those who stole the company flour, said Mr. Laitmere.

Before Crooked-Eye could reply, the young man called Willum stepped forward. He fisted his right hand and pounded it against his left breast with such brutal force that I imagined it leaving a bruise over his heart.

—I do not steal, he said.

The cook turned to him.

—I'm just giving you all warning that Mr. Brewster will have the names of the thieves or there is no work for any more Chilcootans.

The young man's eyes hardened. His right hand dropped to his side.

—Our animals are scarce because you take too many. Our people few because you brought the sickness. Might be we could ask who are the thieves?

Crooked-Eye pulled him aside. In the orange glow of the setting sun he spoke with urgency in their language. Finally the young man stepped back. He turned to leave but not before glaring at the cook once again.

—You tell your boss man—you want to cross our land, you owe us more than flour.

As he strode away, I noticed his sister waiting in the shadows on the edge of the trees. Her brown eyes met mine briefly before she turned away with her brother.

The rest of the group returned to their camp while their spokesman hung back. Although the work crew calls him Crooked-Eye—a nickname which I am certain was born from the fact that the man is so cross-eyed that it is hard to imagine he can even see—Pa calls him "Chief." Instead of being insulted, the name brings a wide grin to the guide's face and he fawns over Pa like a trusted comrade. I suspect that his friendliness is driven less by fondness than by the whiskey Pa brings out at night. The man's affliction does not seem to interfere with his sight, and as he hung around this evening his strange crossed eyes flickered back and forth between the flask in Pa's hands and the woman tending the campfire. After a while he leaned close to Pa and nodded toward the cook's helper.

—You share your drink with me and I will make it so you share that klootchman, he said.

Pa laughed out loud at the offer. He took a large swallow of whiskey and then, wiping his mouth with the back of his hand, he shook his head.

—The trouble with two men sharing one woman, said he, is much the same as the trouble with them sharing one horse. The problem comes when they both want to go for a ride at the same time.

He patted the fellow on the shoulder.

—Don't despair, Chief, he said, grabbing a tin cup from the table.

He threw off the coffee dregs and poured a splash of whiskey into the mug. As he handed it to Crooked-Eye, I leaned close to whisper a reminder of Mr. Waddington's warning about liquor and the Natives.

—Yeah. I recall, said Pa with a snort. Old Waddy said it was unlawful to sell it to them. He never said anything about giving it away.

Pa is not usually given to sharing his whiskey. I fear that this gesture will only make Crooked-Eye want more if the drink has the same effect on him it has on Pa. But Pa is not concerned. He says I am a worrywart. Yet I notice that he keeps his supply of whiskey locked securely in the trunk at the foot of his cot.

Tonight, though, Pa's generosity bought us all an evening's entertainment. Mellowed by the whiskey, Crooked-Eye sat in the glow of our campfire and told tales of his people. He waited until nightfall, as it is the Chilcootan custom to only share stories once the sun is fully set.

And so with the darkening shadows encircling our campfire, I discovered the reason for the look of horror on Rose's face today.

According to our storyteller, the Chilcootan people have a morbid fear of writing. They believe it is bad magic and that the recording of a man's name is a powerful evil which can steal his spirit and bring sickness and death. Two years ago this belief was reinforced after an incident at a place called Benshee up on the plateau. It was there that a trader who wanted a group of Natives to move their summer camp farther away from his post wrote down their names, threatening to bring the white man's disease upon them. Months later they had all perished, and across the plateau thousands of Chilcootans were dead or dying of smallpox.

His words weigh heavy on my heart. No wonder the girl Rose fled at the sight of me writing. I vow not to make the same mistake again and will refrain from making entries in my journal whenever she or any of her people are nearby. From this night on I will keep it hidden away beneath my cot and only bring it out to write in as I do now in the privacy of our tent.

26.

I had to squint to make out the last sentences on the journal page. In the fading light, the kitchen had taken on an eerie kind of quiet. Across the table Grandfather sat slumped in his chair, his shoulders folded forward and his head lowered with his chin resting on his chest. For the briefest moment my breath caught at the stillness of his body, until I noticed the muscles at his temples working as if he was watching something play out on the other side of his closed eyes—and as if what he was seeing caused him pain.

Outside, the rain had stopped, and the late afternoon light darkened the corners of the room. I placed the attached ribbon between the journal pages to mark my spot and reached up for the pull chain on the light above the table. Yellow light flooded the room and Grandfather raised his head. Pretty certain he had nodded off while I was reading, I waited anxiously while he blinked a few times and then straightened up in his chair.

My mind was riddled with questions about what I'd just read. And Willum? Wasn't that the name he had mistakenly called Alan? Before I could open my mouth to ask, Grandfather cleared his throat and said, "That's enough for today."

Should I risk upsetting him with my curiosity? Something inside me said no.

It's funny, the odd things that remain stuck in the mind while important details are lost with the passing of time. Whenever I think about that evening I can still recall the dinner of liver and onions Grandfather and I cooked. We spoke little while we worked side by side, caramelizing the onions and frying the liver to a crisp, just the way he liked it. In Father's absence, except for pan-fried potatoes, we didn't bother with vegetables, feasting instead on thick slabs of buttered sourdough bread still warm from the oven.

Watching Grandfather pick away at his dinner unconcerned, as if the journal entries I had just read him were already forgotten, I couldn't help wondering why, a few months before, he had seemed so set on having me write down some recollection he feared losing.

After a gulp of coffee to wash down the last mouthful of bread, I gently asked again if he still wanted me to do some writing for him.

He pushed aside his half-eaten dinner, took a long swallow of coffee and then cupped the mug between his palms. "Yeah, something's missing in that old journal, all right."

So he hadn't forgotten after all.

He stared into the depths of his tar-black coffee. "There's a gap in the telling, a hole in the truth," he said without looking up. "And I need to set the record straight."

He raised his head, threw back the last of his coffee and said, "But not tonight."

Not willing to let the conversation end so easily, hoping he would offer up more without my having to pry too hard, I searched for harmless questions to keep him talking while we cleared the table.

"Did you ever know the girl Rose's real name?" I asked.

Grandfather smiled. "I did. But I don't recall it. Their language was so hard to my ears that I couldn't even begin to wrap my mouth around her strange-sounding name, much less spell it. For more than one reason, I never attempted to write it down."

"Yeah. I noticed all the misspellings in your journal."

"Hah! You can't fault my spelling. I wrote down the words the way I heard them at the time. My spellings were no more incorrect than those used today. They're all still nothing more than some white man's interpretation of how the Chilcotin language sounds."

With that, he placed his dishes in the sink and retired to the parlour. Once again our conversation had ended abruptly, and I knew that no number of prodding questions on my part would restart it. Before long a static screech came from the other room as Grandfather searched for a radio station.

27.

Most of the time, reception on our Radiola was sporadic at best. During hockey season, we would hold our breaths and count ourselves lucky if we made it all the way through the Saturday night games. For some reason, evenings were best, though, and sometimes we would pick up an American station. From the sound of the voices coming from the other room as I did the dishes, I guessed that Grandfather had done just that and was tuned into some radio play.

I finished washing up and went outside to fetch more firewood. When I returned with an armload and started dumping it into the wood-box by the pot-bellied stove in the parlour, Grandfather shushed me with an impatient wave of his hand.

I unloaded the wood with great care while the CBC announcer asked his listeners to hold for a rebroadcasting of the British prime minister's speech upon his return from Munich, Germany, earlier today. I sat down in Father's chair in awe of the magic of radio waves coming all the way across the Atlantic Ocean, across our entire country, and into our little parlour.

Within moments a British voice crackled into the room. "We are now waiting for Prime Minister Neville Chamberlain to emerge from his airplane here at London's Heathrow Airport … Ah, and here he is now, triumphantly waving a paper above his head …"

A roar from the crowd drowned out his next words. Shouting to be heard above the jubilance, the announcer continued. "Prime Minister Chamberlain is descending the steps to a hero's welcome from those who believe that he has single-handedly averted another European war with his deft diplomacy. He is now about to address the crowd." After the cheers died down, the prime minister spoke.

"The settlement of the Czechoslovakian problem, which has now been achieved, is in my view only the prelude to a larger settlement in which all Europe may find peace. This morning I had another talk with the German chancellor, Herr Hitler, and here is the paper which bears his name upon it as well as mine. Some of you perhaps have already heard what it contains. But I would just like to read it to you."

I could hear the rustle of paper as he read from the document, pausing frequently, as if to let the meaning of his words sink in. When he was done, in a voice filled with pride, he announced:

"We regard the agreement signed last night ... as symbolic of the desire of our two peoples never to go to war with one another again." The crowd in England erupted once again.

And in his chair across from me, Grandfather shook his head wearily.

"My good friends, for the second time in our history," the voice on the radio continued, "a British prime minister has returned from Germany bringing peace with honour. I believe it is peace for our time ... Go home and get a nice quiet sleep."

Grandfather snorted. He pushed himself up from his chair and reached over to turn off the radio. "Get a nice quiet sleep," he muttered to himself. "Hard to do with the sabres of war rattling and clanging all over again."

Although I wasn't even born when what everyone called the Great War ended, I had grown up knowing that it had taken Father across the sea and a world away from the ranch for four long years.

"Dad's too old to go, right?" I asked.

In his bedroom doorway, Grandfather stopped and turned to face me. Confusion clouded his face. "Go where?" he asked. Then without waiting for a reply, the news report apparently already forgotten, he went to bed for the night.

I retreated to the kitchen to wait for Father's return from Kamloops. Partly driven by curiosity, and partly in an effort to push away the nudging fears brought on by Grandfather's observations, I sat down at the table and reopened his journal.

28.

Two more Chilcootans have been hired. Pa insists he needs them to help haul his equipment to the blasting sites and back to camp each night. He was supposed to stay in the forward camp—which moves ahead with each new section of road—but he chooses to stay here with me in the base camp. I suspect that it is less about leaving me alone and more about not leaving his trunk full of whiskey in our tent unguarded that has him make that extra trek back down the trail each day. Mr. Brewster has reluctantly agreed to the arrangement. That too, I suspect, is less about me and more about not wanting to be in the same camp as Pa. The two seem to be at loggerheads whenever they are together. Most of their differences stem from the fact that the foreman still has not let go of his constant complaining about the theft of the flour. The fact that he has yet to uncover the culprits sticks in his craw, according to Pa, and is getting in the way of progress on the road.

—Time to stop flogging that dead horse, Pa told him.

—You do your job, Beale, and I'll do mine, replied Mr. Brewster.

—Then do yours, sir, and let's get this road built. We will soon be entering Chilcootan territory. You might want to rethink threatening them once we're on their land.

—I've worked with these people far longer than you. If we don't show them now who's in control, all our provisions will be at risk of plunder. Then how will we build a road, eh?

Without waiting for an answer, he turned his back on Pa and stomped off with the only Chilcootan he trusts, Chief Talhoot.

—If we're to meet Waddington's deadline we'll be needing to hire more help, whether you want to or not, Pa called after him.

Dismissing Pa's words with a backward wave of his hand, Mr. Brewster kept his course heading up the trail in the evening twilight.

April 2

This morning the two workers Pa chose to carry his equipment up the trail showed up. One was Crooked-Eye. And to my surprise, the other packer is the twin brother, Willum. Mr. Brewster, who arrived at the same time, was taken aback also. He strode across the camp and confronted him.

—You! he said to Willum. I know you.

He turned to Pa. This was the fellow with Klatsassin the day we arrived. I'll be damned before I'll hire any of the war chief's cohorts. Find someone else.

The foreman stomped off. I felt grieved at the thought that with no hope of employment with the road crew, the brother and sister might leave the area.

But to my relief, Pa stubbornly defied the foreman's order. He promised to pay Willum's wages himself. And then—against the cook's loud objections—he saw to it that both men sat down to breakfast before they went to work for the day. I was glad to see the girl's brother eat his fill, for it is clear that he and his sister have gone without for a long time. Although I must say the scowl on his face has not changed since last time I saw him in our camp.

April 5, 1864

With her brother gone during the day I am catching sight of the girl, Rose, more often. Every now and then when I am fetching water or gathering wood along the riverbank I will glimpse her in the distant mist before she quickly disappears into that grey shroud. Once again she has taken to appearing out of the blue on the periphery of our camp whenever I am there by myself. Perhaps it is loneliness in her brother's absence that keeps her returning to watch me from the fringes of the forest, but I like to flatter myself that she is playing with me in her way—flirting, if you will—wanting to be friends, but not knowing how to approach.

Whenever she appears I keep my eyes averted, holding her at the edge of my vision. As wary as if she were a bird about to take flight, I pretend I am unaware of her presence, letting her decide if she wishes to approach. So far she has kept her distance, but once when I inadvertently met her gaze I thought I detected a teasing smirk on her lips that belied my assessment of her timid nature.

April 7, 1864

My patience has paid off. Today I spoke with Rose!

After the day's firewood was chopped and stacked this afternoon, I was left with free time on my hands. So I headed upriver hoping to find some clue as to where the girl disappears to each time I spot her from afar.

I packed some biscuits and a thick slice of smoked beef in my haversack and slung it over my shoulder before striking out. I have been warned against wandering too far by Pa, who worries about grizzly bears in the area—although the cook says it is not the season for them as the salmon are not running in the Homathko this time of year. Still, with all the runoff from the snowmelt swelling the waters, I approach the river with trepidation. I stay high above the rocky banks and pick my way along the edge of the trees keeping well clear of the raging waters. I have come to the realization that my desire to avoid water is not limited to the sea and that I hold far less fear of the lurking shadows in the forest than I do of the river's icy waters. But today I was on a mission.

When I had travelled a distance that I judged would have me close to the area where I have often spotted the girl, I stopped and took my time surveying the landscape. The thickness of the underbrush made it impossible to detect any sign of life beyond the forest shadows—yet as I continued slowly making my way upstream I had the eerie feeling that I was not alone.

In an effort to appear nonchalant, I pursed my lips and practised whistling as I went along. Mercifully, my feeble attempts to reproduce bird calls were swept away by the roar of the waters.

After a time the river widened and its banks stretched out. From a distance the water appears deceptively peaceful. Further upriver the going became easier and I was able to walk along the vast stretches of low bank avoiding the tangle of deadfalls and branches thrown up on shore at every bend.

Away from the deafening roar of the river I could once again hear the now familiar hum of the forest. Birdsong and the rustle of trees swaying in the wind are all sounds that have become the soothing music to which I am content to fall asleep each night and wake up each morning. Each new day I step out from our tent and the smell of the soil beneath my feet satisfies me in a way I have never known before. My new-found contentment only confirms Pa's assessment that I am a "landlubber." His teasing does not bother me, though, because he is right, and I have begun to secretly fancy myself as a man of the earth like the Natives. I am certain I could spend the rest of my life living in the bush. Pa says I will get over that soon enough and start missing a warm bed and running water when the novelty wears off. Perhaps. But what happened today only served to reinforce my growing feelings for this place.

Making my way upriver I continued whistling, trying the repetitive chirp of the chickadee—a common little bird here. After a time I noticed that there seemed to be echoing calls to my chick-a-dee-dee-dee whistles. I slowed my pace and continued until I was certain of it. My calls were being answered. Answered with perfect imitations—too perfect—as if mocking my clumsy attempts. I whistled once more, changing the notes and the tempo. Sure enough, there followed an exact response.

I whirled around and there was the girl, Rose, standing in front of an enormous deadfall which I had passed only moments before.

A victim of wind or bank erosion, the huge ancient tree lay embedded in the forest floor, its branches long since rotted off. Moss covered its thick bark. The root end of the tree—far taller than she—stood upright on the edge of the bank like a giant fist, still clutching uprooted soil and rocks. Tendrils of roots and vines covered one entire side, and it was before this curtain of spring growth that the girl stood as though she had just parted it and stepped out. She was less than a few yards away from me and my breath caught at the closeness of her.

—That's some funny kind of bird you call, she said.

Even now I am embarrassed to write down that I found myself tongue-tied in her presence. After all my imagined visions of this moment—my secret thoughts about the witty things I believed I would impress her with—I was speechless. The foolishness of standing mute made the blood rush to my face and I suddenly felt like a small boy.

With the hint of a smile on her lips she stood there as if she had all day to wait for my response. Finally all I could croak out was a weak hello.

She eyed my haversack with suspicion.

—You got that book in there?

—No. No book. Just some biscuits and beef ...

Now that I had found my voice I seemed unable to stop. Lifting the bag from my shoulder and holding it up, I rushed to explain about the food inside it and how she could have it if she liked.

—Might be that book has bad magic, she said, as if she had not heard my offer.

Before I could think of a reply her eyes narrowed.

—You write down my name?

Of course I have written the name Rose in these pages but I did not feel I was lying when I shook my head and told her that I didn't know her real name.

When I asked her if she would tell me her Chilcootan name she took a startled step back.

—Might be you're gonna put it in that book.

—No. Please, I said, stepping forward.

Afraid she was about to run off, I placed my fisted right hand against my chest in the same gesture I saw her brother do.

—I give you my word that I will never write your Chilcootan name in my book.

I could feel her hesitation as she searched my face for sincerity and I held her gaze.

After a few moments she said something I didn't understand. I leaned forward to hear and when she slowly repeated it I realized that it was her name that she spoke. For the next while she listened patiently as I tried over and over again to wrap my mouth around the strange sounds, the harsh consonants scraping at the roof of my mouth and the elusive vowels rushing over barely opened lips.

For obvious reasons I will not record my interpretation of her name here, but eventually my pronunciation was rewarded with a wide smile. We sat down on a sun-bleached log where I opened my haversack and unwrapped the biscuits and beef. The biscuits had broken apart in my jostling but Rose made quick work of them, crumbs and all.

I made only a small pretense of eating, for I could see that she had an appetite. I tried not to stare while she ate but it was hard not to, as I found her even more captivating close up. Her age is difficult to guess but it is certain she is a number of years older than I, although how many it is hard to tell. I am a few inches taller than she and so hope it is as difficult for her to judge my age and that she sees me as an equal.

After finishing the dried beef, she licked the grease from her fingers one by one as she studied me.

—What do you need that bad magic book for? she asked.

I thought about her question for a moment before answering, for I wanted to be clear in hopes that it would help calm her fear of evil intent.

—I write down things that happen each day so I won't forget.

—Why? Your heart can't remember?

—Not everything.

She stood up and brushed down the front of her deerskin tunic.

—May be enough, I think.

Maybe she's right. Tonight as I record this day I believe I will remember it forever.

April 10, 1864

Rose is getting braver and appears in our camp now even when others are around. We only speak if we are alone, and our friendship remains a secret. A secret I am assuming even her brother is unaware of, for whenever they are in our camp, they both look right past me as if I were not there. And even though Willum does Pa's bidding without question, I notice he regards him in much the same manner.

Last evening I caught Pa once again sharing his whiskey with Crooked-Eye. When he offered the flask to Willum he waved it away, calling it poison.

I have to say I agree with his assessment.

I have said nothing to Pa about my meetings with Willum's sister. Although he turned down Crooked-Eye's offer of a woman, I fear it is only because the cook's helper is not to his taste. And when he has a few swallows of whiskey in him I do not like the way Pa looks at Rose.

29.

Before too long my eyes grew weary from the long hours spent reading grandfather's difficult script, and I began to find it hard to concentrate. I put down his journal and went to bed early but could not sleep. Grandfather's comment about the rattling sabres of war would not leave me alone.

During the past months, he and Father have spent many evenings by the Victrola Radiola listening to the latest news of Germany's annexation of Austria. I had paid little attention, more disappointed in missing an anticipated radio play than interested in the obscure events in a land so far away. Now, Grandfather's ominous words brought home the startling truth—distance would mean little if Great Britain went to war once again.

Maybe it was simply because I hadn't taken notice before, but after that night, it seemed that talk of war cropped up everywhere. It moved from the radio in our parlour to our kitchen table. It crept into customers' conversations in the grocery store, into children's chatter in the schoolyard and even to the harvest dance in the church hall.

For reasons of practicality, we had never been much of a churchgoing family. The cattle didn't know one day of the week from another, so we were often as busy tending to them on Sundays as any other day. Grand-father had always maintained that he met with God every day on the land, and Father agreed. Still, when Mother was here, every once in a while, on a good-weather Sunday, we would all don our finest go-to-town outfits—finest in Mother's opinion, that is—and drive into Sorry to attend the church service. It was more of a social outing for her than the rest of us, Father saying that he got enough socializing at his office desk in The Sorry Grocers on Saturday mornings to last him all week, and Grandfather mut-tering that he had already had enough to last a lifetime.

But they had indulged Mother. Even to the point of attending the church's annual harvest dance. Everyone in the area, adults and children alike, showed up for the November shindig, which was pretty much the last social event of the year before winter set in. The Sorry Grocers always sup-plied the liquid refreshments. The soda pop for the kiddies, along with Dirk's endless supply of adult punch, was a welcome treat at the potluck supper. For years, Father had donated an enormous beef rump, which was buried in the fire pit coals outside of the church hall and roasted all afternoon until it was melt-in-your-mouth tender. His generosity, I suspect, was in part to relieve Mother from contributing her extravagant cream-pie desserts, a mistake she had made the first few years, only to be criticized by the other women who, with hands covering their mouths, had called her a "fancy lady."

After Mother's disappearance we stopped attending the dance, but Dad still delivered the meat to the church the day before. This year none of us had given a thought to attending the event, especially after the visit to the TB sanatorium in Kamloops at the end of September.

Everyone, including Alan, had returned down in the mouth from that trip. Dirk VanderMeer was not doing well. Instead of improving, his condition had taken a turn for the worse. During October and the first half of November, we all worked extra hard during the week, putting our energy into getting ahead of the preparations for the coming winter so that they were free to drive down to Kamloops every weekend.

From his sickbed last Sunday, the storekeeper had begged my father to take his family to the upcoming church social in his absence, citing that he wanted them to have a weekend free from sickness and long road trips. According to Father, Mr. VanderMeer told his wife, "Rose, you go kick up your heels. And you show those ladies who makes the best Gott-damned blueberry-wine punch before they forget, by Gott."

Business at the store had declined for a while after Mr. VanderMeer fell ill. Father blamed it on fear. A team of doctors and nurses had arrived within days of the diagnosis, and everyone who had come into contact with the store-keeper was tested for tuberculosis. All the tests came back negative. Where and how Alan's stepfather had contracted the disease would always remain a mystery. With fears calmed, business picked up some, but never quite to what it was before. The decline of profits worried the ailing man, and he believed that the presence of his family at the harvest dance, along with the goodwill created by the store's generous donations, would help bring back the custom-ers who had started making trips into Quesnel or Williams Lake to shop.

Later, as the date of the event drew closer, when Mrs. VanderMeer told Dad that she really had no heart to attend, he said, "I gave him my word, Rose. If it eases Dirk's mind, I think we should make a showing at the dance at least. He's right, your customers need to be reminded how generous your store is to this community."

Mrs. VanderMeer reluctantly agreed, saying, "Okay. But he's not the one who has to make all that 'by-Gott-damned' punch."

Her attempt at humour fell flat against the worry for her husband etched in her eyes.

In the days before the dance, I laboured over what to wear. In the past, Mother had always insisted on a dress, but I had none that fit anymore, and I had no desire for a new one. Yet I didn't need to be told that my overalls would not do. I knew Father would never say anything about whatever I chose. Still, I didn't want to cause him to endure the women's obvious disapproval if I showed up in dungarees.

How Alan's mother knew that I was struggling with this dilemma I don't know, but it was she who solved the problem. And she solved it in a way that would have me and Father enjoying each and every raised eyebrow in that church hall.

At lunch hour on the Thursday before the dance, Mrs. VanderMeer called me into the backroom at the store.

"When I was a young girl," she said, standing by a garment laid out neatly on the table, "we did many dances together, this dress and me."

She raised her eyes to meet mine. "I thought that on Saturday night you might like to wear it."

Father had often accused me of being unable to resist taking a dare. He said that although he admired my gumption, I would need to be watchful of this trait, as it was of the sort that could lead to trouble if I wasn't careful.

The dare was unspoken in the store's backroom that afternoon, but it was there somewhere between the uncharacteristic grin playing on Rose VanderMeer's lips and the conspiratorial glint in her dark blue eyes.

As it dawned on me what she was offering, I rose to the bait openmouthed, an expletive rising in my throat that was impossible to hold back. "Holy crikey! Really?" I blurted. "Sorry. I mean, yes. Would I ever. Thanks."

I reached down to touch the butter-smooth deerskin, running my fingers along the intricate beadwork at the neck and along the fringed bottom. On the table beside the dress sat a matching pair of beaded moccasins to complete the outfit.

"It's so beautiful," I breathed, barely able to believe her generosity. "I'll take good care of it."

"I know you will."

I was wrong in assuming that my father would have nothing to say about whatever I chose to wear that night. His hands stopped in the middle of adjusting Grandfather's string tie when I came into the parlour dressed for the dance. His startled eyes took me in from head to foot before he gave a slow whistle. "Why, you look lovely, Addie," he said. "So grown up."

I had felt the truth of that earlier as I studied myself in the mirror up in the loft. I had only just begun to notice the changes in my body, and Rose's dress fit as if it were made for me. The soft hide felt like warm silk next to my skin. It draped over my growing breasts without clinging to them and hung down past my calves. The fringed bottom swished across the high-top moccasins, which were only a little too tight on my feet. A faint smoky odour rose from the hide, and I found I liked the earthy scent. When I first saw my reflection, I briefly regretted keeping my hair short, thinking how swell it would have been to have worn it in long braids with this outfit.

Downstairs in the parlour, Father told me to go and stand in the full light of the table lamp for Grandfather. He went back to adjusting his tie, asking, "Can you see Addie, Dad? Doesn't *she* look lovely?"

He often used this tactic, pointedly referring to me as female at each opportunity. It usually brought little result. There was nothing wrong with Grandfather's hearing and I think he simply chose to ignore what he didn't want to consider. But this time he pulled his eyeglasses from his jacket pocket and hooked them over his ears to squint in my direction. I had no idea if he could really see me or if I was just a blur to him, but I spun around, explaining that the deerskin dress belonged to Rose VanderMeer.

He stepped closer, reached up and touched my shoulder. Stroking the soft hide with a gentle hand, he grinned and said, "Well done, Addie. This ought to set the tongues to wagging tonight."

Thinking that the dress had triggered Grandfather's moment of clarity, for the first time it occurred to me that perhaps his calling me boy was partially my fault, caused by the fact that I had been wearing nothing but male clothing for the past two years. But by the time we had driven into Sorry, I was "boy" again.

Before that night, I believed Alan saw me in much the same light as Grandfather. Ever since he had accepted me as an equal, the fact that I was a girl was not an important part of our friendship. But when we arrived at the store on the evening of the dance, although his mother broke out into a wide grin at the sight of me, he looked startled, uncomfortable even, as if realizing for the first time that I really was the "girl" he once teased me about being. He remained mute as we walked across the road to the church hall together, the two of us trailing behind the equally silent adults. Confused by the way he looked at me, or, more correctly, avoided looking at me, I began to question if wearing his mother's dress had been a mistake. But just before we stepped into the pool of light spilling from the hall door, he said in a voice so low I almost missed it, "You look real pretty tonight, Addie."

The words brought a flush of pleasure to my cheeks, followed quickly by something else. Although it felt good to be called pretty—a word that had never been liberally applied to me—I sensed with mixed feelings that our relationship had just altered somehow.

The stir we caused inside the hall still brings a smile to my lips.

It took some time before Grandfather's prediction of wagging tongues took hold. After we hung our coats in the cloakroom, the five of us stood in the entryway of the gaily decorated room. The musicians tuning their instruments at the far end were the first to see us. The screech of off-key notes stopped cold, and as heads turned our way, a hush spread across the room. The abrupt silence hung in the air like a presence, until it was broken by the sound of a low piano chord—the deep notes pounding in a rhythmic simulation of a Native drum beat. Father glared at the piano player. Mrs. Parsons.

Maybe her mockery was aimed at me, maybe it was at Alan and his mother, but as nervous laughter and voices seeped back into the room, Father bent his elbows and formally offered them to Rose VanderMeer and me. We each took an arm and let him escort us across the humming room. After we had taken our seats at an empty table, I noticed a man in an army uniform standing near the piano. Mrs. Parsons was beaming up at him with the same devouring eyes I had seen her cast at my father almost two years ago, and I felt some sympathy for the stranger in our midst. My sympathy waned as the night worn on.

Before long every bowl of vegetables, every platter of meat and casserole of the potluck dinner was empty. After everyone had had their fill of the heavy desserts, the ladies set to cleaning up before the dancing began. It was during that interlude that Mrs. Parsons made it her mission to accompany the army officer to each table and introduce him. Each table, that is, but ours, her bypassing us without so much as a glance causing no heartache on our part. As they walked past, though, the officer looked back over his shoulder at Alan. Then he leaned in and whispered something to Mrs. Parsons.

"No. He's only fourteen," she said, loud enough to be overheard. As they moved on, she added, "Although I have long suspected that he's older. You never know with these people."

From the men who stopped by our table to chew the fat with Father and Grandfather, we learned that the officer was a Sergeant Davenport from the Victoria army base. He was touring the province to speak to young men about military life. His presence caused quite a stir in the hall. Talk of the possibility of war ignited once again and, like a brush fire, leapt from table to table as he made his rounds.

"The army sending out recruiters isn't a good sign," Grandfather muttered to no one in particular.

After the dancing commenced, I noticed a number of ranchers' sons approach the officer at his table. They sat with heads huddled together in order to hear and be heard above the music while their mothers watched from the dance floor with trepidation on their faces.

Before long it was clear that both Grandfather and Alan were getting antsy to leave. Father said we would stay for a bit of music to satisfy Dirk, and then he too would be relieved to call it a night. As the band struck up the "Tennessee Waltz," he pushed himself up from the table. Offering his hand to Rose, he said, "We should have at least one spin around the floor so we can tell Dirk we did."

Of course Alan didn't ask me to dance. I don't know what I would have said if he did. I was just as content as he to stay at the table while our parents took to the dance floor.

I used to love to watch my mother and father waltzing. He would glide her around so fluidly, their bodies moving as one as if melting into each other. How differently he danced now. Stiff and formal, arms held high and holding themselves at a distance, Dad and Mrs. VanderMeer waltzed as if it was a chore. Perhaps it was.

The whispers started at the table behind us.

"Widows and widowers in waiting …"

"… just not proper …"

"… both still married."

As the snatches of conversation melted into the music, and Rose and my father moved woodenly across the floor, an unbidden memory of the last time I saw him dance—the night Evan died—snuck up on me.

Suddenly the room was too warm, the smoke-filled air too stuffy, the bodies too close.

"I'm going to wait outside," I said to Alan. "You coming?"

He rose like a shot and followed me.

Outside, the brittle autumn air hinted of winter's hard-fisted punch. Still, I was glad to be out of the hall's smoky, used-up air. I tugged my wool shawl tighter, glad for the extra warmth of the deerskin dress, and sat down on the back steps. The darkness stretched before us, the night smell-ing of decaying leaves and grass stiff with frost. Beside me, Alan leaned back against the top step to stare up at the moonless, starlit sky.

Inside, the music grew more frenzied, the voices grew louder, as the absent storekeeper's punch flowed. The drone of everyone talking at once carried over the music, making me wonder how they all could have so much to say. That was the thing I liked best about Alan Baptiste. He and I could be alone together, spend long periods of time with neither of us feeling the pressure to fill the silence with words.

Every once in a while, the hall door opened and someone stepped around us on their way to the outhouse, excusing themselves as they did. Finally one of them left the door ajar to let some fresh air in. As blue cigarette smoke leaked out, curling up and around the door sash, a block of yellow light surrounded us. Alan leaned forward and, with his elbows on his knees, lowered his head as if in deep thought.

Inside, the "Beer Barrel Polka" was coming to a grinding end. In the ringing quiet following the final note of the song, Alan turned his face sideways to look at me.

"If I was old enough," he said, "I would go."

"Go where?" Before the question was out of my mouth, I already knew exactly what he meant.

"If war came, and I was old enough, I would join up," he said, his voice low.

But not low enough.

"Hah!" The intended cruelty of the scorn-filled retort sliced through the night. Neither of us turned to its source behind us. We both knew to whom that voice belonged.

30.

The consequence of Mrs. Parsons overhearing Alan's statement on Saturday night arrived in our classroom on Monday in the form of Sergeant Davenport.

That morning, our teacher announced that the officer was there to share his knowledge of the Canadian Army's contribution to Great Britain's military defence during the Great War.

Although Alan and I were never included in any of the history lessons directed at the class, we couldn't help but hear. While the officer spoke, I found myself glancing between him and Mrs. Parsons, and it occurred to me that they were a well-suited pair. Him with his perfectly trimmed moustache and pinched face standing there with his hat held under one arm, looking as if he had a pole running up the back of his uniform and speaking with the arrogance of someone who believed he was the most brilliant person in the room. And her, sitting just as straight-backed at her desk, hanging onto his every word, as if she agreed with his self-assessment.

As he droned on, I questioned why he was there. Most of the students were too young to be interested, and after the initial excitement over the stranger's uniform, they were quickly bored by his litany of rote statistics. When he was done and had departed from the classroom, it didn't take long to realize whose ears this special lesson was meant for.

All during the officer's speech, Alan had sat in his too-small desk at the back of the room, pretending to read. But I could tell he was listening, because not one page of his book was turned.

The fact that he continued to endure that classroom day after day, I believe, was a testament to how much he loved and respected his mother—and my father too, for that matter. Of course, there was always the promise of that unborn foal. Still, I had no idea how much it cost him to remain silent during the rest of Mrs. Parsons' history lesson, which followed after the officer left the school.

Standing in front of her desk, she read out loud from a textbook I had never seen before. After reading the statement "The very day the British Empire went to war with Germany, all across the Dominion of Canada, young Canadian men lined up to fight for King and Country," she looked up, all victory-eyed, and added, "Well … all, that is, except for Native Indians."

She smiled in a way that made me cringe and then headed down the middle aisle, strolling slowly between the desks. "After the loss of so many men in the battle at Vimy Ridge in France," she said, without referring to the book again, "when more troops were needed, conscription—compulsory enlistment—was introduced here in Canada. And Indian bands all across our nation fought to have themselves excluded from it."

At Alan's desk she paused, as if waiting for the meaning of this statement to sink in. "Consequently," she continued, glancing at the top of his head, then turning away, "conscription and recruitment of Indians was prohibited, and they were exempted from fighting for Canada."

She strolled back up the aisle, letting her words trail behind her.

At his desk, still staring at his open book, in a low voice, Alan said, "That's not true."

Mrs. Parsons stopped in her tracks. I fully expected her to whirl around and confront him—he had, after all, accused her of being a liar. Following a heart-quickening pause, within which I could see her struggle to control her breath, she squared her shoulders and continued to the front of the class, choosing to ignore him as usual, dismissing the fact that he was even in the room. She slammed the book onto her desk, the sound ricocheting through the air. Keeping her back to us, she went over to the blackboard and began writing out the grade threes' arithmetic questions, her chalk screeching like a small animal in distress with every stroke.

After lunch, neither Alan nor I returned to our desks. Instead we climbed up to the ridge, where we sat against the sway-back pine tree and watched the wild horses grazing unconcerned among the deer in the valley below.

As the sun's rays cut through the afternoon air, Alan lay back in the yellowed grass below the tree and I joined him, staring up at the sky through the branches. The smell of earth and pine needles drifted on the wind brushing across my cheeks. I closed my eyes and caught myself imagining the wind's soft touch to be Alan's fingers tracing the contours of my face. Startled by this image, my eyes snapped open. I sat up, wrapped my arms around my knees and rested my head on them.

"Mrs. Parsons is an idiot," I blurted, for want of something to say.

Alan shrugged his agreement. After a few moments, he said, "What she said about our people not going to war isn't true. My father, he fought. He fought at that place called Vimy Ridge."

Surprised by his words, I turned my head sideways to look at him. I had never given any thought to Alan having a father, other than Mr. VanderMeer, but I knew he wasn't speaking of him.

"He didn't have to go, my dad," he said, pushing himself up on his elbows. "He volunteered. But when he came back from that war, came back to the reserve, the government said he was gone too long, that he was no longer an Indian."

Staring straight ahead, as if there were reason on the far horizon, he asked, "How can they say a man is no longer an Indian?"

I looked away. I had no answer for something I didn't understand. Instead, I asked what happened to his father.

"He stayed with my mother on the reserve for five years. But she said he couldn't forget that war. Something went bad in his mind over there." He looked down, to his feet pushing at the dirt.

"I'm sorry," I said.

Alan shrugged. "I never knew him," he said. "The year I was born, one night he walked into the bush and froze to death."

I looked away as his dark blue eyes pooled up in contradiction to his dismissive words. For a brief moment I considered telling him about the blue-eyed war chief in Grandfather's old journal. About the girl named Rose, like his mother, and Willum. But I was uncertain if it would make Alan feel better or worse. And in the end I could not betray my grandfather's trust.

All of a sudden, the breeze blowing across the ridge felt colder. It found its way through my jacket, and I shivered against its sting. Before long we headed back down the ridge in silence, the need for words left behind in the icy wind.

I had plenty of words to say to Father and Grandfather, though, as they sat at the kitchen table later trying to eat their dinner. Neither attempted to interrupt me as I ranted on about Mrs. Parsons' history lesson. When I came to Alan's story about his father being told by the government he was no longer an Indian when he returned from the war, Father set down his fork.

"I believe he is referring to the Indian Act," he said. "To a section which states that if a man is absent from the reserve for four years, he loses his Indian status."

"But he was at war! That's not fair."

"Yes. It's quite unfair. It's wrong. Unfortunately, though, it's a fact. But your teacher implying that Native Canadians didn't fight in the war is not a fact. Quite the contrary. I know because I served with more than a few of those men."

Later, after I finished my homework and was gathering up my books from the table, he came back into the kitchen and sat down across from me.

He brushed his hand through his hair as is his habit when he has been thinking and has come to a conclusion. "Tomorrow, why don't you take the day off from school? We'll get our chores out of the way early. Then you and I, and Alan too if he likes, can take a little trip up to Prince George to visit the library and government offices there. Let's just call it a 'field trip' to do a little research for a school project."

If Mrs. Parsons was disappointed at seeing us return to school after a two-and-a-half-day absence, she did a good job of hiding it on Thursday morning. When she caught sight of my father walking in behind us, though, her face fell, and she was unable to control the colour flushing her cheeks. While everyone settled noisily in their desks, Father remained standing at the back of the room.

"To what do we owe this visit, Mr. Beale?" our teacher demanded above the hum of the room.

With his hat in his hands, Father took a step forward, saying, "Addie and Alan have been working on a history project, which they would like to present to the class this morning."

"I have a scheduled lesson plan, sir. I can't hold it up for the benefit of two students."

"This will only take ten minutes," Dad insisted. "I'm sure you can carve that out of the beginning of your lesson, or perhaps add it on at recess or lunch. I can wait right here until then, if you prefer. But I *will* hear my daughter read their report to the class." He hung his hat on a nearby hook and leaned against the wall with his arms folded across his chest as if he had all the time in the world.

"Fine, then," she sighed, then shifted her attention to me. "Go ahead. Do it now if you must."

I rose from my desk, took a deep breath and headed to the front of the class. We had decided, or more rightly, Alan had decided, that I would read the report, which we had both worked on. I was glad to. As Father had said, someone needed to set our classmates straight on the facts that had been distorted. If not us, then who?

Mrs. Parsons sat at her desk and busied herself studying papers. There was a lot of shifting in seats and scuffing of shoes under desks as curiosity took hold of the students. At the back of the room, Father gave me an encouraging wink. I glanced quickly at Alan, catching his brief nod before lowering my eyes to the notebook in my hands.

"Native Canadians and the Great War," I said, reading the essay title. I looked up briefly to let it sink in and then continued. "Aboriginal Canadians have a long history of fighting alongside the British, beginning with the American Revolution and the War of 1812. Once again, in August of 1914, when war broke out between the British Empire and Germany, Indian bands from all across our nation contributed to Canada's war effort. On the home front, many impoverished Native communities donated funds to the war effort. On reserves all across Canada, women knit socks and scarves for the troops and they raised money to send tobacco and candy to soldiers overseas. Many young men, as well as a number of women, left their families and homes on those reserves to enlist. Some Indian bands, such as British Columbia's Lake of the Okanagan Band, saw every single able-bodied man between the ages of twenty and thirty-five march off to war." I couldn't resist stealing a sideways glance at Mrs. Parsons as I read, but she appeared to not be listening.

"According to newspaper interviews," I continued, "most Natives joined up for the same reasons as non-Natives—patriotism, adventure, tradition and the promise of wages during those hard economic times. But join up they did. Exactly how many fought is not known, as the government kept track only of the number of Status Indians who enlisted. However, it is estimated that over four thousand Aboriginal peoples of this land answered the call. In 1915, Duncan Campbell, the deputy superintendent general of the Department of Indian Affairs, stated, 'We note with pride these expressions of loyalty from the Indians and their contributions toward the general expense of the war and toward the Patriotic Fund.'

"Still, it would be incorrect to report that all bands joined in the war effort," I went on. "When compulsory conscription was introduced in 1917, some bands argued for exemption in accordance with their treaty agreements. Consequently, these agreements were honoured, and an order-in-council exempted Natives from conscription ..." I paused to scan the faces of my classmates, wondering if this next statement would shock them as much as it had me, "because Aboriginal peoples were not—*and still are not*—considered citizens of Canada."

Mrs. Parsons let out a satisfied snort.

Ignoring her, I continued reading. "Regardless of this exemption, and the subsequent prohibition against actively recruiting Indians to enlist, they continued to step forward. Following the battle at Vimy Ridge and then Passchendaele, when the call went out for reinforcements to replace the over twenty-five thousand Canadian dead or wounded, many continued to show up at recruitment stations to volunteer. At war's end it was estimated that across Canada, one in every three status Indian males had enlisted."

I was tempted at this point to insert some of the facts we had unearthed during our research. Facts about how some of these men, like Alan's father, had returned home after fighting for Canada to find that their absence had robbed them of their Indian status. Yet they still were not Canadian citizens. They could not vote, and although they were veterans, they were not entitled to the benefits and support that the non-Native veterans received.

I had wanted to include these findings in our essay, but Alan and Father had vetoed me. In the interest of keeping it short and not risking overwhelming our intended audience with facts and figures, in the end, I had agreed. Although, for a brief moment, standing there in front of the class with Mrs. Parsons huffing at her desk, I had to fight the impulse to include this information. I kept my word, though, and sticking to our written version, I turned the page to finish the report.

"In conclusion, during the Great War, both status and non-status Indian soldiers fought for Canada. Many lost their lives in battle. Many were awarded military medals of valour. Throughout the war, and in the years following, the Department of Indian Affairs received scores of letters from their comrades-in-arms and officers commending Native bravery and heroism, causing the department to herald the achievements of Indians on the battlefield and at home. In 1920, Edward Ahenakew, a Cree Anglican priest from Sandy Lake, Saskatchewan, proclaimed, 'Now that peace has been declared, the Indians of Canada may look with just pride upon the part played by them in the Great War, both at home and on the field of battle. Not in vain did our young men die in a strange land. Not in vain are our Indian bones mingled with the soil of a foreign land for the first time since the world began.'"

I closed my notebook. Walking back to my desk in the hushed classroom, I felt every eye on me but kept mine on Alan, who wore a small grin, a rarity to see on his face in this room. My father, still leaning against the wall with his arms crossed, lifted his fist in a thumbs-up.

"Are you quite done?" Mrs. Parsons asked behind me.

"Yes, ma'am," I said, as sweetly as I could muster, and took my seat.

She pushed herself up from her desk. "Well, then," she said brushing down the front of her skirt. "I believe we will take a break so I can rework this morning's interrupted lessons."

She waved a hand at the class without looking. "You're all dismissed for a fifteen-minute recess."

Suddenly everyone was scrambling for the cloakroom at once. In the confusion of jostling for coats and jackets, Alan and I followed Dad outside.

"Well done, Addie," he said at the bottom of the porch steps.

"Yeah, good job," Alan agreed.

"You too," my father said, putting his arm on Alan's shoulder. "I'm very proud of you both. It was an excellent report."

We headed across the schoolyard amidst the whispers and stares of our classmates. "Do you think any of them got it?" I asked.

"Doesn't matter," Alan replied.

Just then Mrs. Parsons' daughter, Enid, approached me nervously. "That was interesting," she said. I waited for the other foot to fall, but with a rush of words, she added, "And I don't care what anyone says, I think you looked real pretty in that Indian princess dress Saturday night." She ran off, leaving me staring after her open-mouthed.

That was the second time in a week someone had used the word pretty in reference to me, and this time left me just as confounded as last.

I hurried to catch up with Alan and Dad, and we all headed across the road to share our excitement with Alan's mother.

Our euphoria was short-lived. We arrived at the store to find Rose VanderMeer standing by the wall phone, the lifeless hum of the disconnected line coming from the telephone receiver in her hand.

From the ashen look on her face, I knew. Mr. VanderMeer was dead.

31.

Our little community was greatly diminished by the death of its store-keeper. The bell above the door rang hollow every time I walked into the grocery store knowing I would never again see Mr. VanderMeer look up and smile at me from behind the counter.

The very afternoon we learned the terrible news, Father took Rose and Alan for one last trip south. At the TB sanatorium outside of Kamloops, they took take care of the business side of death. Dirk VanderMeer's body was brought home to the place we called Sorry to be buried in the cemetery behind the church.

In the days before and after the funeral, the "closed" sign in the store window didn't deter the women of the area. They came with offerings of food and sympathy. If Rose VanderMeer was alone, which she seldom was during that first week, she would come down from her grieving in the living quarters upstairs to answer every knock on the door. More often it was Alan or my father who went to the door to receive the casseroles and offers of "anything I can do to help."

Although we were not family, it felt as if we were, and in those first days Father spent as much time with them as he could. Many of the bolder women approached him as if he were the head of the family and nervously voiced what turned out to be their real concern. Would the store close permanently? Father assured them that as far as he knew, eventually The Sorry Grocers would reopen and continue to operate just as it had in Dirk's absence. Their questions brought a selfish thought slithering into my mind. I couldn't imagine life without Alan Baptiste if his mother chose to close or sell the store and leave Sorry. As it was, Alan's grief took him away from me more than in body. At first I didn't know how to comfort my friend. The death of his stepfather brought back our own family sorrows, and my initial instinct was to leave Alan to his private grieving. Only the recollection of how he had stood by after my brother's death and my mother's disappearance gave me the courage to do the same for him.

The day before Dirk VanderMeer's funeral, Father was going over the details of the service with Rose and Alan when an unfamiliar Dodge station wagon parked in front of the store. Father went downstairs to find Dirk's sister, along with her husband and son, at the door. He ushered the family members upstairs, where Mrs. VanderMeer shyly welcomed them to her home. At first they declined her offer to put them up for the night, saying they would drive into Wells and get rooms at the Jack-Of-Clubs Hotel and come back for the funeral service the following day. But after tea, and many tears on Dirk's sister's part, they decided to take his wife up on her offer.

At the funeral the following day, I could see Mrs. Gleason's resemblance to her brother. She had the same sandy-coloured hair and pale complexion. But looks were the only similarity. Unlike Dirk, she was sullen and quiet and seemed to be content to let her husband do all the talking. Their son, who didn't look all that much younger than my father, also resembled his uncle. But, like his dad, it was soon clear that he, too, liked the sound of his own voice, which had no trace of his mother's or his uncle's Dutch accents.

Mr. Gleason, a Quesnel banker, was a different story. Short and portly, he looked quite comical standing next to his wife and son, who were both a good six inches taller, but his booming voice more than made up for his lack of stature. At the church tea following the service, both father and son were in continual debate over the most uninteresting observations, such as how long the drive from Quesnel took them, how much gas they used, the high cost of this or that. If anyone else slipped a word in edgewise, the two had no trouble adding their opinion to any subject brought forth.

After the last guest departed, Rose thanked Reverend Watts. Then Father, Grandfather and I accompanied her and Alan, along with their new-found relatives, back to the store. Upstairs, while the sisters-in-law sat at the kitchen table in uncomfortable silence, the younger Mr. Gleason took my father aside and informed him that they would take care of the grieving widow now.

Father would admit later that he had an uneasy feeling even then and was reluctant to leave Rose and Alan alone with these people. But what could he say? They were family.

Grandfather put that uneasy feeling to voice in the cab of the pickup truck on the way home when he asked, "Where the hell were those people during Dirk's illness?"

Father agreed that their absence was probably what was bothering him as well. In all the years he had known Dirk VanderMeer, he said, he had only met the storekeeper's sister once. And that was years ago when she and her husband had shown up to "inspect" her bachelor brother's new wife. As far as Father was aware, they hadn't been back since. I couldn't resist chiming in about how I thought Mr. Gleason and his son had seemed less concerned with comforting Mrs. VanderMeer than they had been with eyeing the contents of the store.

"You noticed that, too?" Father said, concentrating on the path our headlights cut through the narrow road ahead.

I said that it was hard not to notice the way those two seemed to take inventory as they walked around the store and residence upstairs. Father nodded in silent agreement.

"Well, no matter," he said after a moment's thought. "Rose has Dirk's last will and testament. He had me draw it up the night he left for the sanatorium. His will is ironclad. He left everything to his wife."

After ten days of mourning, Rose VanderMeer reopened the store. And Father returned to his Saturday morning desk to discover that a will is only ironclad if you can find it.

I went into Sorry with him that day to see Alan, who still hadn't returned to school. We were busy counting penny candy when Dad asked Mrs. VanderMeer to fetch Dirk's will so he could begin the probate process for her. She went to the backroom but returned empty handed.

"It's in the strongbox in his desk," my father insisted. "I put it in there myself." But when he went and checked, he found that the document was not in the metal box, nor was it among the documents strewn about the bottom of the desk drawer.

Rose insisted that she had not moved it. A search of the store and the living quarters, as well as Father's desk, came up empty. He sat back in his chair, ran his hand through his hair and sighed. "This makes it a little more complicated, Rose," he conceded. "But as Dirk's wife, you're entitled to his estate. It will just take a little longer to clean up—and a great deal more paperwork."

The one thing he did accomplish that weekend was to convince Alan to return to working at the ranch the next day. And to school on Monday. I was dead certain he would refuse to go back to sitting in that desk at the back of Mrs. Parsons' classroom. But either the promise of the unborn foal or the lure of the ranch—with all its hard work giving him something to concentrate on rather than sorrow—compelled him.

Much to our teacher's obvious displeasure, on Monday morning he once again squeezed into the desk next to mine, and we went back to being ignored by her except for the lessons she reluctantly wrote out on the blackboard each day.

Father helped Alan's mother file the death certificate in order to start the process of settling her husband's estate in the absence of a written will. Each Saturday after his office hours, he spent time going over the nuts and bolts of the store's business with both her and Alan. Although Mrs. VanderMeer struggled with keeping inventory records, Alan had little trouble learning to do the books, and Father was confident that it wouldn't be long before he could take over the paperwork completely.

Winter settled in. Christmas and New Year's came and went, with half-hearted celebrations. In January, both Alan and I began to count down the days to the birth of his foal.

And then, on a bitterly cold morning at the end of the month, an official-looking envelope arrived in the post office mailbag addressed to "The Manager of The Sorry Grocers." The letter, from a Quesnel lawyer, stated that his client, one Mrs. Helena Gleason, the only living relative of Dirk VanderMeer, was, as his rightful heir, disputing Rose Baptiste's claim to his estate. A handwritten note from Mr. Gleason attached to the formal letter bluntly stated that as an employee of the store, Rose was welcome to continue residing in the living quarters and remain on as manager until the estate was settled, at which time Mrs. Gleason would decide what to do with the business.

Father, who was not one to show his anger, found he had to calm himself after he read what Mrs. VanderMeer's in-laws were up to.

"Don't worry," he told her. "Even in the absence of a will, a person's estate still flows to the surviving spouse. First thing Monday morning we'll call these people's bluff and deliver a copy of your certificate of marriage." He set the letter down on his desk. "Do you know where your marriage certificate is, Rose?"

She shook her head slowly. "No paper says we are married."

"But where did you wed? A courthouse? A church? They'll have records. Who performed the ceremony?"

"My uncle, out on the reserve. We said we are married in front of him. But he's a long time gone now."

"But there must have been other witnesses."

"Only God."

In the days and weeks that followed, Father refused to lose patience over the road blocks he ran into at every turn as he tried to sort out the hornet's nest created by a common-law marriage and the lack of an official will.

Through her lawyer, Mrs. Gleason claimed that there had been no common-law marriage between her brother and Rose Baptiste, but only an employer and employee relationship.

Grandfather was the first one to voice the belief we all held, that it was almost a certainty that the copy of Dirk's will had gone missing at the hands of either Mr. Gleason or his son.

Of course there was no proof, other than the fact that the Gleasons were the only people, besides us, who were in the store at the time. Still, Father believed that his testimony about drafting the document on the day Dirk was taken to the sanatorium, along with the word of the two nurses at the hospital who had witnessed it, would help if it came down to a court case. I realized how serious it was when, with Grandfather's blessing, Father dipped into the ranch reserves and hired a lawyer to represent Rose VanderMeer's interests.

Helpless in the face of this escalating battle of words, during those long winter evenings I sometimes took Grandfather's ignored journal up to the loft and used it as a diversion from the growing fear that two more people whom I had come to love might disappear from my life.

32.

I have become a thief! I've taken to pilfering the camp supplies and stealing food whenever the cook is not around. Taking only small amounts each time—in hopes that it will not be missed—I secret the food away in my tent until I have a chance to give it to Rose. Sharing is no longer a pretense and she takes whatever I offer without comment.

Pa's promise to pay Willum in gold coins when the job is done is all well and good but I am certain that these two have seen the verge of starvation.

I will have to be more careful about raiding the camp provisions from now on, though. The cook has become irritated since noticing yesterday afternoon that the dried plums are greatly depleted. In a cursing explosion, he blamed our neighbours for the theft, claiming he couldn't turn his back for a moment when any of them are around camp. I quickly confessed to eating the missing dried fruit after I woke up hungry in the middle of the night. He scoffed at that explanation and accused me of trying to cover up for the real thieves. My friendship with Rose has not gone unnoticed. But he grumbles that he still holds me responsible given that it is my job to keep an eye on our supplies in his absence—which is often, as our cook spends a great deal of time in his tent when the crew is not around.

I will have to be more diligent, as it wouldn't do to have him voice his suspicions to Mr. Brewster. Our foreman is still deeply perplexed about the missing flour and I do not want to risk adding fuel to his fire of anger.

April 14

The cook is not the only one who has noticed my friendship with Rose.

This afternoon I waited until I heard the duet of snoring coming from his tent before ducking into the provisions shack, where I carefully unravelled the heavy stitching from the top of a burlap sack of beans. Scooping them out by the handful, I dumped the dried beans into my haversack until it was full. I rewove the stitching and plumped up the sides of the bag. When I was done I was certain my plan would work and that not even the sharpest eyes could detect the missing beans. But there wasn't any way to hide my bulging haversack when I stepped outside only to be caught red-handed.

I still don't know why Pa returned to camp this afternoon. But there he stood on the other side of the smoking campfire, his eyes travelling from my startled face to the haversack clutched to my chest.

He sized up the situation quickly, acknowledging my theft with the briefest shake of his head.

—Careful, son, he said. Crimes committed in the name of first love can cast a long shadow.

He turned and headed to our tent.

I didn't stop to consider the meaning behind his words but scurried out of camp to deliver my gift to Rose.

I found her waiting near the giant deadfall on the riverbank above our camp, as I often do. But this time when she spied the bounty in my hands she beckoned me to follow her. I had to duck my head to step through the curtain of roots and vines she had disappeared behind. On the other side I found myself in some sort of semi-subterranean dwelling. The only light came from the opening behind me and from a smoke hole in the sod roof above. As my eyes adjusted to the dim light, I could make out the evidence of life in this underground home— cooking implements set on ledges carved into the earth walls, blankets and fur pelts on either side of the firepit.

—You live here? I asked.

—With my brother, she said, taking a large metal pot from the ledge.

While we emptied the beans into the pot it suddenly occurred to me that if my pa had come home early from the trail, then perhaps Willum had as well. I told Rose that I should leave before he showed up.

—My brother knows you bring food.

—Still, I think it might be better that he doesn't find me here.

I didn't want to admit that I was intimidated by Willum. I can barely admit to myself that although he is probably only a few years older than myself, I feel like a child in his presence.

She seemed to understand, though, and stepped closer. Her dark eyes held mine and I felt my heart quicken as she reached up and laid her hand on my cheek.

—You are a good man, Mister Chance, she said.

At hearing her say my name for the first time—however incorrectly—and feeling the unexpected touch of her hand on my skin, I felt a shiver of shame-filled pleasure wash over me. In fear that she would look down and see the telltale excitement pressing against my breeches, I mumbled my goodbye and rushed out, feeling the fool for doing so all the way back to camp.

Neither Rose nor Willum showed up at our campfire tonight. And I am glad, for Father was unusually surly. Noticing the twins' absence, he asked in a whiskey-slurred voice where my girlfriend was. When I refused to respond he nudged his drinking companion Crooked-Eye.

—The boy's suffering from puppy love, he said with a bark of laughter.

Knowing that his cruelty would only escalate with the night's drinking, I rose from my spot at the campfire. Before I could make my escape Pa reached up and grabbed my sleeve.

—She's a woman, he said in a mocking voice. A woman needs a real man.

I shook off his hand and headed to our tent to retire for the night. It was all I could do to stop myself from crowing that today Rose had called me a man.

33.

As I laboured through Grandfather's detailed journal entries, it was apparent that even as a young man he was a record keeper. Long, wordy descriptions of the weather, the terrain and the progress of the road sometimes made the reading tedious. I often found myself skimming and then having to go back to be certain I didn't miss anything. I inserted slips of paper to mark the passages that wove his boyhood story, instead of facts and figures, intending to read only those marked pages to him when the time was right again.

But his journal and that long-ago world were not enough to keep at bay the reality of the present world: a world filled with the dread of losing my friend if the dispute over his stepfather's estate was lost.

I didn't understand all the legal terms discussed at our table during those months. I only knew that Mr. VanderMeer's assets were placed in the hands of the court until the estate was settled. Fortunately, as the only professional in the area, Father was named as the administrator, and so he carried on as the store's unpaid bookkeeper.

In my eyes, the wheels of the courts moved forward with excruciating slowness. February came and went. My fourteenth birthday, and Alan's fifteenth, passed with little notice. We threw ourselves into our studies, both intent on not disappointing Father when we wrote our final exams in June. Before long, my father's Friday night quizzes at the kitchen table became one more competition between me and Alan.

On the weekends, he continued to work at the ranch. Once the chores were done, he spent all his time out in the barn with the pregnant mare, brushing her copper-coloured hide until it shone like satin. He murmured private words of comfort in his people's language as he groomed her, which eventually caused Father to tease that the foal would be born with its ears perked for Alan's voice.

Beginning in mid-March, as the mare's due date drew closer, he stayed with us full-time so he could be there for the birth. Each morning we reluctantly drove into school, and we returned to the ranch each afternoon, where, before he did anything, Alan hurried out to the barn to check on the mare.

Near the end of the month, he placed a bedroll in the stall next to hers and began sleeping in the barn at night. I begged to be allowed to do the same, but my father, who I have to admit denied me little, refused my pleas. I tried to enlist Grandfather on my side. He, of course, couldn't see the problem with me spending the nights out in the barn to await the birth, but Father held firm.

That year, March had no intention of going out like a lamb. On the last day of the month, the lion returned in the form of a roaring north wind. Still, that evening Alan made his way out to the barn as usual, while I sulked off to the loft.

Hours later, waking to the sound of Father's voice calling up from the kitchen, I scrambled from my bed in the darkness and hurried downstairs.

"Is it born?" I asked as soon as I saw Dad standing by the kitchen door in his mackinaw, holding a lantern in one hand and my jacket in the other.

Without replying, in one quick motion, he tossed me the jacket and opened the door. I pulled on my boots and rushed after him. Outside the wind had died down; a skiff of fresh snow covered the ground. Ahead, Father's swinging lantern exposed his earlier footprints crossing the yard.

Inside the barn the metallic odour of blood and the warm scent of hay filled the air. I came around the corner of the mare's birthing stall and stopped short. My hands flew to my mouth at the sight of the mare standing in the corner of the stall nuzzling her newborn foal. Already up on his wobbly legs, the buckskin colt was searching beneath his mother's belly for his first meal. Nearby, in the flickering shadows, his hands and shirt blood-soaked, Alan stood with a proud grin on his face, as if he were somehow responsible for this miracle.

At fourteen, I had witnessed my fair share of births. Calves and foals, puppies and kittens alike. While the arrival of new life never lost its wonder, there was nothing extraordinary about animal birth on the ranch. But the moment I laid eyes on the wild stallion's offspring, I knew he was special. I won't go so far as to say that long-legged colt changed anything, but in the days and months to come, his presence brought a sense of rightness when wrongness had clouded our lives for far too long.

In June, Alan and I wrote our provincial exams in Quesnel. Any apprehension that our studies would suffer from the excitement over the new colt was laid to rest when we received our final marks in the mail. We had both passed with top honours in every subject. Our scores were good enough that an acceleration of the next two grades into one year was recommended for the coming term. Father offered up this news with complete nonchalance.

"If you two put your noses to the grindstone," he added, "there's no reason you can't receive your high school diplomas in two years instead of four." Excited at the prospect, Alan and I entered our summer break with high hopes.

The long summer wore on with the never-ending work made easier because we had the growing colt, which Alan had named Dancer, to admire at the end of each day.

All the while, the legal battle over his stepfather's estate dragged on, and then ground to a complete halt when the court case was set aside until fall. Our shared joy over the colt, and our great expectations of being freed of school in two years, was tempered by the uncertainty of the Vander-Meers' future. And then July brought an unexpected glimmer of hope.

Although the *Sorry Times* no longer existed, the bush telegraph still relayed local rumours to the grocery store. So it was Rose VanderMeer, the least likely person, who delivered the latest gossip to our kitchen table. The army officer from the harvest dance had been spotted visiting the school-teacher on a number of occasions, and word was that they were courting. If wishing could make it so, I would have gladly been responsible for those two falling in love and marrying. The thought of Mrs. Parsons moving off to Victoria with her soldier husband, and a new teacher taking her place in September, was something I imagined with pleasure for the rest of the summer. But it was clear that it was nothing more than fantasy as August drew to an end and Mrs. Parsons and Enid still resided in the little teacherage behind the school.

And then at the beginning of September, all our sorry little problems, as Father called them, were diminished when, on the other side of the world, in a grown-up version of the schoolyard game of Mother-May-I? the German bully took one goosestep too many.

And Mother England replied, "No, you may not."

34.

On the evening of the third day of September, the Radiola brought the news into our parlour. Britain had declared war on Germany. Seven days later, in a brief interruption of the regular CBC program, came the not-unexpected announcement that the Canadian parliament had approved the request of our prime minister, the Right Honorable W.L. Mackenzie King, to join Great Britain in her efforts in Europe. We were officially at war.

Little changed in our daily lives now that the threat was a reality. The autumn hay still had to be harvested, our winter's wood supply still had to be cut and stacked, the cattle still had to be rounded up and brought down from the summer range. And Alan and I had to return to school.

As we waited with resolution for Mrs. Parsons to ring the school bell that first morning, the younger students jostled about, their chatter filled with excitement over the war. Two boys boasted about older brothers who wanted to join up, and one of the girls said that her mom had cried all weekend long because her brother had run off to the city to enlist. Others, who I suspect had nothing to brag about, brought the adults' summer gossip to the schoolyard. They circled around Enid Parsons as she sat on the school steps, teasing her that she would soon "have a new soldier daddy."

I was surprised that I felt some sympathy for her in their torment, and as I watched, I saw that there was something different about Enid that morning. It wasn't just the lack of frilly dresses, which had been replaced with a plain sweater set and skirt. Over summer she seemed to have changed from a girl to a teenager. Her hair was cut into a short bob that framed her face, a face which at the moment was glaring at the taunting kids with an angry expression not unlike her mother's.

"Buzz off!" she yelled, jumping up and causing them to scatter. Her eyes caught mine, and perhaps the sympathy she saw there brought it on, but a surprising forlornness filled her eyes and she turned away.

It occurred to me then that this girl was done with dolls. For a fleeting moment, I wondered if her sadness was because her mother's friend, or beau, whichever he was, would almost certainly be heading off to war before long. And then another thought struck me: if that was so, then his leaving might add yet another burr to Mrs. Parsons' butt that could cause aggravation for us all, and I dreaded the sound of the school bell even more.

Sure enough, when the time came, it was clear that our teacher's disposition had not softened over the summer. Her eyes narrowed at the sight of Alan and me walking up the school steps. As we filed past her, I saw, not for the first time, the loathing in her eyes. Taking my seat, I wondered once again what he, or I for that matter, had ever done to her to cause so much hate.

While the rest of the students found their places with all the clamour and excitement of the first day of school, Enid Parsons did not go to her usual desk at the front of the class. She stopped at the first empty one at the back, in the row right across from me, and plunked herself down with her arms folded defensively.

Mrs. Parsons settled the class with a look, which I am certain could stop running water in the spring. She welcomed the students back with a long speech about how, now that our country was at war, every man, woman and child needed to do their part. She spoke about the saving of pennies, refraining from waste and supporting our soldiers.

"Some of you in the classroom will soon be old enough to think about enlisting," she said, squaring her shoulders. "We shall see who can rise to the challenge."

I glanced quickly at Alan. He was only fifteen, but she couldn't possibly have meant anyone else. All I could see was the crown of his head above his hinged wooden desk top as he stored his school supplies inside. He finished and slowly lowered the top, his face as blank as our new notebooks.

At lunch break, as we walked over to the store, I said, "Don't let that old biddy goad you into anything foolish."

He shrugged, as if she meant nothing to him. But I knew he had heard her fling down the gauntlet, and I hadn't forgotten the words he had uttered at the dance.

All that fall, the events in our lives and the larger events of the world seemed to race along at parallel speeds. By the end of September, over fifty-five thousand Canadians had stepped forward to enlist in the Armed Forces—Mrs. Parsons supplying the latest numbers to the class each Friday.

At home, Grandfather's condition was deteriorating, his mind growing murkier along with his eyesight. Lately, while Father and I huddled around the Radiola in the evening, whether it was a hockey game or the news, Grandfather no longer seemed to be listening. Each day he added less and less to mealtime conversations. Every now and then he would ask us to pass him something that he couldn't name. "You know, you know," he would say with an impatience he had never had before, "the thing—the white stuff—the shaker thing—" And Father or I would quickly pass him the salt, or a fork, or some other lifelong familiar item, before he could become too frustrated trying to come up with the word for it.

And then, on a rainy day in the middle of October, our lives took a turn that I had long dreaded when Alan and I arrived at the store after school to learn that his mother was no longer the owner of The Sorry Grocers, the only home he had known since he was seven years old. The court had awarded Dirk VanderMeer's entire estate to his sister, Mrs. Helena Gleason.

That evening Father and I drove back into Sorry where he tried to reassure Mrs. VanderMeer, promising to speak to the lawyer in Quesnel about appealing the decision. But even as he was saying it, for the first time, I could hear the despair in his voice.

Later, we drove into the ranch yard to find Grandfather wandering about in the dark in his long johns. Disoriented and confused, as we led him back into the house, like a small child he asked where we had been.

"Remember, Dad?" Father said gently. "We went into Sorry to visit with Rose and Alan VanderMeer."

Grandfather's eyebrows furrowed. He turned toward Father, asking, "Who are they?"

We knew then that perhaps we had averted an even greater tragedy by arriving home when we did. And we knew that never again could we leave Grandfather alone.

After he was settled in his bedroom, I retired to mine consumed with guilt over the realization that I may well have dallied too long and missed the opportunity to keep my promise to him—the promise to record his unwritten memories. Unable to sleep, I pulled his journal from where I'd stashed it in my night table and turned to the last marked page. Sometime in the early-morning hours, I believed I may have found the missing part—the "hole" in Grandfather's past.

35.

April 20, 1864

The days grow longer and the push to gain ground on the road grows more frantic. Each evening the men return at dusk bone tired and often quarrelsome over the possibility or the impossibility of meeting the deadline for Waddington's promised bonus. Most nights they eat supper by firelight and retire to their tents only to rise again in the morning darkness to head back up the trail.

In the pressure to have the work proceed at a faster pace, Mr. Brewster has given in just as Pa predicted and hired more men from the neighbouring camp. A few days ago he brought his own English-speaking guide, Chief Talhoot, to speak to those looking for work. There was much grumbling among the Chilcootans as the chief translated Brewster's message that everyone's wages are to be withheld until the price of the stolen flour is paid off. The foreman turned his back on the disgruntled group and strode into the supply shack. He returned with an armload of muskets, which he dumped clattering to the ground at Talhoot's feet.

—You tell them if they're hungry they can hunt for their dinner, he said.

I wanted to shout out that it isn't more muskets or pots and pans that they need. They need food to feed their families. But like everyone else I remained silent, knowing that my meagre voice would do little to influence a man who could look into the faces of hungry children and deny them even our leftover scraps.

I wonder at the fact that the handful of Chilcootans who have been hired are willing to work in the face of such stinginess. But their desperation and the hope of future compensation have them show up each morning now to pack and carry alongside men whom it is clear they hold in bitter disdain.

I am ashamed to say I suspect that they have reason for such disdain. I have tried to ignore what goes on because it is too awful to admit the truth: that some of the road crew are trading food for unmentionable favours from the Native women. This past Saturday night I saw one of the men approach a girl who was watching our camp from the edge of the trees. He held something up and when she reached out to accept it, his grizzled hand took hold of hers. As he led her toward his tent the light of our campfire flickered across her face—a face that appeared so young it caused me to jump up. But Pa's hand grabbed my shoulder and forced me back down.

—Mind your business, boy, he whispered harshly.

I opened my mouth to protest but he cast me a hard look.

—Don't go getting all high and mighty, he said, the sourness of his whiskey breath full in my nostrils. 'Tis a trade they both want. You should know all about that by now.

Confused and angered by his inference, I jerked away from him. I retired to my tent with the sound of his barked laughter burning my ears.

Since that night I have refrained from pilfering camp supplies. Not wanting to be cast in the same light as Pa's inference or risk having Rose or anyone misinterpret my intentions, I now only bring her food I am able to secret from my own and others' unfinished meals.

April 22

Pa has been gone these last few days, forging ahead on the route marked by the advance trailblazers. With him away and the crew working longer hours, I am left with plenty of free time. I make my escape from camp as soon as the cook is no longer watching. Like chums with an unspoken agreement, Rose and I meet each day on the riverbank near her dugout shelter. She says nothing about my meagre haversack offerings and eats whatever morsel of food I bring. Afterwards, she takes the deerskin pouch she carries everywhere and straps it across her forehead to hang down her back, leaving her hands free to forage.

Who would think that the barren-looking spring soil would offer anything of substance? But every now and then she bends over and roots out tiny plant shoots and either pops them in her mouth or stores them in her pouch. Encouraged by her ease with our surroundings, I follow her wherever she leads. Sometimes we skip rocks in the quieter river waters or scramble up the huge driftwood piles to walk along the logs for no other purpose than the simple fun of it. Often I spot white-headed eagles watching our progress from the treetops. Yesterday I caught sight of a black bear skulking through the woods along the other side of the river. Even though he was a safe distance away, I jerked to a stop with fear. Rose touched my arm to still me and we stood in silence until the beast ambled away into the undergrowth.

—Cook says it isn't the season for bears to come to fish in the river, I said, with what I am ashamed to admit was a tremble in my voice.

Rose snorted.

—Bears are everywhere. They are part of this land. But that bear, he don't want to meet you any more than you want to meet him.

Today Rose taught me how to cut and strip young willow saplings to make an animal snare. I spent most of the morning squatting on the ground with my thighs burning as I tried to place my snare as she has shown me—giving it the perfect amount of tension without having it snap and fall apart in my hands. When at last I got it right, I waited with shallow-breathed patience until the circle snare was finally triggered—catching a fat brown squirrel in its grip. Without hesitation, Rose leapt forward and, taking up a large stone, put the writhing animal out of its misery. She had it gutted before I was even aware that her knife was out of its sheath and in her skilled hands. After the animal was skinned we gathered dry grass and twigs and she sparked a flame with her flint rock—yet another treasure retrieved from her leather pouch. Before long our lunch was roasting on a spit fashioned of sticks above a smokeless fire. It is hard to imagine anything will ever again taste as good as that blackened squirrel which Rose and I chewed down to the bone on the banks of the Homathco River today.

April 23

This morning the artist Mr. Whymper, who has spent most of his time in the forward camp, stopped by ours on his way back down to the Waddington townsite. I was alone, finishing my late breakfast, when he came up beside me and without a word dropped a sheet of paper on the table. I barely had time to acknowledge him before he turned and headed off down the trail—rolls of paintings commissioned by Mr. Waddington under his arm. I soon forgot him, though, when I glanced down at the table to find a pencil sketch of Rose and me sitting on a log by the river. The drawing is so startling in detail that each stitch in her deerskin pouch is clear. Taken aback at the sight of it, I wondered when he had done this. Had the artist become so blended into the scenery these days that I had not noticed him sketching? I quickly rolled it up and took it into the tent to hide away beneath my cot along with my journal. If the writing down of her name causes such fear in Rose I can't imagine what she would think if she sees this drawing which has captured her image so completely.

April 24

Pa has returned to camp. He left Willum up in the canyon for the next few days clearing rock and debris from the latest blasting.

Pa is sour tempered this afternoon, blaming his sullenness on the miles of rough terrain still ahead before the trail reaches the grasslands of the plateau. He intends to remain in camp tomorrow and organize his tools and powder for the next blast. I am disappointed, for I am reluctant to meet with Rose when he is around.

April 25

If the loss of my mother heralded the end of my childhood, then the horrendous events of this day have clinched it. Any pretense of innocence in my life is over at the hands of the closest person to me. My pa. What my eyes have witnessed tonight, my mind will never forget and my heart will never forgive. If there was anywhere to run off to except wilderness I would flee, never to see him again. Instead I find lonely solace in my tent tonight, dreading his return.

Today Pa stayed in camp. In a better mood than yesterday, he began drinking in the early afternoon. Only as I finished washing the evening dishes did I realize he had not shown up for supper with the other men. I headed to our tent to check if he had dozed off. Just as I arrived, the canvas flap was pushed aside and Crooked-Eye ducked out of the opening and brushed by me—a jug of Pa's whiskey under each arm. A quick look inside proved the tent empty and Pa's trunk broken open and ransacked. I hurried back outside to holler after the fleeing guide, demanding that he return the stolen liquor or I would tell Pa.

He stopped on the edge of camp and turned to face me—his toothy grin flashing sinister in the evening light.

—Yeah. You go tell him, he said. You go find him at that place with Rose.

As the meaning of his words sunk in, neither the night shadows nor common sense could have stopped me from rushing out of camp. With only the moon to light my way I scrambled down the riverbank, tripping over rocks and deadfalls in my haste to make my way upstream. Long before I arrived at the hidden entrance to Rose's dugout shelter, I began to dread what I would find.

Pa either did not hear my clumsy approach or was too caught up in his passion to take notice. With his pants bunched at his ankles and his bare buttocks reflecting the firepit light, he let out an animal moan and then slumped forward. Still my mind would not register what was happening. I stood rooted in the opening until from beneath his heaving shoulder Rose's head turned slowly toward me. And I—like a coward—spun away from the emptiness that filled her eyes and fled.

I am ashamed to admit that only after I stumbled back to camp and took refuge in my tent did it occur to me to question what I had witnessed. Had Rose been a willing lover? Or had my drunken Pa forced himself upon her?

April 26

I would not look Pa in the eye this morning. But he paid little mind to my sulking as he readied himself to go to work, his anger over the stolen whiskey still sharp.

Last night I feigned sleep when he finally stumbled back into the tent. I heard him curse as he tripped over his belongings, which I had left strewn on the tent floor. Discovering his ransacked trunk and realizing that he'd been robbed, he roared like a wounded animal. Grabbing me by my shoulders he shook me from my pretended slumber, demanding to know where his jugs of whiskey were.

—Ask your friend Crooked-Eye, I snarled at him.

He flung me back on my bedroll like a rag doll and stormed from our tent. I am certain he woke the entire crew as he thundered through the trees toward our neighbours' camp. But none of the workers rose from their tents to interfere as Pa's shrieked obscenities carried through the night. Even from where I lay I could hear him calling out for Crooked-Eye—threatening him with everything from the wrath of the King George men to bringing the pox upon him for his theft.

If I had not heard it with my own ears I would never have believed that my Pa—who is well aware of the Natives' fear of smallpox—could ever utter such hateful words. In the past I have always blamed his nasty outbursts on the effects of drink and found ways to forgive his hurtful temper when he is in that drunken state. But last night his words came from an ugly place inside Pa that I have always denied existed. His ranting brought no response from our neighbours' camp and he finally returned to our tent, still in a rage. He set to rummaging around in his trunk, muttering to himself how Crooked-Eye had tricked him into leaving camp so he could plunder his liquor.

I gathered up my courage and bolted up from my bedroll to face him.

—No one tricked you into raping Rose, I said.

He whirled around at the accusation.

—Oh no, boy, he said. Not I. I don't have to force myself on any woman.

I stood my ground, glaring at him. When I blurted out that I didn't believe that Rose had willingly lain with him, his eyes narrowed.

—Time to grow up, son, he growled. Do you really believe your measly offerings of food scraps had her befriend you? Well, I'm here to tell you it's the promise of the gold I will pay her brother and nothing more. Those two almost perished last winter. They know what gold will do for them at the trading posts come fall. There's nothing wrong with the lady showing me a little gratitude for giving her brother work.

—Then you are no better than the others who take advantage of their desperation.

But Pa was paying no attention to me. He threw himself back into searching through the mess in his trunk. Relief flooded his face after he lifted a false bottom and pulled out a leather sac. I heard the sound of coins shifting as he opened the drawstring and hastily checked the contents. Satisfied, he returned it to the trunk and replaced the false bottom, tamping it down while still muttering angrily to himself.

—Well, I won't be paying either Willum or Crooked-Eye one bloody copper. It's a sure bet that they were all in cahoots to lure me away so they could rob me.

I crawled into my bedroll and pulled the blanket over my head as if I could shut out his fuming. But confusion and anger chewed at my mind and kept me awake through the long night.

Pa's surliness has carried over into this morning. He sat hunched over his breakfast plate refusing to talk to anyone. While the crew ate in silence, the group of Chilcootan men who show up looking for work each morning arrived. Crooked-Eye strode in with them as if nothing had happened last night. Upon seeing him, Pa jumped up, letting his plate of unfinished breakfast spill to the ground. He rushed at him, shouting a repetition of his bitter threats of last night. To make matters worse, just as he was firing him for being a bloody thief and swearing that neither he nor Willum would ever find work with the road crew again, Mr. Brewster and Chief Talhoot walked into camp. The foreman had come down from the forward camp to hire more Chilcootan workers. Hearing Pa's accusation of theft he took the opportunity to once again ask the group to give up the names of the men who were responsible for stealing the flour this spring. When no one answered he took out a notebook and pencil stub from his shirt pocket.

At Mr. Brewster's insistence, Chief Talhoot reluctantly began telling him the names of each of the Chilcootan men there. As the foreman started scribbling them into his notebook, Willum returned from his two nights at the blasting site. He stared hard at Mr. Brewster and demanded to know what he was doing. Without glancing up, Mr. Brewster replied that he was recording everyone's names and would keep them until he had the names of the flour thieves.

Willum's face clouded over.

—You must not steal our names, he said in a voice dangerously low.

Mr. Brewster ignored him. Stuffing the notebook into his breast pocket, he patted it and turned to his guide.

—You tell these men that I have the power to bring the white man's sickness back to this land, he warned. Tell them all Chilcootans will die if I do.

The group shrank back in fear as Talhoot translated. Mr. Brewster held up a hand.

—Tell them we will not use this power if they work hard to pay off the price of the stolen flour. Today I will hire every man here to work until that is done. And then they will each receive their fair wages and I will tear up this paper with their names.

He stopped and pointed at Crooked-Eye and Willum.

—Except for you two. If our Mr. Beale won't hire you because you are thieves then neither will I.

Willum turned to scowl at Pa.

—Why do you call me a thief?

—There's no more work for you here, Pa yelled. He fished out his lucky twenty-dollar gold piece from his pocket and tossed it at him.

Willum's hand reached up and caught it in mid-air. He opened his palm and looked down at the coin with disdain.

—You owe me more than this, he said.

—Take the rest of your wages in trade for the stolen whiskey.

—I have no use for your poison water, Willum scoffed. He turned away, and after casting a final glare at us all, he left camp with Crooked-Eye skulking behind him.

Surprisingly, the other Chilcootans took up the foreman's offer of work and struck out for the forward camp along with the road crew. Before he headed up the trail I overheard Mr. Brewster's self-satisfied remark to Pa.

—Now that's how you keep these savages in line, Beale.

And Pa, who is usually at odds with the foreman, said nothing.

Today I remain close to camp, venturing to the river only for water. I have seen no sign of Rose. This afternoon I hide in my tent angered at my Pa and ashamed of myself for not protecting her from him.

April 27

I must admit a certain relief that Willum has not returned to our camp since he left with Crooked-Eye. Rose too stays away. Today I watched for her everywhere I went but she is staying well hidden. There is every possibility that she and her brother have left the area. I am too cowardly to check her shelter, but the thought that I may never see her again saddens me.

April 28

A feeling of unease hangs over the crew these last few days. The tension is heavy since Brewster threatened the Chilcootans with smallpox, and any pretense of friendliness between the two camps is gone.

Their women and children no longer hang on the edges of our camp looking for handouts, and our cook is even more grumpy than usual because his woman has not shown up since yesterday. I am left with both her chores and mine now, which helps keep me busy and out of Pa's way when he's in camp. Before he left this morning he told me to stop moping around like a wounded pup and act like a man. I ignore his curt comments and continue to refuse to speak to him. I no longer know my Pa. He is silent and morose but unlike me his concern is not for Rose but for his lost whiskey. Tonight he carefully hoards his last jug. I fear what will happen when it's gone completely.

April 29

I do not know what to make of today's events. Tonight I sit writing by the light of our campfire, trying to make sense of them as Pa snores in our tent. This afternoon I was tossing out the dirty dishwater when I heard a familiar bird call coming from the thicket along the riverbank. I spun around and saw Rose crouched in the underbrush. Startled at the sight of her, I dropped the dishpan and stood gaping at her beckoning me to come closer. I hadn't seen her since finding her in Pa's embrace, and I am ashamed to say that I hesitated. In that brief instant our cook came into sight on the path and Rose was gone. This evening she appeared once again, silently gesturing to me from the shadows on the edge of camp. This time I edged toward her, but before I could open my mouth she held a finger to her lips and then whispered a hurried warning of great trouble coming.

—You must run away and hide tonight.

In anxious whispers she urged me to be gone from the camp before morning light. When I pressed her for a reason she told me that Willum and Crooked-Eye went down the trail and found Klatsassin. They told him about the foreman's threats. According to her, the war chief and his son are now in the Chilcootan camp talking to Chief Talhoot.

—Klatsassin says all the white men must die, she said.

—Why? Why would he say that? I asked her.

—To stop them from bringing the sickness again. To keep them away from our land.

—If this is true, why are you telling me?

—Because you are not like the others. You give without taking.

When I started to plead my remorse for what my pa had done to her, she placed her hand on my chest.

—You are not your father, Mr. Chance, she said. And with a final urging for me to flee, she ducked away and was gone.

By the time I got back to camp the ominous sound of a drum beating in the distance served to reinforce Rose's warning, and I knew I had to speak to Pa whether I wanted to or not. I found him nursing the last of his whiskey. Tomorrow he plans to hike down to Waddington townsite at the head of the inlet to see if he can buy more. When I hurriedly recounted Rose's warning, he scoffed at the idea.

—Don't be a fool, he said. It's just another bloody trick to get us out of camp so they can ransack the place.

I tried desperately to convince him that I was certain Rose was telling the truth, but he waved me off, insisting that I was too lovestruck to know when I was being bamboozled.

—Don't worry, son. Brewster's right about one thing. The Natives are too much in awe of us to do anything foolish.

Frustrated at his response, I tried to warn the cook and the other men, but they too laughed at me for being so gullible. When I pointed out the rising voices coming through the trees, they put it down to the Chilcootans' nighttime sharing of their people's legends. I finally retired to our tent, hoping that they were right. But as I write in my journal I am having a hard time convincing myself that the sounds coming from the neighbouring camp are the sounds of storytelling.

36.

The rest of the page was blank. I quickly flipped to the next and found a final, undated entry.

I am grieved to write the words—Pa is dead.

The entire entry that followed those ominous words was hastily scribbled out to use every last bit of space in the closing pages of the book, making it difficult to read. When I was finished, I was certain that what was missing, whatever happened between April 29 and this final undated entry, was the missing piece, the "hole" in my grandfather's past.

I slowly closed the journal. The ranch house was silent, hushed with that predawn stillness that can make a body feel alone in the world. I switched off my bedside lamp and pulled the covers over my head, hoping sleep would find me and help to hasten the coming morning. But my mind was racing with unanswered questions that Grandfather's words gave rise to. I wanted to run downstairs and wake him to find out what had happened in that huge gap.

Morning seemed to take forever to arrive. I was so keyed up I was certain I could never fall asleep, but I must have, because I woke with a start to the sound of voices in the kitchen below. I dressed hastily and rushed downstairs to find Father and Grandfather preparing breakfast. I sighed with disappointment when I saw Grandfather shuffling between the stove and the table, his head down like a charging bull, as Father talked about driving into Quesnel later today with Rose to see her lawyer.

Ever since Grandfather's memory had become foggy, Father was constantly engaging him in conversation—seeking his advice about the affairs of the ranch at every opportunity. On a good day, he would rise up and answer clearly and competently, as if there were no clouds in his mind at all. During those times, we could almost forget the murkiness that could swell like an ocean wave and wash away even his most familiar memories. There was not much talk of seeking a doctor's opinion. Grandfather was, after all, ninety years old, and on those good days he, and we as well, excused his addle-mindedness as something to be expected.

On a bad day, he would try to hide his confusion by lowering his head and stomping off, muttering under his breath whenever conversation was directed at him.

Grandfather had never been a mutterer. Whenever he had something to say, he spoke clearly in words that anyone could understand. So when I arrived in the kitchen to hear him mumbling incoherently, I knew that today was not the day to seek answers about his past.

Still, when Father went out to the barn later, I found I was unable to resist the urge to try. I sat down across the table from Grandfather as he poked at his barely touched eggs. "I finished reading your journal," I said. "I found the missing part, the hole, you told me about."

He raised his head. His eyebrows came together in a frown over eyes that were little more than slits now. "Hole? Where's there a hole?"

"In your journal entries, I ..."

But Grandfather was back to concentrating on his breakfast plate, and I knew there was no point in trying to push him. I would just have to wait and watch for a better moment. I studied his face, a face creased with years of sun, a face more prone to smiles than frowns. I couldn't help wondering how, and why, he had gone all this time without speaking to anyone, that I knew of, about the events in his boyhood. And why had he chosen to share his journal with me and not Father?

In the following days, I would scrutinize his every move to judge if he was in the present, looking for an opening, an opportunity to gently guide him into the past. In the evenings, when he was settled for the night, I would go to his room, sit next to his bed and read his journal aloud, hoping to jog his memory. I would look up from the pages to search his weathered face for a reaction to the words. And every night, after he fell asleep, I would lean forward to whisper into his ear, "What happened on that last day of April? What happened to your pa?" and then I would turn to the back of the journal and read the final entry.

37.

I am grieved to write the words—Pa is dead.

The horror of his death—the brutal way in which he was slain—haunts me at every moment.

In these past weeks living like an animal in the wilderness I have lost all track of time and distance. I have no idea of the date on this night as my grief finally allows me to record how I escaped death that treacherous morning. Wearing nothing but my woollen long johns, I spent all that day and a shivering night crouched beneath an overhang on the riverbank. When I was certain the murderers had moved on I emerged from my hiding place to find as grisly a scene in our empty camp as anyone could imagine. Even though I had witnessed it the day before I wanted to believe that what had happened was a bad dream. Not a single body was in sight, but the fly-swarmed pools of blood and gore testified to the terrible way in which the road workers died. Grim marks on the ground leading to the river indicate that what was left of their bodies had been dragged off and tossed into the fast-flowing waters. Frantic with the horror of it, I searched through our collapsed tent's canvas folds, hoping against hope to find Pa, but came up with nothing more than my haversack and clothing. And this journal. Nearby, Pa's empty trunk lay upturned on its side. All around, spilled grain and flour was ground into the blood-soaked earth. But the looters had missed the false bottom on Pa's trunk. I quickly retrieved his sack of gold coins, stuffed it into my haversack and hurried away from that gruesome scene. At the ferry landing I found the ferry skiff smashed to pieces. Only the overhead guide wire remained stretched across the river. Staring at those raging waters I saw that my obvious hope of escape to the other side lay in inching my way across the ferry cable above. And I could not do it. I decided that I would rather die trying to follow Waddington's overland route through the canyons and up to the plateau than risk a watery death in the Homathko River.

On my way back upriver it struck me that as horrible as the thought was, I would have to return to our camp to forage for food.

I had not eaten for almost two days. But I spent little time in that miserable place after discovering the cook's stores had been looted and ransacked. I was able to salvage nothing more than some handfuls of dried prunes scattered among the ruins. I stuffed a few—dirt and all—into my mouth, and for the last time I turned my back on that place of death. But before heading up the trail I couldn't resist edging my way through the trees along the riverbank toward Rose and Willum's underground shelter. When I reached the deadfall I crept up to peer inside the opening to find the dwelling abandoned as I expected, the ashes in the firepit the only reminder of anyone's presence. I was about to turn and leave when I spotted something on the dirt ledge that once held Rose's pots and pans. Her deerskin pouch. I scooped it up and quickly looked inside to discover a sack of rice and a few handfuls of beans. Beneath the pouch lay her fire flint and a knife. I threw everything into my haversack and hurried away, confused by the thought that she had intentionally left these things for me to find.

Had Rose been so certain that I would survive that morning?

Miles up the trail at Brewster's forward camp I spotted bodies mutilated beyond description. With a pounding heart, I kept my distance and continued through the canyon in the eerie quiet.

Led forward by the trailblazers' axe marks on trees, I climbed upward in the following days. The going was tough. At some points, my only route across the deep gorge and chasms lay in felled trees acting as makeshift bridges. But my desperation to be away was stronger than my fear.

Since reaching the plateau I have used the sun and moon to guide me eastward toward civilization. Every day and every night and every step of the way I am aware that I am in my enemy's territory. On two occasions I have spotted Chilcootans in the distance wearing clothing that I recognize as belonging to some of the slain road crew. I am certain that they are aware of my presence. But for their own reasons they let me pass.

Early this morning I ran into a man on horseback with a loaded pack mule trailing behind. The bearded Irishman is a trapper who is fleeing the countryside until the Indian troubles—as he calls them—die down. As I walked alongside of him today he told me that a Native friend showed up at his cabin a few nights ago to warn of a rogue band of Chilcootan warriors who are intent on bringing death to all the white men in the territory. I held my tongue and said nothing of what I had witnessed at the road camps.

Although the trapper was surprised to meet me on the trail, he easily accepted my sparse explanation that I had hiked up from the coast headed for the goldfields and had lost my way.

—Aye, lad, he said. Ya must have an angel on your shoulder to have made it through the area unharmed.

He has agreed to allow me to accompany him to the Alexandria ferry, where he will point me to my destination before he himself heads south to New Westminster.

He maintains that we'll be safe once we're on the other side of the Fraser River. That until the colony's new Governor Seymour and his men arrive, this Chilcootan territory is no place for a white man, no matter how friendly the Natives have been to him in the past.

Tonight I sit in his camp grateful for the dinner he shared with me after noting my hollow cheeks and the clothes hanging loose from my frame. I don't know how much longer I would have lasted with only a handful of rice left in my haversack. The few rabbits and squirrels I have been able to snare along the way only left me hungry for more. Now with my stomach full for the first time in weeks, I am able to write in my journal by the light of the Irishman's smokeless campfire while he laments the deteriorating situation between the Europeans and the Indians. My silence seems not to bother my new companion as he talks enough for both of us. In keeping my counsel I am fully aware that I am breaking the sworn oath I made, which has probably kept me alive in these last weeks. But it was a promise made under duress. And I do not mean to keep it.

In my anger and grief of these last weeks I have come to the conclusion that I hold both sides responsible for the horrific events that occurred in the road camp in the early morning of the final day of April. I blame the Chilcootans for the brutal death of my Pa along with the rest of the road crew. And I blame the arrogance of the white men who drove them to it.

So I will bear witness for no one. My oath be damned.

38.

Only in looking back would I be able to see the inevitability of the past catching up with the present.

During the winter of 1939, everything seemed to happen at once. At the end of November, Rose VanderMeer's appeal was denied, and the decision to award her husband's estate to his sister was upheld.

On the afternoon the news arrived, oblivious to this development, Alan and I sat at our classroom desks working on our algebra problems, passing our work back and forth to check each other's answers in the teacher's manual Father had acquired.

Mrs. Parsons was in an unusually light mood that day. Her cheeriness, we would discover later, was due to the fact that her officer friend, who had been up in Prince George recruiting, was visiting. He had arrived in Sorry the night before, and early that morning had gone out hunting. We had no reason to connect him to the late-morning echoes of distant rifle shots, which had caused Alan to pause and raise his head to peer out the window with concern knit into his brows.

After school, we arrived at The Sorry Grocers to find the young Mr. Gleason from Quesnel in the store. Mr. VanderMeer's nephew had come to deliver the official documents himself: documents declaring that his mother, his uncle's sister, was now the undisputed owner of business and building.

The news came as a second gut punch that afternoon. The first blow had occurred only moments before, when a pickup truck with Mrs. Parsons' officer friend at the wheel sped through Sorry. It passed by us in a cloud of road dust, and my breath caught at the sight of the lifeless cargo in the truck bed. As the dust settled on our unmoving feet, I could still hear the antlers rattling against the tailgate, still smell the blood, the animal fear, the death, of the huge buck—our buck—from the ridge.

The incident left us so shaken that we barely took notice of the station wagon parked outside the store. Inside, Mr. Gleason's presence gave us no time to wallow in our sorrow.

His back was to us when we came through the door. He stood in front of the counter, towering over Alan's mother as if he had her pinned there.

"You are welcome to stay on, Rose," he was saying. "Live upstairs with me, in the same manner as you did with Uncle Dirk."

Alan, affronted by the man's words, and his closeness to his mother, rushed over and pushed himself between them. Without hesitation I stepped forward with him.

"This is grown-ups' business," Mr. Gleason said, dismissing us with a wave of his hand. But Alan remained anchored where he stood until the man was forced to meet his gaze. Perhaps it was something he saw in Alan's steely-eyed glare, or perhaps it was Rose VanderMeer's refusal to accept the papers he was waving at her that made Mr. Gleason step back and toss them on the counter.

Just then the little bell above the front door tinkled, and the door opened to reveal Mrs. Watts, the minister's wife. She stepped into the store and then stopped short at the sight of the four of us facing off before the counter.

"Good afternoon, Rose—Alan," she said with a smile. "Hello, Adeline, and uh … uh …"

Mr. Gleason turned and took a step forward, tilting his hat in greeting. "Leonard Gleason," he said. "Nephew of Dirk VanderMeer's—God rest his soul—and the new proprietor of this store."

"Oh," Mrs. Watts replied. "Oh, I …" Clearly taken aback by this announcement, she fussed with the net shopping bag hanging on her arm, saying, "Well, I just have a few things to pick up."

She proceeded down the middle aisle, glancing back at us while Mr. Gleason went into the backroom. The sound of storage doors opening and closing and drawers sliding in and out soon came from the back of the store. Alan grabbed the papers from the counter. He stood reading them as Mrs. Watts finished her shopping. She paid Rose and then hurried out—to spread this latest piece of gossip, I was certain.

Mr. Gleason returned from his snooping and headed over to the desk in the corner. As he jiggled the locked drawers, I stepped forward. "That's my father's desk, and you don't own that."

He picked up Father's engraved sign from the desktop and studied it. "Notary public, eh?" He placed it back down with a thud. "Well, he'll have to find another place for his desk, won't he?"

He strode over to the door, pulled it open and then, with his hand still on the knob, turned his attention back to Mrs. VanderMeer. "Think about my offer, Rose. You've got two weeks to decide."

With that, he stepped out onto the porch, letting the door close behind him. He stood on the other side of the glass for the longest time, his hands jammed in his pockets, rolling back and forth on the balls of his feet, surveying his surroundings. Finally, as if satisfied with what he saw, he turned around, tipped his hat, either to us or to his own reflection, and then made his way down the steps. Before the station wagon pulled away, Mrs. VanderMeer locked the door. For the second time, I saw her hang the "closed" sign on a weekday afternoon. I wondered if it would be the last.

As she pulled down the shade, I said, "Let's go see Dad."

Minutes later, we climbed into the store's van and Alan drove us out to the ranch.

There was little supper eaten around our table that night. Father's reaction to the news was more sad resignation than surprise. But I saw his jaw muscles twitch on hearing of Mr. Gleason's offer to allow Rose to continue working at the store and living in the residence. With him. At the head of the table, Grandfather remained mute, and I wondered if he understood this new dilemma.

By the time Rose finished explaining, it was obvious that she had no intention of remaining on at the store.

The question that was left unspoken, the question hanging so heavy in the air that I wanted to shout it out, was what would she—*what would they*—do? Surprisingly, it was Grandfather who asked, "Where will you go, Rose?"

She thought for some time before answering. "I would like to see Alan finish school here."

"Given Mrs. Parsons' treatment of him over the years," Father said. "I find that rather surprising."

"If we go back to the reserve, the government men might come and take him to the residential school."

An expression of understanding spread across Father's face. "No, Rose, that wouldn't happen," he said gently. "Alan's too old to be forced to do that."

She raised her eyes to meet Father's. "May be. But he couldn't finish school out there," she said. "In Sorry, he can."

"Yes, that's true," Father agreed. "But, although I would dearly hate to see you two leave the area, I have to say that I can't imagine him running into a worse teacher anywhere else."

"I can," Rose said. Then she added quietly, "Sometimes your enemy is your best teacher."

39.

I don't know what I had expected in insisting we go to see my father that day. But listening to the discussion of the situation at our dinner table, it occurred to me that I still held onto the childish notion that he could fix anything. Later, lying in bed, after Alan and his mother went home, I didn't see any way that was possible.

My father spent the following two days in Sorry, helping Rose VanderMeer sort out the tangle of business and the blurred lines between what belonged to the store and what was hers. Fortunately there was some money in a personal account, which had been a joint account when Dirk VanderMeer was alive, and that was clearly hers now. Unfortunately, she had sunk a lot of those funds into store inventory, and it would take more than Father's expertise to sort out that mess.

In the evenings, I couldn't help overhearing him discussing these problems with Grandfather. Discussing isn't exactly the correct word to describe those one-sided conversations, as my grandfather rarely added anything—sometimes even falling asleep in his chair—while Father mulled over the latest issues.

But it was Grandfather who first mentioned the solution. One night, after giving no indication that he was listening, in the middle of Father's thinking out loud about Rose and Alan's options, Grandfather pushed himself up to shuffle off to an early bed. At his doorway he hesitated and then, without turning around, said, "They could live here."

I doubt that the offhand comment was the first time the idea had entered my father's mind, because he nodded to himself in silent acknowledgment. The next morning, Grandfather was still sleeping when I rose in the dark to start chores. It was so unusual for him to be in bed at that hour that we looked in on him twice before going out to feed the animals.

During the next few days, he kept to his bed more and more, saying he just didn't feel up to snuff, toddling feebly about whenever he did rise to join us in the kitchen or parlour.

In hindsight, after what happened the following week, it doesn't take much for my imagination to make the leap from suspicion to believing that his feeling poorly was intentional. On Saturday I stayed home with him while Father drove into Sorry to retrieve his desk, notary seals and papers from the store. He took along a notice to post on the store's cork bulletin board, informing his clients that from this day on he would no longer be doing business there. After the New Year, anyone in need of his services was welcome to drive out to the ranch on Saturday mornings.

When he arrived home late that afternoon, he climbed up to the loft with a measuring tape. I followed behind and held the end of the tape as he ran it across my room, from sloped wall to sloped wall, then from the highest point in the peaked ceiling to the floor—all the while musing about how big this loft seemed to him when he was growing up, and how much smaller it seemed now.

When he was done, he sat down on the edge of my bed and asked if I would mind him dividing the room down the middle, making two bed-rooms out of my one.

"Right now, this is just an idea," he said. "We won't do anything you're uncomfortable with, but, well, I'm wondering how you'd feel about inviting Rose and Alan to share our home for a while? They need a place to live while he finishes school, and with Dad's deteriorating health—and no reflection on you, Addie, but Lord knows we could use a woman's hand around here."

I leaned against my dresser and surveyed the room, trying to imagine it chopped in half by a wall. It occurred to me that this is how the loft would have been divided up if my brother, Evan, had lived. And even though Alan still teased me about being my blood brother, I had mixed feelings about him sleeping on the other side of that imaginary wall. Keeping my confusion to myself, I folded my arms and shrugged my indifference.

And so the decision was made. Within days, the wall was up, and Alan and Rose came to live at the ranch. Father moved into Grandfather's bedroom with the intention of building another lean-to room for Rose VanderMeer on the other side of the parlour in the spring. In the mean-time, she took his room.

As it turned out, for so many reasons, that second lean-to room would never be built.

Over the Christmas holidays, we were spared the gossip in Sorry over our new living arrangements. But I had little doubt that during gatherings from church services to yuletide parties, the town was abuzz with the news that Rose VanderMeer was now the live-in housekeeper on the Beale ranch.

I will say this for the folks in our community, though: they look out for their own. Affronted at the way the store had been taken from Dirk VanderMeer's widow, many customers showed their loyalty to the former owners when Mr. Gleason arrived to take over the business. Later we would learn that those who doubted the rumours went to the store to check for themselves. When they saw that it was true, they turned and left the new owner standing behind the counter, the smile melting from his face. Within weeks, it was clear that—for the folks of Sorry—standing up for their neighbour was of greater importance than simple convenience. It didn't take long before Mr. Gleason realized that his only customers were those picking up their mail, or needing some small staple item. The majority of the store's former patrons began travelling into Wells or Quesnel to purchase the bulk of their groceries.

At the ranch, in many ways it turned out to be a good holiday season. For the first time in years, it actually felt like Christmas. Thanks to Rose, regardless of everyone's initial indifference, the ranch house was decorated with fir boughs and tinsel; popcorn strings and paper chains hung on the branches of a small tree in the corner of the parlour. There were presents under the tree, and a real turkey dinner with all the trimmings on Christmas Day. And Grandfather—who, the day after Rose and Alan moved in, was miraculously back on his feet—sat at the head of the table.

On New Year's Eve, we all bundled up and headed outside to bang on pots and pans in a cacophony of metal clanging at the stroke of midnight. As we ushered in the new year, across the starlit meadows, coyotes and wolves howled back our greeting.

The only discomfiting moment came after dinner the next day, when Rose, who had found what was left of Mother's record collection while dusting in the parlour, asked if we could play some on the Victrola later. I glanced over at Father in the silence that followed her words and saw a flicker of sadness cross his face.

"No," he said, looking down at his empty plate. "No. I'd rather not."

She never asked again.

Alan's mother took her job as housekeeper seriously. Before long, the entire ranch house smelled different. Gone was the musky scent of laundry left sitting too long, as washing was once again done regularly every Saturday afternoon. I found a strange comfort in the forgotten smells of ammonia and vinegar-scrubbed floors, and oiled wood. Every surface sparkled with a pride in cleanliness that had been sorely missing, and which to my surprise was equal to Mother's standards.

Unlike Mother, though, Rose enjoyed being outdoors as much as I did. Claiming it was a freedom she had forgotten in these past years as a store-keeper, she worked alongside us, cutting and stacking firewood, feeding the animals and mucking out the barns and corrals. And when the ice on Sucker Lake was ready, she didn't hesitate to join us in the harvesting of ice blocks.

Almost from the beginning, Rose fit so naturally into our home. Yet I have to admit that I was taken aback the first time she claimed my mother's old armchair in the parlour, which no one had used since she left. Watching Rose settle on the indentations Mother had left in the worn blue fabric made my heart ache in a way that took me by surprise. After a time, though, I convinced myself that it was a relief to see Rose's shape erasing that of my mother.

In the evenings, she would join us in the parlour, her hands in constant motion, either mending, darning or knitting, her knitting needles clacking in background rhythm with the voices coming from the Radiola.

Never having felt compelled to take up any of those womanly chores, in the past I had always left the darning of our heavy woollen socks up to my father. I had felt only the smallest twinge of guilt whenever I watched in fascination as his large fingers delicately pulled the darning needle in and out of a frayed heel. When Rose first took up a batch of our socks to mend, he objected, saying he could do it himself, but she insisted. I believe it was so she would have something to do with her hands on those quiet evenings when there was no radio reception, and the rest of us sat reading.

40.

Alan and I never spoke about the dead buck. Whatever reason he had for not talking about it he kept to himself. But for the longest time, whenever we came across a herd of deer in the fields or meadows, I would see his eyes search the nearby hillsides, hoping against knowing—as I secretly did—that we had been mistaken, that the animal we saw in the back of that pickup truck was not our stag. But of course we both knew it was. I had my own reasons for keeping silent about it. Reasons of guilt, for I could not help but believe that I had condemned the animal in being so foolish as to brand it as ours.

Thank goodness for Dancer. That feisty little buckskin colt went a long way in helping us forget our sorrows. In the past months, I had watched with great pleasure as, beneath Alan's gentle-handed touch, the spindly-legged foal had grown to a high-stepping colt. After Alan moved out to the ranch, he spent every spare moment training his charge, and by the end of December, Dancer was following him around like a puppy dog.

Alan made no attempt to hide his joy in the colt, and in living at the ranch full-time. Every night I could hear his even breathing on the other side of the wall separating our bedrooms, as he slept the deep sleep of the contented. While I, for the longest time, slept fitfully, confused by the growing stirrings in my heart and body created by his nearness.

Even when we returned to school in the new year—arriving that first morning in time to overhear Mrs. Parsons gossiping with one of the students' mothers on the schoolhouse porch—Alan refused to allow it to dampen his spirit.

"Housekeeper! Ha!" the teacher said with no attempt to lower her voice as we approached the steps. "Who do they expect to believe that?"

I stopped short, squaring my shoulders, but Alan reached over and took my hand. Feeling the warmth of his hand seeping through our mittens, I let him lead me forward and up the steps.

On the porch, Mrs. Parsons reached out as we passed and swatted our hands apart.

"Just because your parents live in sin," she said, with a hiss in her voice that straightened my back even more, "does not mean I will allow you to bring it here to my school."

I opened my mouth, but before I could let loose with the response forming on my tongue, I felt Alan's restraint beside me. I clamped my mouth shut and followed him into the cloakroom.

Perhaps our silent defiance that day hastened the beginning of Mrs. Parsons' increased campaign against Alan's presence in her classroom, but at the moment, I felt only pride in our united refusal to be drawn into her mean-spiritedness.

At home, Rose and Alan's presence changed life on the ranch in so many ways. Our suddenly full house, and the sleeping arrangements, meant there were fewer opportunities to try and spark Grandfather's memory about the past. I would take every sliver of our time alone to question him—interrogate is likely the more proper term—about that unsettling last entry in his journal.

Sometimes I fear I pressed too hard. Too often, my rapid-fire questions only served to confuse him, and I would have to back off at signs of his growing agitation. But every now and then he would answer, giving me some tiny puzzle piece that I would scribble down to try and sort out later. Still, by the end of January, I knew nothing more about the missing part of his past than what I had learned from reading his journal.

February of 1940 brought my fifteenth birthday, and Alan's sixteenth. Sixteen! Sure and certain, as Father noted, no other boy had stayed in the Sorry school past the age of sixteen. Alan's continuing to show up only seemed to fuel Mrs. Parsons' growing fury, the flames of which had increased since he and his mother moved out to the ranch.

I had assumed that our teacher's friendship with the army officer, Sergeant Davenport—who continued to visit her from time to time—had erased any unrequited feelings she once held for my father. And perhaps it had, but, by the look on her face whenever she ran into us all together, it was clear that she detested seeing another woman at his side. In particular, Rose VanderMeer. And I have to admit that for a while, I took secret pleasure in our teacher's discomfort in our living arrangements.

Since Alan's and my birthdays fell so close together, we celebrated both on his. After stuffing ourselves on the cake Rose had baked, she brought out a large, brown-paper-wrapped package. I opened it while everyone at the table made guesses as to its contents. I think they all knew but were just playing the game, because when I lifted the lid of the cardboard box and pulled away the white tissue paper, I was the only one surprised by the contents. My hands flew to my mouth as I let out a squeal at the sight of her deerskin dress, the one that she had lent me to wear to the harvest dance last year.

"Really, Rose?" I whispered through my fingers. "I can keep it?"

She nodded with a smile.

I lifted the dress carefully from the tissue, raised it to my face to brush the softness of the deerskin against my cheek. Carefully replacing the garment in the box, I stood up and hurried around to the other side of the table to thank Rose, realizing as I leaned down to wrap my arms around her that it was the first time I had ever hugged her. The awkwardness of her turning to receive the hug, and my face ending up in the folds of hair at the nape of her neck, was lost to Grandfather's demanding from the head of the table, "What is it? What is it?"

Returning to my seat, I saw that he still looked confused even after Father's quiet explanation.

Alan's gift came next. Telling him to close his eyes, Father headed out to the enclosed porch. Brittle winter air seeped in through the open door while he rummaged around outside and then returned seconds later cradling a heavy, freshly oiled saddle in his arms. I instantly recognized the intricate leather carvings on Grandfather's roping saddle and glanced quickly at him. But he was puzzling over something on the cuff of his shirt sleeve and appeared unaware of what was happening in the moment.

Father set the saddle on a stool by the door. "Okay, Alan, you can look now," he said.

Alan opened his eyes. His sharp intake of breath caused Grandfather to startle in his seat.

"Happy birthday," Father said. "We believe you can use this."

Staring open mouthed at the saddle, Alan stood up, saying, "I, uh, I don't know what to say."

"Thank you," his mother prompted.

"Yeah, thanks," Alan said, running his hand over the seat. "It's just that ... well, it's too much ... I can't take this."

"Yes, you can. And you can thank Dad," Father said. "It was his. And he wants you to have it."

The gesture left me both surprised and saddened. Neither reaction came from wanting the saddle for myself, but from realizing what giving it away meant. Even though everyone was aware of the reality, this was an admission that Grandfather would not be roping or riding range—ever again.

Alan's reaction, too, was cause for concern. Although Dad and Rose treated his initial response as being taken aback by the generosity of the gift, when Alan turned to Grandfather and said, "Thank you, Mister Beale," I felt something twist in the pit of my stomach. Because to me, the crooked smile I saw flicker across his face was not one of bashful gratitude, but guilt.

At the head of the table, Grandfather cocked his ear, then leaned toward me and, in a voice loud enough for all to hear, asked, "Who's that fellow again?"

41.

If anyone had asked me later how it was that I didn't recognize Mrs. Parsons' final campaign against Alan right from the start, I could only have claimed that I'd grown complacent about the enemy. Surely I didn't consider her a real threat, a true enemy, in the sense that the word was being used at the time. The enemy was Germany: Adolf Hitler, the war.

If there was ever any talk of Father enlisting again, I was unaware of it. Grandfather's declining health would have at least one positive result. It would keep my father home. At school, Mrs. Parsons reminded us weekly of the brave young men who were signing up all over the country. Although she never spoke to Alan directly, it was clear her remarks were aimed at him, and even though he was too young to join up, I couldn't help but recall his declaration the night of the harvest dance.

As another winter turned into spring, Grandfather grew frailer. He slept later and later. Perhaps because he could no longer gauge the light. For a man whose life once was run by sun-up and sundown, he seemed to have lost track of time. Every now and then, if no one else was about, and if I gauged his mood would allow it, I would read to him from his journal even during the day, in hopes of eliciting some response. But more and more often, whenever I did, he would stare into the dimness of his world and say nothing, and I grew fearful that it was too late.

One evening, when I was reading from one of his favourite novels, I noticed Rose's hands slow at her needlework, her ears cocked to hear the latest instalment. After that, if she was in the parlour when I read a book to Grandfather, I found myself raising my voice in order for her to hear. And then one Sunday afternoon, while Rose was mixing up a cake batter, I went upstairs to fetch *Gulliver's Travels*. When I returned with the book I found Grandfather dozing in his chair in the parlour. Leaving him there, I went into the kitchen and sat down at the table. Without asking, I opened the book and started reading aloud as Rose worked. It soon became routine, with Alan or me taking turns reading to her from whatever novel we were studying. Sometimes she would stop us and ask about something that wasn't quite clear in the narrative. But mostly she would continue working, knitting, sewing or baking. And when each book ended she would always say, "That was a good story." And then ask what book was next.

As spring crocuses blossomed along the driveway, our lives at the ranch settled into a comfortable existence. With Alan sharing the morning and after-school chores, my workload was lighter. We spent hours studying together at the kitchen table. Later we joined everyone in the parlour to listen to the latest news reports from Europe, or to read. Just like a real family. And I foolishly let myself be lulled into believing that it would always be this way.

Perhaps that explains why, at school, I let my guard down. I should have seen it coming, but I was too wrapped up in life at home to be wary.

It started with small things.

I paid scant attention the first time our teacher complained that her new eraser had disappeared.

"Now, did someone borrow it and forget to return it?" she asked the class.

A few days later it was two of her pencils that went missing. "Now, they didn't just sprout wings and fly off," she said, searching her meticulously organized desktop.

When the following week her fountain pen went astray, she stood in front of her desk and crossed her arms. "Well, class, it appears we have a thief in the room," she said, her eyes scanning the faces, landing on none. "That gold fountain pen was very important to me. It belonged to my late husband. And I want it back. Today."

I glanced around the room, wondering who would dare touch her things. The entire class squirmed nervously at their desks, as if all were guilty. Except Alan. He sat motionless in his seat, his face a study in indifference.

At noon we sat out on the church steps, our new spot to eat lunch ever since Mr. Gleason took over the store.

"She wants to call me a thief," Alan said, before biting into his sandwich.

"Why do you say that?"

Alan shrugged and kept chewing, as if he had made a comment about the weather.

Even then I couldn't believe that Mrs. Parsons could be that calculating. "Oh, she likely just misplaced her pen," I said. "It'll turn up."

Alan lifted his shoulders again. "Maybe."

In the cloakroom after lunch, when he slid his lunch pail back into his cubbyhole, I heard a metallic clink as it hit against something in the back. Alan reached in, pulled out the fountain pen and held it up.

His eyebrows lifted in silent "I-told-you-so" resignation. A sudden gasp sounded behind us, and I swung around to find Enid wide-eyed at the sight of her mother's gold pen.

I snatched it from Alan's hand and, before he could object, I marched into the classroom. Mrs. Parsons looked up from her desk as I placed the lost pen in front of her. "You must have dropped this in the cloakroom," I announced, and without waiting for her reply, I turned away. Returning to my desk I kept my eyes fixed on Enid, daring her to challenge me. She took her seat without a word, a smile lifting the corners of her mouth.

At home, Alan and I kept the incident to ourselves. I felt certain that one of our classmates had planted the pen in his cubbyhole, someone's idea of a joke. By the following week I had forgotten it. And then money went missing.

On Friday, Mrs. Parsons announced that some dimes and twenty-five-cent pieces, which she kept in her top drawer, had disappeared.

"Now, this is serious, children. Someone in this classroom has gone into my desk and pilfered my silver."

I glanced around the room. Who could be doing this? It was no longer a childish prank. Across the aisle, Alan shook his head in disgust. And in the desk behind him, Enid, her face scarlet, was glaring at her mother. Enid?

After school, I whispered my suspicion to Alan. "It wasn't Enid," he insisted.

In the following days, I stuck close to the school during recess and lunch hours, hoping to catch sight of someone sneaking back into the empty classroom. For weeks nothing else went missing and I thought perhaps the whole theft incident was at an end.

During the month of May, Alan and I spent every spare moment studying for our final exams. If we aced them and were accelerated again, it would mean that we would have only one more year of high school before graduation. And we meant to ace them. We were so intent on it that we both paid little heed to anything at school. So one morning, near the end of the month, we were taken by surprise when, the moment we returned from recess, our teacher let out an ear-piercing shriek. While everyone froze where they stood, she jerked back from rummaging in the bottom drawer of her desk, holding her purse in her hands.

"My pocketbook is gone!" she cried. At the rising commotion in the room, she grabbed the yardstick and slammed it down on the desk with a loud crack. "Everyone take your seats, and sit with your hands folded in front of you," she ordered.

Everyone moved quickly while she stood smug-faced before us.

"Someone has stolen my pocketbook," Mrs. Parsons announced, her voice now alarmingly calm. "This is not just petty theft now. This is criminal. And I intend to find out who is responsible and report him to the authorities."

A hum of whispers rose from the class as everyone turned to look around. A second whack of the yardstick on the wooden desktop cracked through the air.

"Silence," Mrs. Parsons ordered. "Now, if you don't have my pocketbook, you have nothing to worry about. If you do, I will find you out. Here is what we are going to do. Everyone will leave the classroom and line up outside. Now, everyone rise and exit single file."

Once we were outdoors, she left the students in Enid's charge, instructing her daughter not to let anyone back into the school while she went next door to fetch Reverend Watts as a witness. Perplexed, I stood pondering what had just happened and wondering what was about to.

"She said *him*," Alan said beside me.

"Him?"

"She called the thief 'him.'"

Most of the students in our class were girls, and the three boys were grade-schoolers. In that moment, I realized that Alan was right. Our teacher meant to brand him as a thief.

I pushed my way past the other students and bolted up the porch steps. Enid had beaten me to it. I arrived at the back of our classroom just as she lifted the top of Alan's desk. She reached in and pulled something out. When she glanced up and saw me standing there, she lifted a finger to her lips, lowered the desktop and turned away, her mother's pocketbook in her hand. I backed up slowly and then ducked out of the school only moments before our teacher strode across the yard with the minister in tow.

It all happened so smoothly after that. Smug in her knowledge of exposing the classroom thief in front of Reverend Watts, who also happened to be a member of the school board, Mrs. Parsons asked us politely to return to our desks. While we shuffled inside amid murmurs of confusion, she stood at the back of the room with the minister. Once everyone was settled in their places, she ordered us to all raise our desktops on the count of three.

"One, two, three, desktops up," she called out in an almost cheery voice. Amid the creaking of hinges and questioning murmurs, she headed up the aisle. With only the slight pretense of checking the contents of the other desks, she made her way to Alan's. As if expecting her, he sat leaning back against his seat, his arms folded. After Mrs. Parsons reached his open desk, she stood waiting for the Reverend to catch up. When she finally lowered her gaze, the smirk fell from her face. After a moment's confusion, she reached down and searched through Alan's belongings. Finding nothing, she straightened, turned on her heel and continued up and down the aisles, barely glancing into the other desks.

"Well ... I ..." she stammered to the minister, who followed behind her with a perplexed expression on his face. "It appears that the thief has stashed my pocketbook somewhere else besides his desk as I suspected." Her eyes darted around the room as if searching for an answer. "Maybe we should check the cloakroom."

"Perhaps you should check your desk drawers, Mother," Enid called out.

"My pocketbook is not in my desk," her mother snapped. "It was taken from my purse."

"Maybe you should check anyway," Enid said. "You know how you have been misplacing things lately."

Watching Enid play cat-and-mouse with her trapped mother, I could have stood up and cheered for her.

Reverend Watts raised a questioning eyebrow and nodded toward Mrs. Parsons' desk. There was nothing else for her to do but comply. She squared her shoulders and strode up the aisle, the good minister on her heels.

She opened and closed the desk drawers with quick disdain, as if this was all a waste of time. But before she could slide shut the bottom drawer where her purse had been kept, the minister leaned forward and peered in.

"Isn't that a pocketbook?" he asked.

The blush rose crimson above Mrs. Parsons' lace collar. It seeped up her neck and into her face. Her eyes met Enid's across the room. And the look that passed between them was a stark acknowledgment that Enid was wise to her mother's folly.

"Oh ... why ... yes, yes it is," Mrs. Parsons said. She scooped it up and opened the other drawer to shove the pocketbook back inside her purse. "Thank you, Reverend," she said, slamming the drawer so forcefully it startled even her. "Sorry to have bothered you."

Enid's interference effectively ended the incidents of items going astray in our classroom, and Alan and I finished out the school year with our teacher doing little more than ignoring our presence once again. When our final provincial exam results came, our determination paid off. We had received top honours and were recommended for acceleration once again. Father delivered the results and stood over Mrs. Parsons' desk as she silently signed off on our report cards. We left school that June jubilant with the thought that we would have only one more year to spend with her. Still, all summer I found it hard to trust that she was through with her determination to break Alan's spirit. By then I had come to accept that that was her intent and secretly worried about what else she would throw at him when we returned to school in the fall.

In the end, it wasn't Mrs. Parsons who broke Alan. It was a horse.

42.

It was Enid Parsons who would inadvertently alert us. But by the time we realized the meaning of the alarm bells her comments set off, it was too late.

After the incident at school, Enid became, if not a friend, a tolerated acquaintance. During the rest of the school year, without being invited or asking for permission, she sometimes joined us on the church steps at lunch hour. Since our accelerated program meant that Alan and I had caught up to her grade level, we would all graduate the following year, and so our stilted conversations were mostly about our studies. At best, our newly established relationship was awkward. Still, Enid had earned my respect in the way she had stood up to her mother, and I felt I owed it to her to rethink my long-held judgment of her as a milksop.

Nothing was ever mentioned about her part in ending her mother's vindictive campaign against Alan, but his acceptance of her presence acknowledged his gratitude. Neither she nor we ever voiced the belief that Mrs. Parsons had planted all those missing items in order to implicate him. The only time I ever heard Enid say anything against her mother was one day in the middle of that summer, when I found her sitting on the steps of The Sorry Grocers.

Rumour had it that business had fallen off so badly since Mr. Gleason took over that the store was in danger of closing. Even though that might mean the loss of our post office, none of us at the ranch mourned the thought. I took great pleasure—and I am certain Father did as well—in retrieving our mail and then strolling out of the store without spending a dime, under the cold stare of Mr. Gleason.

On the morning I ran into Enid Parsons on the front steps of the store, he was still trying to make a go of it.

Enid looked so forlorn when I climbed out of our pickup truck that I felt compelled to sit down beside her while Father went inside to fetch the mail. She picked up her bottle of cherry soda and offered me a sip. When I declined, she set it back down and, without my asking, volunteered the information that she was just sitting there waiting for Sergeant Davenport to leave town.

"Don't you like him?" I asked.

"I can't stand the old goat. But Mother is so blinded by her silly crush on him that she can't see that he's not really serious about her."

Surprised by the anger in her voice I raised my eyebrows. "Then why does he visit so often?"

"Because the idiot likes to play cowboy," she said with a sneer. "Whenever he is in the area recruiting, he shows up at our place in his brand new jeans and ridiculous stetson hat, and Mom moons all over him, exclaiming how handsome he looks, when he looks like nothing more than a drugstore cowboy. She's even convinced one of the ranchers to lend him a horse so he can go out riding the range. So dumb."

Since the night Sergeant had shown up at the harvest dance last fall, I had not liked the man. Still, there was little I could say to Enid's complaints, other than to murmur agreement and nod sympathetically. Before long my father came outside with the mail in hand. Climbing into our truck, I felt a small twinge of guilt for leaving her looking so alone on the store steps. The twinge was long forgotten, however, before we reached home.

For me, that summer of 1940 was in many ways a summer of discovery. During those months, my feelings toward Alan grew deeper. It became harder to pretend that they stemmed from a sisterly affection, or a childish blood-brother friendship. Thoughts of him disturbed nearly every waking moment of each day. I often found my mind wandering, wanting to reach out and touch him as I watched him doing the most ordinary of things, or caught myself daydreaming about what his lips would feel like on mine. Startled by these giddy, girlish thoughts, I would push them aside. Living together in the same house meant that I must.

Still, while I kept my feelings in check, I let myself imagine a future in which we were together, doing what we both loved, ranching this land. If I had known then what was coming, how drastically things would change, perhaps, like most fifteen-year-old girls who find themselves falling in love for the first time, I would have acted on those feelings. Instead, I kept close rein on them and worked hard not to let anyone see how besotted I was. In all likelihood, I fooled no one.

Except perhaps Grandfather. Most of the time, he either seemed oblivious to Alan's presence, or was startled by it. Explaining that Alan was Rose's son often caused him such agitated confusion that after a while, we stopped reminding him.

From the beginning, though, he accepted Rose as easily as if she had always lived with us. Now and then he would mistakenly call her Fern, and even when he called her Rose, it wasn't always clear to which Rose he was speaking. She never corrected him.

My relationship with her was easy from the start. She treated me as an equal, as a woman, which I so wanted to believe I was becoming. Sometimes I would let myself consider the fantasy of her and Father becoming more than friends. I found myself imagining scenarios where Mother suddenly decided to return to us, showing up at the ranch house door only to have Rose answer it. In my lingering resentment toward Mother, I imagined the hurt look on her face as she realized she had been replaced. Which of course wasn't true. The sudden reappearance of their wedding photograph was silent testament to that.

Not long after Mother disappeared, when it became clear to me that she was not coming back, in a fit of childish hurt and anger, I had made it my business to get rid of the two photographs of her displayed in our home. I took down the graduation portrait of her wearing her white nursing cap and holding an armful of red roses. And I removed the wedding-day photograph from the sideboard in the parlour and stuck it in the drawer. It reappeared the following morning. For a long while, every time I squirrelled it away, the framed photo would be right back out, sitting on the sideboard the next day. In time Father gave up. For the last two years the photograph had remained out of sight in the sideboard drawer. Then, the week Rose and Alan came to live with us, one day the photograph was back on display. I never knew if it was Father, or Rose in her weekly cleaning, who dusted it off and put it back out, but it was a clear statement by whoever did that my parents' marriage was still valid. In my new-found maturity, I left it there, realizing it was not my place to dispute this silent declaration. Still, sometimes at night, I would find myself listening for footsteps between the rooms downstairs, a part of me afraid that I would hear them, another part disappointed that I never did.

As summer vacation wound down, I sensed an increased restlessness in Alan. By the time September arrived, I was certain he would do anything not to return to that schoolroom. I fully expected he would try to convince his mother, and my father, of the waste of it. But he said nothing. On the Tuesday following Labour Day weekend, once our morning chores were complete, he changed and climbed in behind the wheel of the pickup truck. His reluctance was obvious, though, and I couldn't blame him. I was certain that Mrs. Parsons would find some other way to get to him before she allowed "an Indian" to graduate from her classroom. I sat in the passenger seat watching his jaw work as he drove into Sorry for our first day of school. Which, as it turned out, would be Alan's last.

43.

Alan brought the ranch truck to a jerky stop in front of the schoolhouse. As we climbed out and slammed the doors, Sergeant Davenport crossed the road in front of us. Watching him hoof it over to the store, I understood exactly what Enid had meant when she called him a drugstore cowboy. Grandfather would have laughed out loud at the sight of the hokey western garb and dubbed the sergeant "all hat and no cattle."

Alan laughed, but there was no humour in his eyes. He shook his head and, with a resigned sigh, slung his book bag over his shoulder and headed for school. Walking beside him, I couldn't help glancing back and snorting as the sergeant clomped up the grocery-store steps, his crisp denim jeans tucked into spit-polished cowboy boots, his face shaded by his oversized hat.

Inside the school, Mrs. Parsons greeted our appearance in her usual fashion: by ignoring us. Still, all morning the expression on her ferret face made me nervous. I couldn't help thinking she was not done with Alan and wondering what other devious tricks she had up her sleeve.

When lunch hour arrived, Alan and I went outside and sat on the pickup tailgate to eat our sandwiches in the sunlight. Summer still had a warm hold on the countryside. In the schoolyard, dust clouds rose beneath our classmates' feet. Watching them play their childhood games, I was suddenly filled with resentment at being there. I believed Father and Alan's mother were dead wrong to insist we stay in school, where neither were we wanted, nor did we want to be. It was such a complete waste of time. Like Alan, I desired no future career, no other life, except ranching. I believed we would both be better off working at the ranch than sitting in a classroom under the cruel eyes of a teacher who did not teach. I was about to voice this old complaint when Alan cocked his head toward The Sorry Grocers.

"Store's closed," he said between sandwich bites.

I glanced over my shoulder, and sure enough, the store's window shades were down. The "closed" sign hung in the door. Unusual for the middle of a weekday.

"Maybe he's given up," I said, "hightailed it back to Quesnel."

"No such luck," Enid said, walking up to the truck. "He just went off with Sergeant Davenport this morning. To play cowboy."

She leaned against the tailgate. "Saps," she added and took a bite of her apple.

I smirked at the thought of the grocer dressed up in western garb like the sergeant, but Alan lifted an eyebrow. "Play cowboy?" he prompted.

"The silly fools have gone chasing after horses. Think they are going to rope themselves a wild stallion."

I sat up straight. After Enid had started joining us for lunch last term, Alan and I had sometimes discussed the animals we spotted from up on the ridge. I tried to recall what we had said in front of her.

"Enid," I asked warily, "you didn't tell the sergeant anything about the herd of wild horses, did you?"

She stepped back. "Of course not," she said, looking offended. "I don't even speak to the idiot. I stay in my room whenever he comes calling on Mom ..."

Her face fell. "Oh ... I ... uh," she faltered, and then her words came out in a frantic rush. "I think I mentioned it to her, though. One day this summer she was ranting on about you two always going up to the ridge to ... well, to do 'improper things.' So I told her the only thing you did up there was watch the wild animals in the valley. I could have mentioned the horses. I'm sorry. I didn't think. I didn't mean ..."

"It doesn't matter," Alan told her. "Everyone around here knows about those slicks."

"Oh God," I blurted, looking from her to Alan. "Maybe they're after the buckskin stallion."

Alan shrugged, unconcerned. "Gleason and the sergeant? Those two could never catch him."

"It's not just those two," Enid said. "A bunch of Mr. Gleason's friends from Quesnel went with them. They brought their own horses, and ..." She took a breath and turned to me. "You're right, Addie. I heard him talking with Mother this morning. They're going after a buckskin stallion."

Alan and I slid off the tailgate at the same time.

"Don't matter," he said as we gathered up our lunch remains. "He's too fast." He lifted the tailgate and closed it with a decisive slam. "That stallion's not going to let any man own him."

At that moment the school bell rang. We threw our lunch pails into the front of the truck and headed toward the schoolhouse with Enid.

While she and the other students shuffled inside, Alan and I kept going.

I won't say we raced up that hillside, but neither did we dawdle. I don't know what Alan expected to find once we reached the ridge, but I hoped we would see nothing more than deer, or horses, grazing on the autumn meadow grass below. We wasted no time or breath discussing it as we climbed. I clung to Alan's faith in the buckskin stallion's speed. I had heard him claim on more than one occasion that the horse was "so fast, he could run a hole in the wind." Still, ahead of me, Alan moved up those winding paths with the urgency of uncertainty.

The relentless afternoon sun beat down, and by the time we reached the clearing before the final climb to the summit, sweat was streaming from my forehead, trickling down my back and soaking my shirt.

I stopped to catch my breath, but Alan continued steadfastly upward. When I finally pulled myself onto the ridge, he was standing as still as the lone pine tree, staring down into the valley. With my lungs gasping for air, I joined him to scan the vast stretching meadows below. At first I saw nothing. Not a single sign of wildlife. No deer. No horses. Not one solitary range cow disturbed the peacefulness of the valley floor. And then Alan lifted his arm and pointed eastward. I followed his gaze across the fields to the lonely knoll rising above our family graveyard. I had to squint to make out the hulking forms on the narrow road. They were so out of place that it took a moment to register the unfamiliar pickup truck parked in front of the little graveyard's picket fence. And behind it, a horse trailer. As my mind raced to make sense of this, a sudden movement on the rise above the graveyard caught my eye. After that, everything happened so quickly.

On the crest of the knoll, lit by the harsh afternoon sunlight, the silhouetted form of a horse suddenly appeared. The buckskin stallion. He reared up on his powerful hind legs, his front hooves pawing the air, striking out at the men and horses surrounding him. Tangled lines, like black extensions of the stallion's mane, stretched out to anchor on the saddle horns of his merciless pursuers. There were so many of them. Like characters from some dark tragedy, they played out a silent pantomime of battle between men and beast. The wild horse was fierce in his struggle. He twisted and bucked, throwing his head in a futile attempt to shake loose the taut ropes around his neck. He reared up again, coming down hard, sidewinding so violently that one of the riders was ripped from his saddle and left lying in the dirt grasping for his lost line. The other horsemen held firm while the stallion strained with brutal determination, rearing, kicking and biting, in a savage battle of wills. It was impossible to judge who was winning.

Without warning, in one fluid movement, Alan leapt over the valley side of the ridge. Startled from my numb disbelief, I followed without hesitation, skidding and sliding down the broken shale surface of the almost vertical slope. There was no time to consider what we could do once we reached the valley, but anything was better than watching helplessly. Suddenly my feet went out from under me and I tumbled forward, feeling sharp edges ripping through my clothing, tearing at my skin. I caught a root and pulled myself up. Below, Alan disappeared into the trees.

Once I too entered the timber, I lost sight of the valley. There were no animal paths to follow in this unfamiliar terrain, so all I could do was continue downward. The slope was so steep that many times I lost my footing and had to grab onto tree trunks or branches to stop myself from careening forward. I could hear the sound of distant shouting and I raced in the direction of the voices. It seemed to take forever before I broke out onto a grassy slope above the valley.

I skidded to a stop, horror-struck at the scene playing out across the meadow.

In the clearing in front of the graveyard, the wild-eyed stallion was still struggling with his captors. Even from a distance, I could see the rope cuts in his flesh, the frothing sweat, pink with blood, spraying from his hide. Amid the confusion of dust clouds and flaying lines, a number of the men were now scrambling on the ground with lariats and whips.

I screamed useless threats, knowing that my voice was lost on the wind but unable to stop myself. Even if they could have heard my cursing demands that they get off of our property, my accusations of trespassing and calling them horse thieves, swearing to bring my father's wrath and the Mounties upon them, I doubt if anyone would have paid me any heed.

I threw myself downhill, stumbling once again and somersaulting forward. The world spun around me until I thudded to a stop against a stump. Forcing myself to my feet, I pushed on. By the time I reached the bottom, Alan was halfway across the meadows. On the far side, the raging stallion had been wrestled down to the road, his determined tormentors struggling to force him onto the horse trailer ramp. Lines were passed through the trailer's side rungs and the men on the ground were pulling hard on them, while those still on horseback tightened theirs.

As the stallion fought, bucking and kicking against the restraints, his whinnied cries echoed through the valley. Nearing the trailer, he reared up and one of his hooves slipped through the side bars. As he came back down, I saw with horror that his foreleg remained stuck between the iron rungs. The riders suddenly slackened their ropes. Sensing his freedom in the ease of tension, the horse twisted and rose up yet again. As his trapped hoof pulled free, his hind legs skidded on the ramp—and slipped out from under him. As if in slow motion, he tumbled backward off of the ramp. In that heart-stopping moment, with his legs fighting for foothold in the air, he threw his head around to see his fate rising up to meet him. His back hit the ground first. It seemed to take forever before his twisted body heaved over on its side, his arched neck coming to rest at an unnatural angle. And then the whole world went still. I stood frozen in my tracks as dust settled on the stallion's motionless body.

In the time it took me to scramble across the meadow, Alan had already reached the road. I don't know what passed between him and those men, but they rushed around gathering up what they could and those on horseback rode off. One of the men on foot picked up his hat, banged it against his leg and replaced it on his head. I recognized the stupid new stetson as he tried to approach the stallion. Alan blocked his way. He stood there until Sergeant Davenport backed off—his hands raised as if in surrender—and climbed into the pickup truck. By the time I arrived, everyone was leaving, taking their horses and trailer with them.

As I approached Alan warily, it occurred to me that he had been right in his declaration that the buckskin horse was never going to let any man own him.

Alan gently removed the remaining ropes from the stallion's neck, tossed them aside and knelt on the ground beside him. Believing that the wild horse was dead, I was startled to notice a tremulous rising and falling of his belly. I stepped closer and stood mute while Alan stroked the animal's neck and murmured words of comfort in his mother's native language.

A huge brown eye, white-edged with panic, rolled frantically about in its socket until it came to rest on Alan's face. I will always swear that in that very moment the stallion relaxed, and he remained calm while the light slowly went out of his glassed-over eye.

All my life, I will take comfort in knowing that the last thing the buckskin stallion saw before he took his final shuddering breath was Alan Baptiste kneeling over him, whispering his goodbye.

44.

We buried the buckskin stallion in the meadow beside the graveyard. Late that afternoon, I clung to the back of the tractor seat as Alan drove over the rutted dirt roads on the way to the east valley. Father, Grandfather and Rose followed behind us in the pickup truck.

Everyone, including my grandfather, helped dig the hole beside where the horse lay. We worked in unhurried silence, the only sounds the building of the north wind, our shovels pushing into the dirt and the occasional clink of a blade striking stone. When the hole was deep enough, Alan climbed onto the tractor and gently nudged the body into it, and we backfilled the grave. We placed no marker. In time the meadow grass would reclaim the smoothed and raked patch of dirt, leaving no trace of the animal's final resting place.

When we were done, we stood for a moment, sombre in our individual thoughts, the smell of freshly turned earth in the air. Beside me Alan said, "Now he belongs to the land." Somewhere above us, a hawk screeched his agreement.

Alan lifted his head skyward. He looked up at the circling bird, then back at the dirt mound. And, in a low voice, as if speaking to himself, he added, "Forever."

He was the first to turn away. Sensing his need to be alone, when he headed back to the tractor, I climbed onto the pickup tailgate and rode home in the evening twilight.

The next morning, after our chores were done, Alan remained out in the fields. I waited until it was obvious he wasn't coming before heading to school alone. Nothing was said all week when he kept himself busy, or stayed up in his room, to avoid the moment that Father would drive me into Sorry.

In the following days, Alan kept his grief to himself. Whenever he was not working, he retreated to his room in the loft. He no longer spent hours in the corrals training Dancer. The morning after we buried the stallion, he turned the leggy yearling out into the back field and left him to run free. But if Alan appeared anywhere within his sight, the colt would race over to the fence and run alongside it, nickering and whinnying for his attention.

I felt helpless in the face of my friend's solitary despair. Lying in the dark, every night I could hear him, restless and sleepless, rooting around in his room on the other side of the divider wall. I began to fear I would never see his smile again. Father and Rose left him to himself. Nothing was said the following Monday morning when once again he remained home. But as Monday turned to Tuesday, Tuesday to Wednesday, and he made no move to return to school, I couldn't help notice the fear growing in Rose's eyes. Still, she made no fuss.

All week long, I felt Alan's absence in the classroom. I hated Mrs. Parsons' expression of triumph each morning when I arrived without him. I would hate it even more the following week.

I couldn't blame Alan for not wanting to return to school, for not wanting to sit in that stupid desk under the smirking eyes of our teacher. But there was something deeper than sorrow in Alan's withdrawal, and without knowing why, like Rose, I too was frightened for him. So, Friday evening, when Father and I were alone in the barn pitching hay into the stalls, I took it upon myself to ask if he intended to talk to Alan about going back to school.

Father stabbed the pitchfork into the hay and leaned against it. "Well, Addie, it's really not my place anymore, is it?"

"What about the deal you made with him?"

He thought for a moment. "Now that he and Rose live here, that no longer holds, does it? I can hardly fire him or take away the colt, can I?" He took up the pitchfork again. "No," he mused. "If anything is to be said, it has to come from his mother." He pushed the fork deep into the hay. "We can only hope that given time, he will keep his word to her."

After breakfast Saturday morning, Father and Rose headed down to Williams Lake, he to attend to business at the stockyards in preparation for the fall cattle auction, and she to shop for groceries and ranch supplies. On the way home they planned to take the opportunity to stop in Wells to catch the new picture show, *Gone with the Wind,* playing at the cinema. For a long time I had looked forward with great anticipation to the coming film, which we had heard so much talk about on the Radiola. The hype about the movie, Father maintained, was for many a welcome relief from the depressing news reports of the war in Europe.

At any other time I would have jumped at Father's invitation to join them, but not surprisingly neither Grandfather nor Alan accepted, and I didn't have the heart to go either.

After Dad and Rose drove off, I stood at the kitchen window watching Alan saddle up the roan gelding in the corral. He led him through the gate, mounted and then rode out into the field, a halter and lead rope dallied around his saddle horn. Across the pasture, Dancer raised his head at the sound of Alan's whistle and then galloped over to join him. When he came alongside, Alan leaned over and looped the halter over the colt's muzzle. They trotted across the field, the roan's tail swishing away flies, Dancer's tail held high, matching the proud arch of his neck. I was relieved to see them together, glad that Alan was working with the yearling again. The colt had filled out over summer. With his hide turning a buttery cream, his mane darkening to a deep chocolate, he looked more and more like his sire. Watching them disappear, I remember thinking that the haughty colt could go a long way in healing the ache in Alan's heart.

It never occurred to me to worry as morning turned to afternoon, then afternoon to late day, and they still hadn't returned. It was only when I glanced out the window and spotted Alan and the roan coming through the field, with the colt nowhere in sight, that I felt a familiar lurch in the pit of my stomach. I left Grandfather sitting in his rocker on the porch and hurried across the yard to meet Alan by the barn.

Shading my eyes from the late-afternoon sun, I watched him ride up and dismount on the other side of the corral fence. "Where's Dancer?" I asked while he unlatched the gate.

In no great hurry, he led the roan in and tied the reins to the fence rung. Without meeting my eyes, he lifted a stirrup to loosen the saddle cinch and said, "Left him over in the east valley."

"Why?"

"It's where he's meant to be. He belongs to the land. Like his father."

I stood speechless, my heart thudding in my chest, while he pulled out the cinch strap, heaved the saddle off the roan's back and carried it into the tack room. I knew. Even then, I knew.

When he returned and began brushing down the roan, I dared to ask the question stuck in my throat. "And what about you? Where are you meant to be?"

His back to me, he answered so quickly that any hope—hope that what I feared most wasn't true—was swept away.

"I am meant to follow in *my* father's footsteps."

"You're going." It was not a question but a statement of fact.

Without turning around, he nodded.

"You can't," I cried. "You're only sixteen. You're too young to go to war."

"I'll be seventeen in a few months. The same age my father was when he joined up."

He untied the reins, led the gelding through the gate, removed his halter and turned him out into the field with a slap on the rump.

"Some soldier you'll make!" I lashed out, hurling the insult at his back. "You're such a lousy shot, you can't even hit the broad side of a barn."

He latched the gate and turned to face me. "Don't, Addie," he said. "Nastiness doesn't suit you."

"Don't go. Please," I pleaded. "Stay. Stay here with us. With me. The ranch is your home now, too. It's your mom's home. I thought … I thought that we … that you … wanted to stay here, to live here forever."

He laid his hand on my cheek. The first time he had ever touched me with the tenderness of anything more than friendship. His dark blue eyes, the tiny flecks of brown catching the afternoon light, held mine. "Nothing's forever," he said. "Except the land."

And beyond those midnight-blue irises, deep within the pools of darkness, I saw his steely determination. Determination to leave behind his mother's dreams and my father's expectations. And I saw his plea for understanding.

I wrenched my head from his palm. "I'll tell you what's forever. Dead! That's what's forever. And it won't matter how forever the land is if you die over there."

"If I am meant to, I'll come back." He placed his hands on my shoulders and pulled me close until his lips met mine. The warmth of their touch, a warmth I had imagined so many times, filled me with an overwhelming sorrow. I remained still, my arms at my sides, until he whispered, "Wish me luck, Addie."

If only I had. But instead of wishing him a tearful farewell, instead of returning his goodbye kiss, I reached up and slapped his face. "Quitter!" I said, and I turned on my heel and fled to the house.

Grandfather was still sitting in his rocking chair when I rushed up the steps to the front porch. I stood panting beside him, my frustration and fear turning into anger, as I watched Alan wearily cross the yard.

"What's all the commotion?" Grandfather asked.

"Alan's leaving," I cried. "Rose's boy. Alan. He's running off to join the army. Stop him, Granddad! He's too young. Tell him! Please! Tell him he can't go to war."

Confusion worked the muscles of Grandfather's face, his bushy brows knit together. And then he shuddered so violently that I instinctively reached out to steady him as he pushed himself up, muttering, "No. No. I can't do that."

He shuffled by me, clearly agitated, and I followed him inside. By the time he was settled in his parlour chair, Alan was up in the loft.

Hearing him rummaging around in his room, I went outside and hurried over to the workshop. I dug around in the storage closet, throwing objects aside until I found what I was searching for. Carelessly dumping Mother's things from the green tapestry travel bag, I hauled it back to the house and up to the loft. When I barged into Alan's room he was shoving clothes into an old canvas bag—the same bag he had brought with him the day he and his mother moved out to the ranch.

"Here," I said, tossing the tapestry bag to the floor by his feet. "Take this."

I didn't tell him that the oversized travel bag was once a part of a set that belonged to my mother. Or that she had taken the other with her the day she ran off. I didn't say that I thought it was fitting, that he of all people deserved the abandoned bag, because now he was just like her. A quitter, running away when things got tough.

I spun around and went downstairs and out onto the front porch to sit in the rocking chair. My back stiffened when I heard Alan's footsteps in the kitchen. I stared straight ahead, across the yard, at the fields and shadowed mountains in the distance, until he stood before me, the bulging travel bag in hand, blocking my view.

"Tell my mother—" He hesitated, searching for the right words. "Tell her I tried."

"Ha. You didn't try," I said without looking up. "You were just waiting for any excuse. You knew you were going. I saw it in your face on your birthday when Dad gave you the saddle."

"I tried, Addie."

When I didn't respond, he said, "Tell my mother I'm sorry, but I have to do this now. Tell her that I ask her not to stop me. That it's better if I come back because I'm meant to than because I am forced to ... Tell her I love her."

"Tell her yourself. I won't."

"Yes, you will. I know for her sake you will."

I slowly raised my head and met his gaze with unflinching stony silence.

And in that moment, I saw not the eyes of a sixteen-year-old boy, but the saddened eyes of a man, a man old beyond his years.

"If I …" He glanced away and then back. "If I don't come back," he said quietly, "tell her to look for me in the land."

When I remained stubbornly mute, he touched my cheek and said, "Goodbye, Addie."

If I could go back and relive that moment, if I had it to do over again, I would jump up and throw myself into his arms. I would give him a lover's goodbye kiss, wish him the luck he'd asked for, beg him to look after himself and to come home safe to us. I would tell him I love him.

As it was, before long, and for months later, years later even, I would chastise myself for the icy-cold way I let him take his leave.

I remained staunch in my anger, my arms crossed firmly over my beating chest, as he walked down the steps and across the yard, Mother's green tapestry bag banging against his leg. In the dappled light along our driveway, his hazy form grew smaller and smaller, until it shrank to nothing more than a dark spot on the road and then disappeared.

I sat out on the porch until the setting sun cast a golden glow across the fields and marshes, lighting up the landscape in its orange reflection. And then, in the evening gloaming, I rose and went inside to cook Grandfather's supper.

45.

Alan was right, of course. I told his mother. I repeated his words as I remembered them spoken, keeping the unspoken to myself.

In the hours between his leaving and Rose and Father's return, I had plenty of time to consider what had happened, and how best to relay it. By the time they arrived home just before midnight, I had come to the conclusion that, for Rose VanderMeer, nothing less than the plain truth would do.

Her reaction was both expected and unexpected. Wide-eyed at my blunt announcement that Alan was gone, she sank into a kitchen chair. When I hesitated, she gestured for me to continue, and then listened without interruption until I had no more to say. She gave the smallest of nods, lowered her head and sat staring at her hands. Father stood leaning against the counter, his jacket folded over his arm, waiting for her response. For the longest time, the kitchen clock ticked off the minutes, seeming to grow louder with every stroke, so that I wondered why I had never noticed it was so loud before. After a while, Father straightened up. "I'll go look for him," he said, pulling on his jacket. "If he didn't thumb a ride, he might still be walking."

I jumped up. "I'll come with you."

Rose raised her head. "No. There's no use in anyone going after him," she said. "We didn't see him on the way home. There's no reason we would see him going the other way."

"We weren't looking," Father said.

"I would have noticed my son." She smiled sadly at him. "No. Either he caught a ride, or he meant not to be seen. Either way, he has made a choice, a choice I have to accept."

I opened my mouth to protest, but she turned her attention to me and the words died on my lips.

"I heard the hopelessness of trying to change his mind in your voice, Addie."

"I'm sorry. That wasn't my intention." I swallowed, then added, "But it's true."

"First thing tomorrow," Father offered, "I'll go into Sorry to use Reverend Watts's phone. I still have some contacts in the army. Alan's too young…"

Rose shook her head before he could finish. "He's gone searching for the man he wants to be. When he finds that man, he'll come home."

"It's Mrs. Parsons' fault, she—" I blurted.

"No. That teacher woman is not stronger than Alan," she said. "If anyone is to blame, it's me. My son has the body, the heart, of a man. I tried to keep him a boy for too long. Now I have to do as he asks. I have to trust him."

Father sat down at the table across from her, took her hands in his and held her eyes. "As you say, Rose, he appears to be a man. But he's not yet seventeen. I saw boys younger than that die on the battlefields of Europe not so long ago. Recruitment officers have been known to look the other way regarding age. What will you do if he enlists—if he goes to war?"

"Pray."

I have no doubt she did just that in the privacy of her room that night, and certainly she did in church the following morning.

When they first came to live at the ranch, at Rose's request, we sometimes went to church on Sundays. Our attendance was sporadic at best but more often than in the past. I think it was her way of standing up to the gossip about her position at the ranch. After a while, the only one who cast sideways looks at us whenever we slipped into our pew was Mrs. Parsons.

I remember none of Reverend Watts's sermon the morning after Alan left. But I do recall how I already missed my friend with an aching sadness. With the smell of furniture wax and musty old hymn books heavy in the chapel air, I sat between Father and Grandfather, trying hard to replace my sorrow with anger—anger at Mrs. Parsons, who sat two pews ahead with Enid; anger at the years of cruelty she made Alan suffer. And anger at him for running off when we were so close to being done with her.

Following the service, Reverend Watts stood out on the church porch greeting each of his parishioners as they left. While we waited our turn, Grandfather squinted at the notes posted on the bulletin board as if he could see them.

When Mr. Gleason had taken over The Sorry Grocers, the community message board was removed from the store and relocated to the church. It had remained there on the sheltered porch wall ever since.

Fingering the notices, Grandfather said, "Read some of these to me, boy."

It was an old request. Every time we went to church now he would have me read out messages tacked to the corkboard. With the lack of the

Sorry Times, I suppose it was his way of keeping up with the pulse of our community. He loved hearing what was for sale, or who was hiring help during branding or haying season. Most often the notices were just plain boring, and he would lament how he missed the old newspaper and its creator, Dirk VanderMeer. But that Sunday he made no comment as I scanned the board and read out those I thought he might find interesting.

While Grandfather chuckled over the Barkers' colorful description of free puppies to give away, "half shepherd—and half sneaky neighbour's dog," I heard Reverend Watts greet Rose behind us. I turned just as she took his hand.

"Please pray for my son, Reverend," she said, her voice strong and brave in the asking.

"Why, what's the trouble, Rose?" he asked, enfolding her hand in both of his. And then, while others stood waiting, he listened to her explain as if he had all the time in the world.

Rose made her plea for prayers for her prodigal son with no trace of self-pity or disappointment, her despair second to the fact of his leaving to join the army. While she spoke, our neighbours, Mr. Miller and his wife, moved closer. Mrs. Miller placed a hand on Rose's arm, but it was her husband who spoke up.

"Don't worry, Rose," he said. "Our boy, Ralphie, joined up last September, and he still ain't seen any fighting. He sailed for Britain with the First Canadian Infantry Division in January. We just got a letter from him last week, and he says he and his troop mates are still cooling their heels in England. Says they are all chafing at the bit to join the fray over in Europe, but it's only our flyboys who are in the thick of it. None of the Canadian soldiers have been deployed yet." He put his arm around his wife. "With any luck, this whole thing'll be over before our boys see any action."

"Not bloody likely," Grandfather murmured beside me. I glanced at Rose but felt certain his voice was low enough that she didn't hear.

While the women of the congregation pressed closer, clucking like hens around her, and the men stood nearby assuring themselves that once again the Huns would be defeated and it would surely all be over before too long, Mrs. Parsons strode across the porch. Her back ramrod straight, she made her way around the huddled group.

I watched Rose, who remained unflinching under the teacher's scorching glare, turn her concern to comforting the Millers, and I couldn't help but admire her backbone. Behind her, children played in the churchyard, their pounding feet forcing the sweet smell of grass and autumn dust into the warm air. My gaze travelled beyond them, beyond the schoolhouse and our little town of Sorry, and up to the foothills and mountains that Alan loved so much, and I felt myself smile for the first time since the day before. I saw then how beautiful this late-summer day was. Yesterday had been the same, but I had paid no attention.

Forever after, whenever I thought of the day Alan left us, I would remember it as a day full of sunlight and warmth. But it was really the day after I would envision. The day I saw Rose accepting Alan's decision with dignity and grace—and realized I could do no less. For it was not only me and my dreams that he had left behind. It was his mother, and her love— my father, and his expectations. It was Mrs. Parsons' prejudice, a prejudice that nothing would ever change. And it was his dead father's footsteps he intended to follow. I could only hope that whatever he encountered on his journeys would not lead him to the same fate.

For the longest time I held close to the hope that the ranchers were right, that the war would end before Alan was put in harm's way. But all that month and into the next, night after night, as the Radiola crackled with BBC news reports of German bombs raining down on London, that hope grew fainter and fainter.

46.

I felt Alan's absence every waking moment. I carried it with me everywhere where I went. I felt it when I lay sleepless at night and couldn't hear him breathing in the next room. I felt it in his empty chair in the parlour, at the kitchen table. I felt it whenever I was working outside and glanced up to see deer grazing nearby. I felt it on those afternoons when I skipped school to climb up to the ridge alone. And I felt it whenever I was lucky enough to spot Dancer grazing among the wild horses in the valley below.

Although I missed my friend sitting in his desk next to me at school, I was glad he had escaped that sorry place. And like him, I saw no purpose in being there. I brooded about it, until I came to the conclusion that my father was wrong in his unshakable belief that I should finish out the year. "Hardly anyone in Sorry has ever stayed in school as long as I have," I insisted. "There's nothing unusual about leaving at my age."

"And you're content to be 'usual'?" Father asked.

But he did not insist, as I expected he would, when one morning at breakfast, I finally dug my heels in and refused to go.

He looked over the rim of his coffee mug at my announcement. "I won't force you," he said sitting back. "You're old enough to make your own choices, I suppose." He set his mug down. After a moment's thought, he said, "I know where your heart is Addie. It's with the ranch, and I expect it always will be." He smiled." I'm aware that your intention is to make your life here. And that's all well and good. In truth, I'm glad. But there's a bigger world out there. And you never know what life will bring. I fear that if you choose to quit school now, if you close that door, it will not be easy to reopen."

The protest rose in my throat, but he held up his hand. "I only ask that you give this decision a great deal of consideration. Before you choose, think about how you might feel years from now—perhaps for the rest of your life—if you allow someone else to be the deciding factor in that choice. The truth is, whether or not you graduate in the spring will probably have little effect, if any, on the course of your life. But what will have an effect is how you will look back upon all this later. How you will feel knowing that, after all you and Alan went through in that classroom, you handed Mrs. Parsons this victory just when you were so close to the finish line."

It was the longest, and most wordy, bit of advice Father had ever pressed on me. It worked. After the consideration that he asked of me, I steeled myself to remain in school for the duration. In the end, the decision had more to do with pleasing him, and with not being a quitter, than with my teacher.

Through his army contact, Father found out that Alan had indeed enlisted. He'd ended up on Vancouver Island with the British Columbia Dragoons and was in basic training near Victoria. We took comfort in the contact's assurance that in his opinion, it was unlikely Alan's unit would be deployed anytime soon. If ever. "Unlike the last war, this one is being waged in the air and at sea," he wrote Father. "The foot soldier will play a smaller role."

There was comfort, too, in knowing where he was. But even though we were now aware of his location, Rose asked that we not write to him until Alan himself disclosed his whereabouts. It took constant self-control to keep my promise to wait.

It also took a great deal of talking to myself during those months to keep Christian thoughts in my head at church, and to ignore the desire to slap the smug grin off of Mrs. Parsons' face every time someone asked after Alan. At school, I wanted to shove the letter about his enlistment under her nose. But Enid said that her mother would refuse to admit that Alan had joined up, even if he came marching down the road in his uniform and saluted her.

Every night, those of us left at the ranch sat around the Radiola listening for news dispatches from overseas. Poland, Denmark, Norway, Holland, Belgium, Austria and France had fallen beneath the boots of the Third Reich.

Despite the war in Europe, life at home carried on much the same. I threw myself into my studies. After making the decision to finish out the final year, now more than ever I wanted not just to graduate, but to graduate with top honours. I began to take great pleasure in imagining Mrs. Parsons' face as she was forced to hand me a sheepskin diploma.

All winter during lunch hour, Enid and I would put our heads together to quiz each other as we tromped up and down the snow-covered road, blowing into our mittens. Sometimes I would catch her mother scowling at the two of us from the classroom window. Whenever I alerted Enid, she steadfastly ignored her with a dismissive shrug, and my admiration for her grew.

At home, under Rose's care, Grandfather regained a little of the weight he'd lost. I wanted to believe that he was getting better, but there is no getting better from growing old. More often now he would speak to Rose as if she were someone else. Sometimes it was my mother. Sometimes it was the Rose of his journals. But whether he called her Fern or was speaking to the wrong Rose, she never corrected him.

One afternoon, a week before Christmas, while they were kneading bread dough at the counter, he asked, "What happened to your boy, Rose?"

"Gone off to join the army," she replied.

"No. No. The little one, the toddler. The boy I saw on your hip in Barkerville." His hands stopped working the dough, and as if speaking to himself he said, "No. That's not right. Not Barkerville. Down in Williams Lake, it was." Frowning, he turned toward her. "Is he … is he …"

Rose touched his arm. "It's all right, Mr. Chance. He's all grown up now."

But he seemed not to hear. Shaking his head, he muttered something incoherent—as he tended to do lately when he lost track of his line of thinking—and left the room.

I stood in the archway as he sat down in his chair in the parlour, took up his pipe from the side table and searched for his tobacco pouch with trembling fingers. Rose had finally convinced him that he didn't have to go outside onto the porch to enjoy a smoke.

After he managed to tamp a wad down in the pipe bowl, he struck a match and attempted to light it, but the match burned down before he had drawn the flame in. I went over, lit another and held it steady for him. The tobacco caught a glow, and his mouth filled with smoke, which he blew out in a thin stream while he sank back into his chair.

I'll never know what it was about that moment that made me think of it. Maybe it was his mention of Barkerville that brought his journal to mind. But it suddenly occurred to me that he must have kept more than that single one. Rather than ask him, rather than risk further confusion at a time when I could see his thoughts were already muddled, I went into his bedroom, closed the door and undid the leather straps on the trunk at the end of his bed.

When I lifted the heavy lid, the musty smell wafting from the trunk seemed stronger than I recalled. Inside, the most recent record books, those I'd worked on with Grandfather, were still piled in the right-hand corner where I'd left them. I ignored those and concentrated on the other books stacked in the trunk. I decided to go at the many piles methodically. Working from right to left, I removed the books one by one, flipping them open as I took them out and restacked them on the floor.

Granddad was nothing if not organized, and as expected, I found myself going backward in time in chronologic order. When I had exhausted one pile, I replaced it in the trunk and I attacked the next. After a while I began to notice that the further back in time the record books went, the more detailed his entries. And I became even more convinced that the key to unlocking Grandfather's missing memory was to be found somewhere in these years of old books.

My eyes grew blurry scanning pages until I finally came to an entry about Barkerville. Excited, I sat back to read Grandfather's detailed description of the great fire, which had all but levelled the town, followed by how afterward, at the age of nineteen, he had pre-empted the land for this ranch. It was as if I had found treasure. A wealth of words to read to him.

I don't know how long I sat there immersed in his past, but before I knew it, the light in the room had dimmed and Rose was calling us to supper.

Reluctantly, I closed the book and gathered up the others from the floor. Replacing them in the trunk, I noticed a canvas volume at the very bottom of the only pile I had yet to look through. Like Grandfather's boyhood journal, this book stood out because it was so unlike the ranch record books. If it followed the order in which Grandfather had arranged all the others, it could well be the very one after his leather-bound journal.

I pulled out the battered and stained canvas-covered book, intending to look through it after dinner. Seeing something sticking out from it, I opened the book to find a folded paper pressed between its pages. The brown-edged notice was old, but the printed words beneath the Royal Coat of Arms remained bold and clear.

BUTE INLET MASSACRE!
REWARD OF $250
WILL BE PAID BY GOVERNEMNT, UPON AND for the apprehension and conviction of every Indian or other person concerned as principal or accessory before the fact, to the murder of any of the fourteen Europeans, who were cut off by Indians, on or about the twenty-ninth and thirtieth days of April now last past, in the Valley of the Homathco River, at Bute Inlet.

Dated Government House, New Westminster, 17th Day May 1864
By His Excellency's Command
ARTHUR N. BIRCH   Colonial Secretary.
GOD SAVE THE QUEEN

I dropped back down onto my heels and turned to the beginning of the book.

47.

June 29, 1864, Fort Benshee, Chilcootan Territory

Much has happened since meeting the Irishman Mr. Patrick Nolan. On the morning after my first meal with him I fell ill. I am not blaming his cooking but after my meagre diet of rabbit or a few mouthfuls of rice, filling my stomach with rich food played havoc with my body. During the night I became feverish. Dysentery and vomiting kept me incapacitated from the moment I awoke.

Mr. Nolan has taken pity on me and changed his travel plans. His kindness I can never repay. If not for him I may well have perished in this unforgiving land. Seeing my misery, he loaded me on to his horse and led us back to one of his trapline cabins, where he nursed me in my delirium for uncounted days. His cabin lies very near the Chilcootans' fishing grounds and so he boarded up windows and barricaded the door each night. But for all the time we were there we were left to ourselves.

When I was well enough to travel, the Irishman decided that instead of heading to Alexandria on the Fraser River as planned he would take me to nearby Benshee Lake, where a friend of his, a Mr. William Manning, owns a ranch. Mr. Manning has worked the land for years alongside his Chilcootan wife and is well regarded by the local Indians. So Mr. Nolan believed it to be a safe place to leave me while I healed.

He also believed that William Manning would know the truth about how things stand with the Natives.

If the Irishman doubted that the uprising was as serious as he has been told, his mind was changed before we ever reached his friend's ranch. Making our way across a wide meadow, we drew to a standstill at the sight of a large party of men on horseback riding toward us. A serious-looking bunch they were. The leader introduced himself as Captain William Cox. He is the law commissioner from Richfield and has been charged with hunting down the Chilcootans responsible for the murders at Bute Inlet. He informed us we should go no further. He then gave us the grave news that Mr. Manning has been slain and his house burned to the ground. Cox and his contingent of volunteers— made up mostly of hardened-looking miners from the goldfields—had just finished burying the rancher's remains. Worse yet, he told us that a few days ago, one of Waddington's pack trains out of Bella Coola was attacked. They were on the way to Manning's ranch with provisions and materials for that portion of the roadwork when they were ambushed. Five more were dead at the hands of the same renegade Chilcootans, according to Cox.

The captain handed Mr. Nolan a folded paper. I looked over his shoulder as he read the notice offering a two-hundred-and-fifty-dollar reward for the apprehension of each Indian involved in the massacre of fourteen Europeans.

—You best come along with us, said Captain Cox. Those savages may still be nearby. They could be watching us from the trees at this very moment.

We joined them then and there. For days now we have remained encamped in their hastily erected fort at Benshee Lake awaiting the arrival of the new governor of the colonies, who is on his way up from Bute Inlet with another party of lawmen.

Tonight I am grateful to Captain Cox, who caught me watching with envy whilst he sat writing by the firelight and generously tossed me this canvas notebook. Now while the others sit around the campfire spinning tales about the mayhem in these territories I have something to occupy me besides gazing at the spindly pole stockade surrounding us and wondering how strong it would be against an attack.

The talk these nights has been wild. The opinions among the men as to the reason for the native uprising are many and varied. Most maintain that the Chilcootans murdered the road crew and pack train as well as the rancher, Mr. Manning, simply for plunder. Others opine that they are all bloodthirsty savages who kill just for the sport of it. The call to hang every living Indian wherever they are found is not uncommon. A few dissenters say there must be a fair trial. Then they can string them up. I listen without adding comment.

Mr. Nolan has no trouble voicing his opinion.

—I don't know how British law can be applied to a civilization that has lived with their own ways and customs for centuries, he said.

They may be barbaric in our eyes but our ways may seem just as barbaric to them.

—Are you condoning murder? one of the miners challenged him.

—No. Just stating that wanting to stop the white man's invasion of their territories may have been motive enough. We're the newcomers here. There's something to be said about our European arrogance of believing it's our God-given right to go wherever and however we please.

I could have spoken out then about the things I have witnessed. I could have told them about the careless threats which I heard with my own ears. Threats of bringing a new plague of smallpox to the people of the Chilcootan. I could have spoken up about hungry women and children being denied food. But even though I agree in part with Mr. Nolan's opinion, I ignore my conscience and keep my silence. The image of Pa's cruel death is too raw.

July 6

There is great celebration in our camp tonight. Frederick Seymour, the new governor of the Colony of British Columbia, has arrived with the chief magistrate, Chartres Brew, and his posse of volunteer lawmen. The reinforcements have buoyed spirits that were running low.

Mr. Nolan is well acquainted with Magistrate Brew, who is also an Irishman. He says the peacekeeper is a fair man who won't allow vigilantes to run amuck with vengeance or for reward. Mr. Nolan, for one, is glad that the magistrate is here to balance Captain Cox, who he fears is more likely to shoot first and question later.

Among the arriving party is one Mr. William Buckley from the Bute Inlet road crew! I remember the man only vaguely but he is one of three who I have now learned also survived the massacre! He shows no recognition of me. But that is not unusual. I am certain that given the weight I have lost in these past months along with the length of my hair and sun-darkened skin, I no longer look the boy I was then. Neither am I he.

I was glad to hear of other survivors but said nothing of my escape. It would not do to speak up now when I have held my counsel so long. It would only arouse suspicion as to my motives. Which I am not certain of myself.

July 7

Captain Cox and his crew rode out again this morning while Mr. Brew and his men remain in camp resting from their long journey. Mr. Nolan has also decided to stay at the fort for the time being.

—It's just as safe here with all these lawmen as in New Westminster, says he.

I suspect that he delays his journey for me. And I am glad of it. Neither of us is interested in any reward money, and we both remain in camp rather than accompany Cox's party on their Indian hunt, as he calls it. ·

After seeing the state of camp supplies, Mr. Brew has sent a party back to Bella Coola at the coast for provisions.

July 12

During the nights we are aware that we are not alone. The distant sounds of barking dogs carry to the fort letting us know that Natives are camped nearby. Some of their women have even approached our camp. Out of curiosity or to barter. Perhaps even to spy on us. I do some spying of my own when they show up. Staying hidden, I watch from afar. I am not certain what I would do if I saw Rose among them. But I can't help wonder what became of her. Is she travelling with her brother Willum? Are they with Klatsassin and his war party? But I recognize none of the faces of those who bring fish to trade for sugar.

Magistrate Brew watches them as well. He spoke to one through an interpreter, telling her that our Great White Chief Governor Seymour does not wish to go to war with all Chilcootans. That the King George Men only wish to find those involved in the white men's murders. He asked her to take back a message to Chief Alexis of this territory. He said he knows that the chief and his people are not involved with the renegades. Promising that no harm will come to them if Chief Alexis helps to bring in the guilty ones, he has invited him to come to the fort and meet with Governor Seymour.

Yesterday he received a reply. Chief Alexis will come when he is ready. So far there is no sign of him.

July 18

The supplies from Bella Coola have not yet arrived and provisions are getting low. My stomach is used to going without but Brew's men are not, and tempers are rising. Not just from lack of food but from lack of action. There is little in this fort to keep the men occupied and the heat, the blackflies and the mosquitoes drive them crazy. Many are ready to pack it up and head back to the goldfields if they are not put to use soon.

July 20

Cox's search party has returned to the fort with bad news. Donald McLean, their second-in-command, has been shot and killed! The expert tracker was greatly respected by the men and his death has disheartened all. Cox's expedition caught only distant sightings of the elusive warriors and they have brought back no captives.

Cox and Brew parlayed with Governor Seymour over the next plan of action. Both leaders argued for a plan to retreat until winter sets in and then return when the Indians' food is in short supply. But the governor is having none of it. He insists that the lawmen remain in the territory until the rascals are captured and peace and order are restored to the area. There is much debate over a plan to cut off the access to the Chilcootans' fishing grounds and how to accomplish that.

While the arguments heated up I caught a movement on the crest of the hill above camp. Suddenly there were a dozen or so riders on horseback looking down on us. I grabbed Mr. Nolan's sleeve and he followed my gaze.

—Chief Alexis! he said, loud enough to alert the others.

All eyes turned to look. Nervous fidgeting and whispered curses broke out among the men as three of the riders broke away from the group. With a white cloth flapping from the end of a long stick they trotted down the hill. The one called Chief Alexis stayed behind on his pinto pony watching the envoy approach the fort. When it was clear that their peace sign had been accepted, the chief dug his heels into the horse's flanks and with his musket held over his head galloped at full speed into our camp. The rest followed suit but remained on their mounts as their chief leapt from his before it had come to a standstill.

I scanned the faces of his party and felt relieved when I recognized none of the Chilcootans from Bute Inlet.

Even from a distance Chief Alexis was a sight to see. Dressed in leather leggings and a long blue military jacket opened to reveal a glistening torso, he strode up to the three leaders and asked for the Great White Chief. When Seymour stepped forward, Chief Alexis grabbed his hand and shook it heartily. As to what followed I can only rely on the word of a miner who interpreted their words because to my surprise, Chief Alexis and Seymour conversed in French!

While they spoke the chief grew agitated. According to the whispered words of the miner beside me, Seymour asked him how it is that Chief Alexis allowed white men to be murdered in his territory. Alexis replied that if Klatsassin has made war it is not his business. He said that maybe the white men brought it on themselves.

I understand nothing of the French language but I could read the hostility brewing between them. The talk went on for some time before the chief conceded that Klatsassin and his followers were some bad savages who did not know God.

In the end the chief agreed to stay and share food. Tonight more of his followers have shown up and concern grows over their growing numbers and our diminishing food supplies.

July 21

The pack train from Bella Coola has arrived with provisions. And just in the nick of time. Chief Alexis and his people remain encamped at the fort. The chief is considering the request to encourage Klatsassin to come in for peace talks. For the moment he has agreed to guarantee safe passage eastward for Governor Seymour, who will leave for Alexandria soon. Captain Cox and Brew will remain and formulate a plan for the further pursuit of Klatsassin and his followers.

July 24

Governor Seymour left the fort this morning. As did Patrick Nolan. I bid a sad farewell to my companion and protector. He has decided to accompany the governor and his party to New Westminster after all. I feel well enough now to travel myself, but I have lately become acquainted with a miner from Cox's party who is headed back to the goldfields as soon as this is all over. The grizzly old prospector—a Mr. Willoughby Davis—has filled my head full of stories of his claim on Williams Creek near Barkerville. He says he could use an honest young man such as myself to work it with him. His offer to share in his diggings is an opportunity I cannot turn down. So I will wait and go with him and Cox's men when they move out.

August 8

Not much has happened in these last days. I was beginning to regret my decision not to leave with Mr. Nolan. Finally this morning Brew's party rode out, heading southwest toward the Chilcootan fishing grounds at Tatla Lake. The word is tomorrow we will be on the move as well.

August 9

We left the less-than-ideal safety of Fort Benshee with Cox and his men today. Chief Alexis and a number of his party are accompanying us to Fort Chilcootan. The chief has agreed to speak with Klatsassin if the forward search party encounters him along the way. He will try to persuade the war chief to turn himself and his warriors over to the lawmen. He believes Klatsassin is ready to talk peace because he and his followers are tired of running and hiding on their own land.

August 10

A lone Chilcootan approached our camp tonight with a message for Captain Cox. Klatsassin has sent word that he no longer wishes to make war with the white man. If the King George Men leave the area—if they turn northward—they will remain unharmed. But if they continue southwest he threatens that he and his warriors will be forced to attack … Cox did not hesitate in his response. His eyes remained hard on the messenger while his words were directed to the interpreter.

—Tell your chief that I do not wish to make war either. But we will not turn back. Magistrate Brew and his men are now coming from the west and they mean to kill every Chilcootan man, woman and child. You tell your chief that if he wishes to talk peace for his people he must meet with me at Fort Chilcootan in two days.

August 12, Fort Chilcootan

The war chief wants to talk peace! This morning his messenger appeared in our camp at this abandoned fort. Klatsassin sent a twenty-dollar gold piece with the messenger as a gift for our chief. The sight of the gold coin startled me as it reminds me of the one Pa carried in his pocket as his good luck charm. But I have to push that dark thought aside and concentrate on what is transpiring between Cox and the messenger. From what I understand through the messenger's gestures and his few English words, Klatsassin wants to know what will become of him and his men if they come to talk peace. Cox guarantees that they will suffer no harm if they come peacefully. He promises that their families will no longer be pursued or harmed in any way by the King George men.

The messenger took some time before nodding that he understood. He held up the gold piece. Cox accepted, giving the man a pouch of tobacco to take back to Klatsassin in an exchange of good faith.

August 14

After two days of waiting for the war chief's response, Klatsassin's own son came to the fort tonight. With Willum as his interpreter! I hid away in my tent to watch through a small opening as Rose's brother asked for confirmation of Cox's promise that the warriors' families—all their women and children—would remain unharmed. He held Captain Cox's gaze as the leader assured him that this was true. Willum turned and spoke quietly with Klatsassin's son. Then he turned back to Captain Cox.

—Our people are hungry. Our fishing grounds are meagre. Our animals few. And yet more and more of you come. We cannot fight so many. Our chief accepts your offer of peace for the lives of our families. When the sun has risen tomorrow morning, Chief Klatsassin and those of us who are still with him will come to this place to speak with your Great Chief.

Tonight, as the camp waits for the morning, I cannot find sleep.

I spoke with the prospector Mr. Davis and he has agreed that if indeed the Chilcootans do show up tomorrow to surrender, then it is time to leave and return to the goldfields. It will be none too soon for me.

August 15

Klatsassin, like the entire party of men who walked into our camp with him early this morning, is a far cry from the fierce Chilcootan I last saw at Bute Inlet three and a half months ago.

Willum's claim that their people are starving is no exaggeration. The state of their women and children who are gathered on the grass hillsides outside our camp is no better.

As the warriors made their uncowed approach to the waiting Captain Cox, I grabbed my haversack and bedroll and slunk away to where Mr. Willoughby Davis was saddling up his horse. He is as anxious to get back to his diggings as I am to be away from this place. But I could not resist one last glance backward.

At the sight of the delegation sitting cross-legged on the ground before Mr. Cox's tent, I turned away quickly. But not before Willum's eyes locked on mine. I could still see the challenge in them as I pulled myself up on Mr. Davis's horse and settled behind the little man. He clicked his tongue and the animal stepped lazily forward. At that moment I heard a familiar voice call my name. And in the distance I saw her. How could I not? She stood out among the group of women waiting on the hillside.

But I pretended not to see her there. Pretended not to hear her call out to me. I dug my heels into Mr. Davis's horse and we trotted away.

48.

"Addie?" Father's voice wrenched me back to the present.

I looked up to find him peering around the bedroom door. I hadn't heard it open.

"Dinner's waiting," he said, his eyes travelling from the open trunk to the book in my hands.

"Be right there." I placed the canvas-covered journal inside the trunk and closed the lid.

In the kitchen it was clear that the evening meal had been delayed. I mumbled an apology, which Rose brushed aside, and took my place beside Grandfather. Watching him pick at the dry roast and overcooked peas, I wanted to ask so many questions about what I'd just read but knew I could not. For his own reasons he had chosen to keep his past secret, and it was not my place to bring it up in front of anyone else. And for some reason, particularly not in front of Rose.

While Father passed her the potatoes, he said, "I noticed a 'for sale' sign in The Sorry Grocers' window today, Rose. Made me wonder if you're interested in buying it back."

Beside me, Grandfather's head snapped up.

Rose set down the potatoes, saying that no, she wasn't interested in the store. She met Father's eyes. "I know some people say it's not proper for me to live here. That maybe it's time I move back out west—"

"No!" I blurted, in sudden panic. "What about Alan? If ... when ... he comes back. He'll expect you to be here."

Father set down his fork. "That's not why I brought up the store, Rose," he said, ignoring my outburst. "I'm not concerned with gossips' wagging tongues."

"Don't leave, Rose," Grandfather said, surprising us all. "We need you around here. Our Addie can't brew a pot of coffee to save her soul."

I felt my jaw drop, not at his opinion of my housekeeping skills, which even I agreed with, but because he had just called me Addie.

Rose smiled at him, then turned back to my father. "If it's fine by you, Addison," she said. "I would like to stay until Alan returns."

"Of course it's fine by me. By all of us. We're happy to have you here. But from here on, I insist that we pay you the same wages we would pay any hired hand. You do more around the ranch than any man would be expected to. And to be honest, I'm with Dad. Addie's coffee making aside, I don't know how we'd get along without you now."

Grandfather slapped his hand on the tabletop. "Good! It's settled, then." He pushed himself away from the table and stood up. "This is your home, Rose, for as long as you like. And that's what's proper."

He strode into the parlour, leaving us all speechless at his renewed vigour.

These days there were fewer and fewer moments when he was the Chauncey Beynon Beale of old. But whenever it happened, I was always startled by how clear-minded he was when he jumped into a conversation, whether it was about the ranch, the war in Europe or Rose VanderMeer.

Later that evening, after he was settled in his bed, I followed him to his room and shut the door behind me. Could the newly discovered second journal help him to remember the request he had made of me two years ago? Would hearing me read it spur him on to finish dictating his unfinished statement about the events of April 30, 1864?

I retrieved the canvas-covered book from the trunk, sat down by his beside and turned to the first page.

"June 29, 1864, Fort Benshee, Chilcootan Territory," I began. "Much has happened since meeting the Irishman Mr. Patrick Nolan ..."

Grandfather's breath caught in his throat. I stopped reading and glanced up quickly. The expression on his face had me instantly regret taking him unaware. His brows were knit together; the corners of his mouth twitched with confusion. After a brief silence, he sank back, letting his head rest on the pillow, and, with a slight wave of his hand, gestured for me to continue. Keeping my voice low, I read slowly, checking on him every few sentences to gauge his reaction. All the while, his clouded eyes remained fixed on the middle distance, his body so still that I found my eyes straying to his chest to check his breathing.

For the next half hour, other than the muffled hum of the evening news coming from the other side of the door, the only sound in Grandfather's room was the quiet drone of my voice. With no comment or interruption from him, not knowing if he was listening or had nodded off to sleep, I read him the entire passage about his time in the Chilcotin with the Irishman, Mr. Nolan. It was only after I reached the entries about Fort

Benshee and Captain Cox that I sensed his agitation. Yet each time I hesitated, he gestured for me to continue. Until I came to August 15 and began reading his description of riding away from Fort Chilcotin with the girl Rose calling after him. He lifted a trembling hand.

"That's enough," he said, closing his eyes. But not before I saw the glisten of moisture gathering in them.

In the following days, I looked for opportunities to continue reading to him. But moments when his mind was clear, and we were alone, grew fewer and farther between.

Christmas and New Year's came and went without a word from Alan. I wanted desperately to write to him, to say so many things to him that I had not. But I kept my promise to Rose. If she could wait until he was ready, it was only right that I did the same.

When I returned to school in January, I checked the mail each and every afternoon. But day after day I came away disappointed.

One afternoon near the end of the month, while checking our post office box, Father and I ran into our neighbour, Mr. Miller. The rancher walked outside with us after we retrieved our mail, telling Father that they had taken on a new ranch hand while their son, Ralph, was overseas. He waved over a fellow who was playing in the snow with three young boys.

"He can't enlist 'cause he's got a club foot," Mr. Miller said in a low voice, explaining the slight limp of the Native man walking toward us. "But that don't stop him one iota from being the best wrangler a man could hope for."

While the new ranch hand, Jimmy Sellers, was being introduced, the boys raced around in front of the store, hooting and hollering and pelting each other with snowballs. They all appeared to be the same age, no older than five or six, and looked so much alike that I found myself staring. All were hatless in the crisp winter sun, their shoulder-length hair dusted with snow from their roughhousing.

"Triplets?" Father asked, nodding at them.

"Yeah," answered Mr. Sellers. "A real handful, them boys."

Watching his sons play reminded me of Alan Baptiste when he first came to Sorry, although the triplets appeared to be a bit younger than he had been then.

At that moment, Mrs. Parsons came out of the schoolhouse. Before she reached the bottom step, an errant snowball sailed through the air and struck her square in the middle of the chest. She looked down at the dripping clump, brushed it off with disdain and then cast a scalding look at the triplets.

I can't swear if I actually heard it all the way from the store porch or if I read her lips when she spat out the word "Savages!" before she turned on her heel and headed toward her house.

Clapping Mr. Sellers on the shoulder, Mr. Miller said, "Well, Jimmy, let's hope she forgets that little incident by the time your boys start school in the fall."

Father and I exchanged looks.

The minute we were inside our pickup cab with the doors closed, I asked if he heard what the teacher had called them.

"I can only imagine," he answered, turning the key in the ignition. "But I didn't miss that scowl."

While the engine rumbled to life, I voiced my fear that the new boys would suffer the same prejudices that Alan had experienced in her classroom.

"It's a cause for concern," he agreed, looking over his shoulder as he backed the truck away from the store.

He drove the next few miles in deep thought. Before we turned onto the ranch road, he said, "I'll go in and have a little chat with Mrs. Parsons before they enrol. If that doesn't work, I'll meet with the school trustees if it's necessary."

As it turned out, it wasn't.

49.

The first week in April, a blue envelope addressed to me in Alan's familiar handwriting lay waiting in our mailbox. I held it to my chest and climbed into the truck cab before tearing it open. When I did, instead of the anticipated letter, I found a newspaper clipping. At the wheel Father kept his eyes on the road while I unfolded it.

It was a christening announcement from the *Victoria Daily Colonist*. "What? Why would ..."

And then I noticed the grainy faces in the photograph. Four children stood on either side of their mother's chair. A new baby, lost in layers of a lace christening gown and frilly bonnet, lay in her arms. Behind her, dressed in his army uniform, standing militarily erect with his hat in one hand, the other resting on his wife's shoulder, was the baby's father—Sergeant Davenport.

"Interesting," Father said after I read the announcement under the photograph. "What are you going to do with it?"

"I don't know."

There was no letter, no note, with the clipping. I wrestled with my conscience all evening. I fell asleep that night imagining all sorts of scenarios where I would smugly watch the horror fill Mrs. Parsons' face as I handed her the newspaper clipping in front of the entire class, or as she found it lying anonymously on her desk. By the time I arrived at school the next morning, as tempting as it was to ambush her with this bombshell, I'd made my decision.

Enid Parsons, for her own reasons, which she had never shared with me, detested Sergeant Davenport. At lunch that day, sitting on the church steps, I took the newspaper clipping from my pocket, unfolded it and handed it to her.

She studied it for a moment, her eyes narrowing as understanding dawned.

"I knew it!" she said. "The old lecher."

Instead of confronting her mother with it when we returned to class, as I thought she might, Enid tucked the newspaper article inside a book. And that was the last I saw of it.

Until Easter Sunday.

That Sunday of 1941 was no different from other years. With a twinkle in his eye, Reverend Watts teased his congregation that he could always count on the Birth and the Resurrection to guarantee a full house. Before the end of the service, after the final *amen* of his sermon, he held up his hands, saying, "I have a personal announcement to make this week."

The congregation shifted in their seats, waiting with undisguised curiosity. Except for those of us from the Beale ranch. We all knew what was coming. Two weeks ago, the reverend and his wife had driven out to speak with Rose.

Father had welcomed them inside, and while everyone settled around our kitchen table, I busied myself making tea, questioning whether our minister had been listening to the Sorry gossips and was there to pass judgment on us.

It turned out that his concern had nothing to do with our living arrangements. He and Mrs. Watts, along with his brother, who was a butcher, were considering purchasing The Sorry Grocers. However, he told Rose, they would never consider making an offer if she had any intention of doing so herself. They drove away that afternoon with Rose's blessing to go ahead with the purchase.

That Easter Sunday was the first time I ever heard clapping and cheers in the chapel. As the parishioners filed out after the reverend's announcement, the air was abuzz with relief at the news that the grocery store would once again be owned by one of their own.

Outside, while Rose and Father waited in line to shake Reverend Watts's hand, I guided Grandfather across the porch toward the community bulletin board. But we couldn't get anywhere near it. A crowd, three or four deep, heads bent in muffled conversations, was gathered in front of the wall where the board hung.

As I tried to peer around them to see what the attraction was, Mrs. Parsons—red-faced and huffing like a hen with ruffled feathers—elbowed her way through the bodies and scurried down the steps. As she passed, faces turned to follow her, trying unsuccessfully to control the smirks playing on their lips.

I pushed through the crowd to see, tacked on the bulletin board, the newspaper clipping I'd given to Enid.

Following the Easter holidays, I returned to school to learn that Mrs. Parsons had given notice to the school board. She'd resigned from her teaching post at the Sorry schoolhouse and would not return in the fall.

Instead, Enid informed me with great dismay, her mother now intended to move to Vancouver with her after she graduated. I was filled with guilt that my relief was tempered by Enid's misery.

"I guess it's true that no good deed goes unrewarded," I said wryly, and she laughed with little mirth. Still, I felt bad for her and wondered if she would still have posted that christening announcement with the photograph of Sergeant Davenport's family on the bulletin board for the whole town to see if she had been aware of the consequences.

At the end of June, Enid and I graduated. The school trustees placed great emphasis on having a proper graduation ceremony for the two of us. I would have gladly skipped it, the anticipated pleasure of Mrs. Parsons being forced to hand me my diploma lost to the thought that if Alan had only waited nine more months, he would have been there with us. But my ambivalence was overruled by Rose's and Father's excitement. So in the end I agreed to attend, with one concession, however, for which I did not seek permission.

Mrs. Parsons' face was a grim mask as she handed me my graduation certificate, rolled up and tied with a purple ribbon. Her congratulations for the honours I achieved and the scholarship—which I had won but would never use—crackled in her throat. Her limp handshake, which satisfied the school trustees but fooled no one else, was rudely brief. And my armour against that bitterness on my final day in her classroom was the little bit of Alan I felt was there with me, in his mother's deerskin dress that I was wearing.

Enid and I met a few times that summer before she and her mother moved to Vancouver, where Enid intended to study teaching. We would sit out on The Sorry Grocers' steps and share a soda. It was during these visits that I learned the truth about her contempt for Sergeant Davenport.

"The old goat made a pass at me. When I told my mother, she said I must have imagined it. I could handle him—I just stayed in my room and latched my door when he was around. But what hurt worse was that she didn't believe me." She shrugged. "Guess she does now. She can hardly look me in the eye."

On the day they left for Vancouver, Rose and I drove into Sorry. When I parked the truck in front of the store, Enid waved at us from where they were loading their suitcases into Reverend Watts's van. She finished what she was doing and headed over, her mother calling after her to hurry or they might miss their bus in Quesnel. Without looking back,

Enid said, "Oh, don't get your shirt in a knot, Mother. I'm saying goodbye to my friends."

In that moment, now that it was too late, I regretted that I had not gotten to know Enid better.

As if reading my mind, she hugged me and said, "Who knows? Maybe I'll come back and teach here someday."

Over her shoulder I watched Mrs. Parsons squirm. And when Enid released me and turned to hug Rose, saying, "Give Alan my love when you see him, and tell him thanks for the newspaper clipping," the shocked expression on her mother's face made me smile. It was small retribution for the years of torment she had caused Alan and me. But it was enough.

In the following years, Enid and I would exchange letters from time to time. She would eventually meet and marry a young man from the coast and never return to Sorry. I couldn't help but think that it was Sorry's loss. And mine.

50.

With school days, and the long hours of studying for exams, left behind forever, I was free to devote my spare time to Grandfather. He was ninety-one that summer of 1941, and I could no longer ignore that he was growing frailer with each passing week. His eyes, shrunken into the shadows below his hooded brow, were now little more than slits concealing the clouded irises that once sparkled sky blue. I stopped waiting for days when his mind was clear, and every evening I sat at his bedside reading entries from the newly discovered canvas journal.

There were many nights when he barely acknowledged my presence, but once in a while he would smile at a passage or make some comment that let me know he had been listening. Sometimes I would reread the same passages the following night to see if he noticed. Too often he did not, but every now and then he would catch it, saying, "Nope. You already read that part." But whether he listened with interest or fell asleep to my voice, one thing was clear: these new journal entries caused him no agitation.

Following the entry from August 15, 1864, his writing took up again the day after he walked into the mining town of Barkerville with Mr. Davis and his lame horse. I found much of it familiar, versions of the stories I had grown up listening to on those long winter nights when the electric lights failed in our ranch house. Familiar, but different. His written stories were filled with details that were never included in the fanciful tales he had told when I was a young girl.

For as long as I can remember, I knew about Grandfather's Barkerville days. I knew that he had become the sole owner of a mining claim after his partner died of a heart attack during the great fire of 1868, and that he eventually sold that claim, using the gold he walked away with to homestead this ranch.

What I hadn't known, and was pretty sure my father hadn't either, was that after Grandfather arrived in Barkerville, he became as hard drinking and hard living as any rough and seasoned miner in that wild town.

Every night, as I read him page after page about his life in the mining town, I would try to image him working the claim along Williams Creek during the days and then drinking and dancing the nights away in one of the dozen or more saloons. If I hadn't know better, if I hadn't recognized his handwriting, I would have found it difficult to believe these new entries were written by the same fifteen-year-old boy as the first journal.

In exchange for Grandfather's labour, Mr. Davis had provided lodging in his log cabin, which was built on his claim, and meals, which Grandfather found himself cooking more often than not. He was promised a quarter share of the "mining company," which was little more than a thirty-foot shaft sunk into the ground next to the creek.

Finding that being lowered into that dark and dank hole was as fearsome as the thought of being drowned, Grandfather did all the mule work above ground, working the windlass and the sluice boxes and hauling away the slag, while Mr. Davis went underground with his pickaxe. It was an arrangement that suited them both. According to Grandfather's words, "all the gold we eked from the gravel, ounce by hard-earned ounce, was stored under the floorboards beneath Mr. Davis's bed."

During the daylight hours, when the miners of Barkerville were pickaxing, panning and sluicing and dreaming of castles in the air, the town's wooden sidewalks were quiet. But at night, they would come alive with the rough and hard-working men searching for fun in the saloons and dance halls that crowded both sides of the main street.

I was more than a little surprised when I read about Grandfather's drinking, dancing and gambling. At first, it appeared that he accompanied Mr. Davis to the saloons to protect the old miner from his fondness for the ladies of the night, and their fondness for his gold. But it wasn't long before Grandfather too was drinking with the Barkerville ladies, who were just as apt to have a smoking cigar or pipe in their mouth and a pistol strapped to a thigh under their skirts. Even knowing there was no gold to be had from Mr. Davis's young guardian, they fawned all over him, mothering him or flirting and teasing him mercilessly until he felt his cheeks flush. When there were no paying customers around, they would pull him to the floor and dance with him for free, instead of the dollar they charged the other miners.

On Grandfather's dresser, beside the sepia portrait of my grandmother, sat a grainy photograph of him standing outside of the Go-at-'Em Saloon on the main street of Barkerville. Seeing how tall and handsome—and unlike a boy—he was then, I have my doubts that the ladies' attentions were as motherly as he credited them to be.

All my life I had known my grandfather to be a teetotaller. Reading about his drunken escapades, about him stumbling back to the cabin late at night, or not at all until it was time to start digging in the morning, I couldn't help wondering if he had intentionally followed in his pa's footsteps. Was he drawn into that nightly world of wild revelry to escape the ghosts he never wrote about, but that were there between the lines?

I found it strange that there was no mention of his recent past, or those who occupied it, in this new journal. It was as if his life before he moved into Mr. Davis's cramped one-room cabin on Williams Creek was a clean slate. And then, one night, I came to a passage that changed all that.

Hearing Grandfather's snore, I was about to close the journal when my eye caught the date on the opposite page.

Up until then all his Barkerville entries had been fairly regular, sometimes daily, at the least weekly. But all of a sudden there was a six-month gap. Startled by the date of the next entry, I sat up in my chair and continued reading silently while Grandfather slept.

51.

Barkerville, April 30, 1865

There will be no absolution for my cowardice in not coming forward to speak of the events at Bute Inlet. Today marks one year from that, the most horrific day of my life. And almost half a year from what would amount to be the second worst. October 26, 1864.

The only good to come out of that fateful October morning is that I have sworn off the drink. For if it had not been for my drunken carousing in the months after my arrival here in Barkerville, I may have paid better attention to the gossip in the crowded saloons.

I took to drinking too easily—especially since the love of whiskey was the one flaw in my pa's character that I abhorred. Perhaps I have hated my own self as much and forgetfulness was my intention in numbing my mind with the stuff.

I have not had a drink since the evening of October 25. I shall never forget that date.

With dusk already settling in after the five o'clock sunset, Mr. Davis and I left our diggings to walk down to Martin's Saloon. While we stood at the bar waiting for our drinks, I spied an abandoned *Victoria Colonist* newspaper on the counter. Recognizing the photograph of Judge Matthew Begbie on the front page I leaned over and fetched the paper.

The circuit court judge is a familiar face in these saloons whenever he is in the area. He often appears in the bars still wearing his judicial robes and powdered wig after a day in the Richfield courthouse up the road. Although the barkeeps make no bones about serving me, I am uncertain how this lawman would view it, and so I take no drinks whenever he's about. Being an American citizen and having no knowledge of what the ruling is on my presence in these colonies, I have kept my distance in fear the judge might question my age and family.

But that evening his only presence was in a newspaper photograph. The newspaper from which I learned the horrible news that it seems all of the other miners were well aware of.

Oblivious, I began reading the account of a recent trial in Quesnellmouth. It wasn't until I came to Judge Begbie's statement saying that "regardless of the circumstances of surrender under British law he had no recourse other than to find the savages guilty of murder" that I realized he was talking about Klatsassin and his warriors.

Murder? The day that I rode away from the peace talk meeting out at Fort Chilcootan I understood that the men were prisoners of war. Now they have been sentenced to death!

—I thought you knew, boy, Mr. Davis said. Talk has been of little else whenever the judge bellies up to the bar.

—They were tricked! I heard Cox give his word! He guaranteed no harm would come to them if they surrendered peacefully.

—Tricked they were, Mr. Davis agreed. Came in to talk peace, then while they slept that night a stockade was built around them. They woke the next morning to find they were arrested and charged with murder. But that is not the worst of it, boy. Tomorrow morning they are to be hanged in Quesnellmouth.

I wasted a frantic hour of precious time searching for a horse or a wagon but none was to be had. So I made the journey on foot. With only a crescent moon and starlight to guide me, without stopping to rest I hurried along the same thirty miles of wagon road that had taken us two full days to travel with a lame horse. In mad determination to get there before daylight, I covered the distance to Quesnellmouth in twelve hours.

Still, I was too late.

The sun was well risen when I finally stumbled into the little Fraser River settlement. I raced toward a large crowd gathered at the gaol on the riverbank. As I drew nearer my breath caught at the apparition rising above the heads of the milling crowd—the crossbeams of the gallows with taut ropes stretching downward. Unable to stop myself I pushed through the hushed crowd. And there beneath the trap doors of the platform hung five men. I recognized only four. Brewster's guide, Chief Talhoot. The blue-eyed war chief Klatsassin, and his son. And the man I knew as Willum.

A group of Chilcootans stood in silent mourning before the ghastly sight. I was about to turn away when I caught the glimpse of a familiar profile among the women.

Although her cheeks were fuller and her body filled out since last I saw her, I was certain it was Rose. Without thought I cried out her name. Her head slowly turned and across the distance her eyes met mine. The sorrow drained from her face and was replaced with contempt. This time it was Rose who turned away. She slipped between the surrounding women, who moved in to close the gap left after her and stood forming a solid wall against my following.

I searched the little town for hours but she was not to be found.

Now this six months later every time I close my eyes I see her.

And I see the scornful face of her brother Willum. For even in death his eyes found mine. Mocking me. Accusing me. Forever condemning me for breaking the oath that I made to him the morning my pa died.

52.

The entry was so startling that in the following days I could think of little else. I waited impatiently for a time when I was certain that Grandfather and I would be alone and undisturbed for hours.

That day finally came a few weeks later, at the end of September. The afternoon was sunny and warm, and it took little convincing to entice Grandfather out to the screened-in front porch after lunch when Father and Rose left for Quesnel. I settled him in mother's old rocking chair and went to fetch his pipe and "fixins." Lately he rarely lit it but simply held the smokeless pipe between his teeth out of habit. Asking for his tobacco was a good sign. Once his pipe bowl was aglow, he leaned back in the chair and sighed. For a long while, we sat there side by side, me staring out at the ranch yard, the corrals, the fenced pasture and the haze of mountains beyond. And he puffing at his pipe, staring out at his memory of the same view. The warm air was heavy with the mixed scent of summer departing and autumn arriving, the silence broken only by the sound of birdsong and the creaking of his rocking chair.

After a time, Grandfather took the pipe from his lips, blew out a cloud of smoke and said, "Beautiful."

I didn't know if he meant his smoke, the perfection of the day or simply life itself. I turned to look at his profile, grown sharp with shadows and angles; his skin was so translucent, I could make out the map of spiderweb veins beneath it. And yet, in that face I could still see the strong and competent man who had given me so much; who had taught me to handle a horse and to shoot a gun, to love this land and all it had to offer. He looked so serene in that moment that I glanced down at the canvas journal in my hands and questioned myself. What had I hoped to accomplish by reading him this latest passage, which in all probability would cause him anxiety?

The truth was that Grandfather was having shorter and shorter stretches of lucidity. I had to face the truth—before too long he would be beyond the reach of worry. Did I have the right to intrude on these peaceful interludes by attempting to dredge up the past? Was it simply curiosity? Or was it something deeper that compelled me? I had to admit that curiosity played a part, but there was something more.

I believed that, somewhere deep inside, my grandfather was tortured by the need to tell what he had kept buried for all these years. And I owed it to him to help him do that before he sank into unawareness.

So, as he puffed contentedly on his pipe, I opened the canvas book on my lap and turned to the marked page. Taking a deep breath, I began to read. "April 30, 1865, Barkerville."

Fully expecting Grandfather's resistance, I was startled when he took the pipe from his mouth and said, "Wondered when you were going to get around to that." He felt for the ashtray on top of the apple crate beside his chair, tapped the ashes into it and sat back.

I took that as permission to continue. Grandfather's rocking slowed, and then came to an abrupt stop, while I read about the hanging of the war chief Klatsassin and his followers.

With both hands gripping the chair arms, Grandfather remained perfectly still, listening to his own words from the past tell of his frantic trip to Quesnellmouth, and his arrival—too late—at the executions. It was only when I came to the name Willum that he showed any reaction.

I sensed him stiffen in his chair and I stopped reading, letting the silence settle in the enclosed porch. After a few moments, in a voice so low I had to lean closer to hear, he said, "I should have spoken up."

I reached over and placed a hand on his arm. "Don't you think it's time you told someone what happened that day in Bute Inlet?" I said.

"Yeah. It's time."

Taken aback by his reply, I closed the journal and pushed myself up. "I'll get the notebook and a pen," I said, chastising myself for not thinking of it beforehand. I left the porch and rushed inside, afraid to lose the precious moment. When I returned, Grandfather was chewing on his pipe stem. Once I was settled beside him, he removed the unlit pipe from his mouth and, holding it with both hands, stared down at it as if he could see it.

"If you have ever heard some fool imitate an Indian war cry," he finally said, without raising his head, "and you think you know the blood-curdling sound of terror, you don't, boy. You don't."

He shuddered at the thought.

"Those sounds," he whispered, as if to himself. "Those terrible sounds, they're something you never forget."

He sat unmoving for a long time, then raised his head slowly.

"But it wasn't the war cries that woke me that morning," he continued, without my having to prod. "It was the thunder of musket fire outside our tent. Pa was already on his feet by the time I woke. He pulled back the tent flap and I saw the sleep on his face turn to surprise, then to rage. 'Murderers!' he shouted, just as another musket blast cracked the air. He glanced down at his chest, at the red stain blossoming around the hole in his grey long johns. 'Bloody murderers,' he cried, 'you've killed me.' A second musket ball ripped into his shoulder. But still, he did not fall. He pushed through the opening, like an enraged bull, and stood hurling threats as if that alone would stop the attackers. 'The King George Men will come and hunt you down like dogs,' he screamed. 'They will come and hang you all!'"

Grandfather sighed. "And then ... he simply crumbled to the ground ... a hatchet cleaved into his skull." His lips trembled, and he lowered his head.

I held my breath, waiting. Just when I thought he had reached his limit, that what I was asking him to recall was too painful, he raised his head. Staring straight ahead, as if he could see something in the distance, he continued. "Seeing your own pa cut down in such a gruesome manner should turn a boy into a man. But not I. I scrambled into the tent corner with my bedroll and lay curled up beneath it like a blubbering baby. I shook so violently that I don't know how no one noticed me there as they dragged Pa's trunk outside. The centre pole was suddenly kicked out and the tent collapsed around me. I burrowed deep into the canvas folds, my fist jammed in my mouth to stop myself from crying out in terror. And then, suddenly, a blade sliced through the canvas not inches from my face. A hand reached in, grabbed me by the hair and yanked my head through the opening. The steel fingers wrenched my head back, exposing my neck to the knife edge. I was certain I was a goner. But instead of coming to my throat, the long blade slashed into the canvas, and I was lifted through the opening like a rag doll."

Grandfather's words came faster and faster as if he sensed the urgency to get it all out. My pen raced across the page in an effort to keep up.

"My executioner raised his arm to strike the death blow. I looked into the blackened face and saw that it was Rose's brother. Willum. He threw back his head in a victory cry and flung himself full force on top of me. The blade of his knife sank into the earth a breath away from my temple and he hissed, 'Be dead!' I struggled against his vicelike grip, sobbing and pleading for my life. And then I heard his urgent warning in my ear: 'If you want to live, be still.'

"It took everything I had to force myself to go limp, but when I did, Willum lifted himself off of me. He grabbed me by the arms and dragged me away like a sack of potatoes. Rocks ripped through my clothing and tore at my skin as I was bumped and scraped over the rough-edged ground, but the sight of mutilated bodies along the way numbed my mind to pain. I closed my eyes against the visions and the next thing I knew, I was tumbling through the air. I thudded down on the river's edge, and my eyes snapped open. Willum landed in a soundless crouch beside me. He grabbed me and forced me back into an overhang beneath the bank. I expected he would finish me off right there. Instead, he clapped a hand over my mouth and held me in his vicelike grip until my panicked thrashing ceased. I don't know how long he held me pinned down, forcing me to look into his fierce eyes while the sounds of mayhem carried on above us. When silence finally came, he loosened his grip and growled, 'You tell them King George Men when they come—you tell them we are warriors, not murderers. You tell them to stay away from our land with your sickness and your roads. You tell them that we mean war, not murder.'

"When I couldn't find my voice, he grabbed a fistful of my shirt and thrust his face so close to mine I felt his spittle spray my cheek as he demanded that I swear to carry his message. And so I did. Before Willum left me trembling in that underground hideaway, I gave him my oath. I promised that I would speak his words, that I would tell everyone that Klatsassin and his followers had declared war on the white men to protect the Chilcootan peoples and their territories."

Grandfather swallowed hard and laid his head back against the rocker. I held my breath, stunned by what he was telling me, and by the clarity with which he was recalling it.

"But I broke that oath," he said after a moment. "I said nothing."

I waited for him to continue. After a long silence, I said tentatively, "You were just a boy."

He tilted his head as if he had forgotten I was there. "A boy," he sighed. "Yeah. A boy who thought he was a man but, in keeping silent, proved he was not."

"But what difference would it have made if you had told anyone? Would it have changed anything?"

"Maybe not. But I should have spoken up. I owed that to Willum. And to Rose. Her brother saved my life. Maybe I could have saved his."

I glanced down at the notebook in my lap, at the snatches of sentences I had scribbled in my haste to record his words. I wondered if I would ever be able to decipher them later.

"Granddad? Do you remember a few years ago you asked me to write down a statement about what happened that day in Bute Inlet?" I asked. "I've got the start of that right here. Do you want to finish it?"

"Read it," he said with a wave of his hand.

I turned back to the first page in the notebook. "This is the statement of Chauncey Beynon Beale," I read, "as to the events occurring on the Homathko River above the Bute Inlet, in the Province of British Columbia, during the last day of April in the year of our Lord 1864. The telling comes over seventy years late, but it is no less than the truth as I recall it."

I looked up at him. "That's it," I said, "that's all I have."

The muscles of his jaw worked as if searching for a memory thread. I waited, praying that he would not sink so deep in thought that he would lose himself to it. But after a while he turned his head in my direction and said, "All right, take this down."

Speaking slowly, but with determination, he dictated, "I was present in the main camp of the Bute Inlet road crew on the morning of April 30, 1864 ..."

Fifteen minutes later, Grandfather was done. I handed him my fountain pen and guided his hand to the bottom of the page. After his scrawled signature was added to the statement, he leaned back in his chair and took a deep breath.

I blotted the ink, closed the notebook and glanced over at him. I couldn't tell if he was sleeping or awake. I sat quietly, thinking about all he had just revealed, about how his past had weighed so heavily on him all these years. Now that he had unburdened himself, I was left with the question of what to do with his written statement, let alone the story he had just told me.

Before long a snore caught in his throat, and I went inside to fetch his quilt. As I spread it across his lap he stirred, and then asked sleepily, "Did we get 'er all done?"

"Yes, I think so," I said, retrieving the notebook. "What would you like me to do with it, Granddad?"

"With what?"

"Nothing," I said. "It's okay." I stood up and headed inside.

"You mean the gold?" he called after me.

I stopped and turned back. "Gold?"

"The gold in Pa's trunk," he said, with a trace of impatience.

His pa's trunk? The trunk that was ransacked and left in the Bute Inlet camp?

"Give it to Rose," he said, before I could question it. "It'll help her raise the boy."

I sighed in resignation. "Okay, Granddad."

53.

That was the last time Grandfather ever spoke to me about his past.

In the following days, a serenity came over him, a calmness of spirit, which led me to believe he had found some sort of salvation in his confession. I was not about to jeopardize that. I put away his signed statement, leaving the question about what to do with it unanswered for the time being. I returned the notebook, along with his journal, to the trunk at the end of his bed and went back to reading him the classics in the evening. More often than not, by the time I arrived in his room with one of his favourites under my arm, I would find him sleeping peacefully.

During the day, however, there was a new energy to his step. I was uncertain how much of his vision remained by then, if any. Or if, after seventy-odd years of living in this ranch house, he made his way from room to room by rote memory, rather than sight. But for a while, at least, he seemed to do it with a renewed vigour.

Father was visibly relieved by Grandfather's sudden turnaround. As was Rose. Whenever the weather allowed, she would entice him outdoors once again for long strolls around the ranch yard. I would watch them from the porch, walking arm and arm like two old familiar friends, she pointing things out to him and he nodding and smiling as if he could see whatever she was describing. Even from a distance, he appeared younger, his face more animated, during those walkabouts, and I sometimes wondered what they found to talk about out there.

And then, on an unseasonably warm October afternoon, I was out in the yard among the clotheslines bringing in the wash when they returned from another excursion. Standing among the sheets billowing in the wind, I watched them coming up the road, their heads together in conversation. Neither of them noticed me there unpegging the laundry. When Grandfather spoke I stopped working.

"You shouldn't have run off," he said, turning toward Rose.

"Run off?" Rose repeated.

"That day I saw you with the boy in Williams Lake," he said. "I wish you hadn't run away."

Rose replied with a pat on his arm.

He stopped walking and cocked his head to the side, as if trying to recall something important. "I looked for you, searched for years. I asked anyone I ran into from the Chilcotin. Asked after you. And the boy." His hand fumbled for her hand, grasping it so forcefully, I thought it must hurt.

"I wanted to tell you I was sorry. Sorry about Willum. Sorry about Pa … I wanted to ask about the boy …"

"It's okay, Mr. Chance," Rose said, as if the conversation made sense to her. "Everything's all right." She gently urged him forward.

I finished gathering the laundry, grateful to Rose for going along with his ramblings, and then followed them inside. By the time I arrived in the kitchen, any agitation Grandfather had felt was quelled, and he was sitting at the table stirring his coffee.

While his physical well-being had improved, I couldn't deny the truth: that his mind was slipping further and further away. For a while I considered sharing what I had learned about his past with Father and Rose, so they would understand his confusion. But in the end, I came to the conclusion that it was not up to me to do so as long as Grandfather was alive, regardless of how disjointed his grasp on reality.

Only in looking back, in knowing how swiftly things would change, would I question that decision.

54.

In November, Alan's regiment was deployed overseas. We learned from Father's army contact that his unit had joined the other Canadian divisions in Britain waiting to enter the fray in Europe.

Rose took the news far more stoically than I did, holding onto the hope that the war would be over before that happened. Although I said nothing, a small part of me resented having given in to her request not to write Alan while he was in training on Vancouver Island. Now that we no longer had an address, I regretted it even more. I secretly resolved that if I ever got the chance again I would not ask permission. There was no way of knowing that opportunity was forever lost.

On December 7, we all sat in the parlour listening in shocked silence to the CBC news report of the Japanese air attack on the American naval base in Pearl Harbor, and we knew there was little hope of an early ending to the ever-escalating war.

Our Radiola remained on, even through the static silences, during those bleak December days. We would all rush in from wherever we happened to be the moment we heard the announcer's voice bringing updates of the simultaneous Japanese bombings of Singapore, Hong Kong, Malaya and the American base in the Philippines. It seemed the entire world had gone insane. Unable to pull ourselves away, Father, Rose and I spent hours huddled around the radio. Even though the attacks in the Pacific were nowhere near the European front, as we listened to President Roosevelt's declaration that the United States of America was now at war with Japan, and then two days later, with Germany and Italy, Alan was not far from any of our thoughts.

Grandfather, who at one time would not have hesitated to add his opinion to the news reports, now listened without comment, as if indifferent to the pandemonium. Perhaps that explains why none of us noticed his prolonged absence from his parlour chair one evening in early January. Even Rose, who usually kept a careful eye on him, wasn't alerted until the damage had been done. In hindsight, I would vaguely remember Grandfather getting up and shuffling into the kitchen. I may even have heard the bathroom door creak open, but after that I was so caught up in the

London news reports that I lost track of time. It was only when Rose felt a cold breeze that we discovered the open kitchen door and, after a quick check of the house, realized Grandfather was not inside.

Father grabbed a flashlight, and we all threw on our jackets and boots and rushed out into the freezing night. The first place we checked was the outhouse. Although we'd had an indoor toilet for years, on a few occasions lately, Grandfather had forgotten and headed to the outside privy. Someone usually caught him and rerouted him to the bathroom inside.

That night, footprints in the fresh skiff of snow led straight to the open door of the outhouse. But even from a distance we could see that it was empty. The beam from Father's flashlight scanned across the whitened ground, following a second set of footprints leading away. As soon as I realized the direction they were going in, I ran ahead of the light, slipping and sliding in the greasy new snowfall in my haste to cross the yard.

The door to the icehouse was ajar. As I threw it open, father's flashlight scanned the darkened interior until it illuminated Grandfather's still body lying on the straw-covered ice blocks. For a horrifying second I thought he was gone from us, but then his head slowly turned toward the light, looking dazed and confused, as if waking from sleep. We rushed in and helped him to sit up. Rose, who had thought to bring a blanket, wrapped it around his shoulders while crooning assurances against his weak attempts to pull away from us. Passing the flashlight to me, Father lifted Grandfather— weeping and mumbling incoherently—up into his arms to carry him back to the house. I hurried behind, my heart aching when Grandfather, his words slurred with exhaustion, whispered, "I just wanted to sit with Evan."

None of us slept that night, except Granddad. We kept watch on him while he fell in and out of fitful slumber. By dawn he was shaking with a hard chill one moment, and then burning with fever the next. Even in his growing delirium, he protested against the idea of being taken to the hospital. So while Rose and I kept watch, Father raced into Sorry to call the doctor.

The doctor from Quesnel arrived two hours later. He examined Grandfather, tapping on his back and listening to his chest with his stethoscope. When he was done, he retrieved a bottle of pills from his black bag. "Make sure he gets lots of liquids, and give him these twice a day," he said, handing the bottle to Rose.

Father and I followed him out to the kitchen and stood waiting anxiously while he washed his hands at the sink. When he was done, he rolled his sleeves down, saying, "I'm not sure how much good the sulfa pills will do him. There's little more to be done other than what you're doing. Just keep him comfortable." He shrugged his coat on. "Pneumonia. It's the old man's friend—not the worst way to go."

Startled by him speaking about Grandfather as if he were some old horse or dog whose time it was, I wanted to pummel him right there. Father, too, was taken aback by his nonchalance, but he escorted that doctor out the door, saying, "Well, Doc, we're just not quite so ready to give up on him."

Neither was Rose. She tented the head of his bed with sheets, and for long hours we relayed steaming kettles back and forth to ease his rattled breathing. Against my fear that the doctor was right, that Grandfather might not recover, she calmly led the way. She showed by example, sponging him down when the fever rose, tucking warmed quilts around his shaking body when the chills struck and applying mineral water to his parched lips. We crushed his sulfa pills and mixed them with water or broth, anything to get the medicine into him. Strangely it was Rose's voice he responded to most when she gently urged him to drink.

Time passed in a blur. Around the clock, one or more of us was always at Grandfather's bedside, leaving only to attend to the most vital of ranch work or to try to catch a few moments of elusive sleep. Father looked after the outside chores, while I kept the home fires burning. Rose saw to it that we ate.

Grandfather's fever broke on the fourth day, leaving him frail and weakened. His body slipped in and out of consciousness, his mind in and out of the past. In the following days, during his brief spells of awareness, one moment he might fret about some recent ranch business, and the next become agitated over a long-ago event as if it were happening now.

One afternoon, I arrived at the doorway of his room to discover him clutching Rose's arm with an urgency beyond his strength. "The boy?" he asked, his voice hoarse with effort. "The blue-eyed boy I saw with you. Is he … was he Pa's?"

Offering no resistance, Rose murmured calming assurances as he pulled her closer.

And then, his energy spent, he fell back against his pillows. "I'm … sorry, Rose."

I tiptoed in beside Rose and whispered, "He thinks you're someone else."

But her attention was on Grandfather. Like a mother comforting a child, she smoothed his brow with her free hand and said, "It's all right, Mr. Chance, I forgive you."

Under Rose's soothing hand, the deep lines of anguish slowly relaxed and he settled back on his pillow. Before long, he had drifted off to sleep. After a while, I took her place at his bedside. With my hand on his, I sat listening to Grandfather's rattled breathing, to the ticking of the clock on his night table, the muffled sounds of Rose working in the kitchen. Outside the bedroom window, heavy snowflakes drifted silently to the ground. Suddenly, Grandfather's trembling fingers gripped my wrist. "The gold in Pa's trunk," he said, his feeble voice insistent. "Give it to Rose."

Just as Rose had done, I laid my hand on his forehead and smoothed his brow in an effort to calm him. As I murmured useless promises to do what he asked, he released his grip on my wrist and settled down.

In the early hours of the morning, I nodded off, jerking awake in my chair to see Father sitting on the other side of the bed, his head bowed. Fearing that I had missed the chance to say goodbye, I placed my lips on Grandfather's cheek and whispered, "I love you, Granddad."

I drew back at the sound of soft humming. On the other side of the bed, Father lifted his head. He had heard it too. We both watched Grandfather as the faint but familiar song came whispering over his barely moving lips.

"My ... Adeline ... Sweet Adeline ... You're the flower of my heart ... Sweet Adeline."

It may have been a trick of the dim light, but I believed I caught a trace of his old mischievous smile playing at the corners of his mouth.

And then, he was gone.

55.

Until his death, Grandfather had been the most constant presence in my life. For almost sixteen years, every single night, without exception, I had fallen asleep knowing that he was downstairs. I woke each morning to his certain presence, as sturdy and reliable as the walls of our ranch house. I knew nothing else.

When my brother Evan died, I was still a child, a child struck numb by the pain that cut so deep it left me hollow inside. When my mother disappeared days later, I filled the emptiness she left with anger and resentment. When Alan ran off to war, I filled his absence with fear and regret. But there was no filling the void left by Grandfather's death.

Suddenly the ranch house felt empty regardless of how many people stopped by to offer their sympathy and pound cakes. In an effort to comfort myself, I took to wearing his flannel shirts, feeling his presence in their warmth and his lingering scent. Father, I noticed, did the same.

For the longest time, I didn't know what to do with Grandfather's journals. One afternoon, months after he was laid to rest between Grandmother Beale and Evan in the ranch's little cemetery, while Rose was out tending her chickens, I talked to Father about my dilemma. He sat across the kitchen table and listened without interruption.

When I was done, he leaned back in his chair. "Well," he said, after giving it some thought. "Maybe you should just let it be for a while. I suspect that after all these years, there's no hurry to decide, is there? He entrusted all this to you for a reason. I have faith that when the time is right, you'll know exactly what to do."

I placed both journals on the table between us, suggesting that he might like to read them.

Father glanced down at the old books. After some thought, he looked back up at me. "I don't believe I will, Addie," he said. "If Dad had wanted to share his secrets with me, he had a lot of years to do just that."

"I've thought about that," I said. "I wonder if maybe, sometimes—when he called me boy—he believed he was speaking to you."

I pushed the leather journal across the table. "This is the first one,"

I said. "His life before Barkerville. I thought you might like to know about that missing part of his life."

Father looked down at the book again, studying it as if he could read his father's writing through the leather cover. "Okay, Addie, let me think about it," he said, with some reluctance. "But give me some time. There's no rush, is there?"

I shook my head, realizing that it was too soon for him. I had known the content of those journals long before Grandfather passed away. And no matter how strong Father appeared, he was in mourning. He needed time to heal.

I don't know if he ever read any of those journals. When the right time finally arrived, as he said it would, when I felt I knew for certain what I should do with them, it was too late to ask him.

56.

The war years passed in a blur. The world's escalating beef prices brought unexpected prosperity to local cattle ranchers. Herds were increased in an effort to feed the troops, and everyone was kept busy. With so many of the young men gone, neighbours helped out neighbours more often, forming work crews to go from ranch to ranch during branding and haying season. Suddenly, I was not the only female wearing overalls, as wives and daughters took over husbands' and brothers' roles on the home front. Now, no one gave a second glance to my attire whenever I arrived in Sorry to rush in and check our mailbox—hoping for a letter that would never arrive.

Father learned that Alan's division had been deployed to the Italian front. We listened each night for reports from the European theatre, praying for news of the Royal Canadian Dragoons—afraid to hear it. I fought a growing anger at Alan for not writing, at least to his mother, for not letting us know that he was all right. I knew well that he had never been a long-winded person, but I felt it was just cruel to leave us guessing. Father tried to explain it, saying that wherever his regiment was, it might be impossible to send out mail. Or maybe, now that Alan was in the thick of it, he just couldn't bring himself to write home. He had seen similar situations in the last war. "War is a different world," he said. "There's no explaining it. Some of the boys just couldn't put pen to paper over there." He admitted that he didn't understand it himself—he had taken comfort in writing to his father. "But those boys either couldn't bear to share their feelings, or believed not writing was better than lying about them."

Through Father's army contact we were able to follow delayed progress of Alan's regiment on the Italian front during those years. It was all we could do. In the spring of 1945, after Italy had all but fallen, the Royal Dragoons rolled on to northwest Europe. On April 15, the armoured regiment took part in the liberation of Holland. And then, on May 8, for the entire day, we all but ignored our ranch chores as the CBC radio crackled with news of the crumbling Axis forces in Europe. The three of us sat in the parlour listening to the victory celebrations with bittersweet joy.

Less than a week before, a letter from the war office had arrived informing Rose that her son was missing in action.

She took the news with the same bravery with which she had taken his running off to enlist four years before. Father and I followed her example. It didn't mean he was dead, we told ourselves. The war in Europe was over. Alan would be found in some German POW camp.

Except he wasn't.

Six months after the war officially ended, months after Ralphie Miller and other ranchers' sons returned to the small cheering crowds in Sorry, Alan was still listed as MIA.

It was Father's army contact who brought us the truth. He showed up at the ranch door on a rainy March day in 1946. A career soldier, Sergeant Major Denman had fought alongside Dad during the Great War. He was on his way to Prince George on army business, he said, but felt he owed it to his old army pal to take the opportunity to bring the news in person.

Even against Father's sun-weathered face, the officer looked much older than him. He seemed just plain worn out. He sat grey-faced and formal at our table with his hands wrapped around a coffee mug that he never took a sip from. Speaking haltingly, as if he had been rehearsing what he had to say on the way here, he recounted what he knew about the last day Alan was accounted for.

"On the morning of April 14, his regiment fought their way to the outskirts of Leeuwarden, a city long held by the Germans. According to witnesses, that afternoon, as townspeople started appearing on the streets to celebrate the Allied forces' arrival, Alan looked back across the flat greening fields of the Dutch countryside and told his troop mate that the war was as good as over. He said that there was no sense in any more dying. Said he was going to find himself 'a mountain to climb.' He laid down his rifle and helmet and then headed up the road and disappeared around the bend.

"The trouble was, it wasn't over," Sergeant Major Denman said. "Pockets of resistance still held on. That night the Germans made one last futile attempt. The main assault came from the same direction in which Lieutenant Baptiste was last seen heading." He shrugged, letting the words and their meaning hang in the air.

Rose took this information as good news. She believed Alan was still alive. That like his father, he had lost something of himself in the horror of war. She said she felt that he was out there somewhere, trying to find himself again. "When he does, he'll come home."

"I hope you're right, ma'am," the officer said, and took his leave.

Out on the porch, Father said, "You called him lieutenant?"

"Yeah. He'd just been promoted. The truth is, if it weren't for that promotion, for the lad's exemplary service and for the fact that the end of the war was in sight, he would have been listed as AWOL instead of MIA."

In the months, and then years, following the war, Rose held steadfastly to her faith in Alan's return. She refused to believe that missing in action meant killed in action. I chose to go along with her belief that one day we would look up to see him strolling down our road. As the world went back to normal without any news of him, it was harder and harder to imagine.

Now and then one of us would spot his horse, Dancer, on the other side of the fields across from the ranch house. "He's waiting for Alan," Rose always maintained. I believed that, too. Once, I grabbed a bucket of oats and headed across the field, shaking it before me like Alan used to do. Dancer's ears perked forward, but the moment he heard my whistle, he kicked up his hind legs and galloped off, his dark mane and tail flowing behind. It wasn't me he was looking for.

At first I worried that now that Grandfather was gone, and the war was over with no word from Alan, Rose would leave us. To my relief she soon let us know that if it was all the same to us, she'd like to continue working at the ranch. I suspect it was because she knew how much Alan loved this land, and it was the place that he would return to when he was ready. Father was relieved as well. Running the ranch was a full-time job for the three of us, and "Lord knows," as he was fond of saying, "Rose works as hard as any man."

I still hoped that they would find something more than friendship in each other's company. But even though I listened hard, in all the time they lived together, I never once heard the creak of footsteps on the floorboards between their rooms.

57.

In January of 1948, on the eleventh anniversary of Evan's death, Father saddled up his horse and trotted off in the bright afternoon sunlight. Years later I would come to believe that as I stood at the kitchen window watching him become a tiny black dot against the glaring white backdrop of snow, I felt an ominous sense of foreboding. But that is probably just a trick of memory. Nothing more than the recollections of all the January days that I felt the heavy weight of sadness as he rode off alone—as he chose to do—to visit my brother's grave.

Neither Rose nor I became too concerned as dusk descended. Winter days were short, but the late-afternoon sky was clear, and Father always carried a lantern with him. It was only when his horse cantered into the ranch yard with an empty saddle that we began to fear for him.

Rose would not let me head out by myself. There was no arguing with her that one of us should stay at the house. We quickly saddled our own mounts, reminding ourselves that Father always ground-tethered his mare. Perhaps she had become spooked and bolted, leaving him to walk home in the night.

Beneath a full moon, we followed her hoofprints in the snow out to the east meadows. We dismounted and approached the graveyard, where in the moonlight we found Father, sunk down on his knees upon Evan's grave.

At first I thought he was kneeling there in prayer. But as I unlatched the picket gate and let it creak open, he remained still, his head slumped forward onto his chest.

The shock of discovering my father frozen in death would be too much for tears. Those would come later.

The coroner said that it was a massive heart attack. "As simple as falling asleep," he assured us. I have since imagined that if my father had ever been offered a choice of the way to go, this might be it—to slip from this earth so peacefully, while visiting his son.

58.

Following Father's sudden and unexpected passing, I found myself in the grip of an unshakable lethargy. Unable to imagine a future without him, I fell into a depression so deep that moving through each day was like wading through quicksand. I recalled how, in the days following my brother's death, Mother had to hang onto everything within grasp just to cross a room. And I understood for the first time how overwhelming it must have been for her to carry on without him.

For months, I kept putting off settling Father's estate. It was only after receiving a number of letters from his lawyer, urging me to come to his office to go over the will, that I reluctantly made the trip into Quesnel. At twenty-three, I was not a businesswoman in any sense of the term. Still, I was my father's daughter, and I had heard enough of his conversations with clients over the years to feel certain that probate would be simple enough. I was his only heir, after all. So I was startled to be informed by the portly lawyer that it wasn't that straightforward after all. I listened open-mouthed as he explained that although my grandfather had left everything to my father, and Father's last will and testament left everything to me, at the time of his death, he was still legally married to Fern Beale. Half of his estate belonged to her.

"My mother?" I blurted.

On the other side of the desk, the lawyer nodded solemnly. "Fortunately," he continued, "your father had the foresight to make all the bank holdings joint accounts. So they flow to you. But everything else—"

I remained speechless, considering the implications of what he was saying. Half of the land, the buildings, the cattle? Half of the ranch that my grandfather, my father and I loved so much—and which my mother had hated enough to run away from—was now hers. Surely my father had considered this. And he had let it happen?

"But she left us," I protested. "She's been gone for over eleven years. We've never heard a word from her. She could be dead, for all we know."

The lawyer unhooked his wire spectacles from his ears, then wiped his fleshy hand across his face. He set his glasses down on the desktop, saying, "She's not."

I felt a long-forgotten stone thudded into the pit of my stomach. "How—how do you know?"

He opened the file before him. "Some months ago," he said, staring down at the papers in the file, "your father had me contact an agency to search for her. I don't know what his motivation was. Perhaps he had a premonition. Perhaps he was considering legally ending the marriage—he never said."

He picked up a sheet of paper from the file and slid it toward me. "Unfortunately, he passed away before this came."

I glanced down at the letter, taking in the agency letterhead, then felt myself recoil as my mother's name leapt out from the blur of words below.

"We've just received this report," he said. "She hasn't been notified yet. But by law we must. If you like, we can take care of it. Contact her and let her know the situation, see if she's willing to negotiate a settlement. Or," he raised a questioning eyebrow, "you can go and see her yourself. Talk to her in person. Her address is in that report."

I pushed the letter back across the desk. "No," I said, shaking my head. "You go ahead and let her know. Do whatever it is you have to do. I have no desire to see her."

All the way home I wrestled with the confusion of emotions this new development had created. Part of me was relieved to finally know for certain that my mother was alive. The other part felt a renewed anger at her. And there was now the issue of her legal claim on the ranch. Surely she wouldn't believe she deserved it. Would she? If we continued not to hear from her, was it possible for us to ignore her name on the title, and just carry on? If so, would I have to send her half the profits? Could I buy her out? The money in the bank, the bonds Father had purchased in my name, had left me financially secure. But was it enough to buy her half? If not, would she accept payments over time?

At dinner that night I was about to hash it over with Rose, as I did all the ranch business now, but I caught myself. I had leaned on her enough. After Father's death she had been my strength, even though she had her own sorrows to bear. Not only had the years passed with no news of Alan; now she was mourning the loss of her best friend.

I studied her across the table, noticing the new lines in her brow, the crow's feet around her midnight-blue eyes—the only indication of her private heartache. There was no judging her age, and I had never asked. I'd always assumed she was around my father's age. But even with the streaks of silver that now highlighted her ebony hair, which she still wore in a long braid, she looked far younger than any imagined years.

"Have you ever thought of marrying again, Rose?" I asked suddenly.

She put her fork down and looked up at me.

"Yes. But it's too late now."

"Father?"

She nodded.

"I'm sorry," I said. "I wish he ..."

"Your father was an honourable man," she said, a wistful smile on her lips. "He was always a good friend. And that was enough."

I reached over to place my hand on hers. Even though she never became my stepmother—as I had often dreamed she would—I loved Rose as if she were. Since I was twelve years old, this woman had been the only mother I knew. And that too, I realized, was enough.

Later, I went into Father's bedroom, and, as I had every night since his death, I crawled into his bed and wrapped myself up in his blankets. By morning I knew that I would do whatever it took to buy my mother's share of the ranch, short of communicating with her. I would let the lawyer handle that.

I faced the day resolved to get over my inertia, to carry on—as Rose did each and every day—without feeling sorry for myself.

After the ranch chores were done, I decided to start with permanently moving myself downstairs into the bedroom Father and Grandfather had shared. It was a job I had been avoiding. Even though every night since he died I had slept in Father's bed, I hadn't been able to bring myself to get rid of his things. It all seemed so daunting, so permanent. But it was time. Time to grow up and move out of my childhood bedroom in the loft. With renewed energy, I began sorting through his clothes, leaving the shirts that I wanted for myself hanging in the closet, and carefully folding and packing up everything else. Perhaps Jimmy Sellers and his boys could make use of some of it. I would ask when he came over to help me bring down my wardrobe and dresser from the loft.

Jimmy, the hired hand at the Miller ranch while their son Ralph was away, had been working part-time for us and other ranchers in the area ever since the war ended. The day after Father passed away, Jimmy—and his wife, Mary—had shown up unasked to help around the ranch. Last month, he had agreed to hire on with us full-time. He and the triplets, who were now twelve years old, were busy cutting timber for the log home they planned to build at the west end of the hayfield in the spring. I only hoped that I would still be able to afford him once the lawyer settled with Mother.

After I finished packing away Father's belongings, I decided to dismantle Grandfather's iron bed. Perhaps the Sellers could use that as well.

I leaned over to haul Grandfather's old trunk out of the way, but it was heavier than I expected. I removed all the books and record ledgers and pushed it into the corner. It slid slowly across the floor, as if weighted down, taking far too much effort for an empty trunk. And then it hit me. Wondering why I hadn't thought of it before, I peered inside. Like his pa's trunk at Bute Inlet, maybe Grandfather's had a false bottom. I ran my hand over the cloth-covered wooden sides and along the bottom until I felt an indent. Shoving my finger through, I tugged, and the false bottom lifted as easily as a lid.

I slumped back on to my haunches. Dumfounded, I reached into the trunk to touch the soft leather bag lying in the hidden space. Certain of what it was, with trembling hands I picked it up, feeling the heavy shift of coins inside as I did so. Suddenly Grandfather's journal entries were so much more than words on a page, so much more than a story. I hefted the deerskin pouch onto my lap and opened it, running my fingers through the cache of gold coins inside—his Pa's coins, I concluded, the ones that, as a teenage boy, my grandfather must have carried out from Bute Inlet. I recalled him talking about the gold in his pa's trunk. Talk that I had assumed was nothing more than confused memories. But looking down at the coins, I realized that the only thing he had been confused about was which trunk they were stashed in.

Startled by the find, I sat for a moment considering its implications. Only after I had recovered did I notice a roll of paper tucked against the corner. I picked it up and carefully unravelled it. The sight of the artist's drawing sucked the air from my lungs.

I don't know how long I stared down at the detailed pencil sketch Grandfather had saved for all these years. By the time I stood up on legs numb with sleep, I knew exactly what he would want me to do with his journals.

59.

It took less than a week to read the journals to Rose. Every evening we sat on either side of the silent Victrola Radiola, me reading out loud while she concentrated on her knitting. Not once did the long needles halt their rhythmic clicking, even when I stopped to glance up and gauge her reaction to some particular passage. She added no comment, asked no questions, only nodded silently here and there, just as she had a habit of doing whenever I read from one of the classic novels. After a few nights I began to question my assumptions. Perhaps Grandfather's journals had no more meaning to her other than an interesting story.

On the fourth night, I finished the first leather-bound journal, closed it and started right in on the canvas-covered one. It took less than two nights to read all of Grandfather's entries about his journey to Barkerville, his arrival and new life there. Then I came to his description of his frantic overnight hike into Quesnellmouth and for the first time, Rose's knitting needles slowed. They came to a full stop as I read about his gruesome discovery in the town that is now called Quesnel. I left nothing out, reading his remorseful confession about the Chilcotin girl named Rose and her brother Willum word for word.

"Her head slowly turned and across the distance her eyes met mine. The sorrow drained from her face and was replaced with contempt. This time it was Rose who turned away. She slipped between the surrounding women, who moved in to close the gap after her and stood forming a solid wall against my following.

"I searched the little town for hours but she was not to be found.

"Now this six months later every time I close my eyes I see her. And I see the scornful face of her brother Willum. For even in death his eyes found mine. Mocking me. Accusing me. Forever condemning me for breaking the oath that I made to him the morning my pa died."

Letting the words hang in the silence, I closed the journal and took up the notebook in which I had written the story that Grandfather had told me out on our enclosed porch. As I read his verbal account of that April 30 morning in Bute Inlet, Rose set down her knitting needles. When I was done, I turned to my grandfather's dictated statement. And then, in the stillness of our parlour, I shared it with the only living person I knew for whom it might have some meaning.

"This is the statement of Chauncey Beynon Beale," I read, "as to the events occurring on the Homathko River above the Bute Inlet, in the Province of British Columbia, during the last day of April in the year of our Lord 1864. The telling comes over seventy years late, but it is no less than the truth as I recall it. I was present in the main camp of the Bute Inlet road crew on the morning of April 30, 1864. During my time at the camp—in the weeks that led up to that day—on many occasions I witnessed first-hand the threats of smallpox, starvation and the abuse of the women that was inflicted on the Chilcotin people looking for work with the road company. It is my opinion that these events, and the disregard for territorial rights over the land upon which the road company was about to enter, contributed to the attack on the road crew on the morning of April 30. During the attack, I was not in a position to witness any of the deaths, save that of my father, the powder man, Edwin Vincent Beale, by whose hand I know not. The only face I recognized that morning was the man I knew only by the name Willum. He led me to safety and in that way saved my life. It is my sworn oath and opinion that the attack on the men of the road company by the Chilcotin warriors on April 30, 1864, was an act of war."

I set the book down on my lap and glanced up. Rose nodded slowly, as if in acceptance, then took up her work again.

"Nobody won that war," she said, above the clack of her needles. "They stopped the road, but too many people died. Too much trust was lost."

I reached for the heavy *World Book Encyclopedia* volume and let it fall open to where I had pressed the artist's sketch I found in Grandfather's trunk. Removing the flattened paper from between the pages, I leaned forward to hand it to Rose.

Wordlessly, she laid her knitting down and accepted the drawing—an artist's sketch so detailed, so beautifully done, that I had recognized my Grandfather's teenage image the moment I first saw it. And the girl on the riverbank with him looked so much like the woman sitting before me that she could have been Rose VanderMeer's younger self. Had Grandfather noticed this similarity? Or had his memory and eyesight been too blurred by the time Rose arrived in Sorry? I would never know.

Rose studied the faces, a wistful smile forming on her lips. Finally, in a hushed voice she said, "My grandmother."

"Grandmother?" I blurted. When I first saw the face of the girl in the drawing, I was startled at the strong family resemblance and suspected that it was possible that she was some distant relative of Rose's, but her grandmother?

She nodded. "My father died when I was young. Grandmother Rose raised me," she said, still studying the drawing. "I grew up listening to her stories about that long time ago."

"Is she still alive?" I asked.

Rose shook her head slowly. "She died in 1925."

"Did you know about her and my grandfather?" I asked hesitantly.

"No, not for certain. Not until I heard him talk about Willum did I think he might be the same Mr. Chance of my grandmother's stories." She nodded toward the journal. "The same stories."

I stood up, went into the bedroom and retrieved the deerskin pouch.

"I think this was hers," I said, offering it to Rose. "I believe my grandfather kept it in hopes of finding her again someday."

Rose fingered the leather, stroking it as if it were a live animal. "Yes. It's not so good, like her later work, but I know her stitching."

"It belongs to you, then," I said, sitting back down. "And the gold coins inside. Those were his pa's. I believe he always intended to give them to your grandmother, if he ever found her. Perhaps over the years he forgot about it being squirrelled away in his trunk, but something made him remember. I'm convinced that he wanted her to have it—well, because I think he believed that the toddler he talked about seeing her with all those years ago was his pa's child. Whether that's true or not ..."

"It's true," Rose said quietly. "That boy was my father."

60.

The city traffic was beyond anything I could have imagined. Crossing over the Fraser River into New Westminster, I'd had to wrestle back the rising panic at the sight of the cars pouring onto and off of the Pattullo Bridge.

In all my twenty-three years, the furthest I had travelled from Sorry was to Prince George, a town that at the time had seemed so overwhelming. Nothing had prepared me for this. Vancouver's busy streets, the traffic lights, the stop signs, the nearness of other vehicles, were all completely foreign to me. For so many reasons, everything in me wanted to turn the pickup truck around and head home. But I gripped the steering wheel with renewed determination. I hadn't driven these last ten hours to give up now.

When I'd told Rose my plan, she suggested that I consider giving myself more time to mourn my father before making such a huge decision. But my mind was made up; I knew it was the right thing to do. But now, glancing down at the street map on the seat, I couldn't help feeling apprehension.

A chorus of blaring car horns sounded behind me as I turned onto Victoria Drive without remembering to arm-signal my intention. In my nervousness as I changed gears, the clutch slipped beneath my boot and the pickup jerked haltingly forward to a renewed round of impatient honking. I pulled over to the curb and, after catching my breath, checked the numbers on the newly built homes lining the street. According to the address in the manila envelope on the dashboard, my destination was only a few blocks away.

Hesitantly, I pulled back into traffic. It seemed to take forever before I finally parked in front of the South Vancouver address. I switched off the engine and double-checked the numbers. There must be some mistake. Still, not giving myself a chance to lose my nerve, I grabbed the envelope with the documents the lawyer had drawn up, climbed out of the truck and approached the little corner grocery store. As I did, a school bell rang out from the massive brick and stone building across the street. Sir James Douglas Elementary. The name of the first governor of the Colony of British Columbia brought an ominous reminder of Grandfather's early journals—a large part of the reason why I was here.

Inside the store, she was kneeling behind a glass bakery cabinet, placing a Boston cream pie on the glass shelf. When the bell above the door tinkled my arrival, she straightened up, smoothed her apron and put on a greet-the-customer smile. Our eyes met in the dim light, and we both stood frozen in the moment of recognition. Shock, and something like fear, filled her face. A face so very much like the one I remembered from my childhood that I was taken aback. I had expected her to look much older, yet I couldn't help but feel admiration at how my mother had held on to her youthful appearance—and a twinge of resentment at the same time. Where were the wrinkles of regret, the aged lines of sorrow? Life without us should have taken its toll on her beauty. But it had not.

Her hand went to her mouth as her eyes drank me in. I stood in silence, waiting, refusing to be the one to speak the first words between us in almost twelve years. "Adeline?" she finally whispered. "I ..."

"Addie," I insisted.

"Of course, Addie," she said. "I ... I wasn't expecting you."

"I'm surprised you recognize me at all. I was a child last time you saw me."

It was harsh, and I regretted saying it the moment the words were out of my mouth.

"I'd know you anywhere," she said, her voice barely a whisper.

I squared my shoulders, refusing to get caught up in sentimentality. This would be all business. Holding up the manila envelope, I said, "I came to make you an offer for your share of the ranch."

At that moment the door swung open and a group of children clamoured into the store.

"Recess time," my mother said, flustered. "Please ... please excuse me for a minute."

I watched her attend to the children gathered around the counter, her entire demeanour changing as she bagged penny candy and accepted each coin as if it were the most important transaction of her day. As they all vied for her attention, I experienced a childish twinge of jealousy at their familiarity. Turning away from the scene, I looked about the little grocery store, which seemed so out of place in the city.

How strange to find her here, working in a store so eerily similar to The Sorry Grocers: the same smell of stale water in the pop cooler; the same creek of wooden floorboards underfoot. Among the array of baked goods in the glass display case, I recognized many of the fancy desserts that she used to enjoy making, and a flood of unwanted memories came back to me.

After she waved the last little boy out the door, smiling as he called, "Bye, Miss Wagner," she locked the door.

"You go by your maiden name," I remarked while she watched him cross the street.

"Yes, it just seemed easier." She locked the door and pulled down the window shade. "Let me make some tea," she said, turning back to me, "and then we can talk."

Following her to the back of the store, I said, "I always imagined that you would have gone back to your nursing career."

"I tried, but I couldn't bear to see sick ..." She stopped herself. "Well, at any rate, my brother and I bought this place years ago. It's been good."

In the backroom, she ushered me to a chair at a small chrome table and busied herself putting a kettle on the hot plate. An awkward silence filled the room, which I did nothing to relieve. Watching her fidgeting nervously with the tea leaves, I reminded myself that I needed nothing from her other than her signature.

When she was done, she rinsed and dried her hands, then slathered them with cream from a small white jar she took from the window ledge. I thought I was immune to any feeling toward my mother, that I had hardened myself against her, but the smell of the Pond's cold cream was my undoing. The floral scent brought back long-forgotten memories, and for a moment the heavy curtain of time between us lifted. I could almost feel her massaging the leftover cream onto my tiny hands. The image was so startling that I wanted to bolt from my seat and flee; I wanted to have her take me in her arms, to lay my head against her breast and feel the warmth of her body. I stiffened against the threatening tears and looked away.

Perhaps she mistook the unguarded moment for grief, for I heard her whisper, "I'm so sorry about your father, Adeline."

Sorry? Fat lot of good sorry does. Ignoring the too-late sympathy, I turned back to her and said, "The years have been good to you." Even I could hear the cold edge to my voice.

And then I did what I promised myself I would not. "In all those years," I asked, "did you ever think about us?"

"Every single day."

"Then why? Why didn't you at least write?"

"I always meant to. At first I was too broken. By the time I healed, too much time had passed. It just seemed easier to stay away."

"Easier for you, maybe."

She lowered her gaze. "You're right," she said, studying her hands. "You deserved more." She raised her head to meet my eyes. "But I had to leave. I wasn't well for a very long time after Evan's death. If I had stayed with your father, the misplaced bitterness and anger I felt toward him would have grown and infected everyone, everything."

I hadn't intended to say it, but it slipped out. "It wasn't just him you left behind."

She took a step toward me, and my body tensed against her approach. She caught herself, her shoulders slumping as she leaned back against the counter. "Oh, Addie, if you only knew how desperately I wanted to bring you with me. You are the only thing that kept me breathing then, and for years afterward. But you were your father's child. It would have been un-forgivable, selfish, of me to force you to leave the ranch. Even then it was so much a part of you. I couldn't tear you away from the place you loved. I'm sorry I wasn't stronger," she whispered. "Sorry I was such a coward. Can you ever forgive me?"

I had imagined this conversation so often, imagined her tearful apol-ogy—always expecting that I would spit her "sorry" back in her face—but found I could not. Neither could I bring myself to give her what she needed.

"Did you ever forgive Father?" I asked.

"A long time ago."

"I'm glad," I said, taking the manila envelope from my lap.

She turned to attend to the whistling kettle. While she filled the teapot and set it on the counter to steep, I pulled out the legal papers and placed them on the table.

I waited in nervous silence as she brought out china cups and then filled a plate with iced cupcakes. Did she really think I could eat?

Finally she sat down across from me. "All right, now," she said, smoothing her apron. "What do you need?"

I slid the papers across the table. "This is an offer for your share of the ranch."

She picked up the document, her eyebrows rising in surprise as she read. Before I had a chance to recite my planned speech, she stood, retrieved a fountain pen from a drawer and sat back down. I looked away as she signed, the sound of her pen scratching across the paper seeming to take forever.

When she was done, she slipped the document back inside the ma-nila envelope and handed it back to me as easily as if she had just signed an order with the Fuller Brush man.

But her shaking hands betrayed her as she began pouring tea, spilling much of it into my saucer.

"Did he love her very much?" she asked, filling her own cup.

"Yes," I said. "Rose is family."

I could have told her then that Rose's name on the document had less to do with Father than Grandfather. I could have explained how, after sharing his past with her, Rose and I had drawn up a chart, a family tree of sorts, starting with her grandmother, the first Rose, and my great grandfather, Edwin Beale. How we had figured out that the child he had fathered with her was Grandfather's half-brother—which made Rose and Father half-cousins. I could have told her that putting Rose's name on the ranch title would have been what Grandfather, what Father, would have wanted me to do, had they known.

Instead, I said, "But he loved you more." And I gave my mother the only thing I could give her that day. I told her, "He never stopped loving you."

"Nor I him."

Later, I left her with, if not exactly forgiveness in my heart, the beginning of something like it. Father had been right: holding onto resentment was too heavy a load, and I felt the lightness of it lifting away while we sat making uncomfortable small talk over tea. When she walked me outside, I sensed her reluctance to let me go and her yearning for a farewell hug, which in the end, I found myself rigidly accepting. Before I opened the pickup door, she asked quietly if she would ever see me again.

"That's up to you," I said, climbing inside. "You're welcome if you ever want to visit the ranch."

"Well, it's too late for that, isn't it?"

"It's never too late."

"And Rose," she asked. "How would she feel about my showing up?"

"She would welcome you."

Something in her eyes, in the way she said "Perhaps I will, then," opened a door in my heart that had been closed for far too long.

We left it at that. No promises made. No promises to be broken.

It was only after I arrived home that I discovered she had scratched out the dollar amount of the offer—a more than generous sum for her share, according to the lawyer—and written in the sum of one dollar.

61.

The evening sunlight splashed across the meadow, bathing the fence posts, tree trunks and ranch house in a rich golden glow. Having finished my chores, and knowing that the gloaming would last only a few more moments, I stood leaning on the pitchfork in the barn doorway, enjoying the final rays of the setting sun. In the distance, I could hear the voices of the Sellers boys teasing each other as they hurried home from the creek.

I turned at the sound of the ice-house door opening and Rose emerged, a huge brown-paper package in one arm. Roast beef. The same meal she cooked each and every Sunday without fail, whether it was just the two of us or the Sellers family joined us for dinner.

As she closed the heavy door, the latest batch of barn kittens scurried out from the woodshed to wrap themselves around her ankles. She bent down to pet them, crooning endearments in her melodic language. She glanced up to see me watching, and the smile that crinkled her face flashed across the space between us.

"You might want to check with Mary about dinner tomorrow," I called out. "Looks like the triplets have caught a mess of trout."

She glanced toward the Sellers' log house at the south end of the field, where the three teenagers were crawling through the fence with their catch and fishing poles.

"Still having roast beef," she said with a shrug.

Heading toward the house, she called out, "I saw Dancer behind the corrals a little while ago."

I scanned the north end of the field and the forest edge beyond but saw no sign of the buckskin stallion. Rose still swore every time she spotted the horse that he'd come looking for Alan. In the years since the war ended, she had never lost faith that her son would return. Next week it would be nine years since he went away. Now, on every anniversary of that September day, Rose and I would ride out to the east meadows and hike up to the ridge. We would sit with our backs against the sway-back pine tree, just as Alan and I used to do, and gaze out across the valley. With the sun warming our faces, the wind combing our hair, I would tell her about the first time I came up here with him, about our conversations about the foreverness of the land. And she would affirm her belief that, one way or another, he would find his way back to it.

I chose to hold onto that belief, although with each passing year it was getting harder.

At twenty-five, I knew that most folks around Sorry already considered me to be an eccentric spinster at best. It was not that there hadn't been opportunities. The schoolteacher, Mr. Bennett, who had replaced Mrs. Parsons, was the first to show interest in me. But after my lack of response, the handsome young teacher, whom all of Sorry had fallen in love with from the start, married one of the local girls and settled down there.

After the war, some of the ranchers' sons—who probably recognized a certain advantage at the prospect of merged ranches—had made half-hearted overtures as well. But they gave up easily enough when they realized I wasn't looking for a spouse or a business partner. I already had the two partners I wanted, even though one of those partners was long silent.

When I told Rose my intention to purchase my mother's half of the ranch in her name, she said it wasn't necessary. But for me it was. I owed it to my grandfather. Somehow, I felt that this was exactly what he would have wanted. And I was certain my father would have approved.

Adding Alan's name on the title was my way of affirming Rose's and my belief in his return. If anyone had asked either of us how long we were willing to wait, we would have answered, "Forever."

Rose and I settled into a comfortable existence at the ranch. And I believed, if this was to be my life forever, it was enough. Still, I often found myself thinking about my mother, about that day in Vancouver.

Watching her in my rear-view mirror—the melancholy look that I remember from my childhood on her face—I had almost stopped the truck to go back and accept her invitation to stay overnight. Almost is not enough, though. Still, the last image I have of her, standing on the sidewalk waving bravely as I drove away, is far better than the memory of the torment I saw in her eyes the night before she left the ranch all those years ago.

After I left her, I found my way across town to English Bay, where I walked along a saltwater beach for the first time in my life. I sat for hours on a sun-bleached log looking out over the water, trying to make sense of my mixed feelings. All those years of resentment could not fall away in a single afternoon. In the end, I headed home knowing what Father and Rose always knew—that loving someone does not require their presence in your life. Sometimes forgiveness is simply remembering that love.

She was my mother and always would be. She was family. And just like the land, family is forever. Afterward, though, I vowed that I would not fall into the trap of expecting to see her again, of waiting for her hinted-at visit. I promised myself that I would never again nurse the resentment that expectation brings. Still, I couldn't help feeling disappointed as time passed and I heard nothing from her.

Across the yard, Rose climbed the porch stairs and then stood at the top, taking in the last rays of the evening sun. Up in the sky, thin clouds, like paintbrush strokes across the blue, turned vermilion pink in the dying reflection. As the golden fireball slipped below the distant mountains, the ranch dogs started to bark. They raced off down the road, hearing the sound of an approaching vehicle moments before I did. Both Rose and I turned to watch them, just as the little yellow bus rumbled around the bend.

Last year, the Watts family had replaced The Sorry Grocers' old delivery van with the bus. During the week it was used to deliver groceries to customers, and on Sunday, children to Sunday school.

Shading my eyes from the reflective glare of the sun's last rays in the windshield, I watched the bus, with the dogs running alongside, rumble into the yard. The gears grinding in protest, it came to a jerky stop beside me. The driver's window slid open and Reverend Watts leaned out with his arm resting on the frame. "Good evening, Miss Beale," he called above the noise of the engine.

"You're a little early for Sunday school, aren't you, Reverend?" I teased, brushing the hair back from my face. "And much too late for me."

"Never too early, or too late," he said, passing me the latest copy of the store's weekly flyer. "But this evening," he added with a smile, "I've got a special delivery for you."

"Well, that's very kind of you to come all the way out here," I said, accepting his version of the old *Sorry Times*. "Got time for coffee?"

"I'll take a rain check on that," he said. Then with a mischievous wink of an eye, he added, "But perhaps tomorrow, I'll be seeing the three of you in church?"

Three? It was then I noticed the shadowed figure behind him.

Something familiar in the silhouetted shoulders caused my knees to go weak. Standing in the porch doorway, Rose's hand flew to her breast. The pitchfork fell from my hand, and, of their own accord, my shaking legs carried me around the pointed front of the bus. The doors folded open, just as I arrived on the other side. I stopped short, the blood pounding in my ears, at the sight of the green tapestry travel bag landing on the ground. My eyes travelled up to the face of its owner.

And my heart leapt with a long-denied yearning as a voice I secretly feared I would never hear again said, "Hello, Addie."

Afterword

In 1993, after nearly a century of dispute and deep distrust between the Tsilhqot'in First Nation and the government of the province of British Columbia, a judicial inquiry was ordered to revisit the Chilcotin War and the hanging of five Tsilhqot'in warriors. Retired provincial court judge Anthony Sarich was appointed to look into the relationship between the Native people of the Cariboo-Chilcotin and the justice system of this province, and he found the aftermath of the conflict still lingered.

Judge Anthony Sarich wrote in his findings: "Whatever the correct version, that episode of history has left a wound in the body of Chilcotin society. It is time to heal that wound."

On June 26, 2014, after decades of court battles, in a unanimous landmark decision, the Supreme Court of Canada granted the Tsilhqot'in First Nation land title to 438,000 hectares in the British Columbia territories known as the Chilcotin Plateau.

In the interior town of Quesnel, on the banks of the Fraser River, sits an engraved plaque honouring the five Tsihqot'in warriors who perished there. At a dedication ceremony on October 26, 1999, marking the 145th anniversary of their execution, Aboriginal Affairs minister Dale Lovick spoke of the hangings with apologies, stating, "We should be ashamed and sorry."

Acknowledgements

Once again I wish to extend my gratitude to friends and family for their constant support and encouragement. In particular, my daughter and grammar guru, Tanya Rose LaFond, and my daughter-in-law extraordinaire, Joanna Stiles Drake. Thank you both for all the hours spent reading early drafts. I truly appreciated your eagle eyes and thoughtful comments. They made all the difference. To my son, Aaron Drake, sister, Diane Jonas, friends Juliee Thompson and June Walters and of course my husband, Tom Milner, thank you all for your constant encouragement and belief in this story.

I also wish to acknowledge Jane Silcott, Rebecca Hendry and Kathleen Fraser for your tactful and considered editorial comments and advice. And to Vici Johnstone of Cailtin Press, my gratitude for not letting me give up on this project.

※

This story is a work of fiction as are the characters—with the exception of the historical figures in Chauncey Beale's journal. Any dialogue attributed to these historical figures is either completely imagined or gleaned from research.

Much has been written regarding the events leading up to, and the aftermath of, the so-called Chilcotin War of 1864. In particular I found the following resources valuable in my research:

The Chilcotin War: The True Story of a Defiant Chief's Fight to Save His Land From White Civilization. Mel Rothenburger. Langley, BC: Mr. Paperback, 1978.

The Chilcotin War: A Tale of Death and Reprisal. Rich Mole. Amazing Stories, Heritage House Publishing, 2009.

"Magic in the Homathko Canyon." Henry Solomon. In *Nemiah: The Unconquered Country.* Terry Glavin. Vancouver: New Star Books, 1992.

Provincial Archives of British Columbia, Colonial Correspondence. Matthew Baillie Begbie to the Governor of British Columbia. Including notes on Proceedings. British Columbia Supreme Court: Quesnellmouth, September 30, 1864.

"We Do Not Know his Name: Klatssassin and the Chilcotin War." *Great Unsolved Mysteries in Canadian History.* www. canadianmysteries.ca.

"Aboriginal People in the Canadian Military." www.cmp-cpm.forces.gc.ca.

The Quesnel Museum, Quesnel, BC.